The Idealists

The Idealists

HENRY CARLISLE & OLGA ANDREYEV CARLISLE

THOMAS
DUNNE
BOOKS

ST. MARTIN'S PRESS ⚓ NEW YORK

THOMAS DUNNE BOOKS.
An imprint of St. Martin's Press.

Book design by Scott Levine

Library of Congress Cataloging-in-Publication Data

Carlisle, Henry.
      The idealists / Henry Carlisle and Olga Andreyev Carlisle.
         p.   cm.
      ISBN 0-312-20054-4
      I. Soviet Union—History—Revolution. 1917–1921—
Fiction.   I. Carlisle, Olga Andreyev.   II. Title.
PS3553.A7215   1999
813'.54—DC21   98-44018
                                                         CIP

First Edition: February 1999

10   9   8   7   6   5   4   3   2   I

For
Michael

THE SPHINX SET RIDDLES FOR
PEOPLE WHICH THEY COULD NOT SOLVE AND THE
SPHINX DEVOURED THEM.
—ILYA EHRENBURG

The Idealists

THE STORY OF OUR FATHERS
IS OUT OF THE AGE OF THE STUARTS,
FURTHER AWAY THAN PUSHKIN,
IT CAN ONLY BE SEEN IN A DREAM.
—BORIS PASTERNAK

For many years, my father's story—and my mother's and mine—had seemed to belong to another time, as remote as the reign of the Stuarts and as filled with violence, intrigues, and narrow escapes. My memories were fading, and all that remained were dreamlike images of Paris before the Great War, the villa on the Riviera, Revolutionary Petrograd, the Volga region torn by civil war, Moscow under the Red Terror, the Lubyanka cells, the faces and voices of people long dead, growing ever fainter.

My father, Vasily Nevsky, had been the leader of the Socialist Revolutionaries, by 1917 the largest antimonarchist party in Russia. We were the heirs apparent of the revolutions of 1905 and of February 1917. My father was an idealist. He envisioned a just, democratic Russia based on redistribution of land to the peasants. He could not conceive, until it was too late, that the Bolsheviks, preaching class war and the "dictatorship of the proletariat," would in a few months transform the Russia of the February 1917 revolution into a totalitarian power that would enslave our people and half of Europe for three generations.

For opposing the Bolsheviks after their October Revolution, the SRs were hunted, arrested, interrogated under torture, subjected to sham trials, branded as enemies of the people, exiled, executed, and finally, after banishment or death, obliterated from the annals of Soviet history. In 1918, my father was proclaimed Enemy of the People Number One in the USSR, with a one-million-ruble price on his head. To have spoken his name in Stalin's time would have been to sign one's own death warrant.

Meanwhile, the monarchists—the Whites—condemned the Socialist Revo-

lutionary leaders for their failure to stop the Bolsheviks when power was within their reach. They accused them of having destroyed Russia by undermining a social order established by Peter the Great, leaving it prey to the Bolshevik gangsters.

I did not question this verdict. In spirit, I walked with the ghosts of those who had perished. Sadly, I packed away the mementos we had saved from the past: bundles of letters tied with ribbon; the blood-red coral necklace that had belonged to my mother's sister Ariane; the photograph of my father wearing his floppy peasant hat, standing with Maxim Gorky in dappled sunlight at the Villa Ariane; another of him smiling broadly at our dinner table in the company of solemn-looking SR Central Committee members wearing stiff collars and cravats; the photograph of Ariane standing with her white horse; the ledgers in which my father had written his memoirs. These were the relics of the past from which I had walked away.

My life in emigration began in 1920 in Paris following our escape from Russia. The events of the years that followed passed with the hectic speed of a modernistic movie: my marriage to Kiril Golovin and our magical times together in Paris between the wars, ending on a rainy winter day in 1944 when I stood outside the Gestapo prison at Drancy, realizing that I would never see Kiril again. Soon afterward came my parents' deaths, the lonely years after the Occupation; and my meeting with Arthur Pringle, an American working at the YMCA relief agency in Paris where I was a volunteer.

Arthur and I fell in love, and in 1948 we married. We came to live in the United States, sharing our time between Nantucket Island, where Arthur's Quaker roots ran deep, and San Francisco, where he practiced architecture.

My rediscovery of my Russian past began in earnest some ten years later. It was inspired by a seashell I found on a Nantucket beach—and by Boris Pasternak. In the summer of 1958, vacationing with Arthur on the Island, I read that year's best-seller, Doctor Zhivago. *Pasternak's novel told me that at last Russia was struggling to liberate itself from its past, that Soviet lies were beginning to crumble like old plaster. After a lifetime of political harassment, its author, whose poetry had sustained me throughout my life, had found the strength to tell an impassioned story of Russia in our century. Now the world was listening. Reading* Doctor Zhivago, *I recalled my meeting with Pasternak in 1918 in Moscow in a freezing drawing room with two grand pianos. Now, through his novel, he was saying that all of us who had known those years had to remember our experiences, no matter how painful, so that Russia might one day know itself. Why couldn't I, who had no police agents stalking me, no need to placate hostile officials, remember the past?*

Like Zhivago's, our life during the Revolution was full of coincidences and strange encounters, such as our 1918 meeting with the poet. These events followed a mysterious logic of their own, as if a benevolent spirit were guiding our movements. That summer, I knew that it was up to me to recapture that past life.

At the end of September, we were closing our house, preparing to return to San Francisco. A great equinox storm had swept over Nantucket, followed by a day of icy sunshine. That last morning, I went down to the stretch of sand at Brant Point where I swam every day, and sometimes sat on the rocks near the lighthouse and sketched the harbor. For another year, we were leaving, and I wanted to say good-bye to the Island.

Suddenly, in the sand at the edge of the water, I saw an enormous conch shell that the storm had washed up. It was white, scoured, intact. As a painter, my first thought was what a beautiful still-life subject it would make.

I held the shell to my ear. The surf-roar in its depths reminded me of another seashell, one that my father and I had found on the beach below our villa on the Italian Riviera when I was ten.

Back at the house, I wrapped the shell in tissue paper and packed it in a shoe box to take back to California. I remembered that, in the attic of our house there, I had stored a wicker trunk containing the few things I had saved from my former life, including four scuffed ledgers belonging to my father which I had never opened.

The day after our arrival in San Francisco, I retrieved those ledgers and began to read the fine Cyrillic script slanting upward across the ruled leaves.

The first entry described that rainy night in the winter of 1909, when from our window I watched my father and Boris Savinkov set out for the Azefs' apartment on the boulevard Raspail. Though I had forgotten much else, I remembered that night with an intensity that I could never explain—until then. Reading his words, I could again feel the love that my father and I had felt for each other after his return from the Azefs.

Over the next days, drawing upon those notes, I wrote an account of that night as my father must have experienced it. Only then was I able to begin, little by little, to tell the whole story, as gradually another, earlier Marina Nevsky was revealed, and long-departed souls who I felt had been searching for me all those years began to emerge from the shadows of the past.

Part One

IN THE SHADOW OF AZEF

Chapter One

ON A RAW, GUSTY WINTER AFTERNOON FOLLOWING A RAIN, TWO MEN, neither of whom could be mistaken for a Parisian, met at the gates of the Parc Montsouris and walked rapidly along the rue Gazan in the direction of the boulevard Raspail. They walked in silence, falling in and out of step, for one was tall and solidly built with the long, powerful stride of a countryman, while the other, who used a slim walking stick, was slender and of ordinary height, with the quick precise gait of the city-bred.

The taller of the two, Vasily Ivanovich Nevsky, the leader of the Russian Socialist Revolutionary Party, was one of those large men perpetually at war with their clothes. His heavy shoes splashed through puddles; his loose, fur-collared overcoat, unbuttoned, billowed behind him, the right pocket weighted by a nine millimeter Browning pistol. His astrakhan hat exaggerated the broadness of his Slavic features, which, usually composed and even dreamy, were now locked in determination.

In contrast, his companion, Boris Victorovich Savinkov, a member of the same party's Combat Organization, was nattily dressed in the British manner: black bowler, fitted gray overcoat, black oxfords, gold-handled stick. His pale, narrow face with its trim Vandyke beard was calm. In a shoulder holster, he carried a Smith and Wesson semiautomatic.

On the boulevard Raspail, carriages and cabs rumbled over the wet stones. Oblivious to his surroundings, Vasily stared at the third-floor windows of a blackened apartment building next to a café on the corner opposite the Montparnasse Cemetery. In one of the windows, dull light shone behind heavy curtains.

"Someone's home," said Vasily, suddenly remembering their quarry's wife and the two boys. "We certainly—"

"We'll wait at the café."

"He may be up there already."

Savinkov took out a pocket watch and held it up to the light of a gas lamp. "Then we'll intercept him on the way out. He must have known that Burtsev's evidence would expose him. He must be trying to leave the city, if he hasn't already. We'll wait twenty minutes at the café, then go up to the apartment. If he's there with his family, we'll take him aside and tell him that we've come to help him escape the assassins the Central Committee has sent after him. Then we'll lead him over behind the cemetery. It will be a simple matter."

"And if he's not there?"

With an appraising glance at Vasily, Savinkov slipped his watch back into his waistcoat pocket. "In that case," he said, "I shall await your instructions."

Vasily understood. During the past hour, since the thunderbolt had struck at the trial which had been held in Savinkov's apartment on the Luxembourg Gardens, he had recognized the fairness of the Central Committee's resolution that he, Vasily, should be responsible for punishing the traitor, and he had accepted that duty. It was proper, for it had been Vasily himself who had proposed Azef to fill the position of power and trust as leader of the terrorist arm of the party known as the Combat Organization.

Yet while the task ahead on this night might appear simple to Savinkov, it did not appear so to Vasily.

For the past decade, Vasily had served in an advisory capacity in the Combat Organization, whose operations included the assassinations of Minister of the Interior Plehve and of the Grand Duke Sergei. However, circumstances and, no doubt something in Vasily's nature, had prevented him from engaging directly in acts of violence. The Browning had never been fired.

Now there was no choice. The SRs' leader and chief theoretician, whose brain teemed with sensitive intelligence about the Russian revolutionary movement over the past century, as well as with a broad vision of its ultimate victory, had willingly accepted the role of avenger of the party. Savinkov was Vasily's technical counselor. With Savinkov at his side, the mission's success was virtually assured. No one was more experienced in the execution of revolutionary murder than this dapper, intricate man, this littérateur whose inner nature remained an enigma, despite the clue that he himself had offered: in a remark to a friend—widely quoted throughout émigré circles—Savinkov had declared, "My soul is choked in blood." This utterance had impressed Vasily, for whether it was the calculated effusion of a writer dramatizing himself or an authentic cri de coeur, it was undeniably an arresting phrase. What was not in doubt was Savinkov's success in carrying out the projects of the Combat Organization. The deaths of Plehve and the grand duke had been principally his work, carried out under the directives of the very traitor whom the Central Committee had less than one hour ago doomed to die: Yevno Filipovich Azef.

Suddenly in Vasily's mind flashed an image of the living room of the Azef apartment, which he knew well from numerous visits: the armchair with its yellowed antimacassars, the fringed standing lamp, the upright piano with its melancholy shawl and sheets of French chansonnettes in the scrollwork rack, the chromolithograph of the tsar, its presence so duplicitous.

Vasily could almost smell the stale tobacco odor which impregnated the oriental carpet, the chair, the pocked velvet curtains, mingling with the acrid smell of the traitor's abominable cat. And suddenly in the armchair appeared Azef himself, massive body, short fat arms, balding head, black eyebrows, black beard, obscene scarlet lips. How could they ever have placed their trust in him?

With a stab of shame, he remembered his fiery defense of the Judas. He had excoriated Azef's accuser, feisty little Vladimir Burtsev, chief of SR counterintelligence, who had wagered his life to prove his case against Azef before the Central Committee. And Burtsev had declared calmly, "Vasily Ivanovich, your faith in the Central Committee as a privileged family shielded from criticism by its moral standing has created an atmosphere in which treason has flourished!" And then he had presented irrefutable proof—the confirmation of a conversation between Burtsev and a former chief of the tsar's all-powerful secret police, the Okhrana, on a train traveling between Cologne and Petersburg. There could be no further doubt: for almost sixteen years, Azef, director of the Combat Organization, had been a prized, highly paid agent of the tsarist police, the Okhrana.

Vasily recalled that his wife, Anna, and even his nine-year-old daughter, Marina, had had some sort of vague intuitions about the traitor, though never clearly brought forward and to which in any case he had not paid attention. But Savinkov! No one had ever accused Boris Savinkov of going about with his head in the clouds. He had worked more intimately than anyone else with Azef, planning and carrying out the enterprises of the Combat Organization. How could Savinkov have been taken in?

As they neared the Montparnasse cemetery, in the freshness of the receding rainstorm Vasily caught a whiff of roasting chestnuts. Across the street, in front of the café terrace enclosed by steamy glass, a chestnut vendor was tending his brazier. As they started across the street, Savinkov left Vasily's side and went over to the vendor's cart. There, in a swirl of smoke, he exchanged coins for a newspaper cone of chestnuts. Suddenly, Vasily, whose fault it seemed was to have trusted everyone blindly, trusted no one at all. Why was Boris buying chestnuts when at any moment Azef could pop out of the building and vanish into the night?

Good God, was Savinkov too in the pay of the Okhrana? Had he voted for Azef's death to cover himself, perhaps to secure the assignment of executioner and then allow him to escape? As Savinkov came up to him and offered him a chestnut, Vasily's mind was reeling with this thought which paralyzed the will to vengeance that had possessed him since he had left the apartment on the Luxembourg Gardens.

The chestnut burned his fingers. He juggled it, blew on it, broke it with his teeth, and ate the hot bitter meat. A motorcar chugged by. The chestnut vendor stirred his coals, releasing sparks that swarmed skyward, reminding Vasily of fireflies of a summer night on the Volga. Savinkov watched him closely, seeming to sense his malaise and perhaps his suspicions as well. With his comrade's odd, yellow-flecked eyes on him, Vasily felt that he whose soul was choked in blood was peering directly into his mind, which suddenly was assailed by yet another threatening consideration.

The thought of Azef's wife, presumed to know nothing of her husband's police connections, and of the boys had shaken him. Under no circumstances, he vowed to himself, must these innocents suffer. Yet when he tried to think of an honorable way to shield Azef's wife and children, he could find none. The Central Committee's decision had been clear, the vote unanimous.

Suppressing his qualms, Vasily led the way into the partly filled café, choosing a table with a view of the entrance to Azef's building. He ordered a fine à l'eau; Savinkov, a marc.

Savinkov produced a silver cigarette case and matching lighter. He tapped a cigarette on the case and lit it. Without his bowler, his appearance was altered, for though only thirty he was quite bald. He inhaled deeply, letting the smoke escape slowly through his nostrils. "Are you certain that he should be killed?" he said.

At this moment, Vasily felt that he had entered an alien world which resembled an ordinary Parisian café but in which it was impossible to get one's bearings. "You voted for execution," he said.

"In order to stand by you. But will liquidating Azef serve the party? That should be the only question."

"The Central Committee made its decision."

"The Central Committee no longer exists."

It was true. The Committee, which had included Vasily and Savinkov, had agreed to resign en masse in penance to the party's rank and file for its negligence in the case of Azef.

"It existed when it issued the order."

"My recollection is that the order came after the resignation," said Savinkov. "In any case, the decision is yours."

"I know that very well."

"You are our leader," insisted Savinkov, smiling in a way Vasily didn't like. "You embody in your person the spirit of the Socialist Revolutionary Party."

As the waiter served the drinks, Vasily reflected on Savinkov's words. Their substance did not surprise him, but their falsely deferential tone suggested that Savinkov, with Azef out of the picture, was setting himself up as kingmaker. He tilted back in the tiny metal chair, which barely supported his large frame. At that moment, he caught sight of an astonishingly pretty woman entering the café. She wore a dark fur coat with a cowl, which she threw back as she shook out her blond hair. With her was a fashionably dressed young Frenchman who seated her at a table near them. The woman met Vasily's gaze and smiled.

Savinkov was clinking his glass against Vasily's. "The SR party will triumph, Vasily," said the literary artist whose soul was choked in blood. They drank.

Between the brandy, his comrade's words, and the remarkable young woman at the nearby table, Vasily suddenly felt perfectly capable of carrying out the mission that the Central Committee had assigned to him.

"We have grown weak," Savinkov was saying. "We must profit by Azef's treason to strengthen the party. We must prepare ourselves to assume power."

"Through the Constituent Assembly," replied Vasily.

"Which we must control."

"The people will control the Constituent Assembly. We shall lead them to it."

"If the Combat Organization is revived, the road will be shorter."

"I'll give it some thought," said Vasily, though, at that moment, in his heart he promised himself never again to allow terror to corrupt the SR Party's high purpose.

As the two men talked, Vasily's glances at the young woman became less guarded, and she responded with the softest of smiles, unnoticed by her companion.

When it came to the female sex, Vasily could say that he knew himself well. He was an out-and-out romantic. He loved beauty, mystery, and sensuality in a woman, preferences which did not, however, prevent him from treating with hearty comradeship women in the party whose contempt for the upper classes, along with their fierce assertion of the equality of the sexes, caused them to adopt a severity of manner and an antifeminine dress and hair arrangement. But Vasily knew firsthand that revolutionary dedication and female charm need not be incompatible. His wife Anna was endowed with both. She was also intelligent and kind, compulsively selfless in fact, admirable in every respect. But the young woman at the nearby table reminded him of someone else: slender and lithe, running toward him through the silvery grass near the house with the broad veranda overlooking the Volga.

Anna's sister.

Ariane.

Savinkov glanced at his watch and nodded.

They found the front door to Azef's building unlocked. The hallway window to the concierge's apartment was black. There was a strong smell of stale soup and eau de Javel. Savinkov pressed the minuterie button that illuminated the landings above with pale yellow light and preceded Vasily up the stairs. At the third landing, Vasily took the lead, easing his weight along the creaking floor toward the door at the end of the hall. He drew his pistol. The light went off. The two men groped their way back to the head of the stairs where Savinkov found the light button. They tiptoed back to the door. Vasily raised his left hand to knock. From inside, they heard approaching steps and quickly pocketed their weapons. The door opened a crack. Azef's short, plump wife peered at them, terrified. Then, recognizing them, she threw the door wide open and heaved a sigh of relief.

"Ah, Vasily," she said. "Thank God it's you! And dear Boris. Come in. Anna's here."

As he entered the room, Vasily beheld a scene so unlike the one he had anticipated that at first he could not take it in. In the heavy armchair with the hideous antimacassars, in which he had expected to see Azef, sat his own wife, looking up at him from the book which she had been reading to the Azef sons, five and seven. The little boys sat on either side of her, staring at Vasily, their dark, intelligent eyes seeming to read his startled thoughts.

"What are you doing here, Anna? Marina is home alone."

"I'm paying a call on our friends, Vasily. These are difficult times for all of us."

Vasily found no suitable reply. At Anna's feet, the Azefs' hollow-flanked Persian was pawing at her green suede shoes.

From the opposite wall, Tsar Nicholas II gazed vacuously into the room.

"Have you seen Yevno?" Azef's wife asked anxiously.

"We've not," replied Vasily.

"I expected him home by now. We've just come back from the brasserie. Anna took us there for supper. She's been so kind through this whole horrible misunderstanding." She took Vasily's hands in hers. "Tell me at once. Were you able to clear Yevno's name?"

Out of the corner of his eye, he saw Anna shake her head, confirming that, indeed, Azef's wife knew nothing of her husband's police career. The boys' eyes were full of dread. Vasily hesitated. No, he decided, I won't be the one to inform these children that the rest of their lives will pass in the shadow of their father's infamy.

"Justice has been rendered," he said.

"Thank God!" said Azef's wife, throwing herself into Vasily's arms, sobbing into his chest. The cat, its green eyes suddenly violet, spun away from Anna, clawed at the carpet, raced in a circle, leaped to the piano, and with a single pass of its paw, swept the sheets of music to the floor. Then the cat dropped to the carpet, scampered to a wall, turned, ran, and in a single bound clutched at the fringes of the standing lamp behind Anna's chair, lost its grip, fell to the floor, and began cleaning itself.

Azef's wife had not noticed the cat. Still clinging to Vasily, she was gazing up at him with tears streaming down her face. He could feel her relief and gratitude through her dress.

"Thank you," she said. "Thank you."

"You're most welcome," said Vasily, easing himself out of her arms and nodding to Savinkov, signaling immediate departure.

"Everything considered," said Savinkov, "it might be better if Yevno leaves Paris for a while."

"Yes," agreed Vasily. "There may still be those who wish to do him harm."

"Thank you," she said again. "I'll never forget what you've done for us."

"Are you coming, Anna?" said Vasily.

"I'll read to the boys a little longer. We have to finish our story. Go back to Marina, Vasily. I'll be along soon."

Read to the boys a little longer? Finish their story? Vasily did not always understand his wife. Why would she be reading to the traitor's sons when Marina was alone in the apartment watched by secret police agents? Why did she put the welfare of others, including every sort of unworthy person, before that of her own family? Marina was a precocious child, wise beyond her years, but she was still a child. With a surge of concern for his daughter, he realized that lately he too had been neglecting her. He must hurry home and sing her a song before she fell asleep.

. . .

On Raspail, Vasily and Savinkov walked in silence, watchful, now and then glancing over their shoulders, approaching the café. Their former table was unoccupied. The one where the lovely young woman and the Frenchman had sat was now taken by an elderly couple. The chestnut vendor was gone. The wind had died, and the night had turned bitter cold.

"He must have been warned," said Savinkov at last.

"Who would do that?" said Vasily, keeping his voice even, but thinking, Perhaps you?

"He had friends," said the poet-assassin, glancing narrowly at Vasily. "Do we pursue him?"

"Nothing could be gained," said Vasily. "In any case, the worst punishment for Yevno will be to go on living, for he will never know a moment's peace. As for us, we must report his escape to the Central Committee and begin at once to rebuild the party."

Savinkov smiled. "In Italy?"

Vasily pictured in his mind a stone house with a red tiled roof surrounded by almond and fruit trees and overlooking the village of Alassio and the sea. The sea was blue. The sky was blue. The sun was warm. The air was heavy with the fragrances of sea, herbs, and flowers. For months, long before the source of the malaise within the Paris Central Committee had been identified, Vasily had dreamed of getting away to this house, so full of light and good omens. Anna had found it through her friend Ekaterina Peshkova, Maxim Gorky's wife, long separated from the writer, and who now lived near Alassio with her son Max. In any case, a change was essential. With the Paris SR organization in shambles, Vasily was confident that he could conduct the affairs of the party more effectively and with fewer distractions in the country of Garibaldi, a patron saint of the SRs. Savinkov strenuously disagreed.

"Nothing is final," Vasily replied.

"You're needed here."

Am I? thought Vasily. Why, Boris? So that now you can attach yourself to me as you did to Azef, while immersing yourself in the dubious pleasures of Parisian bohemia?

Thinking of Italy, Vasily could scarcely believe that only a half hour before he had steeled himself to kill Azef in cold blood. Remembering the frightened little boys with Anna, he marveled at his wife's goodness. He thought of Azef's wife. What a calvary awaited her! He thought of his daughter waiting for him at the apartment, and he wondered how much she understood of what was happening. Suddenly, he stopped and spread his arms wide.

"We need space, Boris! Space and sunlight—not intrigue and murder. We must rededicate the party to the honorable service of the Russian people!"

Savinkov's smile darkened. "And will you be closer to the Russian peasants on the Italian Riviera, Vasily?"

"I am close to them wherever I am! I am one of them!"

"So you're going?"

"Nothing has been decided."

"Then I wish you well."

"We'll talk soon. Good-night."

"Good-night."

They walked on. At the corner of Raspail and the rue Boissonade, they shook hands and parted. Savinkov headed in the direction of the Luxembourg Gardens, while Vasily continued up Raspail, hurrying, almost running, in the direction of the rue Gazan, where in the distance the bells of the Church of Sainte Anne were striking eight.

Chapter Two

MARINA VASILYEVNA NEVSKY, A SLENDER GIRL OF NINE WITH A HEL-met of chestnut hair, stood at a second-floor window gazing out between parted curtains at the dark street corner at the far end of the park. Under the gas lamp by the gates, directly across the street, the lanky man wearing a raincoat, a man she had often seen before, was conversing with a gendarme. The solemn bells of the church nearby tolled eight. Her father had been gone for two hours.

It had been a little before six when, out of breath, coat and hat soaked, he had burst into the apartment. Not noticing her sitting at a table in the salon drawing in her sketch pad, he had rushed to his study. Returning moments later and seeing her, he had said in a tight voice, "Mother will be home soon, Marinotchka. Make her a nice picture." Then he had clumped down the stairs, letting the door slam with a rattle of glass. Marina ran to the window and saw him join his SR comrade Boris Savinkov across the street and hurry off with him down the street along the park. Then the lanky man her father had said was an agent of the tsar's secret police—the Okhrana, which worked closely with the French police—had stepped out of the shadows. He watched the two men until they had rounded the corner at the end of the park, and then he took out a notebook and wrote in it.

Marina knew where they had gone. The pieces of the puzzle that had baffled her for days now fit together. Her father and Savinkov had gone to the apartment of the traitor Azef to kill him. From her parents' conversations, she knew about the catastrophe that had struck the party: there was an Okhrana spy in the Central Committee, indeed in the Combat Organization itself, and the party watchdog Burtsev had presented evidence that pointed to Azef, though both her father and Savinkov had at first believed that Burtsev himself was the culprit. Today, the matter was to have been resolved at Burtsev's trial before the Central Committee—not Azef's trial but Burtsev's. Either the accuser would prove his charges, or he himself would be condemned as a traitor.

Marina was now certain that Burtsev had been vindicated and that her father and Savinkov had gone to punish Azef. With his wife and children, he lived in an apartment on the boulevard Raspail, toward which they had set forth. Burtsev lived in the opposite direction.

Marina ran to her father's study and opened the lower desk drawer where he kept his pistol, hoping to find it there. The drawer was empty.

The reverberations of the church bells died. Marina took her sketch pad into the dining room and sat in her father's chair at the round table that filled the room. She glanced across at the photograph of her godfather, Alexey Maximovich Gorky, now the celebrated Maxim Gorky, as a young man, a fierce, friendly presence in his broad-brimmed black hat. She gazed around at the nine empty chairs, remembering when they were occupied by Central Committee members engaged in impassioned conversation, her father's rich baritone rising above the other voices.

Here, very young, she had stolen in and sat on his lap, resting her head against his chest to watch the visitors and feel the power of his voice through his waistcoat. The word he spoke with special force was *narod*, the people. She had imagined that he was King Arthur and his comrades around the table were his knights. No matter that these knights wore shabby business suits instead of shining armor, rode rickety bicycles instead of flowing-maned steeds, nor that several of the most esteemed were women: they were no less noble than the knights of Camelot.

She started to draw two knights jousting on horseback. Sir Percival wore white; Sir Mordred, black. Red plumes crowned Mordred's helmet; Percival's were light blue.

For as long as she could remember, she had known that her parents and their comrades had dedicated their lives to freeing the Russian people from the tsar. Lately, however, she had become aware of another, shadowy side of their lives, at first evident to her only through whispers and abrupt silences when she entered the room. Once again, she relived every moment of the hot, hazy afternoon the previous summer, when her suspicions about the secret part of her parents' world had been confirmed.

She had been standing on the bank of the pond in the Parc Montsouris, tossing bread to the swans, when she noticed three older girls from her school approaching her. She smiled at them, supposing that they no longer resented her for being foreign and getting only good grades and had now come to make friends.

"Bonjour," she had said shyly.

"Bonjour," said the sharp-faced one who was their leader. "Dites, est-ce vrai que vous lancez des bombes, vous?"

They had stared at her wide-eyed, and then had run away giggling.

That evening, she had told her parents about the encounter.

"They asked if we throw bombs. Do we?"

"Marina," said Vasily, "your mother and I have never harmed anyone."

Marina remembered the stern woman in a dark dress with a high collar who had stayed with them the spring before.

"Has Vera Figner?"

From their exchange of glances, she knew that she had guessed right. Her mother started to reply.

"Anna," cautioned Vasily, "Marina is still very young."

"Vasily, you make it sound as if Vera Figner had done something shameful. Her act was one of extreme bravery and sacrifice. Marina will soon be ten, and it's time she knew." And to Marina she said, "She belonged to a group called the Will of the People. They freed Russia of the tyrant Alexander II."

At that moment, it had seemed to Marina that she had always known from Vera Figner's regal bearing that she was associated with some grand and terrible deed.

"She didn't throw the bomb," Anna added, "but she helped plan the assassination. She was arrested and condemned to death, but so many people pleaded for her life that they sent her to the Schüsselberg fortress for twenty years instead. Marinotchka, we all believe that to kill another human being is evil, but Vera Figner had come to see that in Russia, only acts of terror could force the tsar to free the people."

"And the fat man, does he throw bombs?"

Vasily frowned. "Azef is devoted to our cause. He is one of the most valuable men in our party. You mustn't judge him by his appearance."

"But does he—"

"Not himself."

"Then who does?"

Anna said, "The best and bravest people in Russia. Our friend Maria Spiridonova is one. She is now in prison in horrible conditions for having shot a murderous tyrant, the General Lugenovsky, who had cruelly suppressed a peasant uprising in Tambov. That was in 1906 when she was only nineteen. She soon became famous all over Russia, even abroad."

"Did the general die?"

"He survived, but Spiridonova was beaten and tortured. She was saved only because of the protests of foreign socialists. But Spiridonova is only one of many heroes."

Near tears, Marina burst out, "Then if these are the heroes, why don't *you* throw bombs and shoot people?"

Anguished, Vasily said, "Terror is not the only way. It's no longer even certain that it's effective."

"And Savinkov?"

"Savinkov is a skilled revolutionary," said Vasily guardedly. "He takes great personal risks."

"Because he's good and brave?" asked Marina, trying to keep her voice even.

"He is absolutely dedicated."

"More and more to terror itself," said Anna, who made no secret of her mistrust of Boris Savinkov.

"Boris is a deeply troubled man," replied Vasily. "For a Russian in these times, that speaks well of him."

He reached out to Marina and drew her to him. "My dearest

daughter, someday you'll make up your own mind about these matters. Just remember that in Russia, the State is the supreme terrorist. It exists solely to perpetuate itself through oppression of the people. Remember that when you choose your own path in life."

Her parents had talked long into the July night, eager to share with her both their passions and their doubts. They spoke more and more freely, as if they were relieving themselves of a burden. Listening to them, Marina had felt a stinging sense of isolation.

She slid down from the chair and went back to the window. The Okhrana agent had gone. The gendarme was strolling down toward the corner of the park at the end of the street, clanging his stick along the fence. Through racing clouds, moonlight flared on the oval pond.

She tried to think of the bedtime stories her father told her, of the Snow Maiden, the Firebird, of quests and magical transformations, but instead, not meaning to, she thought of the evil witch Baba Yaga who lived in a wooden hut that stood on chicken legs and who ate human beings as if they were pancakes. Fear coiled in her stomach. Where was the Okhrana agent now? He was nowhere to be seen. His nightly surveillance had become, by its regularity, almost reassuring. But now he might have stolen into the building, into their apartment, and slipped into a closet from which he was about to leap out at her. A passing cloud darkened the pond.

Suddenly, Marina imagined that Azef, a fat cigar in his mouth, his thumbs in his waistcoat pockets, was standing behind her in the room, smirking at her.

She dared not turn around. It was so right, she told herself, that her father would shoot Azef. Traitors must die.

Then, at the corner of the park, she saw Vasily hurrying back alone.

Through the swaying trees, the pond was again bathed in moonlight.

The key turned in the lock. The door opened with a shudder of glass. Her father stamped his feet on the mat in the hallway and hung his wet hat and coat on the rack. For a moment, she dared not go to him. Then he opened his arms to her. She ran to him and embraced him, feeling as if she were stepping off a cliff.

"I understand, Papa."

"What do you understand?"

"Where you and Uncle Boris went. You had to kill Azef." She burst into tears.

He drew her to him and held her tight.

"But we didn't kill him, Marinotchka."

She looked into his eyes and saw that he was telling the truth. She also saw that he knew that it would have made no difference between them if he and Savinkov had fulfilled their mission.

When she had tucked herself into bed, Vasily came in and sat on the foot of the bed and sang her favorite song:

> *I brought you the sun, the wind,*
> *And an eagle to play with,*
> *But after three nights,*
> *The eagle has flown home,*
> *And the wind is rumbling back to his mother.*

Chapter Three

From his third-class window seat on the Paris-Genoa rapide, Vasily gazed westward at the violet hills beyond the Rhône as the sun broke through the clouds The fields, the cypress windbreaks, the tawny stone farmhouses with red tile roofs were flooded with golden light. The black, rich soil reminded him of Volga fields.

Anna dozed at his shoulder. Across from him, Marina was gazing out the window.

"Is Alassio as beautiful as this?" she asked.

"More beautiful. It overlooks the sea."

"Then let's stay there forever."

He smiled, yet her words reminded him of Savinkov's galling question about whether he would be closer to the Russian peasants on the Italian Riviera. How could Boris, who frequented racy circles in Montmartre, titillating artists and fops with his notoriety as an assassin, how could he of all people imply that this move to Alassio betrayed a waning of Vasily's revolutionary dedication? On the contrary, after the debacle in Paris, the sea and sun would revive him and clarify his thoughts. He looked out the window.

At that instant, he caught a glimpse of a plowman walking behind a big-hooved chestnut, carving the damp earth into shining clods. Behind the plowman stretched a cypress-shadowed field, and in the distance, on a crest beyond the river, stood the ruins of a château.

The image persisted. It told him that the Provençal plowman was cultivating his own plot of land because his forebears had revolted against the lord on the hilltop.

When would the Russian peasants seize the land?

He remembered being in the room while his grandfather lay on his deathbed, gaunt and defiant. He remembered every detail: the breeze-tossed sunflowers along the broken fence outside the window, the lightning bolts dancing on the steppe beyond the river. And he remembered holding his grandfather's hand and feeling the old man's fury at dying landless on the estate on which he had been born a serf. Then twenty-three, Vasily had stood at the bed across from Anna and her sister Ariane, and as the sunflowers nodded like mourners, out of the anger that boiled up in him then, he had conceived a bold idea.

Throughout the empire, a triple alliance between peasants, workers, and intellectuals would be forged. The land would be given to those who worked it, for the benefit of the entire people. And he swore to himself that he, Vasily, would make it happen.

He would begin on the Volga. He would unite his comrades and fire the spirits of the Saratov peasants. He remembered the power he had felt then, the power of his rage, the power of the river. And now he felt that power again.

The train sped on.

On a balmy spring morning before dawn, there had been at least forty small boats out on the river, their lanterns flickering like fireflies. They glided silently with the current, bathed in rosy mist. It was the first of May, the fiftieth anniversary of the 1848 French revolutionary uprising. Already Vasily's plan was succeeding beyond his wildest dreams. Wherever the flotilla of dories, flatboats, and rowboats made a stop—at Solynka, Rybak, Dubrovka—peasant families assembled, summoned by the pamphlets that Vasily and his comrades had sown throughout the region.

Hundreds had come, lighting bonfires along the reedy riverbanks. At each stop, Vasily had stood on the prow of his boat and addressed the crowd, proclaiming an alliance of peasants and intellectuals which would form along the Volga and then spread throughout Russia, uniting with the workers in the cities.

The peasants responded enthusiastically. They came alive with the promise that the land would one day be theirs. He could still see their faces in the flickering light—their eyes filled with hope for the first time in their lives.

Lights flashed past the window.

Savinkov be damned! Vasily knew in his heart that the move to the Riviera would be beneficial, not only for himself and his family but for the party as well. Since the Azef disaster, the rue Gazan apartment had been searched by the French police, as had Savinkov's flat. Vasily needed freedom from policemen and from the intrigues and bickering of the Central Committee, peace in which to complete his work on the land reform plan. From the Riviera, by correspondence and, whenever necessary, travel, he could rebuild the party. Of course, there would be time for fishing, for since his Volga childhood Vasily had been a passionate fisherman. And there would be gardening to be done as well, and painting and interior repair. He looked forward to strenuous physical labor and long swims in the sea. And he was particularly pleased to be taking Marina out of the corrupting atmosphere of Paris, into the sun and sea air, where she could make friends with peasant children and learn Italian. And Anna, who already spoke the language, would also make new friends, as she always did, and help him with party correspondence.

What a strange thing it is to be Russian, he reflected, how constantly surprising. For example, he himself, known to be a man of humanitarian character, a pillar of the intelligentsia, a worshiper at the feet of humankind, had not so long ago at a café on the boulevard Raspail felt an irresistible desire to shoot his former friend and comrade Yevno Azef.

That impulse—which he could now admit had had little or nothing to do with the directive of the Central Committee—was unaccountable to Vasily. What was clear was the revelation of his daughter's feelings toward him. Believing that he had carried out the assassination, Marina had not only absolved him of guilt but had taken that guilt upon her own nine-year-old shoulders. He was moved almost to tears at the thought of it. She looked up at him now, smiling, her green eyes bright with happiness, sharing in silence her excitement over the prospect of their new life on the Mediterranean.

The wheels clicked over the rails. Vasily was falling asleep when a thought occurred to him that jarred him fully awake.

He recalled that it had been he, not Savinkov or anyone else, who had been responsible for elevating Azef to the position of leader of the Combat Organization. No one else.

In that instant, Vasily vowed that he would make amends to his grandfather and to the millions of other disinherited peasants, living and dead, for his failure of judgment in the case of Yevno Azef. In Italy, he would prepare the Socialist Revolutionary Party to liberate the Russian people.

He fell asleep at last, at peace.

Chapter Four

It was a three-storied stone house overlooking the red tile roofs of the village that rose from the sea. Surrounded by a wild garden of roses, oleander, rosemary, lemon trees, olive, and cypress, the villa backed against terraces of almond trees rising to an upper road built by Julius Caesar and now used only by shepherds, hunters, and lovers. To the north, hills dotted with olive and live oak rolled into the blue haze of the Ligurian Alps. Below the house passed the road that followed the coast from the French border eastward to Alassio and then skirted the Gulf of Genoa to La Spezia. In 1910, this lower road was unpaved and dusty and smelled faintly of vanilla.

An ancient fig tree sprang from a terrace wall near the house. On the day of the Nevskys' arrival, Marina climbed into it and claimed it as her private sanctuary. Its pale gray branches and caressing leaves formed a bower with a view of the terrace, the road, the headlands, the harbor, and the open sea. Through the leaves, she could peer into her father's third-floor study and see him typing on his tall Remington. In the fragrant warmth of the fig tree, she was invisible and safe. Vasily called it Marina's Thinking Tree.

At the Villa Ariane, as her parents had named the house, Marina felt truly at home for the first time in her life. On the rue Gazan, she had always been aware that they were different: they were suspect foreigners, revolutionaries, outcasts. She had grown up defensive of her parents and their SR friends, critical of the French, whose stylish, self-assured world she nonetheless would at times have died to be part of. In Alassio, she made friends with the children of fishermen and shopkeepers. With Anna's help, she soon knew enough Italian to attend school.

On the Riviera, Vasily quickly recovered his spirits and was happier than Marina had ever known him. In the morning, he would work on his political articles and land reform plan, and in the afternoon, he would lose himself in swimming, gardening, hiking in the mountains, and fishing from a dory he had found stored in the villa. With only a few words of Italian, he would sit with the mayor of Alassio and his friends at their café table overlooking the harbor, gaining a place in the lore of the town as the Russian who swam in the sea and wanted to give land to the poor.

That first winter, rains hammered the Ligurian coast. In February, Vasily left the villa to attend SR conferences in London and Zurich. Marina would be alone with her mother for several weeks, and the prospect pleased her. She welcomed the chance to be with Anna and to ask her questions that had been troubling her for years. She hoped that she could penetrate the walls of sadness that seemed to surround her mother.

One rain-swept afternoon, Marina went into the sewing room where Anna was at work and sat near her, watching her feed cloth into the jabbing needle of her Singer machine. In her early thirties then, Anna was quite pretty, with gentle brown eyes and long, light brown hair parted in the middle. Despite her contempt for the landed class into which she had been born, and despite her satisfaction with their simple life, she had never lost her taste for fine clothes. With her small inheritance, she had bought dresses at shops in Paris—one from Worth—and had made others herself: loose gowns of light green, turquoise, or pale red that suited her rounded figure.

Rain brushed the windows. The small room was warmed by a fire crackling in the enameled stove. There was a smell of wood smoke and of the lavender drying on the dresser that would be made into sachets. After a silence, Marina asked her mother why she never spoke of her childhood.

Anna was silent a moment and then said quietly, "It's enough that we had to live it."

"What was Aunt Ariane like?"

Anna got up and opened a bureau drawer. From under folded blouses, she took out a photograph album Marina had never seen before. She opened it to a picture of a young woman in riding clothes standing beside a white horse in a grove of pines. The girl wore a small black hat set back on her flowing dark hair, a jacket with a tiny waist, a long skirt. She stood proudly, with a trace of defiance, one slender hand resting on the horse's mane. Beyond, through the pines, flowed a broad river.

"This is a photograph of a painting done when Ariane was eighteen," said Anna.

"She was very beautiful."

Her mother turned the pages to another photograph, of a two-story wooden house with a deep veranda. At the head of the veranda stairs stood a tall, massively built man holding a shotgun, broken at the breech. His face was in shadow, but his high boots and the brace of hunting dogs at his feet were in full sun.

"Our father. The master of Dubrovka."

Marina studied her grandfather's face. "Was he as severe as he looks?"

"He was a man of his time and place."

"Are there pictures of your mother?"

Anna shook her head. "My mother died when I was five," she said in a voice that invited no further questions.

"Who lives at Dubrovka now?"

"I don't know. Father lost the estate in a card game many years ago."

She showed Marina a third photograph, taken in the same pine grove near the river. Ariane, wearing a sheer summer dress, was holding hands with a handsome young man with a broad, smiling face. It took Marina a moment to realize that the young man was her father.

"Were they engaged?" she asked in amazement.

"They were in love. They planned to elope, but it wasn't to be."

She went to the bureau and from deep in the back of the drawer took out a blood-red coral necklace and handed it to Marina.

"This was hers," she said. "A gift from our father."

Marina shivered. The heavy necklace felt almost alive in her hands.

"How did she die?"

Anna stared at Marina, tears welling in her eyes.

"Your aunt died of the harshness of Russia."

She drew Marina to her and embraced her. Marina felt a surge of love for her mother. For years afterward, the memory of wood smoke and lavender would evoke the mysteries that lurked behind her mother's sadness.

At the villa, as in Paris, the Nevskys received a constant stream of visitors. Socialists came from all over Europe to pay homage to the leader of Russia's largest clandestine revolutionary party. Ekaterina Peshkova dropped by often, sometimes with Max. Vera Figner, recently released from prison, stayed with them twice. Boris Savinkov paid several visits, and when he did, he and Vasily would shut themselves in the studio and talk for hours at a stretch, while Marina, perched in the branches of the Thinking Tree, strained to overhear what they were saying. Though Savinkov called her Marina Vasilyevna, using the formal, grown-up form of her name, and in other ways treated her as an adult, offering compliments and useful criticisms of her drawings, she shared her mother's doubts about him. She resented his superior attitude toward her father.

In those years, their conversations centered on one man: Vasily's political archenemy. Peter Stolypin.

When a revolution had broken out in St. Petersburg in 1905, out of the blue a champion of the hereditary monarchy had appeared, endowed with the intelligence and ruthlessness needed to rescue Nicholas II and his vast, somnolent government from the people's wrath.

Vasily had seen him once in 1905, a black-bearded giant in a glittering uniform riding in an open carriage under the equestrian statue of Peter the Great. Upon the outbreak of the insurrection, Vasily Nevsky had returned to Russia to lead the underground SR Party, hoping to deal a death blow to the Romanov dynasty. By 1906, he had managed to plant the seeds of his land reform plan within the Duma, the creaky parliament forced on the tsar by the uprisings. That year, he had incurred the wrath of the large landowners, of Nicholas, and most especially of Peter Stolypin.

As the tsar's prime minister, Stolypin imposed a land program which was a shrewd, brutal perversion of the SRs' proposal: a redistribution of the best land to the richer, more ruthless peasants, while the majority were driven from the rich black-earth districts of Great Russia to new homelands in Siberia where they might scratch a living from the tundra or, if God willed, starve to death. To enforce his decrees, Stolypin had dispatched execution squads to rebellious villages throughout the empire, arresting real and suspected revolutionaries on an unprecedented scale.

To save his life, Vasily was forced to return to France in 1907.

While Vasily and his Paris comrades guided the SR Party— directing from afar the activities of the Combat Organization— Stolypin ruled Russia with an iron hand, blocking genuine reform. Meanwhile, Nicholas and his wife, the Empress Alexandra, had fallen under the spell of the peasant faith healer Gregory Rasputin, whose ministrations to their hemophiliac son had won him the couple's fanatical devotion. Russia was paralyzed.

Then one day in the summer of 1911, as Marina listened from the Thinking Tree, she overheard Savinkov urging Vasily to authorize the SRs to use terror again to bring about a revolution.

Only a few weeks later, the news reached the Villa Ariane that Stolypin had been assassinated.

The prime minister had been shot during a performance in the Kiev opera house in the presence of the tsar. The murderer was a certain Bogrov, rumored to be an undercover Okhrana informer with links to the SRs. Shortly before the performance, Bogrov was said to have reported an SR plot to kill Stolypin, and since he had exposed terrorist conspiracies in the past, the Okhrana had furnished him with a pass, admitting him into the heavily guarded opera house.

No one believed that Bogrov had acted alone.

Vasily maintained that the man was a double agent in the pay of the Okhrana, but doubt remained, doubt and suspicions of the sort that had colored the Nevskys' lives ever since the revelation of Azef's betrayal. Marina could not put out of her mind Savinkov's plea to her father to revive SR terror.

It was then, at the height of the speculation about the prime minister's assassination, that she had an encounter with Max Peshkov that revealed a side of herself that she had never known before—and did not like at all.

Chapter Five

On that afternoon, to escape the oppressive atmosphere at the villa, Marina had climbed into the fig tree to try to read her future in the changes of the sea and sky. She had been in the tree a few minutes when, from down the road, she heard the snarl of a gasoline engine. The sound grew louder, becoming deafening. A goggled rider, hunched over a black motorcycle, blasted into view and shot by with a roar, disappearing in a cloud of dust. The fig tree shook. Max Peshkov was climbing into its branches.

"That's the most beautiful sound in the world," he said, settling on a branch near her. "My father has promised me a motorcycle just like that for my birthday."

"It's too loud," she said, resenting his intrusion. Gorky's son was fourteen then, with thick dark hair and mischievous eyes. Marina found him handsome but impossibly silly.

"It's the poetry of the twentieth century. Someday, I'm going to have the fastest motorcycle in the world."

"I prefer real poetry."

"What you call real poetry is dead."

She stared out to sea, pretending he wasn't there.

"So," he said, "no more Stolypin. Aren't you jumping for joy?"

"As a matter of fact, I am."

He dropped his voice to a confidential whisper. "I saw you watching your father."

"When?"

"When he and your mother were talking about the assassination."

"So?"

"Maybe he had something to do with it?"

"Get out of my tree!"

"So he did have something to do with it?"

At first, she was too angry to reply. Then she said the meanest thing she could think of.

"It must be sad having your parents divorced."

"Not at all," he said casually. "My parents are still friends. Have you met Andreyeva?"

Gorky's new companion, the leading actress of the Moscow Art Theater, had not been with him on his last visits to the rue Gazan.

"No," she said, adding, "My mother says she's quite pretty."

"Quite pretty! She's the most beautiful woman in the world," he said. "She also speaks five languages. My father knows how to choose women. All great men do." He smiled derisively, adding, "What are you going to do when you grow up? Marry some lucky SR?"

"I'm going to be an artist."

"An actress?"

"A painter."

"Impossible."

"Why?"

"Because there are no good women painters. Never were and never will be. It's a question of biology. Besides, the painting of the past is even deader than the poetry of the past."

"That's stupid."

"It's true. The art of the future will be about speed and power. No more saints and sniveling Madonnas."

"Just noisy motorcycles?"

"And airplanes and rockets. The new art will be about scientific marvels."

"And wars?"

"Splendid wars. The twentieth century will be a test of men's inventions and courage, the beginning of a new world in which only the strong will survive."

"I don't like your twentieth century," she said.

"It isn't mine," he said, moving closer to her, grinning. "It's the one that will happen. A fabulous century of revolution and war."

She glared at him, not replying.

He grinned. "But you needn't worry, Marinotchka; your father will play no role in it."

He had moved his hand from the branch he held, reaching out to touch her, when suddenly with all her force she pushed him away from her. With a startled look, he fell backward through the branches, striking the ground on his back.

Marina was horrified. Max's mouth was open, his eyes staring upward. She thought he was dead. Then slowly he sat up, cautiously testing his limbs. Apparently undamaged, he looked up at her and, seeing her terrified expression, burst out laughing.

"So," he said, "you SRs are as violent as they say. Perhaps you have a future after all!"

The murder of Stolypin in 1911 was a turning point for Imperial Russia: his death deprived the tsar of the one man capable of saving his throne. Power now shifted to the "mad monk" Rasputin and his corrupt cabal. But the revolutionaries' hopes for the fall of Tsar Nicholas II were not yet to be realized.

In October 1912, the League of Balkan States—including Serbia, Bulgaria, and Greece—declared war on Turkey. Austria intervened, thereby reducing the League to a nest of squabbling nationalities. Thus did the Balkans become the tinderbox of the firestorm which would soon engulf Europe.

Meanwhile, life at the Villa Ariane went on much as before. Max and his mother returned to Russia, Max seeming to hold no grudge against me for almost killing him, and when he had gone, I found that I almost missed him. That long winter of 1912–1913, with my father away for weeks at a time, was a lonely, questioning time for me, full of riddles about my changing body and the ever more mysterious world around me. But in March a very special visitor arrived, bringing a fresh breath of life to the Villa Ariane.

Chapter Six

FROM THE STUDIO WINDOW, MARINA WATCHED FOR HER GODFATHER'S carriage. It had been seven years since she had seen Gorky at the Paris apartment. She remembered him as a tall, angular man with a bushy mustache, cheeks like little apples, and blue eyes that seemed to mirror all the love and pain in the world. Today, he was arriving with his companion, Maria Andreyeva. They were on their way back to Russia from the island of Capri.

As the carriage drew up at the steps to the villa, Marina ran down to meet the guests. In his broad black hat, squinting into the bright light, Gorky appeared bewildered, disoriented, like a visitor from another planet. But when he saw her running toward him, he smiled and opened his arms to her. When he embraced her, his cheek pricked and he smelled of tobacco.

"My favorite goddaughter," he said, presenting her to Andreyeva, a handsome, full-figured woman with pale skin, soft red lips, and a crown of sable hair.

On the terrace, Vasily and Anna greeted the visitors. Gorky sniffed the fragrant air with a wince of distaste. "So you too are trapped in this Mediterranean paradise," he said. "I tell you, the sea is even more damnably blue in Capri. But here you have figs this early. And geraniums! So many red geraniums in pots! They're lovely, Anna—but, I ask you, what has any of us to do with blue seas and geraniums when Russia is suffocating under the tyranny of idiots? My God, three centuries of Romanovs! And to think that they're shooting off fireworks over the Neva in celebration of their obscene anniversary! It makes you want to cry."

"How much longer will the people suffer?" asked Andreyeva.

Anna smiled sympathetically. "The geraniums are Vasily's," she said. "The whole garden is."

"It's beautiful, Vasily," said Andreyeva. "Ours seems always to grow wild."

Gorky glowered at the garden. Narrowing his eyes, he asked Vasily darkly, "And I suppose you speak Italian?"

"Only a little. Anna speaks it fluently, as does Marina now."

"As for me, I can hardly croak out a single word. Seven years on Capri and Signor Gorky non parla Italiano. What's far worse, my Russian is slipping. I'm scribbling about my childhood, and though my memories of that horror are all too clear, the words don't come as they used to. It's time I was getting home."

"Aren't you afraid of arrest?" asked Vasily.

"Of course, I've thought about that. I sought Lenin's opinion, and he assured me that the amnesty would be honored. I asked Fyodor Chaliapin too, and he agreed. He said that my international fame would protect me. International fame! As if the regime worried about what the West thinks about it! Maybe they'll collar me the moment I step off the train. But more likely, they want me in Russia to keep an eye on me—to snap their fangs when they feel like it. They think I'll be tamer there than prowling in the West, but they're wrong." Again he scowled at the garden. "Where do you do your writing, Vasily?"

Vasily led the way up to his study. He would have preferred a private conversation with his old friend, but Gorky invited the others to follow them upstairs. He surveyed the spacious room, inspecting the bookshelves.

"Herzen, Rousseau, Marx, Thomas Paine, Tolstoy, Cervantes, Shakespeare, Mark Twain, Jules Verne—and Maxim Gorky." He winked at Anna. "The library of a well-rounded man of our time."

Gorky turned his attention to the pictures on the wall: stiff group portraits of SRs; a chromolithograph of "The Man with the Hoe" by Millet; a reproduction of Repin's painting of Tolstoy, barefoot in a peasant shirt; the photograph of himself that had hung in the dining room of the Paris apartment.

He stared with disapproval at the pictures and then dropped into Vasily's armchair as the others found places around the room.

"So this," he said, "is where the new Russia is being hatched."

"My dear Alexey," said Vasily, "the new Russia already exists. It's an ancient dream in the hearts of the peasants. They want land and political freedom, and with our help they will have both."

"With more bombs under carriages?"

"No," said Anna quietly. "That time passed years ago. The martyrs have shown the way. One day, the people will follow."

"Then may the Lord help them!" said Gorky. He gestured at Millet's peasant. "There you have the Socialist Revolutionaries' idea of a Russian peasant. Well, he isn't a bit like that. You think he's been doing nothing all these centuries but leaning on his hoe and mooning about land and liberty, when in fact he's become brutalized by drunkenness and oppression until he's not a man at all but a beast—worse than a beast because a beast doesn't get besotted on vodka and beat up his wife!"

"You're becoming a jaundiced exile," said Vasily. "When the peasants have land, everything will change."

"Alexey," said Anna, "you've written powerful stories and plays about the simple people. You've spoken of your faith in man. Have you lost that faith?"

Gorky lit a cigarette, dropping the match in an ashtray and watching the flame catch some scraps of paper, flare, then die out. He said, "There'll be no freedom in Russia until Russians are taught to be human."

Again the portrait of Tolstoy caught his eye.

"I had many disagreements with Lev Tolstoy," he said. "I saw him holding back social progress in Russia with his obsession about individual salvation, but when he died I felt that I had lost a father. Russia had lost her father. With his death, I did begin to question my faith in man. I wept for a whole day."

"He did," said Andreyeva softly, adding, "But nothing shook your faith like America, did it, Alexey?"

Gorky's face darkened. "A nation of hypocritical money-worshipers! A new breed of philistines who have lost every shred of human feeling in their mad scramble for dollars! If the future lies in America, then God help the human race!"

Vasily said, "But Alexey, you've also been very hard on the

French, the English, and the Germans. You've accused them all of being greedy, soulless petit bourgeois. So I ask you: who does that leave to build a just society upon, if not our own Russian peasantry?"

"Our own Russian peasantry!" said Gorky triumphantly. "In those words lies the central fallacy of the SR Party. The pipe dream of a marriage between intellectuals and the people!" With his cigarette, he gestured toward the sea. "Especially seductive at a great distance from home. I tell you: turn the peasantry loose in its present state, and you'll be releasing a wolf pack that will tear the country apart!"

Anna said, "You're too harsh. The Russian peasant's body may have been brutalized, but his soul has been strengthened by suffering."

Gorky touched his fingertips together and closed his eyes as if in prayer.

"Please, Anna, I beg you. Do not imagine that suffering strengthens anyone. I know suffering like a brother, and I can tell you that no good comes of it. For centuries, priests and charlatans of all sorts have promised eternal bliss in exchange for agony on earth. It's a cruel deception. Suffering leads nowhere but to misery, viciousness, and death. No good comes of it on this earth or afterward."

"Yet you survived it," said Anna. "You found compassion in suffering and the power to show the whole world what Russian men and women endure."

Gorky lit another cigarette. "My work does not celebrate suffering, as does that of so many of our notable writers—Dostoyevsky is the worst of the lot. My work strikes out against it. Yes, I do have a high ideal of man—or used to—but I have no illusions. There must be a clean sweep of the past and a future built on the laws of history."

"As interpreted by the Bolshevik Party."

"I don't agree with Lenin about everything," said Gorky defensively, "but he's a realist, and Russia cries out for realists!"

Vasily said hotly, "If Lenin is a realist, why does he pin his hopes on a Russian proletariat which barely exists? In basing our hopes on the millions of peasants, *we* are the realists. We are the larger, stronger party. As soon as the tsarist government is overthrown, we'll convene a Constituent Assembly to decide our future."

"Ah!" cried Gorky. "The grand illusion—the Constituent Assembly!"

"You don't mean that! You yourself have said that the best people in Russia live in the hope that one day the country will be governed by a true parliament."

"In a weak moment, perhaps I did. But I'm no longer convinced that our so-called best people are fit to lead Russia anywhere but into a ditch. We need iron-willed revolutionaries, not—forgive me—well-meaning ideologues."

Anna shook her head. "I don't understand, Alexey. Has Lenin so changed you? He's a determined revolutionary, but as cold a man as you are warm."

She gazed wistfully at Gorky, as if at a wayward brother. He smiled at her.

"How good you are, Anna. And you as well, Vasily. I wish I could lock arms with you, travel your path, share your faith, but I cannot. Not that I see eye to eye with Lenin, you understand. We're very different, he and I. He is calculating, and like you he is laying plans—though it's true, I admit, that for the moment he seems lost in the woods."

"One cause, one enemy," said Vasily. "When that enemy is chucked out, all the socialist parties will sit down around a table and hammer out their differences."

"Lenin will never do that," said Anna. "In his mind, no one is right but him."

"Don't underestimate him," said Gorky. "Lenin is a spider weaving a web. He slips but always catches himself and spins the next strand in exactly the right place. In his mind is the whole shape of the web. He knows that the Revolution will be only the beginning. He understands that the Russian people are not ready for socialism. They must first be purged of the poison of the past. They must be taught how to behave like men. Only then will Russia awaken from her long nightmare."

They were leaving the study when Gorky stopped to examine yet another picture on the wall, a charcoal portrait Marina had done of Vera Figner. In Vera's handsome, severe face, Marina had captured the very faith in the revolutionary cause she had so often sought in herself.

"This is the true face of Russia!" Gorky exclaimed. "You have seen through to her soul, Marina. You have the gift of seeing life as it is! I hope you will work hard and become a painter."

Marina glowed with pleasure.

Vasily looked at his daughter proudly, "She's quite a trial to us, Alexey. She does see everything as it is—far too clearly."

The Russia to which Gorky returned in 1913 was in a state of unrest barely suppressed by the tsar's vast network of police. Thousands of peasants uprooted by Stolypin's land redistribution flooded into the cities. Angry at being forced off the land, they formed an ardent core which would rekindle the smothered fires of the Revolution of 1905. In the factories and in the countryside, there was open discontent.

Meanwhile, Nicholas II, never doubting the people's devotion to him, had surrendered his imperial authority to Rasputin, whose followers were emerging as the de facto government of Russia.

Thus, millions of Russians suffering hunger and humiliation found themselves at an even greater distance from the tsar.

In Europe, war loomed. The poet Alexander Blok sensed "the smell of burning, blood, and iron in the air." Nations were arming with modern munitions believed by one French military expert to be too deadly ever to be used. Nicholas's bellicose cousin Kaiser Wilhelm II bristled to wage war for revenge, territory, German glory. Conflicts in the Balkan states would soon provide the kaiser and the Hapsburg dynasty of Austria with the opportunity they had long been awaiting.

On a Sunday in June 1914, in the city of Sarajevo, a young Serbian terrorist shot and killed the heir to the Hapsburg throne, Archduke Franz Ferdinand. This was the spark that set Europe ablaze.

That summer, Germany and Austria declared war on Russia, France, and England. Upon learning of Nicholas's decision to proceed to a general mobili-

zation, the French ambassador to Russia, Maurice Paléologue, noted in his diary, "The part played by reason in the government of peoples is so small that it has taken only a week to release universal madness."

For Russian peasant-soldiers meeting the Germans' superior forces in the fields and forests of Galicia and East Prussia, the war proved an unrelieved nightmare. Ill-equipped, untrained armies led by incompetent generals advanced recklessly, only to be thrown back and slaughtered by the tens of thousands.

For revolutionaries like ourselves, the war was a double calamity. Besides its horror, it aroused the people's patriotic feelings, reconciling them with the tsar and with their own misery. In 1915, socialists representing various countries and factions, my father among them, met in the Swiss town of Zimmerwald to decide upon united action. At that conference, the Bolshevik Vladimir Ilyich Lenin proposed that the soldiers of all warring nations be urged to turn their guns against their capitalist masters. The proposal was defeated. The majority, including my father, approved instead a resolution that called for an immediate armistice. The war went on as before.

In Alassio, the surface of life was barely rippled—until 1915, when Italy entered the war on the side of the Allies. That summer, I stood on the train station platform with my school friends, waving good-bye to young men of the village departing for the battlefields of France and Belgium.

By 1916, the German atrocities and immense Russian losses had persuaded my father that Russia must continue to fight on the side of the Allies against the Germans. He was as yet unaware of the erosion of patriotic feeling among the Russian people.

That winter Rasputin was murdered. The murder in itself came as no surprise. His enemies had been legion. What was intriguing was the identity of the principal assassin. Prince Felix Yusupov was one of the richest, most aristocratic noblemen in Russia, a relative of the tsar and therefore also kin of Kaiser Wilhelm and King George V of England.

The court and the ministries were now split into two rival camps: Rasputin's cronies and the aristocratic friends of the assassins.

The empire was dying.

This time no Stolypin came forth.

The tsar played dominoes.

Chapter Seven

IT WAS THE KIND OF LATE WINTER AFTERNOON ON THE RIVIERA WHEN it seemed that fine weather had come to stay. A breeze from the mountains rustled the almond trees behind the house. Their falling petals reminded Marina of the Parc Montsouris, where, one winter, snowflakes had fallen in sunlight. Now the corpses in the Galician forests would be shrouded in snow, but here the potted orange trees at the edge of the terrace were fragrant with what Anna called their bridal smell.

That afternoon on the terrace, no one was talking about the war. Tomorrow was Marina's seventeenth birthday, and she and Anna were settled in a sheltered corner of the terrace planning a party, deciding on the menu, making a list of the guests who would come from the village. From the third-floor window came the soft clatter of the Remington that filled their days. At the far end of the terrace, his feet up on a chair, absorbed in a book, sat the Nevskys' house-guest. Once in a while, Marina would steal a glance at him. Whatever doubts she might have about him, she was smitten by his good looks and had fallen in love with him. He had wavy black hair, deep-set blue eyes, and the longest lashes she had ever seen. To her, he was a riddle. Most of the time, he was distant and withdrawn, and yet sometimes, unexpectedly, he would smile at her and she would be filled with a kind of happiness she had never known before.

Dmitry Danilov had appeared at the villa six months before, arriving from Petrograd via Paris. Marina had seen him on the road from her window, a tall, lean young man, a rucksack slung over one shoulder, looking for Vasily Nevsky's house. In the rucksack, he carried a letter from Abram Gotz, Vasily's SR comrade, now in Petrograd, commending Dmitry to him as "a young fellow with a head on his shoulders and fire in his heart, the kind we'll be needing if the Socialist Revolutionary Party is not to die of old age."

The letter explained that Dmitry had read Vasily's scholarly articles on the theory of revolution and now sought his help with a study of the French Revolution that he was writing. Like Vasily and Anna, Dmitry was a native of Saratov on the Volga, where his parents had been SR organizers. At the outbreak of the 1905 revolution, during a strike at the railroad works, both had been shot dead by Stolypin's police.

Marina was thrilled at the prospect of living under the same roof with this handsome visitor. At night in bed, thinking of him asleep two doors down the hall, she played a game of wondering whether he would become an older brother to her, or a suitor. By the end of the first week, engaging him with questions about the French Revolution, she had managed to lure him on a stroll with her through the village, where she could show him off to her Italian girlfriends. Marina longed to have Dmitry fall in love with her, but it soon became obvious that he would not do this. From that first walk together, he made it plain that he found people with romance on their minds trivial. Dmitry was in love with revolution. While treating Marina like an insignificant younger sister, he carried on impassioned conversations with her father about revolutions of the past and the great one that would one day come to Russia.

By now, six months later, it was clear to her that Dmitry had won a special place in Vasily's heart, and that her father was now acting as if Dmitry were the rightful child of the family and Marina the outsider.

Dmitry looked up from his book and, finding Marina watching him, flashed a smile at her. The sound of the typewriter stopped. Dmitry glanced up at the studio window. After a moment, the typing resumed. He buried himself in his reading.

"They'll be taking their walk soon," said Marina to her mother in a low voice.

"Why don't you go with them?" asked Anna.

"Because they talk too much."

Anna smiled. She looked over the list of guests she was entering in a notebook. "Shall we invite Angelino?"

Angelino Petrelli was a shy, handsome fisherman's son who had a crush on Marina. Since Dmitry's arrival, she had avoided Angelino's company. Now she decided on a change of tactics.

"Yes," she said loudly. "By all means, let's invite Angelino. And Pedro and Alberto too."

Dmitry did not stir.

At that moment, Vasily, wearing his floppy straw hat, burst through the French doors and out onto the terrace.

"Enough land reform for today," he said, spreading his arms to the hills rising from the curve of the shore to the east. "Come, Dmitry, the mountains are calling. We can resolve our differences about the Jacobins."

"An excellent idea, Vasily! My work is stalled. I find it impossible to think straight about the French Revolution. I'm impressed by Robespierre's determination and disgusted with the Girondists. They talked and talked instead of acting. Perhaps on our stroll we can discuss these talkative people."

"Don't be too hard on talkative moderates," said Vasily. "That's what Lenin calls me: 'a wordy moderate, a veritable Girondist.'" He smiled at Anna. "Of course, it's always possible that he's right."

"Very possible," agreed Anna, "but I like to think that in the future, there'll be more need for moderates than for Lenins."

To Marina's delight, Dmitry then said casually, "Vasily, what about taking Marina along? She can listen while we resolve the contradictions of history."

"Why, of course," replied Vasily. "We need a levelheaded referee. Will you join us, Marina?"

"How can I refuse?" she said.

"Will you come too, Anna?"

"Thank you, no," said Anna with a conspiratorial glance at Marina. "I'll stay here and get our supper ready."

·   ·   ·

Vasily and Dmitry led the way up to the Roman road and started eastward over the uneven stones, the glistening sea spreading out to the south. Marina followed. The men were soon deep in argument.

"Why are you so hard on the Jacobins, Vasily Ivanovich? Think what the French kings were doing to their people! Parisians had to drink from the Seine, which was the city's sewer!"

"Nevertheless, the Reign of Terror was wrong morally, and it was wrong politically. It paved the way for Napoleon."

"The Terror was neither right nor wrong—it was inevitable. When our revolution breaks out, you may have to act in ways that might shock your finer sensibilities."

"Dmitry, nothing will ever force Socialist Revolutionaries to massacre innocent people. Our code of honor forbids it."

"And what if the SR code of honor is swept aside by the laws of history?"

"Laws of history be damned! Karl Marx will always be alien to Russia! Marxism is a narrow, Germanic notion that no Bolshevik tinkering will ever make acceptable! Sooner or later, the Russian people will smoke out those scheming dogmatists!"

Vasily wiped his brow. The wind had died, and the late afternoon sun was raking the limestone cliffs above them.

"Vasily," persisted Dmitry, "the Russian peasant is no revolutionary. He's a wild rebel at best."

"He will become a revolutionary when his eyes are opened. Even Gorky believes that education is the central task of socialism."

"Isn't Gorky in the enemy camp?"

"Gorky pursues his own struggle for the liberation of our people without Lenin's cold obsessiveness."

"Haven't there been enough solitary struggles? Perhaps it's time for some cold obsessiveness." Dmitry kicked a stone in his path, sending it flying. "I feel a need to shoot people and burn manor houses."

Vasily shook his head sorrowfully.

"I'm not joking!" insisted Dmitry. "Many young SRs feel as I do."

They walked in silence through groves of wind-bent pine, catching glimpses of the sea. No one spoke. After a while, they left the cool woods behind them and entered a landscape of boulders and broken stone. Neither thyme nor lavender grew here. The rocky path ended at a sandy open space shaded by a single pine tree. Without a word, Vasily and then Dmitry walked to the tree and touched it, and then started back toward the path. Feeling excluded from what had obviously become a ritual, Marina walked behind them.

"Remember who we are, Vasily," said Dmitry. "We're Scythians of the Black Sea, ruthless nomads. We cook our beefsteaks under our saddles. We skin our enemies alive."

Marina hated it when Dmitry talked like this, as if Russian revolutionaries had to be barbarians. Though she had promised herself to be silent on this walk, she was about to protest when her attention was diverted.

"Look!" she exclaimed, pointing to the west. Emerging from the haze that had settled over the sea, a gleaming white steam-yacht was rounding the spit of rock and cypress, sunlight blazing in her twin rows of portholes.

The white vessel was an unusual sight. With German U-boats prowling the seas, the rare ships that passed were usually gray or camouflaged. As it drew nearer, Marina could hear the strains of a string orchestra. In the yellow light, the yacht looked like a toy painted on the water.

"She must be bound for Cairo," said Vasily. "Let's swim out to her and climb aboard, Dmitry. We'll have a look at the Pyramids, and then travel up the Nile to the Valley of the Gods."

"She's going farther than that. Through the Suez to the Red Sea. We'll cruise to Aden and cut through the jungle to sources of the Nile. Coming with us, Marina?"

"I'll stay," she said. "You'll need a Penelope to listen to your tales when you come back."

When they returned to the house, it had grown cold on the empty terrace. The ship was now so close to shore that Marina could hear the timbres of violins across the water. Under a canopy on the afterdeck, couples in evening dress were dancing, moving in a stillness just ahead of the music, the low sun catching the sheen of the women's satin gowns, the men's pomaded hair, their white dinner jackets. Marina was spellbound. She could see the faces of these beings from another world and when the music stopped, she could hear their voices and merry laughter.

She watched in disbelief, thinking, I would give anything in the world to be one of them! Dmitry would pay attention to me if I were an exotic grown-up beauty.

Suddenly, a tremendous sound shook the air, rattling doors and windows and setting village dogs barking. Then from the ship came the sounds of klaxons, bells, and orders shouted over megaphones. Black smoke and orange flames erupted from the smokestacks. Passengers were pouring onto the main deck, mixing with the dancers, pushing toward the lifeboats. Throwing open the French doors, Anna rushed out onto the terrace

"Quickly!" said Vasily. "We must help those people!"

Down the steps, across the road, the four joined a stream of villagers racing down the pebbly path to the beach. There, the Alassio fishermen were running to their dories, overturned against the cliff. They dragged the boats down the beach and launched them. The mayor, a stocky gray-haired man in his sixties, stood at the water's edge directing the rescue effort; then he launched his own dory and rowed out with the other boatmen. Anna ran up toward a group of women in black who were preparing a shelter and first-aid station in the school just above the beach.

By then, the ship's stern was settling, its bow slowly rising. An overcrowded lifeboat had been lowered, but the cables had fouled in the davits, spilling passengers into the sea. The vessel's angle steepened; the flames that had enveloped it were dying, then flaring again. The first dories were reaching the stricken ship. Passengers were jumping from the deck and being hauled out of the water by the strong young arms of the Alassio fisherman.

A full moon was rising in the southern sky. Silhouetted against the wavering reflections of flames in the water, the returning dories were beaching, their drenched passengers stumbling out onto the sand. Vasily, Dmitry, and Anna assisted them, guiding them up the path to the school. They had just returned to the beach when they saw the mayor's boat approaching with two passengers. One was a tall, gaunt man wearing a tailcoat, and holding a violin and its bow over his head. The other, sitting beside him, was a slender red-haired woman wearing a peach-colored gown, who appeared to have

49

fainted against her companion's shoulder. As the mayor shipped his oars, he called out to Vasily.

"Questi due parlano la sua lingua!"

The dory's bow slid up the sand and stopped. Vasily splashed into the water and gently lifted the woman into his arms. Her eyes were closed; her wet dress clung to her body. From the fingers of her right hand dangled a pair of pink satin dancing slippers. Drenched as she was, she was the most beautiful woman Marina had ever seen.

As Vasily carried her to the beach, the man in the tailcoat stepped out of the boat, raising the violin and bow high over his head. Marina could not take her eyes off the woman in her father's arms. Anna too was gazing at her in wonderment. The man held the fingerboard of the violin to his ear and plucked at the strings.

The woman opened her eyes. Still cradling her in his arms, Vasily looked down at her as if she were a child.

"You'll be all right," he said in Russian.

"Where am I?" asked the woman, also in Russian.

"You're safe," said Anna. "You're with us."

"Kind people speaking Russian," breathed the woman. "Who are you?"

Vasily set her lightly on her feet. In the fading light of the flames, his broad, smiling face shone with sweat.

"I am Vasily Nevsky," he said. "This is my wife, Anna, and our daughter, Marina, and this is our friend Dmitry."

"Vasily Nevsky, the revolutionary?" demanded the violinist with a scowl.

"Vasily Nevsky, the hope of the Russian people, Anton," corrected the woman, wide awake now, her eyes shining. Still holding her slippers, she was tugging at her clinging dress. "I am Tamara Sermus. This is my husband, Anton Sermus, whose music, fortunately, makes up for his bad manners. We are honored."

"Come with us," said Anna. "We live nearby. We'll find dry clothes for you."

Sermus bowed stiffly. "Thank you, dear lady, but we must remain in the service of the prince."

"What prince?" asked Marina.

"Don't be silly, Anton," said the woman, gesturing toward the burning ship. "Obviously, the prince has no need of us now." She turned to Anna. "We accept your generous invitation."

"Tamara!" protested Sermus.

"Stay if you like, Anton," she said. "I am going with these good people. What a miracle to find cultivated Russians on an Italian beach!"

"Run ahead, Marina, Dmitry!" said Anna. "Prepare the guest room. Dmitry, please set a fire in the living room."

When Marina came downstairs after making up the guest-room bed with fresh sheets and a pile of blankets and comforters, her parents had arrived with the newcomers. A fire was blazing in the fireplace. Tamara Sermus, wearing Anna's Japanese kimono, was circling the living room with her arms outstretched. Sermus, wrapped in a red woolen robe of Vasily's that was far too large for him, sat in his host's favorite chair by the fireplace, glaring into the flames. Anna brought chowder and bread and cheese from the kitchen, setting out the dishes on the table near the fireplace. Vasily was starting the samovar on the sideboard. Dmitry stood by the French doors to the terrace, their rippled glass lambent with reflections of the burning ship. He was glowering at Tamara. When Marina came in, he fixed her with a dark look, as if she were responsible for this intrusion, which was certain to interfere with his evening routine: a game of chess with Vasily and a discussion of what each had written that day.

"What a charming house," Tamara was saying, alighting on the sofa. "Such warm emanations."

"What a dreadful experience you've been through," said Anna.

"There was no warning at all."

"I heard on the beach that someone saw a periscope just before the explosion," said Vasily. Beyond the terrace, in the moonlight, they could see the burning vessel, her stern submerged, her bow jutting almost straight up out of the water. "What ship is that?" he asked.

"*L'Étoile,*" said Tamara. "She belongs to Prince Oleg Yusupov of Monte Carlo, an uncle of Prince Felix. He and a party of friends were sailing to the Crimea, intending to journey on by sleeper train to his palace in Petrograd."

"With U-boats in every sea?"

Tamara shook her head sadly, "The elder prince is not a practical man. He lives in a world quite his own. He believed that as a relation of the kaiser he could depend on German respect for the rights of cousinage. It seems absurd now, doesn't it?"

"What matters is that you're safe," said Anna.

Dmitry, who had been studying the visitors, said in an icy voice, "So, you are friends of the Yusupovs?"

Tamara laughed lightly, but with an edge of harshness, Marina noticed. "Oh no, young man, like my husband, I am merely a paid entertainer. A professional dancer. Still, you must realize that the Yusupovs and their friends are a far cry from Rasputin's crowd. What a pity that the very people who might have had some good influence on the tsar will now be returning to Monte Carlo."

"Russia will not be saved by the Yusupovs!" said Dmitry sharply.

At this moment, Anton Sermus rose abruptly. "If you all would be so good as to excuse me," he said, with as much dignity as the oversized robe allowed. "I am exhausted and would like to retire."

"Of course," said Anna. "Dmitry, please show our guest to his room."

Looking unhappy, Dmitry led the visitor up the stairs.

When they had gone, Tamara shook her head sadly, "Poor Anton. I'm afraid his reverence for Prince Oleg and his set has quite blinded him to the changes that will inevitably take place in Russia." She sighed and opened her hands as if in gratitude. "What a pleasure to find myself at last among emancipated people with whom I can speak freely. Lately, I've been forced to behave like a conspirator, but in this company it's impossible for me to conceal my true feelings. You see, I have not always been candid with my husband. I have wanted so desperately to return to Russia in these tragic times, to serve the people in whatever way I could, that I agreed to sail with him on board *L'Étoile.*"

Dmitry reappeared at the foot of the stairs. "You're going to Russia as a revolutionary?" he asked sarcastically.

With a pitying glance at Dmitry, Tamara turned to Vasily, "I'm sure you know of Lunacharsky?"

"Of course," said Vasily. "He and Bukharin are the two truly educated men in the Bolshevik Party."

Marina had heard Vasily speak of Anatoly Lunacharsky, Lenin's friend, as well as Gorky's.

"I was so very, very young," Tamara went on, "so unprepared. A student in Petersburg fresh from my straitlaced home in Tallinn—" She broke off, looking apologetically at Anna. "But here I am, repaying your kindness by boring you to death with my stories."

"I can assure you that you're not boring us," said Anna. "Please go on."

"In any case, I was dazzled by Lunacharsky's brilliant mind. Under his guidance, I became part of a circle of revolutionaries who met in the cellar of a café on the Nevsky Prospect. One of the group fell in love with me. I was terribly naive. For a while, I was happy. Very much in love. I even thought that we would marry. But then one day, without a word to me, he left."

"How very sad," said Anna.

"Tragic," said Dmitry. Anna looked at him reprovingly.

Tamara turned again to Dmitry. "I know you're mocking me, Dmitry. Perhaps when you're a little older and more experienced in life, you will learn something about compassion."

"Pay no attention to him," said Anna. "He's not as boorish as he pretends to be."

"In fact," the guest continued, "it proved to be all for the best. I was able to travel abroad, and in Paris, I met the person who showed me my true direction in life."

"Do you mean your husband?" said Anna.

"Oh dear, dear, no!" said Tamara with a laugh. "That was long before I met Anton. I was blessed—I became a student of the Divine Isadora."

She raised her chin and unfolded her hands in a gesture that evoked the artist of whom she spoke: the American dancer whose unbridled performances and scandalous personal life had captivated Europe and Russia.

"You know Isadora Duncan?" asked Marina.

"Intimately. I studied with her in Budapest. From Isadora, I learned far more than dance. Isadora showed me that art, revolution, and love are one, and that only through art will the Russian people be awakened. That is why I agreed to dance for those worthless aristocrats, so that I could return to Russia and perform for the people. I thought that in time I could make Anton see the beautiful dawn that will one day break over Russia."

Soon, with smiles and good-nights for everyone and effusive thanks to Anna, Tamara went upstairs to the guest room. Marina helped her mother with the dishes, while Vasily and Dmitry set up the chessmen. Marina noticed that none of them, each no doubt for his or her own reason, said anything about their guests or the extraordinary event which had brought them into their midst. She was annoyed with Dmitry for his rudeness. As for her mother, she was clearly so enchanted by Tamara that she chose not to risk any possible challenge to her feelings. When the dishes were put away, Marina kissed her parents, said good-night to Dmitry with what she thought was the right degree of coolness, and went upstairs to her room.

On the second floor, passing the guest room, she heard Tamara's raised voice.

"And you," she was saying, "you don't recognize good fortune when it licks you in the face!"

Then Anton's voice, deep and resentful.

"Nearly burned alive and now stranded with dreamy revolutionaries! I hardly call that good fortune!"

Marina stopped and listened. The newcomers did not bother to lower their bitter voices.

"Are you aware, my friend, that Vasily Nevsky is the head of the most powerful opposition party in Russia?"

"SRs used to throw bombs. Probably still do. They may murder us in our bed yet."

"Nonsense. My poor Anton, be sensible. Can't you understand that the Nevskys can be a very useful connection—whatever happens in Russia after the war?"

"For you, perhaps," said Anton. "As for me, I intend to return to the service of the prince as soon as possible."

Just then, Marina heard a chair scrape the floor. She walked on to her room at the end of the hall.

That night, she could not fall asleep for a long time. She was stunned. The beautiful stranger, who had come to them from the sea like Botticelli's *Venus*, seemed in fact to be a calculating opportunist. She must warn her parents. As for Dmitry, he had apparently seen at once through Tamara's golden aura, as she had not. She regretted her coldness to him. He now seemed farther than ever from her. What could she do to make him fall in love with her? Tamara had been right about one thing: if only she could make him see that art, revolution, and love were one!

Chapter Eight

THE MORNING AFTER THE EXPLOSION, MARINA WAS WITH ANNA IN the kitchen cooking for her birthday party. Anna was rolling out dough for piroshki, and with a glass jar was stamping the sheets into rounds, soon to be filled with the savory mixtures of mushrooms, cabbage, and freshly cut herbs that Marina was preparing. Vasily and Dmitry had gone down to the village for news of survivors of *L'Etoile*. The guests had not yet made an appearance.

"Will you invite the Sermuses to stay on?" asked Marina.

"For as long as they wish."

"I'd be careful," said Marina, and she told her mother what she had overheard the night before

Anna reflected a moment; then she said, "Tamara was speaking to that dreadful husband of hers in terms that he would understand. I'm sure she didn't mean that she thought we were a 'useful connection' in the way you suggest. In any case, we take pride in being useful to people."

And in trusting them, no matter who they are, thought Marina bitterly, remembering her father and Azef.

Sensing her daughter's disapproval, Anna said, "You're an artist yourself. You should understand people like Tamara."

"I do understand them," said Marina, thinking of the Sermuses' angry conversation. Then she added, "And Dmitry does too."

"He was rude. It was so unlike him."

It wasn't at all unlike him, thought Marina. And perhaps he had good reason. But she said nothing. Anna looked grieved. Marina felt uneasy: she had upset her mother, yet it was right to have tried to warn her about the Sermuses. There was no doubt about it: their conversation had been coarse and unfriendly.

Anna spooned filling onto the rounds of dough as Marina folded them, sealed the edges with egg white, and set out the piroshki in rows on a baking tin. Anna put the tin in the oven, and they went out on the terrace.

Lost in a discussion about events on the Russian front, Vasily and Dmitry were climbing the steps just as Tamara, still wearing Anna's kimono, ran outside. Sermus followed her, wearing his rumpled tailcoat and trousers, which were not quite dry. His bad humor of the previous night had not subsided.

"What a glorious morning!" cried Tamara. "How lucky we are to be alive!"

"Lucky indeed," said Vasily. "All the passengers escaped serious harm. They're returning to France on a special train later today."

"Get dressed, Tamara," said Sermus. "We mustn't miss that train."

"But the crew, Vasily Ivanovich!" exclaimed Tamara, paying no attention to her husband. "What about the crew?"

"Unfortunately, several were hurt," said Vasily gently. "And two in the engine room died of their injuries."

"Burned beyond recognition," said Dmitry.

Tamara stretched out languidly on Anna's rattan chaise longue. "How I detest Germans," she said.

Sermus glared at her. "Tamara! You told me that your own people were German barons. You said—"

"You misunderstand everything, Anton," she said with a sigh, shading her face with her hand.

Anna came over and sat next to her. "You mustn't think of leaving. Not before the party."

"I'm afraid we must," said Tamara, starting to rise, then falling back into the chaise. She smiled at Marina. "What do you say, Marina?"

Marina said nothing. Anna looked at her pleadingly.

"Do stay one more night," said Marina reluctantly.

"Very well," said Tamara. "We'll stay for the party. I'll dance for you, Marina. It shall be my birthday present."

Sermus threw up his hands in despair and slumped into a chair. Suddenly, Tamara drew the kimono tightly around her. "But Anna," she said, "I've nothing to wear. My dress is ruined."

Anna said cheerfully, "Marina has a white silk dress I've just made for her. It's a little old-fashioned but quite pretty. Will you lend it to our new friend, Marina? You can wear my mauve muslin. It suits you beautifully."

"Of course," said Marina, determined not to upset her mother, though in fact she was crushed. She had been looking forward to wearing the white dress for Dmitry.

"Then it's settled," said Vasily, starting for his study. Whenever he sensed disagreement between his wife and daughter, as he did now, he absented himself from them as quickly as possible. Tamara now lay on the chaise with her eyes closed, a faint smile on her lips, apparently oblivious to them all.

At the terrace doors, Vasily stopped and turned to his wife. "Anna, my dear, I almost forgot," he said. "Savinkov telegraphed. He arrives on the afternoon train."

Sermus sat up in alarm. "The terrorist?" he cried in a horrified voice.

Tamara sat up. "How fascinating, Vasily Ivanovich. A true legend of our time. I've always wanted to meet him."

Dmitry left the terrace without a glance at anyone, stamping up the stairs to his room and slamming the door.

By midafternoon, Marina and Anna had finished setting out the food on the dining table: platters of golden brown piroshki, mussels with parsley, pickled mushrooms, Sardinian cheese, crusty fresh loaves from the village baker. Marina went out in the garden to cut flowers for bouquets. The light was springlike, the fragrant air still. From the village, she heard the clack of shutters thrown open, the strong voice of a mother calling her child. When she had gathered an armful of mimosa and irises, she set them on the ground by the fig tree and climbed into its branches for a view of the town and the sea.

Then Marina glanced down at the terrace.

Once again stretched out on Anna's chaise longue, Tamara had apparently fallen asleep. Her hand covered her eyes. The kimono had parted, revealing a small, perfect breast. As the sun struck her face, she stirred, and opened her eyes. Marina glanced up and saw her father at a studio window, looking down at Tamara.

At that moment, Marina heard a clatter of hooves. A cabriolet was stopping at the foot of the steps.

Vasily moved away from the window as Savinkov started up to the terrace, followed by the coachman carrying his gladstone bag. Savinkov wore a panama hat, a Norfolk jacket, and carried a malacca cane. Tamara sat up with a start, closing her kimono. The new arrival dismissed the coachman. Anna came out to greet him. He kissed her hand.

"Boris," she said, "may I present our guest, Madame Sermus."

Tamara smiled at him radiantly.

"Boris!" Vasily called down from the studio window. "Up here."

Savinkov bent to kiss Tamara's hand. Then, bowing to the ladies, he excused himself and went up to Vasily's studio.

A wine bottle, cork drawn, and two stemmed glasses stood on the desk. Vasily poured the wine.

"Cinque Terre," he said. "The grapes come from a village perched on a cliff that drops straight to the sea. At harvest time, they lower them into boats in baskets."

Savinkov held his glass to the light, examining the straw-colored wine, and then raised the glass to his host.

"Nothing in this world comes easy, does it, my dear Vasily?"

Vasily touched his glass to Savinkov's. "Or quickly. They've been making this wine ever since the Crusades."

They drank. After a moment, Savinkov set his wine down and went to the window.

"Your visitor is a striking woman."

"Isn't she? Quite extraordinary how she and her husband turned up here."

As Vasily related the events of the previous night, Savinkov gazed down at the terrace. When Vasily fell silent, Savinkov turned from the window and sat across the desk from him.

"I've seen her before, though for the life of me, I can't remember where."

"How could you forget such a woman?" asked Vasily, wondering, Why has he come?

Savinkov seemed to read his thought. "I hope this visit is not inconvenient."

"Not in the least. I'm delighted to see you, and Marina is pleased that you're here for her party."

Savinkov lit a cigarette, inhaled deeply. "What does Marina want from this insane world of ours?"

"She wants it to be at peace. She also wants to be a painter. I think she may have some talent. Gorky agrees."

"Is she interested in that young fellow Gotz sent to you?"

"Dmitry? There seems to be a friendship, nothing more."

"I met him in Paris. He's in thick with a group that wants to shake up the party."

"Maximalists?"

"Terror is not their style."

"What do they want, then?"

"A greater voice in the party. They think they can breathe life into it."

"So they think the party is dead?" asked Vasily.

"What would you expect? They're young. The interesting thing is that their leader is Spiridonova."

"Isn't she still in prison?"

"She was just released."

"I'm glad to hear it," said Vasily. He and Anna had met Maria Spiridonova in 1905—one year before she had shot General Lugenovsky and become a legend of the revolutionary struggle.

Savinkov was studying Vasily through the scented smoke from his cigarette. "But you understand, as far as your Dmitry is concerned, it's merely youthful spirits."

"Does the Central Committee know? What does it think?"

"Very little, as usual."

"And you, Boris, we hear of your bohemian life, your artist friends, your novels, your poetry. Are you still active in the party?"

Savinkov placed his cigarette on the edge of an ashtray and picked up Vasily's heavy brass letter opener, testing its point against his fingertip. "I find that I see things in a clearer light as a poet than as a terrorist." He stared at Vasily as if pondering a problem. "By the way, I saw Lenin in Zurich."

Vasily expressed no surprise. As young men, Lenin and Savinkov had been members of the same underground Marxist group in Petersburg, though Savinkov had long ago renounced Marxism.

"You're still on good terms?"

"We speak. I paid a call unannounced at his wretched little rooms in the shoemaker's house on Spiegelgasse. Isn't it odd that I can remember the lane where Lenin lives, and not where I've seen that stunning woman?"

"How did he receive you?"

"Quite well. It's amazing how my infamous reputation opens doors. Of course, that harridan of a wife of his made it plain that I was wasting her husband's precious time, but Ilyich was almost cordial. We chatted about old times. About Azef and the Bolsheviks' own troubles with police spies."

"What news of Azef?"

Savinkov sighed. "You are out of touch, aren't you? Yevno settled in Germany under a false name and set up shop as a stockbroker. Made a lot of money. When the war broke out, the German secret police found out who he was and arrested him—as a dangerous revolutionary! Can you imagine? As far as I know, he is in prison."

"How I misjudged him," mused Vasily.

Savinkov tapped the letter opener against his palm. "Let's just not misjudge Lenin."

Vasily recalled his meeting with the Bolshevik leader two years before at Zimmerwald.

"He has a bad face," he said.

"Perhaps, but he has the will of a man of destiny. And like Dostoyevsky's Raskolnikov, he believes that to a man of destiny everything is permitted."

"He has no base of power."

"I told him that I would be seeing you."

"What did he say?"

"He asked if you were still the leader of the SRs."

"What did you say?"

"I told him that if anyone was, you were. Then he said the very thing I once told you."

"That I was the embodiment of the party."

"Only I'm afraid he didn't mean it the way I did."

"I'm sure he didn't."

"He's very dangerous."

"To whom?"

"Russia."

Savinkov set the paper knife down on the desk and sipped his wine. As he raised his arm, Vasily observed just inside his jacket the strap of a shoulder holster.

"Berlin!" exclaimed Savinkov suddenly.

"Berlin?"

"That's where I saw Madame Sermus! In the summer of 1909, at the terrace of the Kranzler Café on Unter den Linden. As a matter of fact—now it all comes back—she was with Azef."

"You can't be serious."

"But I am. She looked like a schoolgirl then, and all the more seductive for that."

"You spoke to them?"

"I thought it best not to."

"She was a member of a revolutionary circle. Azef would have been investigating it for the Okhrana."

Vasily remembered Tamara's lightness as he lifted her out of the boat. The bottle was empty. He got up and opened another.

"Odd thing," he said, replenishing their glasses. "She bears a certain resemblance to Anna's sister, Ariane."

"Who died young, you once said."

"Yes."

"Were the sisters close?"

"Very. It was Anna who decided to name this house after her."

Savinkov swirled the wine and then touched his glass to Vasily's. "To dangerous women," he said. He drank, then leaned back in his chair. "I find it restoring to be with you, Vasily."

"A well-earned repose after your clever Parisian friends, no doubt?"

"Gallic cleverness is a bore. You have done well to escape it. Even here in paradise, your feet are planted on Russian soil."

From the terrace, they heard the women's voices.

"Nothing changes," pursued Savinkov. "The war has embalmed Romanov power: it's a rotting corpse that infects everything it touches. The Bolsheviks keep their distance. We must do the same.

The conflict will not be with the cadaver. The death struggle will be between socialists. In that respect, we have an interesting rival in Zurich." Savinkov lit another cigarette. "He should be liquidated."

So this was the object of his visit, thought Vasily, noticing for the first time yellow specks floating in the green irises of Savinkov's almond-shaped eyes.

"I can't agree," he said. "Killing oppressors is bad enough. But a rival socialist—where would it end?"

Savinkov shrugged. "Aux grands maux les grands remèdes."

As if the fields of Flanders and East Prussia were not carnage enough, thought Vasily. He had no wish to reenter Azef's world of murky deception and blood. If he had his wish, there would be no more bombs, no more mangled corpses. From the terrace, he heard Anna calling up to him. Guests were beginning to arrive.

He went to the window. The cool air refreshed him. A full moon was rising over the mountains; the first stars shone. The lantern-lit terrace where villagers were gathering had never looked more inviting. He turned back into the room. "We must continue this conversation, Boris. But now let's go down to Marina's party. Madame Sermus will be dancing in her honor."

Marina was relieved to see her father entering the room. Despite her own and Anna's efforts at conversation, the guests were ill at ease in the house of the foreign socialistas. To Marina's annoyance, Angelino hardly spoke a word to her, but instead stayed close to his male friends. The mayor and his wife and their friends clustered together in a corner of the terrace. No one had tasted the food. The Sermuses had still not yet come down.

As soon as Vasily appeared, the mood of the party picked up. Heartily, in heavily accented Italian, he greeted his guests. Dmitry brought him a glass of red wine. He raised it to Marina.

"My friends," he said, now in Russian. "I wish a joyous birthday to my daughter, who is the age of the century! Inspired by your beautiful country, she wants to become an artist and record that beauty. Let us wish her and her whole generation a future of peace and justice!"

Anna translated. As the guests toasted Marina, Tamara, wearing Marina's white Empire dress of whispering silk, appeared at the foot of the stairs. When she had gained everyone's attention, she stepped into the room with exquisite grace. Sermus followed her, his violin tucked under his arm.

Vasily again raised his glass. "And we welcome our special guests, Anton and Tamara Sermus. Tamara, a disciple of the great Isadora Duncan, has kindly consented to dance for us."

Anna rendered his words in Italian. Sermus bowed stiffly and announced in French that Tamara would dance "Anitra's Dance" from Grieg's *Peer Gynt Suite*. He placed the violin under his chin and raised the bow high over the strings. Tamara stood with her head thrown back, eyes closed. Slowly, she raised her arms, Sermus drew the bow over the strings, and Tamara floated through the room, her arms outstretched like the wings of a bird.

As the dancer dipped, glided, and spun in a swirl of red hair and white silk, Marina at first felt a return of the enchantment that had seized her on the beach when she had first seen Tamara in her father's arms. Then the couple's angry words of the night before echoed in her mind. She glanced at her parents. Anna was watching Tamara with undisguised delight, seeming not to breathe. Next to her, Vasily too appeared captivated.

When Marina looked back at the dancer, Tamara seemed transformed. As the music rose in intensity, her movements became defiant, her face hard, drained of beauty. Her slender arms cut the air like swords; her body had become a weapon.

And at every turn, she smiled at Marina as if in triumph.

When the dance ended, Marina tried to believe that she had imagined what she had seen, but she knew that Tamara's exultant look was meant for her, and that it was hostile. Why was this so, she wondered? Did Tamara somehow know that she had overheard the late-night quarrel? Or was she simply jealous of Marina's youth, her carefree life, her loving parents? Or was it something else altogether that made her behave as she did?

The Sermuses took bows, the company applauded, and Anna wiped her eyes. Vasily clapped loudly, shouting "Brava! Brava!"

Savinkov lit a cigarette, watching Vasily over the flame of his match.

Dmitry came up to Marina.

"Let's go for a walk," he said.

Still trying to sort out her feelings about Tamara, she followed him in silence.

He led her into the shadowy garden, rich with the smell of mimosa. He took her hand and drew her close to him. In the moonlight, she saw that his face was flushed from the wine.

In a cold voice, he said, "I brought you here to tell you I love you."

Marina's dream was coming true, but not in a good way. "You make it sound like a threat," she said.

"I can't stay here any more."

"Because you love me?"

He took her in his arms and kissed her hard. She could taste the wine in his mouth. She felt no love in the embrace for which she had waited for months. Then he kissed her again, tenderly, lovingly, as she had been longing to be kissed. Then, remembering that he was leaving, she drew away.

"Where will you go?" she asked.

"Paris—then Petrograd."

"Your book isn't finished."

"I no longer care about the revolutions of the past. I must be part of what's happening in Russia now."

"Then stay with my father."

"Marina, the revolution won't begin at the Villa Ariane. *Our* generation will free Russia. Can't you feel that?"

"Dmitry, all my life I've lived with people who've hoped to free Russia one day. Of course, I feel it."

"I don't mean other people. I mean you. Can't *you* feel it?"

"All I feel is your anger. Let's go back."

She turned away and walked ahead.

"It's that damned Estonian woman," Dmitry said bitterly, following her. "She's put us all on edge."

On the terrace, couples were dancing to the music of an accordion. Dmitry reached for Marina's hand. Swept by sadness, she said, "You go on. I'm going for a walk."

She went to the Thinking Tree and, tying her skirt at her waist, climbed high into its branches.

I'm seventeen, she thought, and my life is over.

She looked across to her father's study. All the lamps in the room were lit. Tamara stood at an open window gazing up at the sky. Vasily came up beside her and put his arm around her shoulders.

"What a beautiful night!" she said. "I could live here forever."

65

Then Anna came to Tamara's side, and Vasily drew her into his embrace.

Marina looked out above the lights of the village to the stars. She could not erase the picture in her mind of Tamara Sermus's cruel smile at the end of her dance. There was evil beneath their visitor's beauty. And she was bewitching her parents.

"Signor Nevsky!" cried a voice from the road below.

The telegraph operator from the railroad station was running up the steps.

"Che cosa?" Vasily called down.

"Revoluzione! Revoluzione in Russia!"

"E buono, Federico."

"E vero, Signor Nevsky."

"Vero?"

"Vero."

The villagers cheered, pleased that their Russian socialists were hearing the news that they had waited for for years. In the studio, Marina's parents and Tamara were embracing each other in turn.

Marina again gazed up at the night sky, blinded by tears. Revolution in Russia. Nothing would be the same—ever. She felt that her life was being torn from her.

"Marina!"

She looked down. In the leafy shadow at the foot of the tree stood Dmitry, smiling up at her.

"Come down, Marina," he said. "We have a new world to build."

At first, Vasily and Anna did not dare believe that the news from Petrograd was true. Dmitry left at dawn the next morning. Marina found a note under her door:

My dearest Marina,

When you read this, I will be gone. I admire and respect your father, but the time has come when I must make my own way. You have given me reason to take the highest path.

I love you.

Until we meet in Petrograd,
Dmitry

She read the words over and over. Two things were clear: one was that Dmitry did love her; the other was that they were all entering the frightening new era that Max Peshkov had prophesied.

A few days later, when Russian-language papers began to arrive, Vasily and Anna realized that the Revolution had indeed happened and that it seemed irreversible. Feverishly, they prepared to return to Russia—that hitherto mythical land that was home to them, but not to Marina.

$\mathcal{N}$ow the news came fast. By April, the tsar had abdicated. Strikes and rioting were spreading, soldiers were refusing orders to fire on demonstrators, regiment after regiment was coming over to the side of the Revolution, the sailors of the Kronstadt naval base had mutinied, red banners floated over the Winter Palace. The news that the United States had entered the war on the side of the Allies was barely noticed.

As more and more information reached us, we were able to piece together the rapidly changing political situation. In Petrograd, two centers of power were emerging. Occupying separate wings of the Tauride Palace on the Neva, each presented a sharply different face—and conflicting solutions to the task of harnessing the Revolution to a new government for Russia.

Out of the Duma, the tottering parliament functioning under the sufferance of the recent tsars, had sprung the Provisional Government. This body was composed of liberal, so-called bourgeois ministers and included one Socialist Revolutionary, Alexander Kerensky, who was also playing a significant role within the other power center.

This competing camp was the Petrograd Soviet, arisen from the still-smoldering ashes of the 1905 revolution, a volatile conglomeration of socialists of every persuasion. Spontaneously formed, operating under a strong Executive Committee, the Petrograd Soviet was the descendant of the revolutionary councils—soviets—of workers and soldiers organized in 1905 by, among others, Leon Trotsky.

Mistrusting each other from the first, the Provisional Government and the

Petrograd Soviet nevertheless needed each other to stave off the chaos that threatened to engulf the country. They agreed only upon one central principle, mandated by the people: the Provisional Government would be replaced as soon as possible by a Constituent Assembly based on universal suffrage, which would then determine the form of the permanent government of Russia.

Meanwhile, the war continued to exact its enormous toll. In 1916, following the broad retreats of the previous year, the Russian armies—under the direct command of Tsar Nicholas II—had launched a massive counteroffensive. However, by December the overwhelmingly better-supplied and better-led German forces had routed the Russians and driven them out of Poland with catastrophic losses.

Now, in early 1917, the cost of the war was measured not only in battle casualties, crippling expenditures, and lost territories, but also in the demoralization of the civilian population. Prices soared, and production and supply systems stalled. An epidemic of suicides, at all layers of society, spread throughout the country.

Louder and louder, the ominous cry "Bread!" resounded in the streets of Petrograd and Moscow. Tens of thousands marched in protest against the war, the shortages, and the refusal of the tsar to acknowledge, much less to alleviate, the suffering of his people.

The words of an Okhrana agent's confidential report summed up the situation: "An abyss is opening between the masses and the government."

Chapter Nine

OF HER LAST WEEKS IN ITALY, MARINA WOULD RETAIN ONLY RANDOM memories. No sooner had the news of the Revolution been confirmed than the Sermuses had an argument that lasted three days. Anton Antonich demanded that his wife leave with him, but to no avail. In the Nevsky family, declared Tamara, she had found a new life, and she would travel to Russia with them "to help build a better society."

For Sermus, these words were the last straw. He departed the same evening on the night train for Monte Carlo, leaving in the Nevskys' care the intruder toward whom Marina had by then developed a keen aversion. However, she told herself to be patient. In Petrograd, Tamara would surely find better connected protectors than her parents.

That spring, rains once again battered the Italian Riviera. Vasily besieged the SR Party headquarters in Zurich with telegrams, attempting to arrange visas and transportation for their return via Western Europe and the North Sea, but the party's negotiations with Allied authorities dragged on and on.

At last, late in March, he received a wire announcing that at the request of the Provisional Government of Russia, France and England had issued transit visas for him and for his family. After twelve years abroad, the well-known SR leader Vasily Nevsky—together with his wife, their daughter, and an Estonian woman identified as an "artiste"—was going home. Along the Roman road, Marina gathered sprigs of lavender and rosemary, which she tied in bunches to pack with her clothes. Anna was finishing a new plaid dress for her to make up for the white one that she had let Tamara keep.

On a sunny, rain-freshened April morning, they left the Villa Ariane. Before walking out the door for the last time, they went to the living room and observed the custom of sitting together for a moment in silence, to ensure a safe journey.

A horse-drawn carriage took them to the station. From Alassio, they would skirt the coast to Genoa, then travel north via Milan to Zurich. There they would collect their visas and join a convoy of Russian émigrés headed home, skirting warring Europe via Paris, London, and the North Sea, and continuing on to Petrograd.

As the train left the coast, Marina looked back at the Mediterranean one last time, trying to burn it into her memory. Her parents were pouring over Russian newspapers for the tenth time. Tamara sat across from her, buffing her nails, glancing up at her now and then with a sham smile. Marina gazed out the window at the villages, kitchen gardens, vineyards, and woodlands rushing by, feeling that she was being swept into a future that she could neither imagine nor evade.

Only the thought of seeing Dmitry soon again gave her courage. She kept his folded note in her pocket. She wanted to forget how condescending he had been, how rough his behavior at her birthday party. His last kiss and the loving words in his note were all that mattered. Marina was sure that in Russia, where he could now take part in the Revolution, the true Dmitry she loved would emerge. A Dmitry who would understand the depths of her love for him and share it.

In the huge Milan railroad station, she watched coach after coach packed with young Italian soldiers, many no older than she, moving through dusty shafts of sunlight. She wondered how many of them would return.

"Oh, Anna," said Tamara plaintively, "this war is so horrible. A whole generation is being slaughtered!" Anna took her hand, murmuring words of comfort.

In Zurich, Vasily settled the women in a pension near the station and proceeded directly to the Swiss Socialist Headquarters on Ramistrasse. There he made a stunning discovery. That very morning, the German High Command had offered Lenin and his Bolshevik entourage safe passage across German territory. The amazing thing was that Lenin had accepted the offer.

When the Swiss Socialists offered to arrange for similar accommodations on the same special train for Vasily and his party, he angrily declined. While Lenin might arrive in Petrograd earlier, Vasily would get there later but with his and the SRs' honor intact. A few weeks delay was immaterial, he told himself, stifling any doubts that he may have had on this subject.

Having secured places for the four of them on a convoy, he started back across town toward their pension. As he was passing the railway station, through a wire fence he saw Lenin in the midst of a group of people preparing to board the special train. On an impulse, he retraced his steps and entered the station, resolved to confront his rival.

Approaching the travelers, Vasily noticed that, for champions of the proletariat, the Bolsheviks were surprisingly well dressed: the men in formal suits, a few of the women wearing hats with veils. One little girl sported the sort of beribboned sailor bonnet especially dear to the bourgeoisie. The travelers were surrounded by protesters carrying hand-painted signs denouncing them. A young man was shouting in Russian: "Lenin is selling the Revolution for German gold," and "Traitors!"

Lenin wore a black bowler and a fur-collared overcoat several sizes too large for him. In his right hand, he carried a loosely furled umbrella, its handle and his knuckles concealed by the long sleeve of the coat. With the Bolshevik leader was his wife, Nadezhda Krupskaya, and another woman whom Vasily had never met, but whose identity he could easily guess: Lenin's close friend and fellow party worker, Inessa Armand, who had once been an SR. She was even more attractive than Vasily had been led to believe and much younger than Krupskaya, whose dumpy appearance set off Inessa's good looks. In the crowd, he also recognized Lenin's lieutenant Zinoviev, who with his unruly black hair and dark-circled eyes, resembled a Russian nihilist as depicted in a Western newspaper cartoon. The Bolsheviks appeared to be oblivious to the protesters.

Vasily thought it fitting that he and Lenin should meet face to face at this crucial time. Both were socialists, both born on the

Volga. Socialists might squabble with one another abroad, but now they must lock arms. And it was appropriate that Vasily, the leader of the far larger, more popular party, should take the first step.

He pressed through the crowd of protesters and went up to Vladimir Ilyich Lenin.

"Ah, Nevsky," said the Bolshevik leader, his Asiatic eyes narrowing, "how unexpected. I suppose we should be honored that you've come in person to protest our travel arrangements."

"I am not here to protest, Vladimir Ilyich."

"You know my wife, of course."

Meeting Krupskaya's dour stare, Vasily remembered that Lenin's wife could be cordial or hostile depending on her sense of her husband's interests. Hostile now, she nodded to him coldly.

"And this is our friend Madame Armand," pursued Lenin. "Inessa, Nevsky is undoubtedly on his way home to lead the Russian peasant class into a bountiful future."

Inessa Armand was smiling at Vasily in a way that at first seemed friendly, but which, he soon realized, was not.

Gesturing toward the train, Lenin said, "Perhaps you and Anna Petrovna will consent to return with us. It's not too late. There're plenty of seats. I'm sure that getting the Germans' permission would be easy enough."

"We appreciate your offer, though frankly I find these arrangements inappropriate. We shall not depend on Russia's enemies at this time, but will be traveling by way of France and Great Britain."

"Of course. The imperialists strew roses in your path. For us, the road home is paved with thorns."

Vasily met the other's withering smile, determined not to be put off by his sarcasm.

"It's all happened sooner than either of us imagined, hasn't it, Vladimir Ilyich?"

"Much sooner," agreed Lenin. "But both you and I know that the real struggle is only beginning."

"With the forces of reaction."

Again Lenin's eyes narrowed. "With *all* the forces of reaction, including those who do not yet understand that they *are* the forces of reaction."

"The hopes of the people must not be swept away," said Vasily firmly.

"Land and Liberty?"

"Land and Liberty."

"Freedom and democracy?"

"The form of the new government must be decided by the Constituent Assembly."

"Oh yes," Lenin laughed. "In the excitement, one had quite forgotten about the Constituent Assembly."

Krupskaya smiled icily. Inessa Armand was watching Vasily with a look of commiseration.

It's now or never, thought Vasily. "Vladimir Ilyich," he said solemnly, "we have a duty to Russia. All socialist parties must present a single front against—"

An electric bell drowned out his words. The last passengers on the platform began to board.

"The second bell, Ilyich," said Krupskaya, glowering at Vasily.

Ushered by Zinoviev, she and Lenin started toward the train. The little girl wearing the sailor hat, ribbons flying, ran to Inessa Armand, who took her by the hand. The protesters were shouting slogans at the tops of their lungs. A young man pounded his fists on a compartment door. Two Swiss policemen sauntered toward him.

"—a united front against the inevitable counterrevolution," Vasily persisted.

With sudden ferocity, Lenin turned to him. "And against the imperialist war?" Vasily looked at him in surprise. "You see, Vasily Ivanovich, we already have a sticking point."

"Not if we look beyond the war."

"Especially if we look beyond the war."

The bell rang again. Compartment doors slammed shut.

"Vladimir Ilyich!" called Krupskaya.

Lenin was studying Vasily with a look of satisfaction. Then he gripped Vasily's hand in his own clasped hands.

"Auf Wiedersehen, Vasily Ivanovich," Lenin said. "I wish you a safe journey. This conversation has been most enlightening."

He boarded the train as protesters swarmed toward his compartment screaming, "Traitor!" "Spy!" "The kaiser is paying you!" The train began to move. Now many demonstrators were hammering on the doors. The police began to drag them away.

Lenin lowered his window and waved mockingly at the angry

crowd. Then he leaned out and shouted, "Thank you very much, Vasily Ivanovich. You have helped me resolve the last problem."

When Vasily returned to the pension and related what had happened at the station, Tamara wept in Anna's arms. Had they plucked her from one shipwreck only to condemn her to death in the freezing North Sea? When she realized that the Lenins' train had departed and there would not be another, she dried her eyes.

"Very well," she said. "If I must die in your company, I will do so bravely. I have no one else in this world."

In London, they stayed in a rooming house while they awaited instructions to board a train for a secret port: for fear of submarine attacks, no ship departures were announced in advance. Tamara lost no occasion to remind them that they could have chosen the quicker, safer route.

To Marina's dismay, neither Vasily nor Anna seemed to mind her complaints, or notice what a dominant place she now occupied within their family.

Chapter Ten

THE SECRET PORT WAS ABERDEEN. THEY BOARDED THE STEAMER IN the middle of the night, settling on the main deck in preference to the suffocating cabins in the bowels of the ship assigned to third-class passengers. A rumor was circulating that the last ship to sail for Norway had been sunk by a German U-boat. Anguished by the thought that Dmitry might have been on board that vessel, shivering in her spring clothes, Marina drew her coat around her and lay down on folded blankets from the cabin. Now she would have to become her truest self, the brave Marina who yearned for adventure, whose hero was Sir Lancelot of the blue plumes. She would work alongside her parents in helping to establish a just order in Russia. But she could not doubt that someday, however far in the future, they would return to the Villa Ariane when the almond blossoms would be in bloom, and everything there would be as it had been. She fell asleep to the sound of Anna's gentle voice comforting Tamara.

When she awoke, they were at sea. On the open bridge over their heads, a ship's officer was scanning the waves through binoculars. Off their bow, a British torpedo boat was zigzagging into a bronze dawn. The deck passengers were stirring, opening the Thomas Cook food baskets issued to them by the Red Cross in Aberdeen. Anna had spread her blanket over the sleeping Tamara. Vasily stood at the railing nearby, conversing with a long-haired, handsome young man wearing a plaid blanket over his shoulders. Marina remembered seeing him at the rue Gazan apartment. He was Ilya Ehrenburg, a Russian writer living in Paris who knew everyone in and out of émigré circles. From their conversation, Marina gathered that he had heard accounts of Lenin's arrival in Petrograd two weeks before.

"The Bolsheviks staged a reception for him at the Finland Station," he was saying. "Immense turnout. Vladimir Ilyich stood on the hood of an armored car in the beam of a searchlight, clutching a bunch of roses. He delivered a wild speech about the coming civil war in Europe, the death of capitalism. It stupefied everyone."

"Was there no protest against his getting to Russia with German help?" asked Vasily.

"Not from that crowd," said Ehrenburg. "They greeted him like a hero. Later, at the Kshesinskaya Palace, where the Bolsheviks are encamped, he stunned his own comrades. He attacked the Petrograd Soviet for playing into the hands of the bourgeoisie. He told them that the Provisional Government must be liquidated, that a separate peace with Germany must be concluded at once, regardless of what the Allies might say. Peasants would take the land by force; workers would seize the factories. Only the proletariat and the poorest peasants would then have a political role, led of course by the Bolshevik Party. And then the bombshell: there would be absolutely no alliances with other socialists! When his followers heard that, they decided that Vladimir Ilyich had lived too long in the West and had lost touch with reality."

"So he opposes free elections?"

"He opposes everything except his own Marxist schemes."

"In that case," declared Vasily, "Lenin has consigned himself to a minor role in this century's history."

At that moment, Tamara awakened, frowned, and languidly stretched her slender arms toward the sun. Marina, next to her, looked out across the dull sheen of the gray-green swells off the bow. The torpedo boat escorting them was gone. The ship's captain had joined the officer on the bridge. On the afterdeck, someone was playing American ragtime on a harmonica. Marina opened her basket and nibbled at a hard biscuit, sipping the hot tea that Vasily and Ehrenburg had brought up from the galley. Tamara sat up and embraced her knees, her loosened copper-red hair streaming down her back. The ship's engines throbbed. Everyone knew that on the calm sea, they would be an easy target for a U-boat.

A white gull balanced in the air over their heads. As Marina looked up at it, she saw a tall man in a sumptuous sable coat standing at the railing of the bridge. He was about sixty years old, with thick silver hair and a muscular face. He was looking down at Tamara. Ehrenburg and Vasily had noticed him too.

"Lianozov," said Ehrenburg. "They said he was aboard."

"Can he be returning?" asked Vasily.

Hearing the name, Tamara looked up and met the admiring gaze of the man in the sable coat.

In those years, Stepan Georgevich Lianozov was known as the Russian Rockefeller. He was an international financier who, under the protection of the Romanovs, had been reaping immense profits from his investments in international banks and munitions cartels.

With the agility of a younger man, Lianozov descended the companionway and greeted Ehrenburg. Ehrenburg introduced him. The man of finance then accepted the invitation of the head of the Socialist Revolutionary Party to sit down next to him on a blanket spread out on the gently rolling deck.

"What brings you on this dangerous voyage?" asked Vasily. "Did you have business in England?"

"I also have business in Petrograd. As must you."

"Yes, and I expect that we'll find changes there."

"And I expect that you are returning to make still more changes—perhaps as a candidate for a ministerial post in the new government."

"If that is so, you are better informed than I am."

"I make it my business to be informed, Vasily Ivanovich. I am acquainted with sensible men in the Provisional Government. Should you become a member of it, I know that they will do their best to keep your radical propensities in check."

"Let them try!" said Anna vehemently, sitting up. "Only the SRs can get Russia out of the mess you people have made of her!"

Tamara looked pained. "Must we always talk politics?"

"I meant no offense, Anna Petrovna," said Lianozov calmly. "I have been advocating reform for years. But unfortunately, the Rasputin cabal and the obtuseness of poor Nicholas and his Teutonic consort have stood in the way of improvement. So now instead of reform, we have a revolution."

"And how will it all end, in your opinion?" asked Ehrenburg.

"This may be the SRs' moment of destiny," said Lianozov. "Vasily Ivanovich, of late I have followed your party's activities closely. The human potential of the SRs is enormous. Were it to be used shrewdly—with less idealism and more practical sense—you might yet become Russia's leaders."

"And we will," said Anna.

"In itself, revolution is a sickness," said Lianozov with a lingering look at Tamara. "Russia is an ailing child which must be cured. Unhappily, the disease is so advanced that the cure must be dictated from abroad by the Western powers."

Tamara, who had been frowning thoughtfully, suddenly flashed a smile at the visitor, then lowered her eyes. Pretending not to have noticed, Lianozov went on: "Of course, I could be mistaken. It is just possible that with the closing of factories and the lack of transportation, starvation will bring the Russian people to their senses. Especially if the SRs were to act wisely. Only time will tell."

Anna said hotly, "You speak like an enemy of the Russian people!"

"You are mistaken. I and a few others like me are the country's best hope. Who else can lead her into the modern world?"

"I can well imagine what your modern Russia would be like," said Vasily.

"Can you? Frankly I doubt it."

"A paradise of free enterprise and cheap labor. The peasantry condemned to slave for landlords wintering in Monte Carlo. A brutal, soulless Russia."

Lianozov threw back his silver head and laughed. "Vasily Ivanovich, don't you see that Western civilization is at the dawn of a new age of scientific progress and industry? When this war is over— as it soon will be—we shall witness an explosion of industrial growth. America will lead the way; Europe will follow. In our own time, most families will have electricity, a telephone, perhaps even a motorcar. I've spoken to Morgan in New York and the Rothschilds in London and Paris, and they agree. The question now is whether Russia will flourish as part of the industrialized world or stagnate in isolation. Russia must cast her lot with the West. Capitalism is the only path to the future."

Anna said, "The Russian people will never entrust their fate to Western bankers and industrialists. What you really want to do is crush the Revolution."

"No, dear lady, only redirect it," said Lianozov with an indulgent smile, "toward the authentic one. I shall be discussing this matter with my friends in Petrograd."

"Stepan Georgevich," said Vasily in a strained voice, "I am a man of the Volga, proud of my peasant ancestry, and I declare: unless you are stopped, men like you, with your greed disguised as service to progress, will end by making even the Bolsheviks appear reasonable. I tell you that should I be appointed to the Provisional Government, I shall do everything in my power to thwart you and your kind. The new Russia must be ruled by the Russian people, not by you."

Lianozov looked at Vasily with a fixed grin, his face a threatening mask.

"We shall see," he said. "But take care that you SRs are not the ones to lend credibility to extremists on both sides." He rose and, after a long appreciative look at Tamara, turned again to Vasily and said, "Au revoir, Vasily Ivanovich, it has been a pleasure chatting with you. I had always wanted to meet the man who permitted Azef to escape the wrath of the SR Party. Such kind hearts are rare in Russia." And with an easy wave, he left them.

Chapter Eleven

THE TRAIN SQUEALED TO A STOP IN THE CAVERNOUS FINLAND STATION, the compartment doors flew open. In the smoky green light, a crowd surged toward the train. Someone shouted "Nevsky!" Vasily raised his arms, and a cheer went up, cries of "Nevsky! Nevsky! Land and liberty!"

Anna stepped down onto the platform, speaking to those who had come to greet the returning exiles, touching their hands. She was home. Marina searched the sea of faces for Dmitry.

"There's Gotz!" called out Vasily. A slender, pale-looking man of fifty wearing a gray astrakhan hat was pressing toward them. Vasily stepped down and embraced him.

"Marina, this is Abram Gotz, my very dear friend, the heart and soul of the SR Party."

"Of course, of course," said Gotz. "And I suppose it's me these people have come to see."

Then Marina saw Dmitry in the crowd. He was pushing toward her, smiling, no longer the troubled, distant Dmitry whose image she had never been quite able to erase from her mind since their last days in Alassio. She was in his arms.

"I've missed you," she said.

He kissed her, then held her at arm's length, looking at her with a wild excitement in his eyes that she sensed at once was not on her account. "And I've missed you," he said. "You won't believe the great things that have been happening here!"

Behind them, Tamara still stood at the open compartment door, looking lost and vulnerable. Dmitry glanced at her, then at Marina with a knowing smile, which told her that his feelings against Tamara had not changed. Anna saw her too and went to her and took her hand, helping her down. Gotz and his SR comrades were clearing a path for Vasily through the jubilant crowd, leading him under red banners emblazoned with gold letters—LAND AND LIBERTY and IN STRUGGLE, YOU WILL GAIN YOUR RIGHTS— toward the station's packed, smoke-filled main hall where a podium had been set up.

As he entered the hall, Vasily held out his hand to Anna. Tamara still at her side, she came up beside him. Marina and Dmitry followed them. The crowd cheered and applauded. A platoon of soldiers presented arms; a band struck up "The Marseillaise," the hymn of freedom that had become the anthem of the Russian Resolution. A woman thrust a huge bouquet of red carnations into Vasily's arms. Marina heard Gotz shout into his ear, "Ten times bigger than Lenin's reception! Ten times!" Then Gotz went up on the podium.

"Comrades!" he called out. "This is a proud day for the Socialist Revolutionary Party, a proud day for our country. Vasily Nevsky has come home, bearing the gift of Russian land and the liberty that is the sacred right of every human being!"

A tremendous roar filled the hall. Vasily took Gotz's place at the podium, embracing the flowers, looking happily at the exuberant audience of workers and clerks, soldiers in gray, peasants in sheepskin hats and belted blouses, their kerchiefed wives and children huddling beside them. At last, they fell silent.

"Comrades, we have a great task before us—"

At that moment, a side door burst open, and a small band of men and women carrying red banners rushed in. At their head was a burly man with a heavy, flushed face, wearing a visored cap.

"Uritsky," Dmitry whispered to Marina. "The Bolshevik strong man."

Vasily continued to speak. "—but if the land is to belong to those who work it, they must defend it against the invaders. A German victory would crush the Revolution."

"Down with the imperialist war!" yelled Uritsky. "Down with

the Provisional Government! Factories to the workers! Land to the peasants! You don't need Nevsky to dole the land out to you!"

Indignant voices rose in answer. "Traitors! German spies! Let Nevsky speak!"

Vasily shouted, "There must be a lawful program! If the land is seized by force, there'll be anarchy for generations!"

A peasant shouted, "Hurrah for Nevsky! He'll give us our land. Hurrah for Nevsky!"

The uproar grew wilder. The Bolsheviks waved their banners. There was scuffling. Again the band struck up "The Marseillaise." With an obscene gesture at the crowd, Uritsky led his gang out of the station.

Now Vasily could speak without interruption, and his rich voice filled the hall. The SR party would prevail, it would assure Russia of a fruitful, just future. The audience listened with rapt attention, applauding whenever Vasily spoke the words "Land and Liberty," the sonorous SR slogan from an earlier revolutionary past. Marina was filled with pride. For the first time, she was seeing her father as the leader the people loved and needed.

Then, on a signal from Gotz, an honor guard led Vasily and his party outside to a black Panhard sedan parked in front of the station. With Gotz at the wheel, they sped across the Alexandrovsky Bridge toward the heart of the city.

From the bridge, Marina had her first impression of Petrograd. The sight took her breath away. The enormous stone palaces which lined the Neva, the Peter and Paul fortress-prison jutting into the broad river, produced an effect of superhuman splendor. She remembered Vasily telling her that Petrograd was built on the bones of hundreds of thousands of serfs who had erected Peter's town on the swamps along the Neva, but she pushed this thought out of her mind. She wanted to savor the dreamlike grandeur of the city.

As they drove along the embankment, Gotz pointed out a park enclosed by a tall, elegant, wrought-iron fence.

"The Summer Garden," he said. "Once a playground for the aristocracy."

"And there's the Winter Palace," said Vasily. "No longer the tyrant's stronghold."

"And the Hermitage," said Marina, recognizing the immense palace from engravings she had seen.

"I was there yesterday with Gorky and the art curator, Andrey Baranov," said Gotz. "Gorky's latest mission is the preservation of art treasures. They're cataloging the collection and preparing to ship it to Moscow should Petrograd be threatened by a German invasion. They need volunteers."

Tamara said, "Anna, perhaps I should offer my services. You know how stupid I am about politics. Art is my world."

Dmitry raised his eyebrows in mock wonderment.

Gotz drove along the Neva past the Admiralty, turned left onto Galernaya. He came to a stop at the gates of a small park surrounding a diminutive palace in the Baroque style.

"The Petrograd residence of the tsar's uncle, the Grand Duke Andrey," said Gotz. "For the time being, this will be your home."

Just then, an automobile overtook them and sped on toward the palace.

"Kerensky," said Gotz.

"Obviously a man in a hurry," said Vasily.

"On the go night and day," said Gotz. "For better or worse, our minister of justice has become the dominant force in the Provisional Government, while keeping a foothold in the Petrograd Soviet. In fact, Alexander Kerensky may well be the one man who is holding the country together at the moment."

"Beware of him, Vasily," said Dmitry. "He's a friend of the landowners and the capitalists."

"Abram," said Vasily, ruffling Dmitry's hair affectionately, "I see that you've failed to bank the fires of extremism in our young friend."

"In the opinion of many," said Dmitry solemnly, "the Petrograd Soviet is now the only rightful government of Russia."

"The Petrograd Soviet is an insane asylum," declared Gotz, "while the Provisional Government is paralyzed. Kerensky keeps both from flying to pieces while the people starve and the Bolsheviks circle like vultures. Look, there's our busy lawyer now."

Kerensky, hatless, wearing a military tunic, jumped out of the still-moving car and ran up the palace steps two at a time, ignoring the small crowd at the stairway.

"Who are all those people?" asked Tamara.

"Petitioners," said Gotz. "Peasants waiting for Vasily."

"What do they want?"

"Land. Now."

As they drew up to the palace entrance, in the depths of the park they saw peasant families encamped around open fires. They looked just as they did in Marina's childhood picture books. Even in the mild spring weather, they wore sheepskin coats and felt boots. The women, heads wrapped in flowered scarves, were tending blackened pots steaming over hot embers. Here, thought Marina, were her father's people, who once sought justice from the tsar and now sought it from him. Vasily got out of the car, and petitioners swarmed around him.

"Comrades," he said in a hoarse voice. "I've come home after a long journey. Early tomorrow, I'll hear your cases one by one. The SR Party understands your needs and the injustices you have been suffering."

"We depend on you, Nevsky," said a toothless old man solemnly. "This time, we will be heard!

The others got out of the car and with Vasily started up the palace steps.

Grumbling, the crowd moved aside to let them pass.

A liveried butler with a flaring white mustache stood in the doorway. Inside, the entrance hall was flanked by two stuffed black bears with raised paws and bared teeth.

"Vasily Ivanovich Nevsky and his party," said Gotz.

"Monsieur Nevsky," said the butler, bowing stiffly. "Mesdames, Messieurs, please follow me."

Dmitry took in the elegant surroundings with a mistrustful look, while Tamara gazed around the mirrored foyer in happy surprise. She spread her arms and twirled, admiring her multiple reflections. Stopping before the butler, she asked, "Where is the grand duke?"

He looked her over with practiced eyes. "His Highness is at his hunting lodge in the Crimea, Madam, if he has not already gone abroad. I presume that you are a member of Monsieur Nevsky's party?"

"She most certainly is," said Anna.

"I must leave you now," said Gotz. "We've much to discuss, Vasily. We'll begin tomorrow. Dmitry, we're due at the Tauride Palace in twenty minutes."

Dmitry said good-bye to Marina. "Tonight and tomorrow, I have urgent meetings," he told her. "If you like, I'll come for you the day after tomorrow and show you the city, as I promised."

"But should you take the time?"

"I'll make time," he said, ignoring the irony in her voice.

"Until the day after tomorrow then."

"About ten, if that's all right."

"It's all right."

Gotz was already at the door. Dmitry hesitated, unwilling to leave on the note that had just been struck. He came back and kissed her on the cheek, then went out the door, following Gotz.

The butler led the new arrivals up the broad, curving stairway to a suite of small rooms crowded with Louis Quinze chairs and sofas, a canopy bed, marquetry tables.

"So tiny," said Tamara. "Who occupies the duke's quarters?"

"The minister of justice and his party," said the butler and abruptly fell silent. In the doorway stood Alexander Kerensky, his right hand resting inside his tunic in the manner of Napoleon, his left extended to Vasily.

"Vasily Ivanovich," he said, "welcome back to Russia. At this historic hour, we need you. Russia needs you."

"Alexander Fyodorovich, I shall try to live up to that trust. Who would have thought at Zimmerwald that we would meet again so soon? May I present you to my wife and daughter and to our friend, Madame Sermus."

Kerensky bowed to Anna. "There will be work for you too, dear Anna Petrovna. Everyone knows of your valuable efforts on behalf of the party."

And to Marina, "Welcome, my dear. The youth of Russia holds her future in its hands."

He kissed the air above Tamara's hand. "Charming," he said. Suddenly, he stepped back, clapping his palm to his brow. "But this is impossible! These tiny rooms! I had no idea there would be so many of you. You'll be packed in like sardines." He turned to the butler. "Can't something more suitable be found?"

"These rooms are all that remain, Your Excellency."

"How unfortunate," said Kerensky.

"Please don't upset yourself, Alexander Fyodorovich," said Vasily. "We'll manage. I'll leave the grand duke's chambers to you. In any case, I'm not so sure how soundly I'd sleep in a grand duke's bed."

The butler suppressed a smile.

To Marina, their arrival at the palace on Galernaya was a moment of deliverance. Never again would her parents inhabit the shadowy realm where Azef had lurked. From now on, they would serve their country openly, honorably, exiles no more. And she would stand by them, together with Dmitry.

Chapter Twelve

EARLY IN THE MORNING ON HER THIRD DAY IN PETROGRAD, DMITRY
came for Marina at the palace. Wearing her new plaid dress and a
white beret, she waited for him outside the entrance under a chestnut
tree. To her delight, Dmitry admired her appearance.

"Very pretty," he said, noticing the beret. "A snowflake in May."

Under a turquoise spring sky, they set forth through the leafing
park and into the city. On a stone bridge over the Moika Canal,
they stopped and gazed down at their reflections in the slow-moving
water.

"Who are those two people?" she asked.

"Free citizens of Petrograd," he said, taking her hand. As they
walked together, Marina felt light as air, thinking, Dmitry loves me.

They entered an immense square. Across from them stood an
eighteenth-century colonnaded building painted a deep ocher red.
Marina was impressed by its harmonious blend of Italian exuberance
and Russian majesty, which shone through the forbidding color.

"The Marinsky Theater," said Dmitry. "Last month, those who
died in the Revolution were honored here. It was an unforgettable
event."

From Ehrenburg, Marina had heard about this memorial, the
first official ceremony to be held in the capital since the Revolution.
Vera Figner had been the guest of honor.

Dmitry led Marina up the stone steps to the theater's main entrance. On either side of the open doors, they saw posters announcing a forthcoming benefit concert to be given by the celebrated actor and operatic basso Fyodor Chaliapin. From the lobby, they could hear a piano being tuned in the depths of the theater.

"I've always wanted to hear him sing *Boris Godunov*," said Marina.

"No doubt it will be a splendid occasion," said Dmitry dryly.

"Don't you find the story of Boris Godunov a timely one?"

"The Figner evening honored revolutionary martyrs. This is sure to be a pretentious social affair. A throwback to the past."

"The posters say that it will be a benefit for frontline military hospitals," persisted Marina.

"It's sponsored by the Provisional Government," said Dmitry. "Need one say more?"

Inside, the empty theater was dark but for the glow of a single electric bulb suspended over the stage. As they walked down the aisle, Dmitry pointed to the central box, now draped with a red flag.

"The tsar's box. On the night of the concert, it was occupied by political prisoners just back from Siberia. To their right sat the foreign ambassadors and to the left the members of the Provisional Government in frock coats, already relics of another era. They don't speak for the people, Marina."

"Who does?"

"The Petrograd Soviet, the sponsors of the ceremony. The Petrograd Soviet is the heart and soul of the Revolution. Its members filled the orchestra rows, while the rest of the theater was packed with bourgeois, anarchists, workers, students, soldiers, peasants, foreign spies, merchants. You'd think that nothing could unite such a crowd, but when Vera Figner walked on stage and the band played "The Marseillaise," the whole theater came alive with a sound never heard in Russia before: the sound of freedom. This is how the whole city feels today. There is exultation everywhere. Nothing will ever be the same again here."

At that moment, Marina noticed a small, slender woman dressed in black coming slowly toward them down the center aisle. Her face was heavily powdered, her huge, mascara-laden eyes fixed on them.

"You are right, young man," said the woman. "Nothing will be the same. But Russia will not be free."

"Who are you?" asked Dmitry.

"Once I was Kshesinskaya." She gazed around the empty theater. "Here for the last time, I am Kshesinskaya."

Marina looked at her in amazement. All her life, she had heard this name spoken with contempt. The reigning prima ballerina of Petersburg, Mathilde Kshesinskaya, had been Tsar Nicholas's mistress before his marriage, and later the mistress of two of the grand dukes. Now with her made-up eyes and whitened skin, she looked incredibly old.

"I used to bring audiences to their feet in this theater, yet Vera Figner's performance was greater than any of mine. The terrorists have triumphed." She fell silent, smiling at them sadly. "You make a beautiful couple. I hope that your lives will be happy, but I fear for you." She sighed. "As for me, I am leaving Russia. Lenin speaks every day to the rabble from the balcony of my palace. If men like him are the future, I want no part of it. Farewell, my dears, and may God bless you."

She walked back up the aisle.

When she had gone, Dmitry said, "There goes your precious past."

"I feel sorry for her."

Dmitry rolled his eyes. "Because she lost her palace?"

Thinking, How simple everything is for him, Marina did not reply.

Recrossing the Moika Canal, they followed a street lined with stone townhouses which stood vacant, their doors and windows boarded up. Dmitry walked with a buoyant stride, and Marina fell in step with him, trying to see the city that he was seeing.

They were crossing St. Isaac's Square toward the Hotel Astoria when a white open automobile with brass headlamps as big as dinner plates drew up at the glass-and-marble entrance. Behind a uniformed chauffeur sat Stepan Lianozov and Tamara Sermus, both wearing motoring dusters. The doorman opened the door, and Lianozov stepped down and helped Tamara out. As they started up the steps, she met Lianozov's crinkled smile with a coquettish, reproachful look. He put his arm around her waist. She slipped out of his grasp, and at that moment caught sight of Marina and Dmitry. For an instant, she seemed discomfited. Then, with a toss of her head, she let her escort take her arm and guide her into the softly glowing lobby.

"Who is that with her?" asked Dmitry.

"Lianozov. The armaments millionaire."

"She hasn't been wasting her time. Has your mother seen through her yet?"

"She refuses to." She hesitated, adding, "As does my father. They seem to adore her."

"It will end badly."

"I know," she said, "and there's absolutely nothing I can do about it."

Making their way down Nevsky Prospect through a shuffling gray crowd, they passed under an arch and entered the vast square before the Winter Palace. Below the sculpted figures and urns on the roof, a huge red banner billowed in the restless air. They came out on the embankment and looked across the river to the fortress of Peter and Paul, the golden spire of its church gleaming against the pale blue sky.

"Another relic of the past," said Dmitry. "The dungeons have been opened to the public. Spiridonova showed me her cell."

They strolled on in silence. Marina had heard that the Revolution had freed its heroine Maria Spiridonova from prison. According to Gotz, she was now a leading member of the radical wing of the SR Party.

"You know her well?"

"She's a comrade." They started across the Palace Bridge. "We share the same ideas. We disagree with the Bolsheviks on certain issues, but in fact we're closer to them than to the SR old guard."

"Such as my father."

"Such as all of them."

"What a pity. What is she like?"

"Spiridonova?"

"Yes."

"A woman of our time," he said. He gestured toward the equestrian statue of Peter the Great on Senate Square. "One of our generation that has ended the reign of the tsars."

"She must be over thirty," said Marina.

"She's thirty-one. What difference does that make?"

"You said 'our generation.'"

"I meant anyone who can feel what's happening in Russia and be part of it!"

At the end of the bridge, Kshesinskaya's pink brick palace came into view. A crowd was standing in the sparse shade of budding lindens listening to a man wearing a visored cap and a winter suit, addressing them from a balcony, gesticulating with violent thrusts of his arms.

Marina recognized the speaker from photographs she had seen— the bald head, small beard, high cheekbones, slanting eyes.

At her first view of her father's archrival, Marina's heart sank. Lenin radiated power.

"Comrades, you're being deceived!" he shouted in a harsh, guttural voice. "As we stand here, the gentlemen in the Provisional Government are plotting to continue the war, crush the Revolution, and set themselves up as your masters!"

The audience grumbled menacingly.

"But they're afraid of us, comrades. They're afraid of us Bolsheviks for one reason: because we speak for you. As for these lackeys of capitalism, they are scheming to pack you off to die in the imperialist war for the benefit of their industries. They get rich; you get killed."

A roar arose from the crowd. Lenin's small eyes scanned the grim faces.

"Comrades, Russia has had her fill of bogus socialists claiming to be the guardians of the Revolution. These so-called liberals tell you that everything will be settled at the Constituent Assembly. My friends, beware. Their freedom is not your freedom; their war is not your war."

The crowd had fallen silent, the frail shadows of the lindens wavering on their faces.

"My friends, your enemies resort to desperate tricks. They appeal to your patriotism—and to your well-known respect for the law."

Laughter rippled through the crowd.

"But be careful, my friends. Their latest trick may finish you off. These so-called socialists in the Provisional Government are in league with the capitalists and the landowners, men like Vasily Nevsky who are conspiring with Kerensky to snatch the Revolution away from you!"

"Never!" someone shouted.

"Comrades, be vigilant. We Bolsheviks promise you bread, peace, land. Through us—only through us—you shall have them! All power to the Soviets!"

In a sudden movement, Lenin raised his arm over the crowd.

He quickly left the balcony. His audience roared its approval.

Marina and Dmitry walked back across the bridge in silence. Marina was outraged. Like Dmitry, Lenin made everything seem simple when nothing was simple! He lied about her father, and the mob believed him.

"We have much to learn from him," said Dmitry.

"You and Spiridonova?" Marina prodded.

"I and every revolutionary."

"So you agree with what he said about my father?"

"Your father has more to learn from Lenin than most!"

"How to deceive people with simpleminded slogans? I thought you were Vasily's friend."

In a self-assured voice, Dmitry said, "I am his friend, but he must understand that there can no longer be a truce with the bourgeoisie. Thousands of SRs agree with Lenin on that point. Spiridonova will be bringing the issue out into the open."

"And you'll take her side."

"I'll take the side I think is right. Why must you reduce everything to personal terms?"

As calmly as she could, she said, "Because I believe in personal terms. I believe that what happens to people one by one is the most important thing in the world."

"It's amazing," said Dmitry. "We're witnessing the birth of a new society, and you can't see beyond our own little lives."

"Lenin's not interested in anyone's little lives. Can't you see? He's only interested in power."

"Of course he's interested in power! How can socialism be built without power?"

"He's not interested in socialism either." She felt that she was losing Dmitry. "Not as we understand it."

"It seems that you and I don't understand anything the same way."

"I mean as my family understands it," she said, surprised by her own words. "We know what we mean by socialism."

"Have you read Lenin?"

"Of course I've read Lenin," she lied. "But hearing him speak makes me realize how dangerous he is. When my father talks about the people, there's love in his voice. When Lenin does, there's only hatred. He is turning people against one another."

"It's amazing how you twist everything around."

Feeling like a spectator of her own action, Marina turned and walked away from Dmitry without looking back. At the end of the bridge, he caught up with her.

"I'm sorry," he said. "I didn't mean that."

"Mean what?"

"That you twist everything around."

"Don't I?"

He smiled. "Yes, but not always." He reached for her hand, and she let him take it.

They came to an open space surrounded by gardens and stately neoclassical palaces. The tall wrought-iron gates of the Summer Garden stood open. Inside, they walked along a broad alley between rows of statues shaded by ancient trees.

They sat on a carved stone bench under a willow near an armless statue of Artemis. The park smelled of damp earth and wood smoke.

A blond peasant girl and a young man with a pistol tucked in his leather belt strolled past them hand in hand. A family of peasants was encamped around a dry fountain. In the willow, a thrush was singing. In the distance, Marina and Dmitry heard shots. The thrush fell silent, then resumed his song.

Marina looked up at the bird. "What do you think he makes of all these strange people in his park?"

"He'd better get used to them."

"Or die?"

"How can you be so indifferent to what's happening?"

She remembered Lenin on the balcony.

"I'm not indifferent," she said. "I'm afraid."

She was swept by sorrow. "Why are you wasting time with me?"

she demanded. "Why aren't you at some important meeting with the Woman of Our Time?"

Dmitry took her hand. "Because I love you, and I want to marry you when you grow up a little."

He took her in his arms and kissed her. For a long time, they held each other. Marina wished their embrace could last forever.

"I have no plans to grow up," she said at last.

"Then I'll have to marry a silly child."

"I don't promise anything. Where do you live?"

"Not far."

His rooms were on the seventh floor of a building off Liteiny Prospect. In the sunless courtyard, an old man peered at them through a grimy window. They started up the stairs. On the first landing, a woman with dark, sunken eyes opened her door a crack and stared at them as they passed. On the floor above, a child was crying. As they neared the skylight over the stairwell, a man and a woman were arguing in angry, throttled voices. On the seventh floor, Dmitry unlocked a narrow wooden door and let Marina into a garret room with a red tiled floor, furnished with a writing table and two worn armchairs. There were books on plank shelves, and a cast-iron stove. In a second room were more bookshelves and a narrow brass bed.

Dmitry laid a fire in the stove. Marina went to the window and gazed out across the rooftops to the hazy western end of the city where they had started their walk that morning. At Petrograd's northern latitude, this was the season of White Nights, when dusk merges with dawn and days go on forever. She was seized with doubts. She had invited herself here, giving Dmitry reason to believe that she wanted him to make love to her. But did he really love her? Did she love him? Their kisses in the park only made it harder to know.

He came to her and took her in his arms.

"I love you, Marina."

"And I love you," she said, hoping to find out from the words whether they were true. The voices of the couple in the apartment below rose angrily, then fell silent. From across the river came a long rattle of gunfire.

Dmitry kissed her, then held her close. Over his shoulder, she noticed a red shawl thrown over the back of the chair near the table.

A woman's shawl with a long fringe. She studied it for a long time while he held her, a feeling of numbness overtaking her. Gently, she drew away from him. She knew that it would be best not to say anything. The day had already been too full of revelations, but she could not restrain herself.

"Whose is that?" she asked, nodding toward the chair.

Dmitry glanced at the scarf and shrugged. "A comrade left it," he said matter-of-factly. "Friends often come here to do party work and stay late."

Then he took her by the shoulders and said in a solemn voice, "One day, Marina, we'll be together forever. I love you." And mimicking Kshesinskaya's voice, he added, "I hope you will be as happy as I once was." Despite herself, Marina smiled, and he kissed her again and again, but Marina no longer enjoyed his kisses. She felt cold. She wanted to leave.

In a horse-drawn cab, Dmitry accompanied her through the soft green late afternoon back to the palace. As they passed the Marinsky Theater, Marina asked in a casual tone, "Will you be going to the Chaliapin concert?"

"I expect so."

"I thought you didn't like social affairs."

"I don't."

"Will you be escorting Spiridonova?"

"She'll be there. People don't 'escort' people any more."

"They don't?"

He smiled broadly. "Except in your case."

"Come for me at eight."

At the palace, she found Anna and Tamara in her parents' diminutive bedroom. Tamara, wearing the white dress, stood at the window. Anna's face was a mask of grief. The small suitcase she had bought for Tamara was open on the canopied bed. The pink dancing slippers lay on top of her things.

"Tamara is leaving us," said Anna.

Tamara turned back into the room and stared at Marina accusingly; then she spoke to Anna. "Dear friend, I won't be a burden to you any longer. I came to you with nothing, and now I leave as

I came. In any case, there is no place for me now in your important new lives. You've been kind to me, Anna. I'll never forget you."

"But where will you go?" asked Anna. "How will you live?"

Tamara clasped her hands. "I shall go wherever my art is appreciated. I've always managed to support myself. I'll teach dancing. Or perform useful work. Caring for wounded soldiers perhaps."

This was too much for Marina. "Or millionaires," she said.

"Marina!" said Anna.

"Tamara knows what I mean."

"Spy!"

"She was with Lianozov at the Astoria Hotel."

"And what of it? Have I lost the right to choose my friends? As a matter of fact, Stepan is sending his motorcar for me. It should be here any minute."

Anna looked bewildered. "My dear Tamara, of course you can choose your friends. But Lianozov represents everything we deplore. We thought you shared our ideals."

"You weren't listening, Mother," said Marina.

"There, you see!" said Tamara, "Your daughter has hated me from the beginning. In any case, it's true. I am an artist, and politics means nothing to me! This ghastly revolution is destroying everything beautiful in life. I respect Vasily, and you, dear Anna. You are good people, but hopelessly impractical. Stepan is a realist; he moves in the highest circles. He knows that the Allied powers will not permit Russia to sink into barbarity."

"The sick child must be cured," said Marina.

"Exactly!"

"And so you'll be enjoying the fruits of Western capitalism with the realistic Stepan."

"If he'll have me—and he's left little doubt that he will." She held out her hand. On the fourth finger was a large ruby set in gold.

Marina heard the rumble of a powerful automobile approaching. Anna, who had come up to Tamara ready to embrace her, said, "I thought he had a wife in Paris."

Tamara rushed to the bed and closed her suitcase. "I refuse to be humiliated any longer. From this moment on, I am free of all of you!"

She yanked the suitcase off the bed and strode out the door, slamming it behind her. Anna buried her face in her hands.

"You shouldn't be so harsh with people," she said to Marina. "I'll miss her terribly. Whatever you think, she has a beautiful soul."

"What did she mean—'our important new lives'?"

"Where have you been all day? Haven't you heard? Your father has been appointed minister of agriculture in the Provisional Government. What a shame that Tamara is leaving us just now."

Marina went to her mother and put her arms around her, trying to comfort her. Over Anna's shoulder, she caught a glimpse of Lianozov's driver in the courtyard below, holding the door of the white phaeton for Tamara. At that moment, the black ministry sedan appeared through the trees and drew up beside Lianozov's car. Vasily got out and spoke to Tamara. Then, as the chauffeur was helping her into the open car, Vasily stepped back and blew her a kiss.

That aerial kiss would haunt Marina for a long time to come.

Chapter Thirteen

FOR THE CHALIAPIN RECITAL, MARINA ASKED HER MOTHER TO LEND her the green chiffon dress with velvet trim at the neck which Anna had bought at Worth in Paris before the war. She intended to look devastatingly beautiful and make Dmitry forget Spiridonova.

"Isn't it a bit too grown-up for you?" Anna had asked.

"Of course, if you'd rather wear it . . ."

"Oh, no. I have my lavender dress."

It turned out that the green chiffon, taken in, looked so becoming on Marina that Anna's reservations were dispelled. Marina suspected that her mother was pleased by her show of interest in clothes, which perhaps eased Anna's guilt over having given Marina's birthday dress to Tamara in Alassio. Putting on the green gown, Marina could imagine that she belonged to her mother's childhood world on the Dubrovka estate. She was reading *War and Peace* and had assigned the romantic role of Prince Andrey to Dmitry.

As for Vasily, the question of his attire was a delicate one. At first, he had accepted the suggestion made by Prince Lvov, the head of the first Provisional Government, that on formal occasions, members of the cabinet wear frock coats. However, Vasily was one of only two socialists in the new government, and the only one of peasant origin. What would it say to his constituency, the millions of Russian muzhiks, if he appeared at the Marinsky in a frock coat?

That question was complicated by the fact that Kerensky, the other socialist in the government, would be wearing his own idiosyncratic uniform, a stark military tunic without markings of rank, perhaps symbolizing revolutionary authority or, more simply, its wearer's sense of self-importance.

It had crossed Vasily's mind that for the occasion he might dress as he had during the heady days of the revolution of 1905—as a peasant. If symbolism was the order of the day, that would be symbolism indeed! He mentioned the idea to Anna. Her reaction was immediate and emphatic.

"Wear a frock coat."

The next day, Vasily visited a shop dealing in secondhand clothes, where every style of evening wear, military uniform, and riding habit was to be found at bargain prices. He chose a top hat, striped trousers, and a gray coat which, though it required no alterations, looked odd on him in the shop's mirror, as if his body was protesting against such formal constraints. Who, he wondered, had this elegant coat belonged to? What triumphs had he scored? What defeats? What had become of him? Was he sipping tea at a hôtel particulier in Paris? Or had his bloated corpse floated out to sea on the Neva?

And where would Vasily himself be a year hence?

However, by the night of the concert, he had put such speculations out of mind. At the stroke of eight, Anna on one arm, his top hat tucked under the other, he started down the staircase of the grand duke's palace. Catching sight of himself and his wife in the gold-framed mirror on the landing, he had the clear impression that for better or worse, he looked every inch a minister, and Anna a minister's wife. As for Marina, she discovered to her delight that the green gown transformed her: she was no longer a girl but a young woman of the world, mistress of her fate.

Trying not to think about the red shawl, she had gone downstairs to wait for Dmitry. Gotz was to drive them to the Marinsky. Dmitry was to come at eight. Remembering his discomfort on his previous appearances at the palace, she decided to meet him at the door herself. In the foyer, she glanced at her reflection in the great mirrors on its walls. With her Aunt Ariane's blood-red coral necklace at her throat, her dark hair combed forward into points at the sides, she looked lovely. She danced a few steps, showing multiple lovely

Marinas in the mirrors, but then stopped abruptly, remembering Tamara prancing here on the day of their arrival.

The doorbell rang. She opened the heavy oak doors flanked by the stuffed bears with their raised paws. Gotz and Dmitry stood there looking at her in surprise. Abram wore a three-piece black suit, Dmitry a dark collarless corduroy jacket and a visored cap, the street wear of revolutionary Petrograd. She could not decipher Dmitry's reaction to her. Was he seeing a stylish Parisian, an overdressed seventeen-year-old, or perhaps a betrayer of the revolution?

Gotz spoke first. "You look charming, Marina," he said. "And so very grown up. Are the minister and his lady ready?"

At that moment, Vasily and Anna appeared on the staircase.

"You do look very nice," Dmitry said to Marina, in the same emotionless tone he had used in the garden at the Villa Ariane when he had told her that he loved her. Sulkily, he turned to meet her parents, looking them up and down in silence.

As they squeezed into the Panhard, the sky over the city was still a light opalescent blue. Horse-drawn cabs, carriages, and automobiles were converging at the entrance of the floodlit Marinsky. Throngs of spectators were waiting there for a glimpse of the government's guests. They recognized Vasily at once and cheered. He doffed his top hat to shouts of "Land and Liberty!" In the lobby, he and Anna spoke with other frock-coated members of the government and their wives. To her annoyance, Marina noticed that Dmitry was watching them with a derisive smile, which he made no effort to hide.

Suddenly, a slender woman with a narrow face, her movements purposeful yet graceful, came up to him. Dmitry kissed her hand in what was for him a most unusual display of formality. Though Marina had seen Maria Spiridonova only in a photograph that Anna had shown her in Alassio, she recognized her at once. The revolutionary heroine's severe, narrow face showed her prison years. She wore a high-collared white blouse tucked into a long narrow gray skirt. Thrown casually over her shoulder was the red, fringed shawl Marina had seen in Dmitry's apartment. Marina's annoyance turned to rage.

Spiridonova spoke to Dmitry in a lowered voice, and then turned to her.

"You must be Marina."

"I am," she said coldly. "And you must be Maria Spiridonova."

"You paint, Dmitry tells me."

Before Marina could reply, Spiridonova turned back to Dmitry and said, "You'll be there?"

"Of course I'll be there," he said, glancing at Vasily, who was conversing with Kerensky.

Spiridonova examined Marina for another moment, then received Anna's embrace.

Marina now was certain that there was more than party camaraderie between Dmitry and Spiridonova. You paint pretty pictures, she seemed to be saying, while we offer our lives to the Revolution and suffer prison and death. Dmitry has spoken to me about your painting because Dmitry and I talk about *everything*. Because I sleep with him.

As Vasily was ushered upstairs, Anna, Dmitry, and Marina were shown to the front of the orchestra section. Spiridonova with other younger party members took seats several rows behind them.

"Where are you and she going?" Marina asked Dmitry, trying to appear calm.

"To a party meeting."

"Will my father be there?"

"As a matter of fact, he won't. This is a special meeting of comrades, not an official one."

"Is Spiridonova convening it?"

"Yes."

"Do my father and Gotz know about it?"

"They're not involved. The official one is next week."

"It sounds like a conspiracy."

He glared at her. "I thought you weren't interested in politics."

"I wasn't until now," she said. Turning from him, she gazed around the theater. Above them, she saw her father take his place in the box reserved for the members of the Provisional Government. The central box next to it, formerly that of the tsar and his immediate family, was unlit and empty. In the box facing that of the Provisional Government ministers, once reserved for the grand dukes and duchesses, Marina recognized Lianozov seated among sash-bosomed ambassadors and medal-bosomed military officers, with their wives in glittering low-cut evening gowns. Where, she wondered, was Tamara? Would Lianozov, who had a wife in Paris, dare bring her to this gala?

The back rows of the orchestra were filling with soldiers, students, and workers who had been allocated free passes by the government. Many of the soldiers were veterans with bandaged limbs, their shabby gray uniforms contrasting with the resplendent uniforms of the officers.

Near them in the orchestra, members of the Petrograd intelligentsia were slowly taking their places. Marina recognized the writer Anton Golovin, a friend of Gorky whose dark good looks were known to every Russian in those years from picture postcards. Next to him, no less handsome than Golovin, sat a man with curly gray hair and pale blue eyes, the poet Alexander Blok. Marina was thrilled by the presence of these writers, personal deities in Anna's and her lives. For a time, she forgot her anger. Next to Blok sat a stunning-looking dark-eyed young woman in black.

"Akhmatova," said Anna.

Marina knew many of Anna Akhmatova's poems by heart. "The best of them all," she said.

Members of the orchestra were filing into the pit and tuning their instruments. Turning and looking up at the first balcony, Marina noticed Lenin. Next to him was Moisei Uritsky, whom she remembered from their arrival at the Finland Station. She drew Dmitry's attention to them. As they watched, Lenin shook his fist at the Provisional Government box and said something to Uritsky that made him laugh. Behind Lenin, his pince-nez glasses gleaming in the half-darkness, sat Leon Trotsky. Vasily's fiery Marxist adversary in many debates at socialist congresses in Western Europe, Trotsky had recently returned from New York and was rumored to have allied himself with Lenin.

At that moment, a small, familiar-looking woman next to Trotsky leaned forward and spoke to Lenin: Marina recognized Ekaterina Pavlovna Peshkova. Lenin motioned to her to sit next to him, but she shook her head, stood up, and left the balcony, reappearing moments later at the rear of the orchestra section, where she settled next to a group of students. Marina pointed her out to her mother.

"I had a note from her," said Anna. "She's here from Moscow for just one night, representing the Red Cross."

"They're all here," said Dmitry, studying the Bolsheviks in the balcony. "The entire leadership."

"I recognize Lenin and Trotsky and Uritsky," said Marina. "Who else?"

"The man in the leather coat is Yakov Sverdlov, one of their best organizers. The fellow with the pointed beard is Felix Dzerzhinsky, a Polish aristocrat, said to be a fanatical revolutionary. The one sitting alone beyond him is Josef Stalin, a Georgian nobody seems to know and nobody seems to like."

"And who's that next to Dzerzhinsky, who looks like a schoolteacher?"

"That's Anatoly Lunacharsky, your friend Tamara's former mentor."

"The Bolsheviks are *your* friends," said Marina, her anger boiling up as she remembered Lenin's scathing words about her father.

"Russia's friends," said Dmitry with a teasing smile. He glanced back at Spiridonova.

In a flash of exasperation, Marina said, "Why don't you sit with her? It's obvious that you want to."

The houselights started to dim. Marina regretted her words the moment she had uttered them: she had left Dmitry no way out.

"It's true," he said, "I do want to sit with her."

As the lights faded, he got up and walked up the aisle and settled next to Spiridonova.

In the darkness, Marina silently started to cry. She felt utterly drained of feeling. Through her tears, she saw a spotlight suddenly illuminate the huge red curtain. The first bars of the death scene from *Boris Godunov* sounded, the curtain parted with a soft purring, and Chaliapin appeared, spreading his arms wide in a gesture that seemed to fill the theater. Even before he began to sing, the spell for which he was famous was cast. Marina dried her eyes with her handkerchief. Damn Dmitry! she thought. I will not let him spoil this evening, when Chaliapin is singing for me, for my parents, for all Russians like us!

Though the portly, handsome singer wore not the royal robes of Boris Godunov but a tuxedo, he *was* the doomed tsar. The enemy was at the gates, and like Nicholas II, he would never be able to pass on his crown to his beloved young son. Soldiers and sailors, students, and dignitaries sat in awe as the tsar bared his guilty soul and prepared to meet his terrifying, exemplary death.

Marina would never forget Chaliapin's Godunov. Just as she was losing Dmitry, she was seeing the old order die. What lay ahead was obscure and menacing, like the Time of Troubles following Godunov's death when Russia was left in chaos for many years.

The parted curtain cast a reddish glow on the dying Tsar Boris. At that moment, a stirring in the balcony caused Marina to glance back. In the section occupied by the Bolsheviks, Dzerzhinsky was standing to make room for a woman in a low-cut ball gown of golden lace who settled between him and Lunacharsky.

Tamara.

On the stage, Tsar Boris drew his last breath. Solemn chords mourned Marina's past happiness, when Dmitry was hers and Russia's future was bright.

*B*y June, the buoyant mood in Petrograd had changed to one of brooding unrest. On street corners, in public squares, in factories and barracks, people talked darkly about some momentous event that was about to happen. The whole city was waiting.

Angry women waited in endless lines for dwindling rations of bread and kerosene.

Peasants who had flocked to the city waited for a proclamation granting them land.

Soldiers waited for orders to go to the front, holding day-long meetings to decide whether they would obey such orders when they came.

The deposed tsar, a captive in his palace in nearby Tsarskoe Selo, waited to be allowed to leave for sanctuary in England with his family, unaware that his cousin King George V had declined to receive him.

Conservatives waited for a military dictator to impose order, many of them secretly hoping for a German occupation that would save Russia from anarchy.

Millions throughout the former empire eagerly awaited the convocation of the Constituent Assembly, which was postponed—and then postponed again.

Everyone waited—except Kerensky, the one man in Petrograd who still believed that he was the predestined leader of Russia.

Alexander Kerensky was exhausting himself in a personal crusade to inspire Russia's demoralized armies to launch an all-out offensive against Germany and Austria. "You carry peace, law, truth, and justice at the end of your bayonets!" he was telling the ill-supplied, ill-fed, badly led soldiers, to whom his appeals for ever greater sacrifice sounded more and more like the ravings of a lunatic.

Chapter Fourteen

ON JUNE 14, THE MEETING THAT WOULD DECIDE THE POLITICAL ORI-
entation of the Socialist Revolutionary Party convened in the main
salon of the grand duke's palace. From the upstairs landing, Marina
watched Dmitry come in with Maria Spiridonova and her following
of a half-dozen young SRs. It was the first time since the Chaliapin
concert that Marina had seen Dmitry. She thought that he looked
pale and preoccupied. She waited for the room to fill; then she came
down the staircase and took a chair in the back row.

Presiding at a long table against the mirrored far wall of the
salon, Vasily and Gotz faced a restive audience of about a hundred
rank-and-file members seated on small gilded chairs. Dmitry, Spiridonova, and her friends occupied the front row. Gotz got to his
feet.

"This meeting is called in response to the decision by certain
SRs to break away and form an independent party, to be known as
the Left Socialist Revolutionaries. I call upon Maria Alexandrovna
to explain this unusual proposal."

Spiridonova rose and faced the audience. She looked determined
and more handsome than Marina remembered her from their encounter at Dmitry's, her long hair loosely braided, her red shawl
tied casually around her waist.

"Under our present leadership, we SRs have made unacceptable
compromises with the reactionaries. Nevsky has worked for many
years on the land bill only to have it sabotaged by other members

of the Provisional Government. Kerensky pretends to be the guardian of the revolution while in fact he's become a guardian of privilege."

"Get to the point!" called out an older man sitting near Marina. "Are we to understand that you people favor an alliance with the Bolsheviks?"

"Indeed, we do!" replied Spiridonova. "In many ways, the Bolsheviks are better socialists than we are."

"Maria Alexandrovna!" pleaded Gotz, "you forget that Lenin rejects all coalitions with other socialists. Unite with the Bolsheviks, and they'll eat you alive!"

"We'll never let that happen!"

"Maria Alexandrovna," said Vasily, getting up so as to be heard throughout the room, "your accusations unfortunately are not without foundation. However, for us SRs, an alliance with the bourgeois in the government is a bitter political necessity. We fought to overthrow the old tyranny; now the first order of business is to combat the new tyranny that the Bolsheviks may well impose upon Russia if they're not held in check."

The younger SRs seated around Spiridonova greeted this warning with jeers. Dmitry rose to speak. "You know how much I respect you, Vasily Ivanovich," he said in an overwrought voice, "but we cannot accept your position. The Bolsheviks want power, yes, but only to clean up the problems inherited from the tsars. Unlike you, they favor a peace settlement with Germany. They—and not you—have a vision of a world freed from exploitation of the working class."

"And what about the peasantry? Two-thirds of Russia," demanded Vasily.

Spiridonova stood up beside Dmitry. "We believe as you do that the new Russia will spring naturally from its rural roots. With the Bolsheviks, we will be traveling parallel roads. We shall be representing the peasants; they, the workers. We are the Left SRs, and as of this moment, we declare our independence—of the Bolsheviks, and of you!"

The room was silent. Shaking his head sadly, Gotz rose and said solemnly, "This has been an historic afternoon—the unity of our party has been shattered when we need unity most.

"If there is no further business, this meeting is adjourned."

Gilded chairs scraped as the assembly rose and started filing toward the doors. People spoke to one another in guarded voices. There was none of the exuberant chatter that usually erupted at the close of SR gatherings.

Marina saw Dmitry searching the room—perhaps for her. She slipped out the door and hurried upstairs so as not to have to speak to him. She did not wish to risk another rejection from him in the presence of Spiridonova. As it was, all that had happened between them was a lovers' quarrel. She had provoked him; she had rejected his lovemaking. He was proud and obstinate, yet one day, she was certain, he would come back to her, as the Left SRs would eventually return to the fold of the party. She tried to tell herself that she despised Spiridonova as much for breaking up the SRs as for luring Dmitry away from her, but she knew that it was not true. Her older rival's red shawl haunted her day and night.

Chapter Fifteen

MARINA CROSSED GALERNAYA AND WALKED WESTWARD ALONG THE
Neva embankment. From the broad stone seawall, she watched the
orange sun pulsating in the pale green sky over the river. The Gulf
of Finland shimmered in the distance, "The Seagate of the Neva,"
Anna Akhmatova had called it in her poem to Alexander Blok.

What if Blok were suddenly to appear at her side? He was said
to be living nearby. Perhaps the poet could explain the riddle of
her being seventeen in this grand, chaotic city where the sun never
set, and answer the questions of whether Dmitry would ever return
to her and whether her father would fulfill his mission?

For a long time, she gazed out over the gulf. An easterly breeze
carried the strains of military music, which rose and died with the
wind. There were no other strollers on the embankment. There was
no poet at her side. The voice of the dying Tsar Boris echoed in
her mind.

She was worried about her father. Throughout Russia, the word
was spreading that the peasant minister was about to save the country. His reputation was growing as the author of the land bill and
as the guiding force behind the one great hope of the dispossessed
millions, the Constituent Assembly. His reputation as a man of
compassion was also growing. At the Ministry of Agriculture, he
received petitioners and was attentive to each one of them—to the
woman who demanded his help in divorcing a nasty husband; to

the inventor of a fantastical agricultural machine; to the young peasant on his way home from the front, unburdening himself of tales of horror. He listened to them all, and they looked to him, believing with him that the Constituent Assembly would right every wrong, but Marina feared that his faith in it was blinding him to the forces which were gathering against the Assembly and against him.

As for his land program, bureaucrats of various allegiances were opposing the very notion of land cooperatives. Why bother? Why set up yet another administration? Why not let the old pre-revolutionary zemstvos, the provincial councils working under well-understood restrictions, carry on their quiet, civilizing mission?

But the greatest threat to her father's plans, Marina knew, was the war. The distant trumpets of the military band on the Field of Mars reminded her that every day more young men were being inducted into the army and sent off to the front, from which it was said that not half would return.

And, as often as not, the last words they would hear before leaving for the front would be Kerensky's frenzied harangues, celebrating their impending sacrifice in the name of Russia. Kerensky was the most ardent opponent of her father's land bill, the most ardent supporter of the war.

Kerensky argued that were the bill to become law, soldiers by the tens of thousands would throw down their arms and rush home to claim their share of land. And so, instead of promoting agrarian reform, the Provisional Government had recently authorized the summary execution of all deserters from the front.

Anna, a staunch opponent of the death penalty, was deeply shocked: "Is this what the Socialist Revolutionary party stands for nowadays: the murder of peasant-soldiers?"

And yet Marina understood the SRs' fear of peace without victory: if Germany won the war, its first act would be to restore the Romanovs to their throne, ending all hope of democracy in Russia for generations to come. The promise of the Constituent Assembly would vanish. Still, if only her father would take a clear stand against the slaughter, as did Lenin! The sight of so many mutilated soldiers wandering aimlessly through Petrograd was unbearable.

She started back toward the palace. Ahead, on the seawall, she saw Vasily coming to meet her.

Wearing his London-tailored blue suit, a black homburg over

his wavy hair, his small graying beard neatly trimmed, her father looked like any fashionable Petrograd gentleman. But as he came up to her, she saw that he was exhausted and—she knew at once—deeply troubled.

"What happened, Father?" she asked, taking his hand.

"I've just come from the Field of Mars," he said wearily, "from listening to Kerensky addressing the soldiers leaving for the front today and delivering what amounted to their funeral oration. It was grotesque. Two of them tried to bolt but were instantly caught."

"Can't you do something?" demanded Marina.

"I can. I will, as soon as the Constituent Assembly establishes a legitimate government."

"Father, more than half of your callers at the Ministry are deserters. They look to you. No one else in power wants to help them. Unless the government ends the war and gives them land right away, the Bolsheviks will do it. Lenin tells them what they want to hear—'bread, land, and peace.' Above all, peace."

"I know that all too well," Vasily said softly. "Let's walk a little, Marinotchka," he said. "Like we used to do on the beach at Alassio where we found that beautiful shell."

They started along the embankment in the direction of the palace, strolling in silence. Then Vasily stopped and, taking Marina's hands in his, said, "Long ago, I made a promise to your Aunt Ariane that I'd never abandon the struggle for a free Russia. Later, your mother and I made the same promise to each other. I'm determined to keep it, but if I were to leave the Provisional Government now, I'd be giving up what power I have." He clamped his hands together. "We should be conducting nonstop negotiations with the Germans, no matter what Kerensky says. If only we could convene the Constituent Assembly tomorrow!"

He searched her face.

"You who see things clearly, what do you think I should do? Break with Kerensky? Leave the government?"

"I think that you should keep your promise."

He drew her to him and stroked her hair.

"I will, Marinotchka," he said. "I swear I will. And I shall keep my word to you. What we're going through now is only the dark before the dawn. You'll see."

That night Marina could not fall asleep. Her father had been wrong: in the White Nights, there was no dark before the dawn. At three in the morning, beyond the muslin curtains of the bedroom, the city still shone with pale, eerie light. As she was beginning to drift to sleep, she thought that she saw Spiridonova's red shawl hanging at the window. Or was it the reddish glow of the sun rising higher in the sky? Her whole body ached. Dmitry loved another woman.

Chapter Sixteen

MARINA'S MORNINGS WERE SPENT HELPING HER FATHER AT THE MINistry of Agriculture, screening the petitioners who came to talk to the muzhik minister in ever growing numbers. In the afternoons, in their apartment, she worked with Anna on administrative plans for the still unscheduled Constituent Assembly. Helping her parents kept her busy, but in this unearthly, waiting city, more frightening with each passing week, with the springtime she had shared with Dmitry now a memory, and with no word from him, Marina felt that her heart was breaking.

Then, in early July, she received an unexpected letter:

> *My dear goddaughter,*
> *The art treasures of the Hermitage are imperiled by a possible German onslaught against this city, and by the ignorance of our people, who are capable of destroying them at any moment in an outbreak of brutish wrath.*
> *As a member of a commission formed to safeguard our national artistic legacy, I have taken the liberty of telephoning my old friend Andrey Baranov, curator of the Italian section there, proposing you as a volunteer to help catalog the paintings before their eventual shipment to Moscow.*
> *Working for Baranov, you'll be advancing your art education under one of the most distinguished art historians in Russia. If you*

wish to avail yourself of this opportunity, please call at the Hermitage
as soon as possible.
  I embrace you.
  Gorky

Marina's spirits soared. The next morning, she hastened to the Millionaya entrance of the great palace on the Neva, where a guard at the door took her name and announced her by telephone. Soon another guard ushered her up the Baroque main stairway to the second floor. He escorted her through room after room of paintings by Italian masters. As they walked by them, with a pang of delight Marina recognized some of the paintings from reproductions. At last, they came to a high-ceilinged office whose French windows opened onto the river and the Peter and Paul fortress. At an enormous eighteenth-century desk inlaid with ivory and rare woods sat a small, elderly man with a pink, childlike face, blue eyes, and bushy white hair. Andrey Baranov stood up when Marina came in, and with a courtly bow, he offered her his chair at the desk.

"Marina Vasilyevna," he said, "do sit down please at this desk, which once belonged to King Louis XVI of France, and write something for me."

Bewildered, Marina sat down at the huge desk. Before her were a pen, a sheet of paper, and a massive bronze inkstand entwined with cherubs.

"What shall I write?"

"Anything that flies into your head. I want a sample of your handwriting."

Marina wrote "Land and liberty" three times. Baranov looked over her shoulder and nodded in approval. "Come with me," he said.

He hurried her back through the rooms through which she had come, walking so fast that she could barely keep up with him. Abruptly, he stopped before a painting of a beautiful young woman in gleaming armor holding a sword in one hand, a severed head in the other. Her eyes were downcast, but she was triumphant. The beauty of the picture caused Marina to sigh with pleasure. Baranov was watching her closely.

"Giorgione's *Judith*," he said. "The tsar never knew what he had. His German curator thought it was a Moretto. As you know, there are very few authentic Giorgiones in existence."

The old man led her to another, smaller painting on an easel at the far end of the room.

"It's wonderful," said Marina, admiring the beautiful Madonna against a richly painted background with classical columns.

"Leonardo," he said, beaming at Marina, his lively eyes sparkling. "*The Benois Madonna*. It's an honor to present one lovely Italian lady to another."

Back in his office, he seated Marina across from him at the royal desk and looked at her for a moment without speaking.

"You're very young," he said at last, "but Alexey Maximovich speaks highly of you. I happen to be a great admirer of your father—a leader of great imagination and spirit. Gorky tells me that you want to become a painter, that you love great pictures, and I see that you do." He broke off, watching her with his head cocked to one side.

"I do," she assured him.

"Especially Italian ones?"

"Especially Italian ones."

"Then we'll be great friends."

From then on, all day, Marina sat across from Andrey Baranov, taking down his descriptions of the paintings, their size, and catalog number. She took intense pleasure in this Aladdin's cave of treasures: da Vincis, Filippo Lippis, Caravaggios, Titians, and her favorite, Giorgione's *Judith*. She felt safe. She felt needed. For hours on end, she did not think of Dmitry, nor about the future.

On a warm, hazy morning early in July, as Marina was walking to work along the Neva embankment, she met a crowd of students carrying red banners bearing Bolshevik slogans. Some wore pistols at their belts; others carried rifles.

"Come with us!" a young man called out. "We're going to the Tauride Palace to support the Soviet. The Bolsheviks are taking over from the bourgeois!"

"I can't," said Marina. "I have work to do."

"What kind of work?" demanded the young man.

"At the Hermitage," said Marina, realizing as she spoke how her reply would be received.

"We're making a revolution, and you have *work* in the tsar's picture gallery?" shouted the young man derisively.

Marina hurried down Millionaya without looking back.

She found Baranov in his office talking on the telephone. Through the French windows, she saw another, larger crowd surging eastward along the embankment, their shouts growing louder. Baranov hung up the phone.

"Gorky wants to see you," he said, seemingly oblivious of the noise outside. "Something about a family friend. I could barely make out what he was saying. In any case, you must go to see him. Do tell him that our work here is proceeding on schedule." He glanced past her to the open window. "And do be careful. The city is going mad."

Chapter Seventeen

MARINA KNEW THE WAY TO GORKY'S HOUSE. SHE HAD GONE THERE
once before, some days after the Chaliapin concert and her parting
from Dmitry. She had been seeking her godfather's counsel, only to
find that he was away in Moscow. On the Troitzky Bridge to Vas-
ilevsky Island, she made her way through an unruly crowd of workers with gaunt, angry faces, fists raised, shouting Bolshevik slogans.
She hurried past Kshesinskaya's palace, half-hidden by the lindens
in full leaf. She rang the bell at Gorky's apartment. Max Peshkov
opened the door.

He wore a tan sweater with moth holes that had been darned
with red wool. At twenty, Gorky's son struck her as being better
looking than ever, though somewhat dissipated. His breath smelled
of liquor.

"Do you still climb trees?" he said.

"Do you have the fastest motorcycle in the world?"

"As a matter of fact, I do. Come for a ride with me."

"I'd love to, but I'm here to see your father."

"This is his day for beautiful women," said Max, and he led her
through an officelike room where people were seated at desks, typing.

"The staff of *New Life*," said Max. "My father's notorious magazine that's shaking up the Bolsheviks."

As they came to the half-open door of the study at the end of the hall, Marina heard distant gunfire. In a low voice, Max said, "If you're wise, Marina, you'll ask my father to speak to Lenin about protection for you and your parents. He's hiding in Finland, but he'll soon be back. Everyone knows that he's planning to do away with the Provisional Government."

He pushed open the door to his father's office and motioned to her to enter; then he left her abruptly.

Gorky stood at a window looking out at the Neva. He was wearing a red silk Chinese robe and Chinese paper slippers. The spacious, airy room was lined with shelves of books and oriental porcelain cups and figurines. On a desk cluttered with papers stood a telephone and several framed photographs. He gave no sign that he had heard Marina come in.

"Alexey Maximovich," she said softly. She could not see him clearly against the light, but when he turned toward her, she was startled by how he had aged since his visit to Alassio. His face was lined, his hair gray.

"How long has it been, Marina?"

"Four years."

"In four years, you've become a lovely young woman and I a decrepit old man. It's not fair."

He came to her and embraced her.

"Baranov tells me that I was right about you."

"I'm grateful for the chance to work at the Hermitage. It's a wonderful opportunity."

Gorky nodded. Suddenly, he began to cough, a deep racking hack. She looked away, studying a photograph on the desk of a handsome young man with wavy dark hair and beautiful, deep-set eyes.

"Yes, yes," Gorky said when he could speak again. "Along with a legacy of barbarism and ignorance, the tsars left us some of the world's most magnificent art. What do you think of these fine compatriots of ours? Wouldn't you rather be back in Alassio?"

"Not any more. I belong here."

In the street, a truck raced by at high speed. Gorky went to the window, shaking his fist as the noise of machine-gun fire filled the room.

"Look at them," he said. "Young men with trembling hands firing into the air with no idea of what they're doing or what they want. Soon they'll be shooting into crowds who don't know what they want either. And they call this freedom! It's not freedom—it's chaos!"

He sat down at his desk. "I fear for your father and for his land bill," he said. "Machiavelli said that a good man cannot be a great man, and while I detest that cynical Italian, I fear that in Vasily's case, he may be right." He looked at her sadly. Again, he was seized by a coughing fit. He noticed that she was looking at the photograph on his desk. "Another good man," he said. "Kiril is the son of my friend Anton Golovin, and is another godchild of mine. He's with his father in Finland now, but when he returns to Petrograd, you must meet him. He loves painting too, and for his sins he wants to be a writer.

"I'd very much like to meet him," said Marina.

"His father and I used to be like brothers; now we no longer speak. Our young men are drowning in blood, and like that idiot Kerensky, Anton Golovin wants them to die to save our national honor. National honor! And to think that he once portrayed the madness of war more powerfully than anyone else." Looking solemnly at Marina, he added, "It may be that the children of prophets will have to save their fathers."

After a moment, Marina said, "Is Kiril Golovin the friend you mentioned to Baranov on the telephone earlier today?"

Gorky brightened. "Oh, no. I was speaking of your family friend."

"Dmitry Danilov?" Marina said eagerly.

"No. She was here this morning. A remarkable woman. Madam Sermus!"

Marina was dumbfounded. "Tamara Sermus is no friend of mine," she said in a low voice. "Why did she call on you?"

"Hasn't she told you?"

"We haven't seen her lately."

Gorky peered at Marina. "Her name is on a list of former Okhrana agents."

Marina felt a rush of vindication, an unashamedly joyous feeling.

"She told me everything," pursued Gorky. "She sat where you're sitting now and told me the story of her life. I will write about it one day! It's a story of our time!" Gorky clapped his hands exuberantly.

"What did she tell you?"

"Everything! How she ran away from her stifling bourgeois home, how Isadora Duncan opened her heart to life, love, art! How she discovered her revolutionary calling in the Lunacharsky circle and fell in love with a young Bolshevik. How Azef forced her to report on the group, telling her that if she refused, the Okhrana would kill the young man she loved."

Marina was silent.

"What have you against the poor woman?" Gorky asked after a moment. "She is so fond of your parents! She asked me all about them and their circle of SR friends. I told her that they were wonderful people."

"Did she tell you about Lianozov?"

"Yes, as a matter of fact, she did. She told me why she took up with him. She told me how the Okhrana had forced her into an intrigue between Rasputin's supporters and his assassins. And about the torpedoed ship and the miracle of her rescue. She said that your mother opened the door to a beautiful new life for her."

At that moment, the telephone rang. Gorky answered it, frowning. Marina could hear an excited male voice crackling in the receiver. Then Gorky hung up.

"Now we'll see whether Lenin is still in control of this mob he's stirred up. What was I saying?"

In an even voice, Marina said, "You were telling me how my mother opened the door to a new life for Tamara Sermus."

"Yes indeed! And she also told me how some devil in you caused you to make life with your family impossible for her, forcing her to prostitute herself, to sell her soul and her body."

"Tamara Sermus lied," said Marina, trying to remain calm. "She threw herself at Lianozov only because she believes that my father has no political future."

"Are you telling me that Madame Sermus had designs on your father?"

Marina blushed. "On my mother also."

Gorky hunched forward in his chair. "Madame Sermus wanted to get her name stricken from the list of former police agents which is to be published by the government. She also wants me to 'reinstate her in the Nevskys' good opinion,' as she put it. She was in tears. 'You must help me,' she pleaded. 'I'm young. All I wanted to do was save the man I loved—must my life be destroyed because of that?' I told her—truthfully—that it was not in my power to have her name removed from the Okhrana list, but she didn't believe me. She spoke of the goodness of man and how Christ had taught us to forgive sinners, and how I was known all over the world for my compassionate soul. She—"

He broke off and went to the window again.

"It never occurred to me that she was not sincere. But from what you say—" He hesitated, then continued as if speaking to himself:

"She wore a black summer hat with a veil, black gloves, a low-cut black dress. Pulling off a glove, she touched a ruby ring she wore as if it were causing her pain. 'Please help me,' she said. She lifted her veil and, blushing and smiling, removed her hat. She seemed to know that the sunlight was caressing her arms and shoulders." He turned from the window, looking at Marina with a distracted expression.

"What happened then?"

As if appealing to her, he said, "She actually asked me if I wanted her to be my *fille de joie*?"

"What did you tell her?" said Marina in disbelief.

"I refused, of course—as gently as possible. She's very beautiful, and I'm not so old as not to feel tempted, yet my heart went out to her only in pity."

He returned to his desk. "I told her that while I could not clear her name, I could perhaps help her find some respectable position that will permit her to rehabilitate herself. I thought of *New Life*, but she knows nothing of politics and had spoken of her love of art—"

Marina saw her dismay reflected in Gorky's eyes.

"I didn't know of your feelings about her," he said. "I gave her a letter to Baranov. The final decision is his. Had I known—"

Back at the Hermitage, Marina ran up the central marble staircase flanked by gilded statuary and gray jasper vases and hurried through the Italian galleries toward Baranov's office. She had reached one of her favorite rooms, luminous with the warm siennas, reds, and greens of the Venetians. On the wall to the right hung one of the most celebrated Titians in the museum, *Mary Magdalene Repentant*. Next to it was Veronese's *Descent from the Cross*.

Marina heard a clicking of heels on the parquet floor. Tamara Sermus appeared at the door of the Venetian room. She was wearing the black dress Gorky had described, a black shawl, and a broad black hat with a veil. For years afterward, Marina would wonder whether the revulsion she felt at that moment might have sprung from some evil streak deep within herself. On the wall behind Tamara was the contrite Mary Magdalene, but there was nothing repentant about Tamara.

In a low voice, she said, "You'll regret this, Marina."

"Exactly what will I regret?"

"Telling that old fool not to engage me."

"If Doctor Baranov refused to engage you, it was his own idea," Marina said quietly.

"Then he'll regret it!" From the Millionaya side came the sound of machine-gun fire, causing the tall French windows to shake. "Do you know what that shooting means?"

"No. And neither do the people shooting."

"It means the Bolsheviks are taking power. It means that I don't have to be afraid any more."

"Perhaps you should be afraid. You spied on them for the Okhrana. For the tsarist government. For Azef."

"I didn't do it for Azef; I did it for love. They'll understand, even if you can't. Only *petits bourgeois* worry about past mistakes. The Bolsheviks will accept me for what I can offer them—*today*. They're realists."

Marina remembered Gorky in Alassio, a celebrated Russian realist calling Lenin a realist. Obviously, in Russia there were many kinds of realists, and all they had in common was that they were all unlike the Nevskys.

"Realists like Azef and Lianozov?"

"Azef and Lianozov are the past. The Bolsheviks are the present—and the future."

"So now you are part of the beautiful dawn that will one day break over Russia."

Tamara smiled. "I loathed you from the first moment I saw you!"

With a rising sense of exhilaration, Marina said, "Thank God Baranov sees through you, even if my parents don't!"

"He'll pay dearly for it—and so will you!"

Drawing her shawl around her, Tamara strode past Marina and

out of the Venetian room. Marina went to the window and after a moment saw her come out onto Millionaya. A gray sedan that Marina had never seen before drew up at the entrance. Tamara got in in back, and the car drove off. Marina hurried to Baranov's office. The old man was standing at his desk, looking distressed.

"I'm sorry, Marina," he said as she rushed in. "I simply cannot engage that friend of yours. She has no feeling for paintings, Italian or any other."

"Madame Sermus is no friend of mine."

"I guessed as much! She's very ordinary."

Through the open windows, they heard voices shouting, "Bread! Land! Peace! All power to the Soviets!"

Baranov shut the windows. "We're closing the Hermitage for a day or two, Marina," he said. "For the safety of the collection. You must go back to your parents. A mob is converging on the Petrograd Soviet at the Tauride, a much bigger crowd than anyone expected."

"My father is going there today. I'll try to find him and ride back with him."

Baranov looked at her with concern. "Please take good care of yourself, my young friend. When this is all over, there must be someone left in Russia with a feeling for Italian paintings."

Chapter Eighteen

SUMMER STORM CLOUDS WERE GATHERING AS THE PANHARD CREPT
through the dense crowd on the Moika embankment. Swallows
wheeled in the darkening sky. The air smelled of rain. On both
sides of the car, demonstrators peered in the windows. Some, recognizing Vasily, nodded and touched their caps, while others shook
their fists at him. Hunched over the wheel, Gotz was anxious.

As they turned into Liteiny Prospect, the mob around them
became more hostile. Grimacing faces loomed at the windows,
mouths shouting curses.

"We'd better turn back, Vasily," said Gotz.

"Courage, my friend," said Vasily. "History will be made at the
Tauride today."

"That's exactly what I'm afraid of."

By six o'clock, the eastern end of the city was bathed in eerie amber
light. Thunder rumbled in the sky over the Neva. Human streams
flowed slowly through the streets, converging on the domed, freshly
repainted Tauride Palace. As the Panhard inched into the courtyard
through the main gate, Vasily realized that the members of the
Petrograd Soviet inside the palace were now prisoners. Only one
man, shouting from the top of the white marble steps, was restrain-
ing the surging crowd. With his Mephistophelian black beard and
glittering pince-nez, Leon Trotsky was a commanding presence, and

yet Vasily sensed that his old adversary was barely in control of his audience.

Vasily and Gotz made their way to the side entrance of the palace. A frightened young guard barred their way with his rifle. Beyond him, Vasily could make out scurrying figures, faces livid in the bluish light of the vestibule.

"Let them in! Get them out of the doorway!" shouted a tall, broad-shouldered man waving a revolver. Vasily recognized the Bolshevik in charge of palace security. "Keep out of sight, Nevsky!" he screamed. "Show your face out there, they'll kill you on the spot!"

"He's right, Vasily Ivanovich," said Nikolai Sukhanov, coming up to Gotz and Vasily. Sukhanov was an old friend, one of the more moderate leaders of the Petrograd Soviet. He was disheveled, his face dripping with sweat. "No one's safe here today." He picked up a telephone from the guard's table and shouted into it, "Get me the commanding officer of the Provisional Government troops! The commanding officer—" He stared reproachfully at the receiver and then slammed it back on its hook. "The goddamned line's dead."

Standing out of sight of the crowd, Vasily could see Trotsky on the steps, jabbing the air with his clenched fist, shouting, "The time is near, comrades! Be patient. The time is near!"

"The time is *now*, Comrade Trotsky!" someone yelled.

A chorus of voices took up the cry. "Now! Now! Now! Others began a new chant until the courtyard reverberated with waves of sound. "Lenin! Now! Lenin! Now!"

Then another wild cheering went up, and Vasily saw armed sailors, wearing white hats with red pom-poms, pushing their way through the throng toward the palace.

"Sailors from Kronstadt! Lenin must have sent them!" exclaimed Sukhanov in dismay. "His agitators must have been working on them day and night."

Suddenly, a flash of lightning illuminated the vast, moving crowd. The sky cracked open. Thunder shook the city, and a hard rain fell. At that moment, a voice from the crowd called out, "Nevsky!"

A roar of voices answered, "Lenin!"

But other voices joined in until the courtyard echoed with rivaling cries of "Nevsky!" "Lenin!" "Nevsky!" "Lenin!"

Vasily went out onto the steps.

There was silence.

"Comrades—" he began in his strong, deep voice, as heavy rain-drops struck his face.

Just then, a burly, full-bearded peasant standing at the foot of the palace steps yelled, "Take power, Nevsky!"

An uproar followed. Vasily shouted, "Comrades, you hold the Revolution in your hands! Deputies from all over Russia will be gathering here to form a new government. The Constituent Assembly—"

The bearded peasant shouted back, "We've heard all that crap before! Take power *now!*"

Breaking out of the crowd, the peasant rushed up the steps. Bringing his face close to Vasily's, he seized him by the shoulders and began to shake him, shouting, "Take power, you son of a bitch! Take the power while you can!"

When the man let him go at last, Vasily felt a staggering sense of helplessness. Where were the regiments that had pledged their support to the Provisional Government? He had personally established no links with them, counting on the fact that the majority of rank-and-file soldiers and sailors were SR sympathizers. But without the regiments, he had no power other than his own voice.

At that moment, he felt strong arms seizing him from behind, grasping his legs, toppling him. As he struggled to stand, he caught a glimpse of Marina nearby. Then he felt himself being lifted high into the air, and then dropped and dragged down the marble steps. Two sailors forced him head first into the back of an automobile waiting at the foot of the stairs. The car began to move; then a heavy blow shook the vehicle. A man had leapt from the steps onto its hood. The man began to shout, Vasily recognized his voice. It was Trotsky.

"Kronstadt sailors are the pride of the Revolution!" he yelled. "Don't dishonor their name! Which one of you will murder Vasily Nevsky? Let the muzhik minister go!"

Far away, Vasily heard a band strike up "The Marseillaise." Someone shouted, "Here are the troops! The Provisional Government troops are coming!"

Vasily felt his abductors shift their weight away from him. He was dragged out of the car onto the cobblestones. Marina was beside him, helping him to his feet.

By then, the rain had become a downpour. In a receding wave, the crowd was moving away from the palace.

As he started back to the Panhard with Gotz and Marina, Vasily saw the Provisional Government troops march into the courtyard, singing. Members of the Soviet came out on the palace portico, their voices joining with those of the men below.

> *Allons, enfants de la patrie,*
> *Le jour de gloire est arrivé*

When they reached the gate, Vasily looked back across the court-yard.

"I should be up there with them!" he said. "I must go back!" But Gotz and Marina were easing him into the passenger seat of the Panhard.

$\mathcal{T}$he storm that scattered the demonstrators at the Tauride Palace did not lift the mood of apprehension that weighed upon the city. A new rumor—or rather an old rumor lent new currency—was spreading through Petrograd. Lenin was a German agent.

Secret dealings between Lenin and certain intermediaries in Stockholm had come to light, dealings aimed at securing German support for a Bolshevik takeover of Russia. Vladimir Burtsev, the SR counterintelligence expert who had once exposed Yevno Azef's connection with the Okhrana, had investigated the case, uncovering evidence that Lenin's acceptance of the German offer of the special train was but the tip of the iceberg.

The publication of these allegations caused a momentary reversal of the Bolsheviks' fortunes. Conservatives blamed them for instigating the demonstration during which more than four hundred innocent people had been shot or trampled. Radicals blamed them for not taking advantage of the uprising to bring down the Provisional Government.

Meanwhile, Kerensky's military offensive against the Germans, after initial success under the Cossack general Lavr Kornilov, faltered and became a rout, then a massacre.

On July 19, the Provisional Government issued warrants for the arrests of Lenin and of his lieutenants. Trotsky and Lunacharsky were imprisoned, but Lenin managed to go into hiding, changing apartments nightly.

Shaving off his beard and disguising himself as a railway employee, the Bolshevik leader crossed the border into Finland and hid in a hut deep in the woods. There, he reflected on the Bolsheviks' mistakes; wrote letters, articles, and declarations; and waited for the next opportunity.

Kerensky, now prime minister, resided in the Winter Palace, sleeping in the tsar's bed, working at the tsar's desk, riding in the tsar's Rolls-Royce Silver Wraith, granting ceremonial audiences. For most SRs, including Boris Savinkov, who had returned from Paris to become deputy minister of war, it was clear that the Revolution had yet to find its true leader. To their dismay, General Kornilov was emerging as the man on horseback who could crush the Bolsheviks and restore order. His Battalions of Death were hanging deserters and suspected German sympathizers at the crossroads.

Throughout July and August, the Provisional Government was paralyzed by a three-cornered intrigue involving Kerensky, Kornilov, and Savinkov, whose role was, as usual, murky. For Vasily Nevsky, the situation was becoming intolerable. He was dismayed at the sight of General Kornilov strutting up the Nevsky Prospect, flanked by his Turkestan bodyguards with their outlandish domed hats and flaring red coats, slashing the air with scimitars. Kornilov was a fearless military leader, but he was also, my father believed, an ignorant bully with the heart of a lion and the brains of a sheep.

But Vasily's attempts to alert Kerensky and Savinkov to the danger had been in vain. Not only had the gates of the capital been opened to Kornilov, but the Provisional Government had by now effectively cut itself adrift from the Revolution.

The time had come for my father to go directly to the people.

Chapter Nineteen

THE MORNING OF SEPTEMBER 1 WAS BREEZY AND SUNNY, A MILD LATE-summer day. At nine o'clock, the Panhard drew up at the main entrance of the Winter Palace. Warmly greeted by the guards, all SR comrades, Vasily walked up the marble stairs to the Malachite Chamber on the second floor where the prime minister convened formal meetings. That morning, he intended to inform Kerensky that, as a socialist and as a Russian, he was obliged to resign his post in the Provisional Government.

As Vasily entered, Kerensky, Savinkov, the minister of finance, and a well-known armament manufacturer were standing around an operator seated at a telegraph machine at one end of a long conference table. The machine was clicking. Kerensky, his face suffused with greenish pallor, looked up at Vasily with open hostility.

"Alexander Fyodorovich," Vasily began in a grave voice, "it is with regret that I—"

Kerensky clutched at his head. "For the love of God, this is no time for speeches! General Kornilov is advancing on the city. This is civil war!"

"A crisis of great complexity at the very least," said Savinkov, "requiring restraint on the part of each one of us."

"What is the traitor saying now?" Kerensky asked the telegrapher.

" 'Come at once to my headquarters. Together we will crush the Bolsheviks.' How shall I reply?"

"Treason!" cried Kerensky. He paced rapidly back and forth in front of the huge green fireplace of the Malachite Chamber. "Tell him that I'll come but that his troops must remain where they are."

The telegraph clicked. Kerensky glowered at Vasily.

"You bear a heavy responsibility for this, Nevsky."

Vasily was outraged. "What are you saying? I vigorously opposed the appointment of that counterrevolutionary butcher as commander-in-chief. Now you're surprised that, with an army behind him and the support of every reactionary in Russia, he wants to take over the country!"

"I'm onto your tricks!" shouted Kerensky. "Instead of rallying the SR Party behind me, you've turned it against me with your prattling about the land bill and the Constituent Assembly! Damn the land bill and damn the Constituent Assembly! They shall not be your stepping-stones to power!"

In an even voice, Savinkov said, "We all must endeavor to remain calm."

"And you!" screamed Kerensky, turning to Savinkov. "You suggested that I promote the general in the first place—I can now see why!"

"I only went along with your own decision, Alexander Fyodorovich."

"You proposed him long before the damnable thought ever occurred to me! I am surrounded by conspirators!"

Vasily took a deep breath. "Alexander Fyodorovich, with the interests of my country uppermost in mind, I have decided—"

The telegraph began to click out a message.

"What does the son of a bitch say now?" demanded Kerensky.

The operator read out the message as it came over the wire: " 'General Kornilov has the honor to offer the post of minister of justice to Mr. Kerensky, and to Mr. Savinkov that of minister of war, in the new government which will be formed upon General Kornilov's arrival in Petrograd at the head of his army'."

"*His* army!" shouted Kerensky. "High treason! Call out the regiments! Declare a state of siege!" Then he turned to Vasily. "Get out!" he shouted. "You are hereby dismissed from my government!"

"You can't dismiss me! I have already resigned from your odious government!"

"Enough! I've heard quite enough to have you arrested," shouted the prime minister as the arms manufacturer came up to him and spoke to him in a low voice. Savinkov drew Vasily aside.

"Am I to assume that you're unwilling to ally yourself with us in insuring the success of the Constituent Assembly?"

"With Kornilov at the head of the government?"

"Who else? As you can see, the prime minister is no longer in control of himself, much less of the country. Surely, you understand that Kornilov is only the means to an end."

"As is everyone, isn't it so, Boris? Never! The Assembly will not be presented to the people by a military dictatorship!"

Savinkov smiled. "My congratulations, Vasily. You are at last free of corrupting associations. Free to go to the peasants with a pure heart and lead them out of captivity."

"And you—you have found a new moral code and a new leader."

"Yes, and as a matter of fact, I advise you to leave the capital before the general arrives. Lavr Gregoryevich is not noted for making fine distinctions between Bolsheviks and high-minded socialists."

"If I do, Boris, it will be to rally the people under the banner of democracy."

"In that case, Vasily, let me leave you with one thought: as I once risked my life and poisoned my soul to destroy tsardom, I now dedicate myself to destroying the Bolsheviks. It is my sole ambition, and it should be yours and every decent Russian's as well."

Savinkov touched his bald forehead in a casual salute and rejoined the others.

The following day, with General Kornilov threatening the capital, and unaware that a Bolshevik coup was already in progress, Vasily boarded a morning train for Saratov. His brain was flooded with memories of flickering lanterns on the Volga so long ago, when he had first proclaimed to the peasants of the Saratov district his vision of the black earth belonging to its tillers. Now he would return to them, his brethren, and proceed to fulfill his pledge, first in Saratov, then throughout the country. As he took a place in a compartment, he felt secure, certain of his mission and also of his personal safety, for in order to elude agents of the two factions bent on destroying him, the Reds and the Whites, he traveled in disguise: a long belted shirt, a floppy-eared cap, and a scraggly false beard.

*N*ikolai Gogol, the Russian satirist, might have invented the Kornilov rebellion.

The aspiring dictator with the slanting Kalmuck eyes who saw himself as the savior of Russia from Bolshevism would in fact assure Lenin's triumph.

At the same time, Alexander Kerensky, the prime minister who imagined that he alone held the country together, was emerging as the symbol of its dissolution.

In September, both Kornilov and Kerensky made the crucial mistake of assuming that the February revolution was dead.

So when the short-lived alliance between Kornilov, Kerensky, and Boris Savinkov disintegrated into an open rebellion led by Kornilov against Kerensky's Provisional Government, the people of Petrograd saw the naked face of counterrevolution.

Once again, the center of power swung to the Petrograd Soviet, which by then had moved from the Tauride Palace to the Smolny Institute on the bank of the Neva. Meanwhile, Bolshevik leaders were fanning the people's discontent, awaiting a signal from Lenin.

The Kornilov rebellion failed; the general was arrested. Kerensky was heard pacing the tsar's suite, humming arias from Italian operas.

Overnight, the Bolsheviks emerged from the status of fugitives from justice to become heroes to the soldiers and factory workers. The first phase of the Bolshevik insurrection was in progress. Citizens in the heart of the city noticed nothing unusual, but in the barracks and in the Vyborg district to the northeast, *agitators were covertly bringing tens of thousands of disgruntled workers and soldiers into the Bolshevik camp. The slogan "All Power to the Soviets" now meant "All Power to the Bolsheviks."*

On September 12, a Bolshevik resolution was passed by the Petrograd Soviet, proclaiming Russia a republic with an administration made up exclusively of socialists. The workers were to control the industries. Peace with Germany was to be concluded at any price. The following month, a Congress of Soviets would convene in the capital.

Unlike the Constituent Assembly, which was to be based on universal suffrage, the Congress would chose its representatives from the local soviets of workers and soldiers who were falling in line with the Bolsheviks.

Always a harsh month in the northern capital, October of 1917 was merciless. Rain fell incessantly. Soggy winds swept down from the Gulf of Finland. Icy mist rolled through the dimly lit streets. It was dark from mi-dafternoon to late morning. Electric power went on at six in the evening, off at midnight. Wood and candles were impossible to procure. There were long lines for food and kerosene. An epidemic of robberies broke out. Armed citizens stood guard in the courtyards of apartment buildings.

For the working people of Petrograd, the most unbearable spectacle was that of life in the city's fashionable quarters returning to normal. The Kornilov revolt had permitted the well-to-do classes to take heart. They began to frequent their old haunts—restaurants, cabarets, theaters. Resourceful women improvised teas and dinner parties. But by the middle of the month, the workers' expectation that something momentous was about to happen had given way to fear that nothing at all would happen, that the Revolution had come and gone, leaving them to face the winter without food, fuel, or hope.

In the Winter Palace, Kerensky brooded over the chaotic state of the country and wept. Sequestered in a tiny flat in the working-class Vyborg district, Lenin reached a decision that would change the world.

Chapter Twenty

VASILY PRESSED AGAINST THE COLD, RAIN-STREAKED WINDOW OF HIS third-class compartment on the Petrograd train in a vain effort to disengage himself from his seatmate, who had fallen asleep, snoring, on his shoulder. For several hours after leaving Moscow, this man, whose name was Petrov, had been swigging vodka from a bottle that now rolled around on the floor to the lurches of the train. The other occupants of the compartment, four hard-faced men in overcoats and caps, darted mistrustful glances at Vasily, who wondered whether they had recognized him.

He was all too aware that his peasant disguise made him conspicuous. There was not, in fact, a single peasant aboard the train. From remarks they had exchanged, he gathered that his fellow passengers were Moscow factory workers recruited by the Bolsheviks to serve as delegates to the Congress of Soviets at the Smolny that night. Just before he had passed out, Petrov had proudly shown off his red pass to the Congress's first session. Moreover, Vasily was certain that the man was not a worker, but a clerk of some kind, one of the dregs of the former tsarist bureaucracy recruited for the occasion as honorary members of the proletariat, whose dictatorship Lenin would be soon proclaiming.

"Good God," thought Vasily. "How could I ever have left Petrograd at a time like this? Lenin is placing all his bets on the

Congress of Soviets, contriving to circumvent the Constituent Assembly altogether. I've let the wolf into the sheepfold!"

The compartment door slid open, and a round-faced Bolshevik agitator, a university student, announced the latest report from the capital, carried by the Bolshevik-controlled telegraph to stations up and down the line.

"Great news, comrades!" he announced. "Trotsky's Military Revolutionary Committee has secured the State Bank and the Central Post Office. The Winter Palace will soon be ours!"

The hard-faced men cheered dutifully. Petrov continued to snore on Vasily's shoulder. The agitator smirked at Vasily. "Unfortunately for you, comrade," he said, "it is confirmed that the Soviet of Peasant Deputies is not participating in the Congress. You may as well go home to your potatoes."

"You're right, comrade," said Vasily, feigning good humor as the others in the compartment grinned. "My potatoes need me more than Lenin does."

Now, he thought, I *must* reach the Congress in time to make a stand. He prayed that Gotz had received the telegram he had sent, asking that he meet him at the station and drive him directly to the Smolny.

"As for the rest of you," the agitator went on, "you have the honor of participating in the final hours of the victorious struggle against the oppressors. Upon arrival at the station, you will be issued orders. Obey them strictly, comrades; the fate of the revolution depends on you."

The agitator closed the door and moved on to the next compartment. Vasily gazed at his own weary reflection in the window. There was no doubt in his mind: his trip south had been a bad mistake. He now saw clearly that, while he had persuaded himself that he was traveling to Saratov to rally the SRs and Volga peasants in a united crusade, he had, in fact—at least to some extent—given into his longing to return to his childhood home, to see the Volga again, to stand on the wooded bank where he had courted Ariane, to lie down in the tall grass of the steppe, drawing from the warm earth the strength he would need in the months ahead. But now there were no months ahead, only weeks, perhaps hours. For the sake of a few balmy late-summer days on the Volga, he had compromised the SR mission. How Savinkov would laugh at this new sentimental escapade!

And worse: as the train crept northward into the autumn twilight, Vasily had the feeling that when he left the capital, he had not been acting of his own free will. It was as if he, together with the snoring Petrov, the agitator, everyone on the train, everyone in Petrograd, everyone in Russia, had fallen under the spell of a sorcerer who bore the face of Lenin.

His friends in Saratov, Jacob and Bella Stern, had warned him about the Bolsheviks' subversion of the government regiments. They had also reported a rumor that former Okhrana agents, turned Bolshevik, had received orders to track Vasily Nevsky down and assassinate him.

But he had not allowed the news from Petrograd to spoil his homecoming. The comradely atmosphere at the SR meetings organized in his honor in towns along the river had captivated him, as had the rapturous welcome he had received from the peasants in the countryside. The early-morning fishing parties, when the pink dawn made him feel like a young man again. The people, the steppes, the forests, the great river herself had reclaimed their son.

He had foreseen his future. In a year or two, he and Anna and Marina would settle in a datcha overlooking the Volga, near Dubrovka perhaps. He would fish every day with his old friend Pavel Pavlovich. He would establish cooperatives for the benefit of the farmers. He would cultivate a model vegetable garden.

Next to him, Petrov snorted, fell silent, began to wheeze. The man's pass to the Congress had slipped partly out of his coat pocket. The passengers across from them had also fallen asleep.

A fresh shower rustled at the window. Vasily could make out scattered lights at the outskirts of the capital.

It's not too late! he told himself. Tonight, he would speak out and alert right-thinking socialists all over the world to what was happening. Vasily eased the red pass from Petrov's pocket and slipped it into his own.

As the train pulled into Nikolayevsky Station, a crowd swarmed toward it, and people tried to board even before it had come to a halt. They looked like well-to-do citizens, with servants dragging their steamer trunks, making way for the tight-lipped masters and their weary-looking wives and children. Fastening the flaps of his cap under his chin, Vasily fought his way along the quay against the tide of travelers.

Outside the station, a snarl of automobiles and carriages clogged Nikolayevsky Plaza, their drivers cursing each other, headlights blinding Vasily. He saw that streetcars were running, slowly as usual, with people clinging outside—but they were running. Then he saw the Panhard. Gotz had received his telegram.

The familiar black sedan was parked by the equestrian statue of Alexander III in the center of the plaza. Vasily splashed through puddles toward the car. Its headlights came on; the passenger-side door flew open. Vasily got in next to the driver and slammed the door.

The man at the wheel was not Gotz.

A second man was in the backseat.

Vasily's impulse was to open the door and run. But before he could do so, the driver flicked on the overhead light.

"Shut that off!" barked the man behind them.

As the driver obeyed, Vasily had time to recognize him. It was his old friend from Saratov, Gerhardt Schwartz. He had also caught a glimpse of the unshaven, furious-looking young man in the backseat.

"Where's Gotz?" asked Vasily.

"Opening the Congress," replied Schwartz calmly. "He sent me in his place."

Schwartz and Vasily had been schoolmates. A descendant of Volga Germans, Schwartz was the son of a blacksmith. Vasily remembered him as a vigorous, good-natured youth with whom he had shared enthusiasms for fishing and for revolution. In recent years, a rank-and-file SR, Schwartz had lived in Petrograd because his true passion turned out to be motorcars. He was a master mechanic and a professional chauffeur, who donated his services to the SRs.

"And who is the comrade with us?" asked Vasily in an even voice.

Schwartz hesitated. "A specialist from Odessa."

"Never mind who I am!" said the man in back. "Get moving!"

"Comrade Schwartz, take me to the Smolny," said Vasily.

The young man laughed. "Don't worry, Mr. Ex-Minister. The Congress will get along without you. Drive where I told you, Schwartz!"

Schwartz pulled out into the square and accelerated, veering into Nevsky Prospect.

Ahead of them, a flash of light filled the sky. A sound like rolling thunder reverberated through the city.

"The cruiser *Aurora*," said Schwartz. "She went over to the Bolsheviks. She must be firing on the Winter Palace."

"It won't be long now," said the man in back.

Vasily was stunned. Shelling the Winter Palace? It was monstrous! Un-Russian!

Through the inverted arcs of the windshield wipers, he could see the bright lights of the avenue. Restaurants and cafés were still open, doing business as usual. Disaffected soldiers and workers in black blouses, with red cockades in their caps and rifles slung at their shoulders, stood at street corners, jeering at the well-dressed passersby who tried to ignore them.

An armored car drew abreast of them. Pulling ahead, it forced Schwartz to a halt. A man wearing an officer's overcoat jumped down from the turret and aimed a flashlight in Schwartz's face.

"All of you, out!" he ordered. "We're commandeering this vehicle in the name of the Military Revolutionary Committee."

The specialist from Odessa got out and angrily thrust a document into the officer's hands. While the officer was reading it in the beams of the headlights, Schwartz whispered to Vasily, "They intercepted your telegram. They sent this fellow to kill you. At the Annichkov Bridge, I'll slow down. Then you must jump out."

"What about you?" asked Vasily under his breath.

"I'll be all right. You're the one they're after."

In the meantime, with a respectful bow, the officer had returned the document to the young man from Odessa, who got back into the rear seat of the car.

Schwartz let in the clutch and shot forward, speeding down the rain-slick avenue, weaving in and out of oncoming traffic.

"Slow down!" commanded the young man.

But the Panhard raced ahead, narrowly missing a truck filled with soldiers. When the rearing horses at the Annichkov Bridge came into view, Schwartz jammed on the brakes. The heavy sedan skidded sideways. Vasily opened the door and rolled out into the night.

He sat up on the damp cobblestones. His sheepskin coat had cushioned his fall. Down the avenue, there was no sign of the Panhard. He knew then that his old friend Schwartz had given his life to save his.

"I must get to the Smolny and denounce these Bolshevik murderers," Vasily told himself. "They must be stopped."

Suddenly, he was aware of shadows whirring swiftly past him like huge owls in a forest. Watching their silhouettes in the misty glow of streetlights ahead, he saw that they were soldiers on bicycles. He realized that this regiment of armed cyclists—along with a small Cossack unit, some untrained cadets, and a battalion of women—were the sole defenders of the Winter Palace.

And therefore of the Provisional Government.

Why was the bicycle brigade pedaling away?

Vasily hurried on, trying not to think about Schwartz, checking to make sure that Petrov's pass was still in his pocket, hoping that Liteiny Prospect streetcars would be running.

It was nearing five o'clock in the morning when Vasily jumped off the Number 17 tram at Smolny Square. Every light in the huge Smolny Institute was blazing. Arc lights on the roof swept the courtyard, where automobiles and armored cars with red flags at their fenders sped out into the city while others returned like bees to a hive. Evidently, the Bolsheviks had seized every motor vehicle in the city. At the outer gates, Red Guards and soldiers warmed themselves at a bonfire. Within the inner gates, cordwood was stacked up as a barricade. Machine guns garlanded with cartridge belts flanked the entrance. Others were positioned on the roof.

Vasily presented his pass to a young sentry, who glanced at it and then looked him over. "You're late, Petrov," he growled.

Vasily's heart sank. Had the Congress already adjourned?

Inside, the Smolny was bedlam. Shabbily dressed, hollow-eyed men and tired-looking women were hurrying in all directions. At an improvised buffet where tea was being served, Vasily spotted Uritsky, who recognized him across the foyer. Vasily walked into the Assembly Hall, relieved to find that the Congress was still in session.

In the smoke-filled hall, every seat, every window ledge was occupied by workers and soldiers. At the podium, an old acquaintance of Vasily's, the Bolshevik leader Kamenev, was reading out a list of government officials arrested that day at the Winter Palace. The platform behind the speaker was occupied by Bolsheviks.

In the audience, Vasily spotted Maria Spiridonova and several other Left SRs. Dmitry was not among them. The opposition seats were almost all empty. Then he saw Gotz making his way toward him. They embraced.

"I thought I'd never see you again," said Gotz. "A nasty-looking little man sneaked into the back of the car just as Schwartz was leaving to pick you up. There was no way to stop him."

"He was supposed to kill me, but I'm afraid he's killed Schwartz instead," said Vasily. "What the devil has been going on here? Where are our people?"

Gotz sighed. "Walked out."

Vasily could not believe his ears. "Walked out of the Congress?"

"When it became clear that Lenin's crowd was trying to take it over, they left. They thought they could stop them by denying them a quorum."

"A quorum!" exclaimed Vasily in desperation. "As if these bandits would give a damn about a quorum?"

Gotz shrugged. "No one could imagine what happened next. Trotsky got up as our people were leaving the hall. He shook his fist at them. 'To those of you who are walking out, we declare: you are pitiful, you are bankrupts, go take your rightful place on the rubble heap of history!' Come with me; I'll show you what we now have to deal with."

Gotz hurried him back into the packed foyer, down a corridor, and through a door inscribed "Ladies Classroom Number 4."

Just as they entered, at the far end of the large room, an overhead light came on. Vasily saw people sleeping all around them, on the floor, at school desks cluttered with documents. The young woman who had pulled the cord of the ceiling light said in a shrill voice, "Wake up, comrades! Fifteen minutes is up! Back to work!"

Sleepers stirred and resumed their labors like automatons, typing documents, proclamations, decrees.

In the pale electric light, Vasily made out two men stretched out side by side on the floor. One, still sleeping, was wrapped in a woolen overcoat drawn over his head. His heavy black shoes, scuffed and unshined, lay beside his stockinged feet. The other, who wore a leather coat, was awake, staring at Vasily with his head propped on his hand. It was Trotsky.

"I'm sorry that you weren't present at the Congress," he said. "My words were meant especially for you. It's all over for you in Russia."

At this moment, Uritsky and the thin young man from Odessa appeared in the doorway.

Uritsky looked expectantly at Trotsky.

Sitting up and studying Vasily as if he were a chess problem, Trotsky said, "You have served Russia in spite of yourself, Nevsky. You may be proud of your contribution. We have adopted your land program as the first decree of *our* new government." He called out to Uritsky, "Let this man go in peace. He no longer matters."

Then he shook the sleeper next to him.

"Wake up, Ilyich," he said. "It is time to announce the birth of the Socialist order."

Chapter Twenty-one

FIVE DAYS AFTER THE COUP, ON OCTOBER 30 THE BOLSHEVIKS REQuisitioned the grand duke's palace. To avoid surveillance by Lenin's secret police, the Cheka, the Nevskys spent November and December with a succession of SR acquaintances in the capital, a day or two in one place. Every night, teams of leather-coated Chekists swept the city, arresting suspected counterrevolutionaries and then driving them off to prison or shooting them on the spot. All over Russia, citizens suspected of opposing or questioning Bolshevik authority were being killed by the tens of thousands.

But even as Lenin presided over the birth of the Red Terror, he did not feel secure enough to cancel the Constituent Assembly. Nor did he yet dare order the arrest of his popular rival, Vasily Nevsky.

Despite Bolshevik intimidations, local elections had been held in November. During the first weeks of January, from all corners of the country, the elected deputies to the Assembly were arriving in Petrograd, where they were greeted at the railway stations by the orchestrated hostility of Bolshevik Red Guards.

At dawn on the morning of January 18, 1918, Vasily awakened to the sound of distant rifle fire. He had been dreaming that he was clinging by his fingertips to the edge of a cliff. From the abyss below, a voice had thundered, "Take power, you son of a bitch!" He had struggled frantically to pull himself up, but his fingers kept slipping, until he lost his grip.

Next to him, Anna was still asleep. Vasily sat up. In those first instants, he had no idea where they were. The room was cold. Through the partly frosted window, he saw in the distance the dome of the Tauride Palace, bathed in rose light. Then he remembered. They were in the garret rooms of a house on Sergeyevsky Lane. Soon Gotz would be coming to drive him to the palace for the opening of the Constituent Assembly.

He looked down at Anna. She was his loyal friend, his faithful supporter, never faltering in her faith that one day love and justice would flower in Russia.

How could a man not cherish such a wife?

But then how, in this Russia, could he draw guidance from someone who was as oblivious to evil as he was himself?

Across the room, Marina too was sleeping, her face nestled in her dark hair. As Vasily studied with admiration this mysterious woman-daughter, it struck him that she was the bravest of the three of them. He and Anna were sustained by their revolutionary ardor, but Marina had to face the perils of their lives with—what? With nothing more than love?

He pulled on his blue serge trousers and went to the window.

Beyond its snow-covered park, the Tauride was ringed by soldiers. Were they the regiments who had promised their support, or were they loyal to the Bolsheviks?

Anna stirred, opening her eyes.

"Is it time to go?"

Vasily went to her and stroked her hand. Marina too was awakening.

"You mustn't come, Anna. It's too dangerous, for you and for Marina. You both must wait for me here."

Anna smiled sleepily. "Of course, I'm coming," she said. "Someone has to look after the president of the first elected parliament in the history of Russia."

"I'm not elected yet."

"You have the votes."

"Lenin has the guns."

Marina was getting up, preparing to leave with them. Anna said gently, "You must wait for us here, Marina. There's no reason for you to go."

"There's every reason," said Marina. "When will you understand that this is my fight too?"

"We do understand," said Vasily. "And we are proud of you."

Gotz left them at the main gates of the palace. Double files of deputies in the native dress of various nationalities—Ukraine, Georgia, Azerbaijan, Bashkiria, Kazakhstan—were approaching the gates. At their head strode a huge bearded man wearing heavy boots and a flowing brown coat trimmed in gold. Vasily recognized Gavril Andronovich Zorin, First Secretary of the Peasants' Soviet of Bashkiria, with whom he had struck up an acquaintance at a secret SR meeting in Moscow in 1905.

"Gavril!" he called out to him. "At least I have one friend here."

"You've a hell of a lot more friends than that, Vasily," Zorin shouted back, gesturing toward the deputies who recognized Vasily and raised a cheer.

Meanwhile, another gray crowd was converging toward the gates—boisterous, rough-looking men wearing soldiers' overcoats their caps cocked back on their heads. Many were armed.

Lenin's proletariat, thought Vasily.

"Ready for a good fight, Vasily?" asked Zorin, throwing an arm around Vasily as they met.

"With you, I'm ready for anything. But where are the regiments that were supposed to guard the Assembly?"

"The Bolsheviks sabotaged their trucks. The bastards are leaving nothing to chance."

Vasily remembered his encounter with Lenin at the Zurich railway station and felt a resurgence of strength: today, regiments or not, he would prevail.

He and Zorin led the deputies across the courtyard, up the palace steps, and into the foyer adjoining the great hall where at nine o'clock the Assembly was to convene.

It was two minutes to nine.

Vasily glanced around in astonishment. The immense foyer was packed with a noisy, drunken mob: Red Guards, soldiers, sailors, street ruffians. At the foot of the stairway leading up to the galleries, Uritsky was handing out passes, turning back anyone who appeared sober or orderly. A buffet near the stairway was serving free vodka.

Followed by Zorin, Vasily led the deputies into the main hall.

There, one by one, they took seats at desks to the right of the podium. The galleries were already packed with boisterous spectators. Bayonets glinted in the smoky light. Armed Red Guards and Latvian mercenaries fiercely loyal to Lenin surrounded the podium and ringed the hall. Vasily found chairs for Anna and Marina just behind the section reserved for the SR deputies; then he sat next to Zorin at a desk in the front row. In the din, they waited for the Bolshevik leaders to arrive.

After almost an hour, Marina heard a loud cheer in the foyer that was taken up by the drunken rabble in the galleries. Lenin and his comrades walked in briskly. The cheering exploded into a roar of shouting, whistling, and the thumping of rifle butts.

Behind the Bolsheviks, the diminutive and grave-looking Spiridonova entered, her red shawl around her shoulders. Next to her walked Dmitry. Marina held her breath. Dmitry was staring straight ahead, seeming dazed.

Lenin settled at a desk in front of the podium, while the other Bolsheviks took places near him. Turning in his chair, he scanned the rows of SR deputies with a look of amused contempt.

When the uproar subsided, Zorin stood up. "By Russian custom," he shouted, "the oldest member present chairs the opening session!" At Vasily's urging, a white-haired elderly man sitting near him rose and walked unsteadily to the podium, on which stood a heavy brass bell.

Derisive shouts and catcalls filled the hall. "Shvetsov," Anna said to Marina. "Returned from twenty-five years at hard labor."

Shvetsov picked up the bell and rang it with all his strength. He started to speak, but the clamor drowned him out. "Comrades," he cried out, "have some respect for those who have sacrificed their lives so that we could meet here today."

The jeering only increased. Shvetsov held his own for a few moments, smiling and patting the bell humorously. Suddenly, one of the main organizers of the October coup, Yakov Sverdlov, blackbearded, broad-shouldered, wearing an open leather jacket, rushed up to the podium and seized the bell from the old man's hands. Shvetsov again tried to speak; then he shrugged and stepped down. Shaking his head sadly, he returned to his desk.

Sverdlov picked up the bell and clanged it vigorously. "Comrades, our revolution began with the Soviets," he shouted, "and it must proceed with the Soviets. A Soviet republic represents a higher form of democracy than a so-called parliamentary democracy. It is the only path to pure socialism," he said, pointing to Vasily, "not to the false socialism of the SRs, who have been repudiated by the true revolutionaries in their own party!"

The galleries and the left side of the hall applauded. Sverdlov raised his hand, calling for order. "Comrades, I move that this assembly adopt the following resolution: 'In accordance with the orders of the Council of Peoples' Commissars, the Constituent Assembly acknowledges its duty to form a plan for the reorganization of society.'"

There were mingled cheers and boos. Zorin stood up and yelled, "This is out of order! Our first business is to elect a president of this Assembly!"

Lenin spread his arms wide and yawned.

"The vote! The vote!" protested the SRs.

Sverdlov glanced at Lenin, who shrugged in contemptuous assent. Sverdlov conducted the vote.

"Maria Spiridonova, candidate of the Left SRs. Those in favor?"

Bolsheviks and Left SRs raised their arms. As Marina watched with a sinking heart, Dmitry hesitated, then slowly raised his hand.

"Vasily Nevsky, candidate of the SRs. Those in favor?"

At that instant, Lenin nodded toward the galleries. Riflemen on either side of the hall and in the galleries leveled their weapons at Vasily. At first, no one moved. Then Zorin's hand shot up. One by one at first, then in a wave, SRs and other non-Bolshevik deputies raised theirs. In a mocking voice, Sverdlov announced the result. By an overwhelming majority, Vasily had been elected President of the Constituent Assembly. Vasily bounded up to the podium, smiling defiantly at the leveled rifles.

In a voice that resounded throughout the hall, he declared, "Comrades, for the first time in our history, elected representatives of the people are meeting to shape the destiny of the motherland. The Constituent Assembly must now mold itself to the people's will."

"Bourgeois lackey!" yelled a Bolshevik deputy.

"Judas!" called out another.

"Shoot the son of a bitch!"

"All power to the Soviets!"

Vasily spoke over the din. "This assembly is not the servant of the Bolsheviks. This Assembly holds the sacred trust of all the people. It belongs to no single party—"

Angry yells interrupted him but he persisted. "It does not even belong to the Socialist Revolutionary Party, though in fact we speak for the majority."

Rifle bolts clicked in unison.

"We must act for the millions who have yearned for this moment, for the millions who have given us their vote—and especially for the millions yet unborn whose fate will be determined by what happens here today!"

Turning again toward the galleries, Lenin shrugged elaborately. There was laughter. Vasily stepped down and started toward his desk. Red-bearded Nikolai Bukharin, the Bolsheviks' leading theoretician, took his place at the podium. His accusing finger followed Vasily to his seat.

"Comrades," he said, "there goes a ghost from the past. For incredible as it may seem, ex-minister Nevsky does not exist in the present. He has failed to understand that a new Russia was born in October and that there shall be no returning to the past, that the past is dead. Indeed, the ex-minister has failed to grasp the central fact of this century: that the Bolshevik Party is leading the exploited classes toward genuine socialism! The only power in Russia, now and forever, is Soviet power!"

Zorin rose and thundered, "This Assembly is the only lawful authority in Russia! It belongs to the people, not to your Latvian riflemen! Listen to its president!"

Vasily stood up. There was a determination in his bearlike stance that filled Marina with pride. Next to her, holding her hand, Anna watched her husband, scarcely breathing.

"Comrades," said Vasily forcefully, "just as many of you have traveled great distances to come here, so has all of Russia traveled a long, painful road to reach this hall. But here in the streets, and, even in this chamber, we are met by Bolshevik guns. Why? For one reason, and one reason alone: because the Russian people have rejected the Bolsheviks, and the Bolsheviks are resisting the will of the people!"

Over angry protests, Vasily called a recess. It was almost midnight.

When the session resumed, heated debate went on for another six hours. As Marina gazed around the huge hall studying the faces of the deputies, she thought, How sad it is that the best men from all over Russia have come here with the highest hopes, only to see Lenin and his gang crushing those hopes, making certain that all the years of meetings, the dreams, the prison terms, the striving for justice would come to nothing.

Once again, Vasily stood at the podium. "If the majority of this Assembly agrees," he said solemnly, "we will proceed at once as a coalition to create a new Russian state."

"Coalition!" cried Sverdlov. "What coalition? We'll never join in coalition with the bourgeoisie!"

In a ringing voice, Vasily shouted, "The Constituent Assembly will now proceed to execute its lawful mandate!"

Lenin rose to his feet and started toward the exit, followed by the other Bolshevik leaders. To Marina's surprise, the Left SRs did not move from their seats.

As the last Bolshevik walked out, she silently prayed that her father would adjourn the session. Instead, over the bedlam, Vasily conducted the discussion and the voting on a dozen resolutions. He was about to call for the vote on his land bill when Sverdlov appeared in the doorway.

"This assembly is illegal!" he shouted. "The Executive Committee of the Peoples' Commissars of the Soviet Republic will charge with the crime of counterrevolution every deputy who does not vacate this hall at once!"

The Left SRs conferred among themselves and then rose and slowly filed out of the hall, Dmitry last.

Now the mood in the galleries was frenzied, reckless. Marina was certain that, should a single shot be fired, there would be a massacre. Then, with a feeling of disbelief, fear, and pride, she heard her father declare, "We will now proceed to vote on the form of the future government."

At that moment, a sailor came up behind Vasily and tugged at his sleeve. "I have received orders from the People's Commissars. You've got to stop now. Everyone must go home. The guards are tired."

"We're the only representatives of the people here," declared Vasily.

"Doesn't matter," said the sailor. "You can't stay. The guards are tired."

The electric lights blinked on and off and then went out altogether, plunging the hall into darkness. However, some of the deputies had come prepared. They lit candles they had brought with them. Now the great hall of the Tauride Palace resembled the inside of a church. Vasily declared, "I move that this Assembly adopt a republican form of government for Russia!"

By candlelight, the motion was carried unanimously.

At last, Vasily stepped down from the podium. The high windows of the hall were turning a murky gray. A cold, foggy dawn awaited outside. A strong hand gripped his shoulder. It was Zorin.

"Take good care of yourself, friend," he said.

"You take care of yourself too, Gavril. It isn't over."

Though exhausted, Vasily felt a sense of elation. Lenin had sabotaged the Constituent Assembly, yet for the first time, the seed of democracy had been planted in Russia. If it took a hundred years, he swore to himself, that seed would bear fruit.

The crowd from the galleries was noisily pouring down the stairway. As he reached the foyer, Vasily saw Anna and Marina and caught up with them. Then he noticed Dmitry pressing toward him. Was he at last returning to the SR party? Dmitry came to him and leaned close to his ear.

"For God's sake, Vasily, don't go to your car!" he said and melted into the crowd.

Chapter Twenty-two

Vasily led Anna and Marina along deserted side streets, skirting mounds of snow-covered dead horses left unburied since October, taking a roundabout way back to Sergeyevsky Lane. In the garret apartment, he threw off his coat and rushed to the window, staring at the Tauride Palace, barely visible in the gray morning light.

"A disastrous night," he said, "fateful not only for Russia but for the rest of the world." He turned back into the room, his eyes shining. "We must turn this defeat into victory. We must drive out these gangsters! The time has come to plant a government of the Constituent Assembly on the Volga!"

That night, as she packed, Marina discovered in her suitcase a bouquet of lavender that she had tucked there before leaving Alassio. Its sharp, sweet smell reminded her of the Villa Ariane. She found it hard to believe that less than a year ago, she had lived in Italy in a house overlooking the sea, concerned only about whether or not Dmitry loved her. In the freezing kitchen, her parents were discussing the journey ahead, trying to buoy each other's spirits. Marina and her mother would travel on passports in Anna's maiden name, Dubrovin. She was to be Marina Dubrovin, whose father had been killed in the war. Vasily would use a false passport prepared for him by the party. Together, they would journey to Moscow, where

Vasily was to meet in secret with the city's SR leaders. Anna and Marina would go on to Saratov ahead of him to find a safe refuge for the three of them.

In the spring, when the Volga had thawed, they would travel north to Samara, an SR stronghold. In Samara, Vasily and his comrades would establish a new central government of Russia.

Such was the plan. It filled Marina with dread.

Vasily was burning SR documents in the kitchen stove when there was a rap on the door. He stepped into the adjoining bedroom, Marina opened the door. Dmitry stood on the dark landing.

For an instant, she was filled with joy. Then quiet fury took possession of her.

"Where have you been since July?" she demanded. "Why have you come now?" Vasily came back into the kitchen.

Dmitry's attention was fixed on him. "Uritsky's at the Smolny, getting Lenin's signature on a warrant for your arrest. You must all leave this apartment immediately!"

"Then you too are in danger," said Anna.

"I want to help you."

"Why?" asked Marina coldly.

"Marina—" warned Vasily.

"Let's go to the Elenskys," said Anna.

"You must stay away from your SR friends," said Dmitry. "Your movements have been tracked since October."

"By whom?" asked Marina.

Dmitry glanced uneasily at Anna. "Cheka agents," he said. "There's no time to lose. Come with me to my flat."

Dmitry's rooms looked smaller than Marina remembered. She watched him lay a fire in the small cast-iron stove, as he had done in the spring when she had invited herself to his apartment. He looked up at her with longing. She turned away. The fire blazed but would not warm the room. She and Anna spread their overcoats on the floor and lay down. Vasily and Dmitry conversed in low voices by the stove. Dmitry was defending the Left SRs' alliance with the Bolsheviks. When Vasily started to tell him about their plan to go to Saratov, Marina cast her father a warning glance. Dmitry noticed it.

"Marina," he said. "I'm sorry about what happened tonight. But you should know that I'm not about to betray the Nevskys."

She was falling asleep when she heard steps on the stairs, then three rapid knocks. Dmitry opened the door. By the light of the stove, she saw Spiridonova in the doorway. As Spiridonova came into the room, she loosened the fringed shawl she wore over her coat and, without a glance, dropped it on the back of a chair near the table. As she must have done a hundred times, Marina decided.

Vasily asked in a low voice, "Have you achieved everything you wanted, Maria?"

"Vasily, we will do what you failed to do—give the land to the peasants."

"The Bolsheviks will never let you. They fear and loathe the peasants."

"The needs of the peasants will be met. If not, we shall use our old Combat Organization tactics. There are daring revolutionaries among us." She looked quickly at Dmitry. "Be sure of it, if the Bolsheviks betray the peasants, we Left SRs will make them regret it."

"The Bolsheviks will destroy you," said Anna. "You threw away whatever power you had when you joined them."

"On the contrary, we've become indispensable to them. As for you, Vasily, I have Lenin's word of honor concerning your safety. You and your family have nothing to fear provided that you leave Petrograd at once." She turned to Marina. "I hope you understand that, Marina—you have nothing whatever to fear."

She picked up her shawl, and drawing it tightly over her coat, she left the apartment.

At noon the next day, they were walking in misty sunlight toward the Nicholas Station at the eastern end of the Nevsky Prospect. In their winter overcoats, they blended with the passersby, the war-weary, starving inhabitants of Petrograd. Dmitry was helping carry their bags. Crossing the square in front of the Marinsky Theater, Marina remembered Kshesinskaya, wondering if she had reached Europe. She thought of her walk with Dmitry. Less than a year ago, he had told her that the city belonged to the two of them—together.

On the platform, she led him away from the others.

"Come with us," she said. "Work with my father. If the SRs stay together, they can still save the Revolution."

"They?"

"We, damn you! Come with us."

"My work is here."

"With Spiridonova."

"With the Left SRs. Spiridonova is a courageous woman, and I share her ideals, but that's all there is between us."

"She has blinded you. You're helping the Bolsheviks wipe us out!"

"What happened at the Constituent Assembly was a disgrace, but the fact remains that the Bolsheviks are building the first just society on earth, and we must help them." He took her hands. "Join us, Marina. Stay here with me."

"They'll destroy you! They'll destroy Russia! Don't let them do it! Come with us!"

Vasily and Anna had boarded the train. Vasily lowered a compartment window and called to Marina.

With an anguished look, Dmitry started to speak. The final bell drowned out his words.

Their hands slipped apart. Not looking back, she stepped aboard the moving train.

Chapter Twenty-three

In Moscow, they spent five days in a second-floor flat at Number 131 on Kuznetsky Most, that once-fashionable shopping street near Lubyanka Square. During the revolution of 1905, Vasily had hidden from the police in this apartment, which belonged to a married couple, both concert pianists, SR friends of Vasily's. Recently, they had fled to Odessa to seek passage abroad. Their departure had evidently been sudden—they had left closets full of clothes, books on the shelves, musical scores on the piano racks, and in a drawer, a rare treasure: a box of twelve candles.

While Vasily met with his SR comrades, Marina and Anna escaped the unheated apartment into the empty streets, eerily silent now that the ringing of church bells was forbidden and people stayed indoors for fear of arrest. Refuse and human waste befouled the courtyards. Walls were plastered with proclamations announcing rationing of nonexistent meat, sugar, soap, and kerosene; freshly printed lists of members of the former wealthy classes drafted to work in battalions; warnings that speculators would be shot on the spot; posters proclaiming Down with Illiteracy and The Enemy Never Sleeps.

On the eve of Marina and Anna's departure for Saratov, Anna went with Vasily to a party meeting in a distant section of the city beyond the Moskva River. Marina stayed in the flat alone. By the fading light of the kitchen window, she had started to trim a few half-rotten potatoes when she heard a knocking at the door, not the agreed-upon two double-knocks, but three strong raps.

She lit a candle and went into the dark, icy foyer.

"Who is it?" she asked.

"I want to see Yegor and Liza," came the muffled reply.

She realized that she should not have spoken—what if it was the Cheka? The voice was insistent.

"Please let me in; it's urgent."

She held up the candle and opened the door. A man who could have been twenty-five or thirty stood before her. He was tall and had a long, oddly handsome face. The mixture of shyness and expectancy in his manner told her at once that this was no Chekist.

"They've left the city," she said. "Are you a friend of theirs?"

"A close friend. And you?"

"My name is Marina. My parents and I are using the apartment for a few days."

"I want to borrow a book. Nietzsche, a man with terrifying ideas. I need it for something I'm working on. May I look in the library?"

They went into the salon where two grand pianos, black and enormous, stood side by side. The young man looked around the room.

"It's strange," he said. "I can almost hear Yegor and Liza playing the fantasia together. Now they've gone, like everyone else."

He sat at a piano. "Do you know it—Schubert's Fantasia in F Minor?" Closing his eyes, he began to play softly. Then he stopped. "It's written for two pianos. Nobody plays it better than Yegor and Liza. What a pity they've left. Moscow needs their music. Of course, they had to leave. They're SRs, and they're arresting SRs. And you too, Marina Vasilyevna, you must be an SR."

"I am."

"Then I pray God that you can get away quickly." He studied her intently. "You look like Antigone holding that candle. I shall always remember you."

He got up and took the candle from her and went into the small library off the salon. Soon he returned with two volumes.

"I found the Nietzsche—and this is for you." He handed Marina a thin book within a maroon paper cover. "I'll get my friends another copy when they come back." He handed her the candle. "Looking at you, Marina Vasilyevna, I'm certain you will be saved.

You will live out your life in a beautiful country, a country as green as your eyes. There you must hear the fantasia in full. It's about our life after the storm. You're still very young. You'll live to see it." He went to the door. She opened it for him. He looked at her for a long moment and then disappeared down the dark stairs.

She held the candle to the book. It was *Over Barriers*, a collection of poems by Boris Pasternak.

On the morning of the sixth day in the apartment on Kuznetsky Most, they once again observed the Russian ritual of departure, sitting down for a moment of silence before going out the door. However, this time Anna and Marina were to take the train for Saratov alone and wait for Vasily at the house of their old friends Jacob and Bella Stern.

As Vasily and Anna laid plans for a return to their birthplace, speaking in whispers, Marina sensed that, as had happened during the Azef affair in her childhood, secrets were being kept from her. They were secrets that had to do with events that had taken place on the Volga twenty years before, events that still haunted her parents, and at the center of which was her Aunt Ariane.

Part Two

AND THE SPHINX DEVOURED THEM

Chapter Twenty-four

THE KAZAN RAILWAY STATION WAS MOBBED WITH TRAVELERS FLEEING the freezing, famished city. Waves of bodies surged toward the train as it drew up at the platform. The coaches were already filled with passengers who somehow had already managed to board. The crowd around Marina and Anna swept them toward a boxcar fitted with plank tiers, a conveyance known as a "Maxim Gorky" because Gorky had ridden such freight cars in his adventurous youth. On it was a sign: CAPACITY: 8 HORSES OR 40 PEOPLE.

They climbed into the cavernous interior and crawled over bundles and trunks, arms and legs, finding at last a corner in which to spread their blankets.

Most of their fellow passengers were soldiers. They spoke in a harsh slang that Marina could barely understand, and they stared with open curiosity at the women in their foreign-made clothes. When the heavy door of the boxcar rolled shut, they were in darkness, but for the occasional flare of a match illuminating a battle-weary face and the smoky glow of an iron stove at the far end of the car. A soldier began to sing in a rich, bass voice. For the first time, Marina heard the song that was sung throughout Russia in those years.

Red apple,
Where are you going?

You've rolled to the trenches,
You've rolled to the forests,
If you roll to the border,
You'll never come back.

In "The Song of the Little Apple," Marina recognized the spontaneous voice of the people, expressing the confusion and cruelty of the times. The red apple of the Revolution kept rolling on, but where would it stop? Uncertainty was all that united Russia now, but in this simple song were glimmers of hope.

Red apple,
Where are you rolling?
If you roll to the Volga,
You'll live forever.

As the wheels clicked over the tracks, Marina began to distinguish the faces of the men around them.

A young soldier sitting near her said, "This war is horrible. No one who hasn't been in it knows how horrible. And it's all for nothing."

A deep-voiced man spoke, "It's the tsar's war, and we're stuck with it."

A bearded man said, "The Bolsheviks will pull us out of it."

The deep-voiced man said, "If they don't, we'll pull *them* out!"

"What kind of talk is that, comrade?"

"It's plain as day, brother. We chucked the tsar. We chucked Kerensky. If Lenin doesn't suit us, we'll chuck him too."

"You sound like a bourgeois," said the bearded man. "Be careful, comrade. You're on thin ice."

The singer broke in:

My good little apple,
You're on thin ice.
The Bolsheviks are winning.
Little apple, they'll catch you.

Laughter filled the car. In the silence that followed, the young soldier spoke in a hollow voice, "For three days, we marched through shell bursts. We ran out of bullets. With our rifle butts, we clubbed our officers to death. And all for nothing."

The train clicked over the tracks. The deep-voiced man said, "All that matters now is the land. Nothing else."

The bearded soldier said, "Lenin gave us the land in October."

"And he took it back in November along with our crops. He stole the SRs' plan. It was Nevsky's plan, and a good one too, until they wrecked it."

"Nevsky got nowhere with it," said the bearded soldier. "He was just one of Kerensky's grave diggers."

"You're wrong, brother. Nevsky was the best of the lot, a peasant like us. If only he'd been the leader instead of that blowhard Kerensky, things would be different. But now they say he was murdered in Petrograd the night they closed the Assembly."

Anna spoke out. "Vasily Nevsky is not dead."

There was a silence. The deep-voiced soldier asked, "How can you be so sure, comrade?"

"I saw him in the street in Moscow—days after the Assembly."

"Then he's on the run," said a new voice. "And he better not stop running."

There was a silence; then the deep-voiced man said, "He's a Volga man. If he's alive, that's where he'll go."

For no reason that Marina could understand, the mood of the soldiers turned hostile. In the smoky light, she could see them grinning like wolves. One, sitting near her, took off his gray cap and began combing lice out of his hair into a newspaper on his knees, killing them one by one with his lighted cigarette, looking up at her and leering. Another was cracking sunflower seeds between his teeth, spitting the shells at her feet.

"And who are you?" the young soldier asked her, emboldened by the others. "Where are you going?"

"My name is Marina Dubrovin. I'm going to Saratov," she answered in a friendly tone. "What's your name, comrade?"

"Misha," he said in a shy voice. The other soldiers laughed at him.

Marina's candor won them over. As quickly as it had arisen, the men's hostility passed. They took Marina and Anna under their protection. At the water stops, they helped them out of the car.

They filled their teapot with boiling water and shared their bread with them. They turned their backs when one of them relieved herself by the tracks.

The train rolled on through the endless white landscape. Now and then, the steam whistle sounded a long, haunting cry.

On the fourth day, they reached Saratov.

Our arrival in Saratov in March 1918 coincided with the signing of the Brest-Litovsk treaty between Russia and Germany. Under its terms, humiliating ones for Russia, the fledgling government gave up vast regions of the tsar's empire—Poland, Latvia, Lithuania, part of Belorussia—and recognized the autonomy of Georgia and the Ukraine. That same month, fearing that despite the treaty, the Germans might occupy Petrograd, the Bolsheviks moved the capital of the now much-reduced country to Moscow.

With only a small loyal following, confronting enemies within and abroad, they knew that their authority was hanging by a thread. In the Don region, a "Volunteer Army" was forming under experienced White army officers seeking to destroy the Red regime. In the Far East, another White army was massing on the Manchurian border, backed by the Japanese and threatening to occupy eastern Siberia. To the north, British and French troops, soon to be joined by Americans, were landing at Murmansk and Archangel in a campaign henceforth known to Russians as The Intervention.

As a response, Lenin unleashed the Red Terror throughout the country. This was the terrible 1918 springtime of hunger, disease, arrests, and random executions. It was during this time that the seeds of civil war planted in October began to bear their deadly harvest. For three years, war would sweep across the length and breadth of Russia, darkening the skies with the smoke of burning villages. Civilians would experience the horror of modern combat coupled with the barbarity released in an oppressed people whose hopes of liberation had been raised and then dashed.

Chapter Twenty-five

ON THE QUAY OF THE SARATOV RAILWAY STATION, ANNA AND MARINA pressed through a crowd of soldiers and refugees and headed toward the waiting room. At the entrance, scrutinizing the arriving passengers, stood a man wearing the floor-length leather coat of a Chekist. He had a reddish face from which most of the nose was missing. Next to him, Marina noticed a gangly young man with elfin features framed by a mass of auburn curls. The young man smiled at her. The noseless Chekist was studying her closely. The curly-headed man tugged at his sleeve and whispered something in his ear that made him laugh and look away. Dragging their suitcases, Marina and Anna crossed the waiting room and left the station. They were faint with exhaustion.

Jacob and Bella Stern lived in a residential section of Saratov called The Lindens. Anna remembered the way to their white stone house. It was tightly shuttered and looked abandoned. She knocked at the door. A frail, white-haired man opened the door a crack and stared at them without a sign of recognition.

"Jacob," said Anna, "have you forgotten me?"

The old man opened the door wide, looked up and down the street, picked up their bags and hurried Anna and Marina inside. Closing the door behind them, he embraced Anna, kissing her on both cheeks. "Anna, my dear, I never thought the day would come when I wouldn't recognize you."

A short, plump woman with an open round face, her black hair touched with gray, came into the entrance hall.

"Annitchka!" she cried out, her eyes filled with delight as she and Anna hugged.

"And this is Marina?" said Jacob Stern, taking Marina's hands in his. "You are most welcome in this house, my dear."

Turning to Anna, he asked, "And Vasily?"

"Still in Moscow. We're here to find a safe place for us to live. He'll join us soon."

The Sterns looked at each other. Leading the visitors into a cozy library warmed by the fire of an enameled stove, Jacob said, "Bella, quickly bring us some tea and something to eat. Our friends must be famished after their journey."

At the kitchen door, Bella turned to her husband. "Tell them, Jacob."

Jacob Stern spread his hands in a gesture of helplessness. "Alas, you've come to the least safe house in the city. I'm no longer at the Gymnasium. They ordered me to teach Karl Marx, and I refused. So now besides being a Jew and an SR, I am also a parasite." He shrugged. "As a consolation, I am writing about a Jew who believed that evil is an aspect of God's perfection beyond man's understanding. Sometimes, I wonder whether Spinoza wasn't giving God too much credit."

Bella returned, carrying a tea tray with a platter of black bread, salted fish, and a bowl of pickles. "Stop feeling sorry for yourself, Jacob," she said. "Find chairs for our guests."

They sat at a small table next to the stove. Among the framed pictures on the wall facing her, Marina noticed the photograph of Ariane standing with the white horse, the same photograph that her mother had shown her in Alassio. She wanted to ask the Sterns about Ariane, but they were speaking about the present.

"Saratov is no longer SR territory," said Bella. "We meet in secret now." She hesitated, looking anxiously at her husband.

"I tried to warn Vasily when he was here last fall," said Jacob. "He was in danger then, and he will be again if he returns."

Anna, glowing with pleasure at seeing her old friends, was determined not to hear their warnings. "This has always been SR territory," she said. "I'm sure that when spring comes the people will clear the Bolsheviks out. Then our party will reconvene the Constituent Assembly."

Bella shook her head. "You haven't changed a bit, Anna."

"What could be more endearing than our friend's optimism?" said Jacob. "We're happy you are here, and we will try to help you."

Marina never forgot the comfort of their first evening at the Sterns—the warm stove in the library, a long bath in a spotless bathroom, fragrant sheets under a fluffy down comforter, the chance to launder their clothes. After the boxcar, it had seemed like Paradise.

Their presence in Saratov did not go unnoticed. The next day, visitors came calling at the Sterns', all claiming to be loyal followers of Vasily Nevsky. Jacob had gone out, but Bella, Anna, and Marina served them herb tea in the library. A wrinkled old woman brandishing a lorgnette claimed that in her youth she had been an intimate friend of the great nineteenth-century Russian revolutionary writer Alexander Herzen in Geneva. A rough-looking man with a red beard said that he was a cousin from Tambov, "closer to Vasily than a brother," though Anna could not remember her husband ever speaking of a relative in Tambov. A slender blond young man announced with a languid movement of his hands that he had come "to put his life in the service of the forthcoming savior of Russia, Vasily Nevsky."

Any one of them, thought Marina, could be an informer.

One visitor in particular aroused her suspicions: the elfin-faced young man with auburn curls whom she had noticed at the station in the company of the disfigured Chekist. Sitting across the room near the picture of Ariane, he was smiling at her as if they were old friends. Despite her misgivings, she returned his smile. He came over to her.

"You're very pretty," he said.

"And you're very forward."

"Yes, but it's all right. I'm a poet. Poets are permitted to say what they're thinking."

"What if you had found me plain?"

"Then I'd have lied in my teeth."

"How do I know you aren't lying now?"

"Instinct. You must have wonderful instincts."

"I do."

"Then trust yourself."

She laughed. "You certainly are sure of yourself—"

"Sergei. Sergei Sergeyevich Lomov."

She glanced toward the blond young man who was now sitting at her mother's feet.

"Do you know him?" asked Marina.

"We've met."

"What do your instincts say about him?"

"Dangerous."

"An informer?"

"Far worse. A bore. A great believer in the rights of man. He will bore your mother to death. And your father too, when he gets here."

Concealing her fears, Marina smiled. Everyone here seemed to know that Vasily was on his way to Saratov. "My father is hardly an enemy of the rights of man," she said lightly.

"That's different," said Sergei. "From everything I know about him, your father is a radiant spirit. And you are too, Marina Vasilyevna. Tell me, do you have a special friend, someone you're crazy about?"

"I did."

"No more?"

"You ask so many questions. Are you a Chekist?"

"I'm not," replied Sergei evenly. "However, I know all of them around here. I earn my bread as a telegrapher. The Reds shot the only other telegrapher in the district, so my services have become indispensable. The hand of the poet is all that keeps the Saratov Cheka in touch with the outside world."

"Who was the man at the station with you?"

"Malyevich. Ex-Okhrana. Arrested by the tsar's police and imprisoned in the Petropavlovsk fortress. That's where he lost his nose to rats. For some reason, the experience caused him to become a fanatical follower of Dzerzhinsky."

"What makes you think my father is coming to Saratov?"

"It's common knowledge," he said and, lowering his voice, added, "You mustn't stay in this house. Do you like poetry?"

"Very much."

"Blok? Akhmatova? Pasternak?"

"Pasternak most of all. I met him in Moscow."

"Marina, you have met a great man," said Sergei. "Wherever the Russian language is spoken, Boris Pasternak will be remembered as the poet who captured the bloom of the first, the real Russian Revolution. Nothing better will happen in our time."

Remembering her walk with Dmitry in Petrograd, Marina said, "No, nothing better will ever happen."

Sergei glanced across the room. "Your mother."

"What about her?"

"She doesn't trust me."

"Should she?"

"Decidedly not. I have designs on you."

"What kind?"

"I want to be your cavalier servant. Please think about it."

Sergei swept an imaginary plumed hat to the floor, and then went over to speak with the elderly friend of Herzen.

Late that afternoon, after the visitors had gone, Jacob returned home with the news that he had found a safer place for them.

"It's an abandoned schoolhouse north of the city. No one will know. I'll take you there tomorrow."

The schoolhouse stood in the middle of a snowfield sloping gently down to the Volga. Its small peaked cupola identified it as a chapel, though under the Provisional Government it had served as a school, offering free instruction in reading and writing to peasant children and their parents. Several weeks before, the Soviet authorities had closed it.

Marina and Anna were quickly settled in their new quarters, which they heated only at night so that chimney smoke would not betray their presence. From their SR friends, Jacob and Bella had collected blankets, kitchen utensils, provisions, a log here, a sack of groats there. The couple came to see them at night, bringing supplies and news: reports of the interminable trench warfare along the Franco-German front, of the civil war spreading throughout the country, of famine and epidemics, but never news of Vasily.

Nor was there any word of Dmitry.

As one freezing, gray day succeeded another, Marina and Anna diverted themselves as best they could. In the evenings, Anna would translate aloud the *Georgics* from the dog-eared volume of Virgil which she carried with her wherever she went. Her favorite passages were those that evoked the poet's love of the farm where he had spent his youth. Marina knew that these stanzas, which made her think of Alassio, reawakened in her mother memories of Dubrovka, her parents' estate, which lay tantalizingly close by, a short day's walk to the north.

Since childhood, Marina had treasured her parents' descriptions of Saratov as a city bathed in silver light; their recollections of the wharves where wanderers spun tales of their adventures; of the Gymnasium where Vasily had made his first revolutionary friendships and met Jacob; of his great friend Pavel, a fisherman who lived on the river and told stories of pirates and ghost ships, and who knew every turn of the Volga as far north as Kazan.

But now Saratov was closed to them. For beyond the field that stretched below the schoolhouse, the river Volga, the mythical mother of Russia, was a steel-gray ribbon of solid ice. Marina and Anna were waiting for the spring thaw, yet the lingering winter provided them with breathing space.

At night, sitting by the stove, Marina found that here, in her homeland, her mother was sometimes willing to talk about her past. Her sister, she told Marina, was a gifted storyteller. In her stories, Ariane was able to transform their childhood, which was ruled over by their brutal father, into a fairyland. She knew the secrets of the forest, of the swift-moving river, and of the people who lived along the river's banks.

It had been Ariane who had first made Anna aware of the terrible legacy of serfdom. She had inspired those feelings in Vasily too. After her death, he and Anna had together vowed to keep her spirit alive and help bring about the downfall of the dark Russia that had destroyed her.

By April, the skies cleared, and throughout the long days, the curtainless schoolhouse was flooded with sunlight. Now they could hang their wash outside on the lilac bush near the back door. They could air their winter clothing.

Then one morning, Marina heard a sound that she thought was artillery fire. But when she looked out over the river, she saw gleaming floes rising upon one another and sliding away as they moved slowly downstream. The spectacle took her breath away: the river was casting off its frozen shroud.

"The thawing of the Volga was always a time of celebration," Anna told her. "In the old days, there were bonfires and music and dancing along its banks."

The lilac bloomed, a scraggly garden broke through the damp earth, the marshy fields below the house flooded and began to green, reeds sprouted along the bank, and soon the Volga turned a deep blue. At twilight, snow-white cranes winged north. In the early morning, a nightingale sang in the lilac bush, its song awakening in Marina a longing for Dmitry. Hearing the nightingale's song, she wanted him to come to the schoolhouse and take her in his arms.

Chapter Twenty-six

THE MORNING OF THE FIRST OF MAY WAS WARM AND CLEAR. MARINA
and Anna were sitting on the stoop of the schoolhouse. Fluffy
clouds coasted across the sky. A steamboat chugged upriver, its stern
paddle wheel leaving a sparkling wake. On the towpath, a horse-
drawn cart was nearing the schoolhouse. When it started up the
field, Marina recognized the driver.

Anna saw him too. "The young Chekist," she said.

"Sergei Lomov is not a Chekist."

"I hope you're right."

So do I, thought Marina.

"Dear ladies," Sergei called out as he drew up in front of the
schoolhouse. "I bring you greetings from Vasily Ivanovich!"

"Where is he?" asked Anna.

"Upriver at the house of his friend Pavel, a friend of mine as
well. I didn't dare bring Vasily Ivanovich here."

"When did he arrive?" Marina asked joyously.

"Early this morning. We knew he was on his way. There'd been
a telegram from the Moscow Cheka."

"Who is *we*?" demanded Anna.

"Your humble servant, the Hermes of the Nether Regions, and
the Saratov Cheka. The telegram said that he'd boarded a train
disguised as a peasant. Mercifully, however, Malyevich has been on
the lookout not for a peasant but for a priest."

"What do you mean?"

"To be very precise, my dear, mistrustful Anna Petrovna, I mean that in transcribing that message at the Cheka telegraph office at the railroad station, I took the liberty of changing the word *peasant* to *priest*."

"Won't you be found out?" asked Anna.

"It's quite possible, in which case I'll plead incompetence. A highly credible defense these days. In any case, you should know that Vasily Nevsky is not traveling as himself, but as an SR friend of his, Alexander Orlov, from Moscow."

"But he must have told Pavel?"

"Especially not him. He doesn't want anyone to know a secret that the Cheka could extract under torture."

"But the old man must have recognized him," said Marina.

"But he didn't. It's been thirty years, and besides, your father is disguised and Pavel is almost blind. He welcomed him as Nevsky's friend Orlov and lent me his horse and cart to fetch you. We must go before Malyevich finds out that no holy father will be arriving in Saratov today."

It was raining lightly when they reached Pavel's isba, half hidden in a grove of pines along the river. As Sergei drove the cart up to the door, Vasily, wearing a peasant blouse, ran out to them and lifted Anna down from the cart, taking her in his arms and then catching Marina in his embrace as she jumped to the ground.

"My dear ones!" he said. "A dream come true! It was right here along the river that I had my first revolutionary experiences—in 1898, twenty years ago to the day. And now to be here with my family and our generous young friend. But come, Pavel is anxious to meet the wife and daughter of Alexander Orlov."

"It's good of you to take us in in times like these," said Vasily to their host. They were settled around the stove on which a pot was simmering, filling the isba with an intoxicating smell of herbed fish stew. "Vasily Nevsky remembers you; he often speaks of his Volga days."

The old man opened the door of the stove. Firelight danced in his milky eyes. "He used to come here as a boy," he said. "He loved to fish, and I taught him some tricks. He was a good fisherman and could have made his living from the river, but even then he had strong feelings about what was right and wrong for the people. I wasn't surprised that he became a revolutionary." He picked up a poker and stirred the fire. "They say he's on his way here."

"The Volga is where his friends are," said Anna.

"His enemies too," said Vasily. "It's where they'd come looking for him."

The old man squinted at Vasily. "Did you hear about the price the Bolsheviks put on his head?"

"What's he worth to them?"

"Two hundred thousand rubles."

"That's a fortune."

"With two hundred thousand rubles, a man could live like a prince for the rest of his life. But for Nevsky, it's a bargain. The Reds know that he's the one man who might rally the peasants and run them out of Russia." Again, Pavel stirred the fire. "The question is whether Nevsky himself knows it."

"Nevsky knows it better than any man alive," said Vasily emphatically. "The Bolsheviks stole the Constituent Assembly in Petrograd; he's determined to get it back in Samara."

"I hope you're right, but some say he was abroad too long and has lost touch with his own people." Pavel looked at Vasily; it was as if he were trying to peer through the clouds in his eyes. "Once before, here in the district, he forgot who he was."

"When was that?" asked Anna in a low voice.

"When he fell in love with the daughter of old man Dubrovin, a landowner upriver. For a time, he forgot everything else in the world."

"He married her," said Vasily firmly. "Her name was Anna."

"I'm talking about her sister Ariane. He fell in love with her first, and no good came of it. She was a roussalka."

"A water nymph?" asked Marina, fascinated.

Sergei said, "On the Volga, a *roussalka* is a maiden who sits naked on the riverbank combing out her green tresses and singing softly in the moonlight, luring travelers to her palaces of emerald and pearl at the bottom of the river."

"Nevsky told me about Ariane," said Vasily. "She couldn't have been a roussalka; it was she who died."

The old man was silent. At last, he said, "Dying is a roussalka's most powerful spell."

No one spoke as Pavel ladled out bowls of fragrant stew. He cut slabs of black bread and passed them around on the blade of his knife.

"They say things are bad in Moscow," he said.

Vasily shook his head sadly. "Thousands are dying there of cold, starvation, typhus. The Cheka is shooting anyone they choose to name as a class enemy—'harmful insects' Lenin calls them. The main interrogation prison on Lubyanka Square is busy night and day."

"So that's where the Red Apple is rolling," said Marina.

"No one dares protest—no one except Gorky. So far, Lenin puts up with him because of his fame abroad."

"Did you see Dmitry in Moscow?" asked Marina as casually as she could.

"We passed in the street. He didn't recognize me."

"Was he with Spiridonova?"

"Yes. And with others too. Spiridonova, by the way, still imagines that the Left SRs can remain independent of the Bolsheviks."

"And what about Tamara?" asked Marina.

"I saw her also," said Vasily reluctantly, "at a distance on Lubyanka Square. She was with Dzerzhinsky's lieutenant, Peters."

"Who is this Tamara who travels in such dangerous company?" asked Sergei.

"A friend of the family," said Vasily, not looking at Anna.

"They must be threatening her," said Anna.

"I don't doubt it. What they're saying about the Cheka's methods is appalling."

Marina watched her father, wondering whether he really believed that Tamara was being forced to keep company with a leading Chekist against her will.

"In these times, it's wrong to judge people too quickly," said Anna.

"In these times," said Vasily, "it's impossible to judge them at all. Peshkova, for instance, is on good terms with the arch-Chekist Dzerzhinsky. What do you make of that?"

Sergei got to his feet. "When Gorky's former wife lies down with the lion, all must be for the best. But speaking of the charming

Dzerzhinsky, I must be leaving. The Cheka never sleeps, and neither must its unwilling servant."

Marina and Vasily and Anna followed their visitor outside.

"How can we express our gratitude?" Vasily asked him.

"You trusted me. That's enough."

"I trust you too, Sergei," said Anna.

"I'll try to see that you never regret it."

Her parents bade Sergei farewell and went back inside. Marina stayed outside with him. She had wanted to say good-bye to him alone but now could find nothing to say. The rain had stopped, and she looked out across the river where the moon's silvery reflection wavered in the swirling water.

"Thinking about your special friend?" asked Sergei.

"How did you know?"

"May you find each other one day."

"You're very kind," she said. "His name is Dmitry. A Left SR." Suddenly, she was overcome by sadness. Again she looked out across the river.

"You love him so very much?" he asked softly.

"I don't know," she said. "I used to think he meant everything to me. But perhaps it was an illusion."

He took her hand and kissed it. "Some of us live our whole lives on illusions—and are grateful for them. Good night, Marina."

"Good night, Sergei," she said. "You are a true cavalier servant."

He touched his imaginary hat and then turned and started down the towpath toward the darkened city.

The Nevskys stayed on at Pavel's, waiting for news from the north. What they learned from their host's fishermen friends was discouraging. Bolshevik brigades were being dispatched up and down the river to requisition the peasants' stocks of grain. Peasants who resisted were subjected to bloody reprisals. Civil war and the Red Terror were closing in around them.

Then, one evening, Jacob Stern walked into the isba. He and Vasily fell into each other's arms.

"The Reds are retreating!" Jacob announced. "Samara has fallen to the SRs! You're needed there, Vasily. The Whites must not be the ones to defeat the Bolsheviks. You must go north at once."

"Where are the White forces?" asked Anna.

"Siberia. Battle-tested tsarist officers have formed an army under Admiral Kolchak."

"Are the people with them?" asked Marina.

"More and more," said Jacob. "The Bolshevik grain raids bring fresh recruits to the Whites every day." He hesitated. "Moreover, they have a proven weapon," he continued in an anguished voice, "the cry that for centuries has rallied people, 'Kill the Jews!' Unless they're stopped, that cry will soon echo up and down the Volga." He fell silent; then after a moment he added, "Some SRs are said to be considering an alliance with the Whites. You must prevent that, Vasily."

"I'll go at once," exclaimed Vasily.

Pavel stood in the doorway.

"I'll help you get there, Vasily."

Vasily looked at him in amazement.

"Didn't you hear me? I said I'll help you get to Samara."

Vasily went to the old man and embraced him. "How long have you known?"

"Ever since you spoke about Dubrovka," said Pavel. Then he turned to Anna and bowed. "My respects, Anna Petrovna." And to Vasily, he said, "I've a friend who works on a steamer leaving tomorrow at dawn. He'll get you on board."

"Marina and I will be going too," announced Anna.

"No, Anna," said Jacob. "There's fighting up and down the river. You and Marina must wait here until the SRs' government in Samara is established."

"I'll send for you as soon as I can," Vasily assured her. "It won't be long."

"We'll be cut off from each other," protested Anna. "How will we keep in touch?"

Vasily hesitated. Then Pavel said, "My friend on the steamer can deliver messages."

Vasily put his hand on his friend's shoulder. "How can I thank you for everything you've done for us, Pavel?"

"Easy, my friend. Just give Russia back to her people."

Chapter Twenty-seven

MARINA WATCHED THE STEAMER DISAPPEAR INTO THE MIST UPRIVER, wondering whether she would ever see her father again. When she had asked him what would happen if the Bolsheviks retook Samara, he had said that it was unlikely that they would. But if they did, he and his comrades would travel beyond the Urals and establish the government of the Assembly further east, perhaps in the city of Omsk. Peasants all over Russia, he had assured her, would rise up and support them. Time was on their side.

July was sultry. By noon, the sticky air was yellow with mites. The Sterns had stopped coming. Anna and Marina were cut off from news except for what Pavel picked up from other rivermen. There were rumors of anti-Bolshevik Allied forces sweeping down from the northern port of Murmansk.

August came; the days grew shorter. One morning, Pavel drove his cart to Saratov, hoping to bring back some coal for the following winter. When he returned that evening, Anna and Marina saw that he was troubled.

"The Reds are shooting people," he told them. "At the ravine between here and town. Hundreds, they say."

"SRs?" asked Marina.

"Many SRs. Others too."

"Dear God," said Anna. "I hope they haven't taken Bella and Jacob."

"I'm afraid you're no longer safe here."

"We're grateful to you for sheltering us this long, Pavel," said Anna, "but it's time for us to try to join Vasily. We'll be leaving for Samara at once." She glanced sternly at Marina to ward off her objections.

"Father hasn't sent for us yet."

"But I know he wants us. Can you get us passage on a steamer, Pavel?"

"Impossible," said the old man. "Ever since Vasily slipped past them, they search every vessel."

"Then we'll go by road."

"It's two hundred and fifty miles to Samara. There're armies on the march. Starving refugees. Bandits. Bolshevik raiders."

"Vasily needs us. Could your friend on the steamer still get a message to him?"

"I think so."

"Then we'll let him know that we'll be going north to Samara. On the way, we may stop off in Khvalynsk, where I have a cousin. Vasily knows him. Mikhail Borovsky."

"If you're so set on going, I'll lend you my Pasha and my cart for the trip," said Pavel.

"We might not be able to return them," said Anna. "How can you do without them?"

"I'll manage. They'll be my gift to the Nevskys—and to the Revolution."

That evening, Pavel helped them load their belongings and provisions of carrots and potatoes from his garden and dried fish and a sack of millet seed from his larder. Together, they led Pasha down to the river and hid the horse and cart in a willow grove. Then, as they did every night, Anna and Marina spread their blankets on the floor of the isba. Pavel started to pull off his boots.

"You'll be stopping at Dubrovka?" he asked.

"We will," said Anna. "Do you know who lives there now?"

"Only ghosts," said Pavel, and he bade them good-night and climbed up into the loft above.

Shortly before daybreak, Marina awakened to the sound of an engine idling outside. She got up and went to the window. Two men holding lanterns were stepping down from a truck. As they started toward the isba, Marina recognized one of the men; the noseless Chekist, Malyevich, whom they had seen at the station when they had first arrived in Saratov. The other, in military garb, was a younger man unknown to her. Anna had awakened. Dragging their blankets, Marina hurried her mother out the back door and into the thicket of lilacs. Anna started to speak, but Marina touched her finger to her lips. The Chekists burst into the isba.

Through the open door, Marina saw the darting lights as they searched the room. They found Pavel in the loft and ordered him to come down.

"Where are they?" Malyevich shouted.

"You can see for yourself that I am alone," they heard him say calmly.

"You're lying!" yelled the other man. "We know that Nevsky's wife and daughter are living here! Where are they?"

"I don't know. They left yesterday."

"That's a lie!"

The intruders ran outside and around the house, passing close to the lilac bushes. Marina and Anna held their breaths, shivering in the morning chill. Angrily, the men stomped back into the isba.

"All right, old man!" Malyevich shouted. "We'll teach you to keep company with people who shoot Comrade Lenin!"

"Lenin's dead?"

"Wounded in an assassination attempt two days ago. A filthy SR plot. Ilyich will live, but your friends won't when we catch them."

"They couldn't have had anything to do with it. They were here."

"Nothing's impossible these days," said Malyevich. "If Comrade Peters says the Nevsky women did it, they did it, no matter where they were. If he says ten thousand other people did it, then they did it, and they'll pay for it!" The Chekist laughed. "What about this old crock? Shall we shoot him?"

Malyevich hesitated. Then he grumbled, "There'll be time for that. Put him in the truck. We can use another hostage."

Taking turns at the reins, Marina and Anna traveled along a smooth, sandy road through a pine forest that seemed never to end.

They were silent, grieving over Pavel's arrest. They had been the cause of it. And for what? wondered Marina.

The road had left the river, but by midafternoon they began again to catch glimpses of blue through the trees. They found themselves back on the towpath. Anna was driving when they came to a village in a pine grove near the water's edge. Smoke plumed from several of the chimneys, but there was not a soul in sight. Anna pulled up in front of one of the isbas.

"This is where Vasily's grandfather lived."

The door of the isba slowly opened, and a wrinkled old woman with gnarled hands stood staring at them. Baba Yaga, thought Marina.

"Good evening, babushka," said Anna. "We're on our way to Dubrovka. Can you tell us who lives there now?"

The old woman only glared at them; then she stepped back and closed the door.

After a moment, Anna nodded toward the picket fence behind the isba. "There used to be sunflowers there," she said. "Everything is in shadow now."

They had just left the village when Pasha pricked up his ears. Wagons were rumbling toward them through the trees. In the first sat a man and a woman with round faces the color of earth, their eyes suspicious as they passed them without speaking. The wagon was loaded with tables and chairs, silver candelabra, and paintings. Two more wagons followed, their wooden axles groaning. Each was packed high with furniture and household objects. The driver of the last wagon was a fat, flat-faced youth who stared at them, grinning. Beside him sat an old peasant with a narrow face and small red eyes. Abruptly, the young man skewed his wagon in front of them. Marina, who was driving, tugged at Pasha's reins. With a heaving of their heavy loads, the other wagons creaked to a halt. Through the trees, smoke was creeping toward them.

"Who are you?" demanded the old man.

"Travelers to Samara," said Anna.

The young man was smiling steadily at Marina.

In a strong voice, Anna said, "I am the wife of Vasily Nevsky, and this is our daughter. We're on our way north. Please let us pass."

"The muzhik minister?" asked the old man.

"Yes."

He looked at them a long time. Then he said, "We believed Nevsky once. He said the land would be ours. It was a lie. The tsar was bad, the Bolsheviks worse, and the SRs do nothing. Now we're taking what belongs to us ourselves. We're letting the Red Rooster loose. Tell Nevsky that."

At a nod from the old man, the smirking driver let the women pass.

Marina looked at her mother. Anna was ashen, staring fixedly ahead. The air tasted of smoke.

"What's the Red Rooster?" asked Marina.

At that moment, they were leaving the forest and starting down a broad field sloping to the river. An orchard ripe with fruit had been hacked down by the road. On a rise above the meadow stood the manor house Marina had seen in the photographs. Smoke was billowing from its upper windows.

"That's the Red Rooster. Vengeful arson. It was once our home," said Anna in a dead voice.

Pasha reared in his traces. Marina dropped to the ground and held his bit. When she had calmed him, she and Anna walked over to the house. The front door was open. They went inside.

Everything in the downstairs hallway and parlors was smashed: rosewood cabinets, upholstered chairs, a jewel-encrusted Venetian mirror. Vellum- and leather-bound volumes had been ripped apart and hurled to the floor. Curtains were pulled down. A grand piano was tipped up on its keyboard. The parquet floor was littered with broken glass and china. Over the marble mantelpiece hung the oil portrait of Ariane, familiar to Marina from its photograph. The painting was much larger than she had imagined, and there was another difference. She went up to the painting and stood before it, bewildered. In the photograph, the beautiful young woman's long hair had been dark. In the painting, it was copper red. Marina was suddenly seized with panic. Anna too was staring at the painting. Smoke was pouring down the staircase, filling the salon.

"We must go, mother," said Marina. "Quickly."

They ran outside and back to the cart. Marina took the reins. They started down the meadow toward the towpath; Pasha lunged in his traces, his ears thrust forward as Marina struggled to hold him in check. When they reached the road and looked back, the house was engulfed in flames. Guided by Pasha and the starlit river, they continued north.

That night, they camped in the open, tethering Pasha to the cart in a fragrant grassy field sloping toward the river. Anna had hardly spoken since they left Dubrovka. Marina could not put out of her mind the fact that the girl in the painting bore a strange resemblance to Tamara Sermus, but she said nothing to her mother. As they finished their meal of potatoes, Anna said, "Poor Pavel. I'll never forgive myself for causing his arrest. He has no chance now."

"Why do you take it all on yourself?" asked Marina. "If it was your fault, it was mine too."

"I brought you here," insisted Anna.

Smiling, Marina took her hand. "You brought me into the world."

Anna squeezed her hand. "And now I've brought you into my world. My poor Dubrovka. If only you could have seen how beautiful it was when Ariane and I were children."

"Tell me more about your lives then."

Anna sighed and then began to speak, slowly at first, then in a flood of words, as if a dam within her had burst. "My father loved Ariane, and this was her undoing. He loved her too well. He loved her with a passion that blinded him to everything else. Ariane came to fear him and to hate everything about him: his authoritarian manner, his cruelty to the servants, his drunken rages, and especially his possessiveness toward her." She broke off, cupping her face in her hands.

"If it's too painful—"

"It's time you knew. At that time, Jacob was our tutor. It was he who introduced us to the ideas of the Socialist Revolutionaries." She paused. "He also introduced us to your father."

"And he and Ariane fell in love," Marina added quietly.

"He was everything she had dreamed of in a man, not the least his revolutionary ideals. At the time, he was staying at Pavel's isba and would come to Dubrovka secretly. Vasily and Ariane would meet at the stables and walk through the woods and along the river.

"Jacob and I became their intermediaries, helping them to arrange their meetings. Then one afternoon, at a time we should have been having a lesson, my father saw them walking together by the river."

Anna closed her eyes. Again she spoke slowly and with difficulty. "My father had been drinking all day—he was out of his mind. He found Jacob and drew his hunting knife, threatening to kill him if he didn't tell him who the man was who was seducing his daughter. Fearing for his life, Jacob revealed Vasily's identity. As soon as I heard my father's angry shouts, I ran down to the river to warn the lovers. When Ariane returned to the house, my father locked her in her room. Then he went on drinking and raging in his study until he passed out late at night.

"The next morning at dawn, I went to his study and lifted the key to Ariane's room from its hook without waking him. I brought bread and milk and unlocked the door. Ariane was packing her clothes. She asked me to go to Pavel's and tell Vasily to meet her that night in the woods and take her away from Dubrovka forever. I went to Pavel's and found Vasily there. He was overjoyed and promised to come for her.

"But that night my sister and I waited at the agreed-upon place in the woods until daybreak, but he did not come.

"I told Ariane that Vasily loved her and that he would come for her soon. Something unexpected must have kept him away. She seemed to believe me. At least I thought she did, so I left her." Anna paused again, closing her eyes and slowly shaking her head as if in disbelief.

"It has occurred to me since, many times, that I was far more jealous of Ariane, and of Vasily's attraction to her, than I was willing to admit to myself. And that was why I left her alone when she needed me most."

Transfixed, Marina listened in silence.

"Early the next morning, I went to her room. When I opened the door, I found her lying across the bed in a tangle of bloody sheets. Her face in the dawn light was as beautiful as it had been in life. Our father's hunting knife lay on the floor. My thought was that he had murdered her, as in his drunken rages he had sometimes threatened to do."

Anna suddenly burst into tears. Marina put her arm around her.

"I never thought I would tell this to a living soul," said her mother at last. "I thought I would live with it all my life, alone."

"It's better this way."

"There was blood evidence," said Anna in a dead voice, "that our father had raped my sister. And from the way the knife had fallen from her hand to the floor, I was certain that she had then taken her own life."

"How terrible," said Marina, hardly breathing. "Does Father know this?"

"Eventually, I told him that she had killed herself, only that. The day before her death, my father had denounced Vasily to the authorities as a revolutionary. The police had seized him. That was why he had not come for Ariane."

Anna was silent for a moment; then she went on.

"Several months later, when Vasily was released from prison, he came to the woods by the river to mourn Ariane. We met there by chance. We grieved for her together, and we came to love each other through our love for her. That fall, your father asked me to marry him. Soon afterward, we eloped and went to live in Paris where you were born the following year."

"What happened to your father?"

"He sank into a drunken depression. I hardly saw him at all. He shut himself in his study for days on end, only coming out at night to go gambling and drinking. That was when he lost Dubrovka to a neighbor in a card game. The next day, he shot himself with his rifle."

Again she hesitated, and then went on in a firm voice.

"All this happened in another time that's gone now. Even my memories of it are almost dead. And who knows, now that Dubrovka is no more, perhaps at last I am free of them."

Marina thought of the painting in the smoke-filled room. It would be ashes by now.

"Why was your sister's portrait still in the house?"

"The new owner of Dubrovka never lived there. According to Pavel, the owner believed that it was haunted. It was locked up for many years; then it was at the mercy of the villagers and the Red Rooster."

Anna started to cry softly. Marina sat up and hugged her.

"I understand why you never told me this before, but I'm glad you did now. Now it won't stand between us any more."

"Never."

Marina hoped that she was right, but the vision of the portrait of Ariane standing with the white horse lingered threateningly in her mind.

Her aunt had been a roussalka.

Chapter Twenty-eight

FOR FIVE SWELTERING DAYS, THE TWO WOMEN DROVE NORTH ALONG the western bank of the Volga, taking back roads, skirting villages, and hoping that, with their shawls wrapped around their heads, they would be taken for local peasant women. Late each afternoon, they camped in the fields, letting Pasha graze while they bathed in the river, brewed tea from linden flowers, and roasted potatoes and carrots from their dwindling supply.

On the morning of the sixth day, they drove through an immense field of sunflowers that reached to the river. A milestone showed that Khvalynsk lay just beyond the horizon. Ahead of them a cloud of dust rose, and minutes later, out of the dust appeared cavalrymen wearing peaked hats. Marina's heart sank. In Khvalynsk, they had hoped to encounter SR troops. These were Red Army men.

Marina guided Pasha off the road and reined him in. Riders with dust-encrusted faces stared down at them as they passed. Soldiers on foot followed, sunburned young men in dusty uniforms, appearing exhausted yet proud. Horse-drawn artillery pieces and supply wagons came next. The very last wagon was filled with young women wearing bright kerchiefs, their lips and cheeks rouged, laughing and singing in shrill voices. They called out to them.

"Join us, ladies!"

"It's your womanly duty!"

"Climb up on the wagon with us!"

Long after the army had gone out of sight, Marina could still hear the women's bright voices echoing across the fields.

All her life, the memory of the peak-hatted cavalrymen in the dusty sunlight and of the merry women following them would linger in Marina's mind like a dream. Yet, it had not been a dream. On a hot summer day in 1918, south of Khvalynsk, in search of her father, she and her mother had encountered the troops of the fabled Red general, Chapayev, marching to victory through fields of sunflowers.

Across the undulant steppe, Khvalynsk rose into view, then dropped out of sight like a vessel on a heaving sea. They passed people leaving the town, some on foot, some driving wagons loaded with possessions.

"The Reds have taken Khvalynsk!" a young woman called out to them. "The People's Army fled without a fight."

"The Bolsheviks came from the north," said Marina to her mother. "They must have taken Samara."

"Not necessarily," said Anna firmly.

"Do you think your cousin will receive us, now that the town is occupied?"

"He's a decent man," said Anna, taking the reins from Marina. "It's his new wife we have to worry about. I'm told that she's difficult."

The Borovsky house, one of the town's more imposing stone buildings, stood on a rise overlooking the river. Stern topiary shrubs surrounded it like sentinels. Doric columns painted white framed its entrance. Anna and Marina opened the gate and went up the steep front steps. A stout woman of about forty appeared behind the screened door. A small white poodle barked, jumping and scratching at the screen.

"Elena Borovsky?" asked Anna. "I am Anna Dubrovin, a cousin of your husband."

Staring with disapproval at the horse and cart by the gate, the woman smiled coldly. "Quite impossible to know who anyone is these days." Then her smile vanished. "But if you're Anna Dubrovin, then you must be Vasily Nevsky's wife!"

"I am," said Anna calmly. "My daughter and I are on our way to Samara. We need a place to stay for a few days. Is Mikhail at home?"

"You must have been followed here by the Cheka."

"No one has followed us," said Anna.

Elena Borovsky reflected. "It's extremely inconvenient, but I suppose I can let you stay for a short time. Mikhail is away, and the Reds are requisitioning rooms all over town. Now I can tell them I need our spare one for members of my family."

She took the poodle in her arms and let them into a hallway opening onto rooms filled with furniture polished to a high shine; overstuffed chairs; and sofas covered in dark red brocade. The whole house smelled of wax. She led them up two flights of hardwood stairs to a small bedroom under the eaves.

A washstand with a basin and a water pitcher stood in a corner of the room. Marina already missed their daily swim in the Volga and sleeping under summer skies. In this waxed house, she felt trapped.

When they had washed, Marina went downstairs to tend to Pasha. The mistress of the house met her in the hallway. "I had the horse taken to Red army headquarters," she said with a look of satisfaction.

"You had no right to do that!" cried Marina.

"I had no right not to. It's the law. Horses are being requisitioned."

Upstairs, Marina told Anna what had happened. "We'll never see Pasha again," she said bitterly, "and we're stuck with that hideous woman. I'd rather be with Chapayev's girls following the soldiers!"

Anna was as dismayed as Marina. They had both grown fond of Pasha. "We'll have to continue north on foot," she said. "At least we'll be less conspicuous."

There was a rap on the door.

"Please come down and have a cup of tea with me in the dining room," said Elena Borovsky through the door.

"Thank you," replied Anna with feigned warmth.

"We've got to get away from here," whispered Marina.

"We will. Soon."

. . .

"Real tea," announced Elena as she filled cut crystal glasses set in filigreed silver holders. Then, lowering her voice to a conspiratorial whisper, she said, "My husband joined the SRs. Don't tell a soul, or I'll be shot."

"We won't breathe a word," said Anna.

Elena studied Anna and decided that she was sincere. "We won't have to endure this occupation for long," she went on. "My husband says that the Whites will soon bring back the monarchy."

A grandfather's clock ticked in the hall.

In a quiet voice, Anna said, "Elena, we SRs are fighting for democracy, not for the restoration of the tsars."

"Then my Mikhail is fighting in the wrong army for the wrong cause," exclaimed their hostess indignantly. "And so are his friends. Is it possible that you haven't heard what happened at Yekaterinburg?"

"We've had no news for days."

"The tsar, the tsarina, their daughters, and the young tsaryevich were butchered there by the Bolsheviks. They even slaughtered the tsarina's pet dog." She took her poodle into her arms and hugged it. "There is the crowning triumph of your precious revolution!"

The next morning, Anna and Marina learned that the road to Samara was closed to civilians. It was rumored that the city was still in the hands of the SRs but about to fall to the Bolsheviks.

As days passed and the weather turned cold, they observed changes in the Red Army occupiers. The soldiers who had entered the town singing joyous songs of liberation now glowered at civilians with suspicion. Townspeople seldom left their houses, and when they did, they moved about furtively, speaking to each other in guarded voices, inflaming the soldiers' mistrust. There were tales of people disappearing. As Soviet control over Khvalynsk tightened, stories began circulating about yet another foe of the Reds, a formidable army sworn to destroy them and the Whites alike. The Greens.

Their leader was Antonov.

The legendary Green army was made up of bandits, Cossacks, adventurers, idealists, and peasants outraged by both Bolshevik and White abuses. The Greens offered no revolutionary doctrine, no promise of a bright future, only the swift justice of saber, pistol, and rifle. To the peasants of the Volga, their leader was a hero. Antonov, a great lover of women was a burly, black-bearded man with long flowing hair. In strength, horsemanship, and courage, he had no equal. Unpredictable and merciless toward his foes, he would enter a town, plunder the property owners, and kill the Bolsheviks, and the next morning he would celebrate his victory in a village fifty miles away. The Greens would dance with the women of the village, Antonov more lustily than any of them. Songs and the music of accordions echoed across the steppes. Yet, when Red detachments arrived, they found only a few peasants amusing themselves at a peaceful rural gathering. Antonov? The Greens? No one had ever heard of them.

Like the rest of Khvalynsk's respectable citizens, Elena lived in dread of Antonov's army, which now was said to be riding southward along the Volga toward the town. No less frightening were reports concerning the Red raids of neighboring villages in search of caches of grain. The Bolsheviks were seizing their crops, including their reserves for next year's seeding. Hoarders were shot on the spot. Civilians were taken hostage at random and executed, ten for one, in reprisal for the killing of Bolsheviks.

As fall neared, Anna and Marina had, for the present, no choice but to stay on in Khvalynsk.

In 1918, the Bolsheviks' man of the hour was Leon Trotsky.

From his headquarters in an armored railroad coach, with forays into the countryside in a Packard touring car, the People's Commissar of War had succeeded by summertime in marshaling ragtag remnants of former tsarist regiments, Red Guards, and young worker and peasant recruits into a formidable fighting machine known as the Red Army. Wearing a peaked hat with a red star, a thick belted coat, gauntlets, and heavy boots, Trotsky inspired his soldiers with fanatical loyalty to the October Revolution, while shooting draft dodgers, deserters, malcontents, and participants in unauthorized retreats—commanding officers and commissars first.

It was Trotsky, executing Lenin's plan known as "War Communism"—total commitment to the survival of the Bolshevik regime—who saved it from its many enemies during its darkest hour.

Among his fiercest foes was Boris Savinkov. Fanatically dedicated to the destruction of the Bolsheviks, the former SR assassin commanded a small but well-trained and highly motivated army of White irregulars. That summer, he managed to encircle Trotsky's railway headquarters and cut off his communications with Moscow. Though this action caused a serious disruption of the People's Commissar's command, it was not a fatal one. Once again, by going in the right direction but not far enough, an SR had come close to halting the Bolsheviks' momentum but had failed.

The Left SRs, the Bolsheviks' only political allies in 1917, had become their enemies by 1918. Outraged by the wholesale executions of peasants,

Spiridonova's faction had reverted to the terrorist tactics of the days of Azef. The Left SRs assassinated Moisei Uritsky, the head of the Petrograd Cheka. That was the same day, August 30, 1918, a young woman named Fanya Kaplan had shot Lenin twice in the chest, seriously wounding him.

After that, waves of massacres broke out over all of Russia.

Chapter Twenty-nine

IN THE LATE AFTERNOON OF OCTOBER 1, 1918, VASILY STOOD AT THE window of his room in Samara's Grand Hotel, gazing across the rooftops of the city to the dusky meadows and woods beyond. He was thinking of his wife and daughter. He missed them and feared for their safety. Anna's message telling him that they had left Pavel's isba and traveled north filled him with anxiety. Had they reached Khvalynsk before the Reds got there? Had the Borovskys been there to receive them? Where were they now? And here he was in Samara, forced by Red Army advances to travel east beyond the Ural Mountains, to Omsk or perhaps to Siberia, to try to regroup the SR forces.

As he thought about his wife and daughter, he remembered, unwillingly, the little lie he had told them last May at Pavel's house. It was not even a lie, merely an incomplete truth. Even if it was a kind of deception, there was no harm in it, because it was without purpose and therefore innocent. Yet, it had puzzled him, even as it did now. When Marina had asked him about Tamara, he had said that he had seen her at a distance on Lubyanka Square in the company of Yakov Peters. And this, as far as it went, was entirely true; he had recognized Tamara's companion for having had him pointed out to him in the street recently by an SR comrade. What Vasily had not mentioned was that Peters and Tamara had parted company at the Lubyanka gates, and then she, keeping out of sight of the

Lubyanka windows, had walked rapidly all the way around the square to where Vasily stood in the shadows of a doorway. She had looked pale and distraught, yet still very beautiful.

"Vasily, you must help me!" she had said in a soft, frightened voice.

And she had told him a story that at any other time would have seemed fantastic to him. She told him that she had foolishly let herself become intimately involved with Peters and now found herself entrapped by his murderous jealousy, drawn into deadly Cheka intrigues, and in fear for her life.

"No doubt you could improve your position considerably by turning me in to your new friends," Vasily had said dryly.

She stared at him with a pained expression. "How can you say this? I would never do that, Vasily! Never! I'm caught in an evil world, and I want nothing more than to be with you, to stand by you! By dear Anna! The weeks in Alassio and coming here with you were the happiest times of my life. Whatever happens, I want to be with you!"

He didn't know whether to believe her. Nevertheless, an unexpected feeling of desire had crept over him as he remembered her lightness in his arms when he lifted her out of the dory in Alassio. But he told her only that he would soon be leaving Moscow for the East. At that moment, two Chekists came out of the Lubyanka gates, ambling in their direction. Tamara took his hand and held it hard.

"Take me with you, Vasily," she pleaded. "Please take me with you!"

Before he could reply, she had read his answer in his eyes.

"We'll meet again," he told her, as the Chekists drew nearer.

"When? Where?" she demanded.

Vasily reflected. Lately, he had thought no further ahead than the Ural Mountains. "Whether our cause is successful or whether it fails, should I survive, I shall return to Moscow."

"But how will I find you?" she asked urgently, glancing at the Chekists.

Her desperation was undeniably authentic, decided Vasily. How indeed would she find him? Where was he to roost in this devastated city? Which SR friends had survived? Which would receive him? Then he remembered the key in his pocket.

He had carried it with him since the previous winter, as a kind of good-luck charm, a talisman to assure him that there would be some sort of life for him and for Anna and Marina in the future. It was the key to the apartment with the two grand pianos on Kuznetsky Most. Lord knows who would be occupying it now, but with the dual epidemics of disease and arrests, there were many empty flats throughout the city.

The two Chekists were almost upon them. Tamara put her hand on his sleeve, her eyes pleading. His stubborn feeling of desire unremitting, Vasily was about to whisper the address—131 Kuznetsky Most, second floor—when he remembered Savinkov's toast in Alassio.

"To dangerous women," the ex-assassin had said.

Vasily had touched Tamara's shoulder. "We will find each other," he said, and they had parted quickly in opposite directions.

Vasily looked around the room. It was the best in the city's finest hotel, though it was furnished with only one bed, which he shared with his comrade Volsky, who now lay asleep across it, snoring like a horse.

Vasily sat down at the small writing desk near the window. For a moment, he contemplated the picture over the desk, a chromolithograph of the Château de Chillon on Lake Leman shrouded in crepuscular mist, a study furnished by the hotel management to replace the framed photograph of Lenin which had decorated the room during the Bolshevik occupation of Samara. Contemplating the picture, Vasily recalled his trip to the Swiss mountains at Zimmerwald in 1915, when revolution had seemed like a mythical event fated always to happen in the future.

A knock at the door startled him.

"Visitor to see you," said the SR on duty at the door. "States his name as Golovin."

"Anton Golovin?" asked Vasily in surprise.

From the hallway, a strong, youthful voice answered, "His son, Kiril."

"Show him in."

The guard admitted a tall, slender, strikingly handsome young man with thick waves of dark brown hair. His resemblance to his celebrated father, Russia's most famous living writer after Gorky, was—as far as Vasily could judge from photographic postcards—remarkable.

"A pleasure to meet you, Kiril Antonovich," said Vasily, pointing to a chair near his desk. "Gorky has often spoken warmly of you."

"As he has of you, Vasily Ivanovich," said the young man, sitting down, "and of your wife and daughter. Marina is a great favorite of his."

"How may I be of service to you?" asked Vasily, using a formal turn of phrase inspired by the young man's elegant bearing.

Volsky snorted, rolled over, snorted again, and was still.

"I am here on behalf of someone who wishes to meet you," said Kiril, ignoring the obstreperous sleeper. "Antonov."

Vasily leaned back in his chair. Could it be that Golovin's son was a member of the Greens? In the eyes of the SR leadership, the Greens were dissipating the peasants' revolutionary energies in mindless pillage and mayhem. But then perhaps Antonov, through the offices of this young man, was seeking an alliance with the SRs. Here was a possible yoking of the peasants' anger with the lawful government of the Constituent Assembly—potentially a powerful, democratic alliance.

"I will meet with Antonov gladly," he said.

"He asked me to tell you that he will receive you at our camp outside the city. I brought a horse for you."

"My comrades and I are setting forth for Omsk tomorrow morning."

"You'll be back in time. We too must leave in the morning."

In the waning light, Vasily and Kiril Golovin rode westward out of the city, through a broad meadow toward a dark oak forest silhouetted against the sunset. Kiril eased his horse into a canter. Vasily did the same, concentrating on keeping a proper seat.

As they entered the dense forest, Kiril slowed his horse to a walk. After riding for a long time at this pace, they saw firelight in the center of a clearing. Suddenly, a roar of laughter that seemed to come from a hundred throats reverberated through the woods. Vasily felt uneasy. Had he let this beguiling youth lure him into a den of desperadoes?

"Don't be alarmed," said Kiril, reading his thought. "You're Antonov's guest. No harm will befall you."

As they rode into the clearing, Vasily easily identified Antonov. A giant of a man, with thick hair to his shoulders and a full beard, he was standing by a bonfire addressing his men, several hundred of them, sitting in circles around him. He turned to the new arrivals.

"Welcome, Nevsky!" called out the leader of the Greens in a booming voice. Arms outstretched and moving with a heavy, rolling gait, he walked toward Vasily.

The two men embraced. Then Antonov held Vasily at arm's length, peering into his eyes. Finally, as if he had seen everything he needed to see, Antonov clapped his visitor on the shoulders with both hands.

"Come, Mr. Minister," he said with a broad grin, "let's drink and talk and get to know each other." He led Vasily to a place in the circle around the bonfire. They sat cross-legged, surrounded by Antonov's lieutenants. Kiril was at the leader's right. Antonov brandished a bottle.

"To the muzhik minister," he called out. "A son of the Volga who has traveled far and thought big thoughts!"

A deep, reluctant growl answered him. Antonov drank and then passed the bottle to Vasily. Vasily raised it high. "To the Greens," he called out. "To the champions of a free Russia!" He drank. The powerful brew burned his throat. Another chorus of growls echoed his words.

Vasily was beginning to pick out individual faces among Antonov's men, wolflike and menacing and yet filled with pride in the brotherhood of the Greens. It struck him that if these were outcasts, so was he himself an outcast now, as indeed were all worthy Russians. He rose to his feet.

"Comrades," he said, "it is true that I have traveled far and have thought deeply about the fate of our country, but here among you I see the future: citizen soldiers springing from the Russian soil to liberate her. Tomorrow morning, my comrades and I set forth for Omsk to plant our banner in the east. I leave Samara confident that you will thunder over the steppes up and down the Volga, upholding the new government of the Constituent Assembly!"

Silence greeted his words. The bonfire crackled.

After a moment, Kiril said, "Vasily Ivanovich, few among us know what the Constituent Assembly is."

"And those of us who do know," said Antonov, "want nothing to do with it." He got to his feet, towering over Vasily.

"Vasily Ivanovich, we fight the same enemy, we with guns and sabers, you with words. We all say, 'No to the Reds, no to the Whites,' but what has the Constituent Assembly been, but words? The people have no more use for assemblies; they cry out for a chieftain. Are you that man? If so, your strength is here, on the Volga. In Siberia, if you're not brought down by the Bolsheviks, the Whites will swallow you alive."

"I must take that chance," said Vasily. "All the rebels of the past failed because they had nothing to offer the people but blood. The SR way offers them freedom. Why not travel the same road, Antonov? My words and your sabers."

Antonov grinned. "Mr. Minister, your words are no doubt as strong as my sabers. What I fear is that, should we join forces, my sabers would become as strong as your words." His men echoed his laughter. He seized a bottle and raised it. "Let's drink to our separate stars, Vasily Ivanovich. Tomorrow, you go to the east, and we to the south. Though we both want the same thing for Russia, I do not think that our stars will meet again."

"How far south are you going?" asked Vasily.

"To where we are most needed. Khvalynsk."

Chapter Thirty

ATOP THE HILL BEHIND THE BOROVSKY HOUSE, THERE WAS AN ANCIENT churchyard surrounding a white stone chapel shaded by a stately larch tree. During that fall of 1918, Marina went there often with her sketch pad. From the churchyard, she could see all of Khvalynsk, the cobbled streets, the wooden houses with scrollwork eaves, the white church with its golden cupolas, the town hall on the market square, the wharves jutting into the river. To the west, the steppe stretched in pale waves to the horizon. For an hour or two each day, Marina could believe that she would live out her life in a beautiful green country, as Pasternak had promised, but now her sketch pad was almost filled. Her life was running out like her drawing paper.

One late October afternoon, a cool wind was gusting from the north. The larch tree was scattering its golden needles on the graves marked with wooden crosses. Another winter was coming. Marina was sketching the chapel, absorbed in her work.

After a while, she began to feel cold. Glancing out at the river, she noticed a gunboat, a red flag taut at its sternpost, cruising swiftly downstream. She thought that the vessel would cruise by, but it heeled and turned upstream toward the wharves where a steamer was docked, gray smoke swirling from its stacks. Even before the lines were fast, a stocky man waving a pistol ran down a gangplank, leading a dozen soldiers carrying rifles. With a rush of fear, she realized that these were Bolshevik grain raiders. The stocky man led them into one of the brick depots across from the wharves.

In the distance, she could make out workmen bent under the weight of heavy sacks, prodded by the riflemen, lugging their burdens on board the gunboat. One worker stumbled, letting his sack fall into the water. The stocky detachment leader drew his pistol and ran up to the man and shot him, kicking his body off the gangplank.

To the west, Marina noticed a plume of dust rising from the steppe. A double column of horsemen seemed to rise out of the parched earth, galloping toward the town. At their head rode a huge man with a black beard and flowing hair.

The Greens, Marina realized, and their leader Antonov. As she watched the riders racing across the steppe, she thought, Now Elena Borovsky's nightmare is coming true. But Marina herself was no longer afraid.

The Greens reached the outskirts of Khvalynsk, firing their pistols into the air as they clattered over the town's cobbled streets. They drew up in front of the town hall, where the Cheka was headquartered, dropped from their horses and ran into the building. There was a long volley of gunfire. Minutes later, Chekists began filing out, hands over their heads. Townspeople appeared from doorways and courtyards, cheering the Greens and cursing their captives.

Marina ran down the steep lane toward the house. She was nearing the front gate when she saw a man on horseback galloping up the hill toward her. He reined in his lathered horse.

"The Borovsky house," he called to her as he dismounted. "Do you know it?"

"It's just down the hill," she said.

Leading his horse, he came up to her. His face was caked with dust and sweat. "You're Marina Vasilyevna?"

"I am," she said. He wiped his face with his kerchief and looked up at her again. Suddenly, she recognized him.

"And you're Kiril Golovin. I saw your photograph in Gorky's office."

He looked at her, searching her face and then smiling warmly. "He said that we would meet."

"He told me the same thing."

Nearby, there was a burst of gunfire. Marina barely heard it. She was looking at him as if she'd known him all her life.

"I saw your father in Samara," said Kiril, breaking the spell. "He told me that you and your mother might be at the Borovsky house."

Marina felt as if Gorky himself had sent this young man to her rescue. Was he the Knight of the Round Table she used to draw in her childhood? The white knight with blue feathers on his helmet?

"I must speak with your mother," the young man said in a determined voice. "I have an urgent message for her from your father."

Marina led Kiril down to the Borovskys' gate. There he tethered his horse, and she led him up the steps and into the hallway. Anna was coming down the stairs.

"Mother, this is Anton Golovin's son Kiril. He's seen father in Samara."

Kiril went to Anna and kissed her hand. "An honor, Anna Pavlovna."

"How is he?" she asked anxiously. "Is he all right?"

"Vasily Ivanovich is in excellent health, and he sends you his greetings."

"Thank God," said Anna softly. "We'll soon be seeing him in Samara."

Kiril spoke firmly. "Anna Pavlovna, your husband wants you to know that by now he will have left Samara and started east toward Omsk. His wish is that you return to Moscow and wait for him there. In any case, it would be extremely dangerous to travel north right now."

Looking distressed, Anna started to protest.

"I'm sorry, but there's very little time," said Kiril in a gentle voice. "I'm here with the Greens. At any moment, there'll be reprisals for our raid. I've heard that there's a steamer leaving for Saratov within the hour. Perhaps the last one for a long time. Please pack immediately, and let me take you to the wharf. Vasily Ivanovich would want me to do this." To Marina, he added, "I want to see you again. It's very important."

At that moment, Elena Borovsky burst into the hallway, her poodle barking at her heels. She folded her arms defiantly and stood before them, glowering at Kiril. Marina noticed that, for the first time since she and Anna had been staying in the house, the double doors to the dining room were closed.

"How did he get in?" she screamed.

"Kiril Golovin is a friend," said Anna.

"I want nothing to do with your friends! He's one of *them*! Did your hear the shooting? It's all your doing! I hate you! You must leave at once!

To Marina's surprise, Anna replied in an even voice. "Come with us, Cousin Elena. You're no longer safe here. The Bolsheviks will be taking hostages and shooting them. We're leaving for Saratov. Please pack what you can and come with us."

"Come with you! Leave my house and come with you?" shouted Elena. "You must be mad! All the misfortune that has befallen our poor country is the fault of you liberal fools! As my husband says, 'They let the genie out of the bottle, now they're surprised that they can't stuff it back.'" With a triumphant smile, she rolled open the dining-room doors.

On a snow white lace tablecloth, a table was set with gold-rimmed china, crystal glasses, and heavy silver. Tall white candles in silver candelabra.

"The time has come for us to learn to live in peace with the Bolsheviks," Elena announced. "I've invited the commissar and his staff to dinner here tonight. They'll be here at any moment." She went to the sideboard and began to set out lace doilies and cut-glass finger bowls.

Anna and Marina went upstairs and threw their belongings into their bags. As they came downstairs, Elena was lighting the candles on the dining-room table. Kiril and Marina hurried Anna outside. At the gate, Kiril untied his horse and handed the reins to Marina. He picked up their suitcases and started down the street toward the wharves. As they left the house, Marina looked back. In the fading afternoon light, she saw two leather-clad Chekists open the front gate and start up the steps to the screened door.

For years afterward, she asked herself: Were they members of the commissar's staff? Or were they uninvited guests?

Chapter Thirty-one

THE HORN BLARED, HAWSERS SPLASHED, AND THE STEAMER WORKED out into the current. Anna and Marina found a sheltered place on deck among their fellow passengers—peasants, Red Army soldiers, and the new breed of refugees: dispossessed members of the propertied class trying to be invisible. As the river bore them swiftly downstream, Marina heard a chorus of male voices at the bow of the vessel. She and Anna made their way forward. A circle of Red Army soldiers were singing:

> *Red apple, red apple,*
> *Where are you rolling?*
> *Red apple, red apple,*
> *Winter is cold.*

She went up to the railing and looked down at the dark, racing water. Where was her father now? Had he reached Omsk? And Dmitry? And Kiril Golovin? More than ever, she believed that her godfather was a miracle worker who had put Kiril in their path to save them from death in Khvalynsk.

The Red Army men sang late into the night. Marina and Anna made a nest out of their blankets and fell asleep to the strong, plaintive songs of a Russia that perhaps no longer existed.

• • •

When they awoke, the vessel was steaming past the pine woods of Dubrovka and the meadow where the house had been. Nothing remained of it but its four chimneys. Soon, smokestacks and onion-domed churches of Saratov glowed in the pale sunrise ahead.

"We mustn't linger in Saratov," said Marina. "Let's get to Moscow as soon as we can."

Drawing their shawls around their heads, they disembarked and followed side streets to the railway station. The ticket booths were closed. No schedules were posted, no railway employees were in sight. Exhausted and hungry, they went into the waiting room and settled on a bench under a poster:

COMRADES, BE VIGILANT. THE ENEMY NEVER SLEEPS.

Marina looked around the waiting room and noticed a mottled glass-paneled door with black lettering:

TELEGRAPH OFFICE
No Admittance

She went to the door and listened, hearing the quick, dry clicking of a telegraph key. She knocked. The clicking stopped. A blurred figure appeared on the other side of the glass. The door opened, and Sergei, wearing earphones that gave his elfin face a comical appearance, stared at her without a sign of recognition. Then he saw Anna on the bench. He turned again to Marina, this time with a look of recognition, and whispered, "Meet me in back of the station." He took off his earphones and, closing the door behind him, crossed the waiting room and went outside.

Moments later, Marina and Anna followed him. Without a word, Sergei led them along an alley between rundown wooden ware-houses, into a courtyard, down a flight of stone stairs, and through a small door into a dark, clammy room. He lit a candle in a niche in the wall, and Marina saw that they were in a narrow cellar with a vaulted ceiling. Smoke-blackened icons filled the corner to the right. The frigid vault smelled of moldy stone and incense. Though they were wearing heavy woolen coats and shawls, the damp cold chilled them to the bone.

"This was a Khlysty meeting place," said Sergei.

Marina had heard Vasily speak of the Khlystys, a secret sect whose members called themselves the People of God and sought spiritual perfection through ritual sexual orgies.

"They say Rasputin used to come here," Sergei added.

"Where are the Khlystys now?" asked Marina.

"They've all been shot. It seems that there's no room for religion or promiscuity in the new society, much less for both at once. They died like most of the Saratov elite, including all the SRs who did not flee. Your friends the Sterns were among them. I'm so very sorry."

Anna buried her face in her hands and burst into tears. Marina embraced her.

"Have you heard anything about my father?" she asked in a hesitant voice.

"Dear ladies, I'm happy to tell you that though Admiral Kolchak's coup succeeded and the Whites now control Siberia, the Cheka reported recently that Vasily Nevsky and several other SRs slipped away from them. Without an army, with both the Cheka and the Whites pursuing him, Nevsky is still determined to rally the peasantry behind the Constituent Assembly. It's mad. It's impossible. It's marvelous. In a word, it's Russian."

"It's not at all impossible," said Anna firmly. "When the Reds and the Whites have exterminated each other, Vasily will help establish the government the people have wanted all along."

"If only he could," said Sergei. "If only he could enter every isba in the country and in his rich voice tell the peasants his dreams for their future! As it is, his message is lost in the vastness of the motherland."

"We had hoped to join him in Samara," said Marina. She was seized with a feeling of utter hopelessness.

"We'll meet with him in Moscow," said Anna. "I'm certain that he'll rejoin the SR underground there."

"Anna Petrovna, I'll try to help you get to Moscow, but first I must give you two words of warning. First, you must not count on there still being an organized SR underground in Moscow. Second, I have not forgotten your speaking of your friendship with Tamara Sermus. I must advise you to be extremely wary of this friend of the family. For some time now, she has been the mistress of Dzerzhinsky's man, Yakov Peters. Peters has more blood on his hands than does any other Chekist, though close on his heels is his rival,

Martyn Latsis. Peters and Latsis compete to impress Dzerzhinsky with their sadistic accomplishments, notably the torture and execution of hundreds of prisoners in the Lubyanka cellars. So please be careful. The reward for Vasily Nevsky is now a half million rubles."

Sergei held his watch up to the candle in the niche. "Right now, I must see about getting you tickets for tonight's train to Moscow. Normally, this would take days, even weeks, to arrange, but miracles have been known to happen to the Nevskys." He looked at Marina. "In fact, one will happen when I return—I have a happy surprise for you."

He left. When he returned a half hour later, the cold was beginning to numb them.

"You'll leave for Moscow tonight," he said. "The comrade in charge of tickets is drunk, and his wife has a weakness for me. But first, dear ladies, about that surprise. A friend of yours has been staying in my study. Please come with me."

They followed Sergei into the dark courtyard and up steep, creaky stairs to an apartment in the back of a ramshackle wooden building. He opened the door to a room filled with books from floor to ceiling. On the floor, pillows were strewn on a Turkish rug. A coal-oil lamp was burning on a desk scattered with papers.

A man was sitting at the desk. He stood up as they came in. It was Dmitry.

At that moment, he appeared to Marina as she had often seen him in her dreams, smiling secretively, his dark eyes shining from under his thick lashes. He kissed her, and she felt as though she were falling back in time, as though she had reached the end of a perilous journey, as if everything would be all right from now on. But Sergei was addressing them solemnly: "Dear friends, we have little time before we must leave for the station. Come to the kitchen with me, dear Anna Petrovna. Let's share some secrets and leave these tiresome young people to themselves."

When they were alone, Dmitry took Marina in his arms. "Marina, I have something important to tell you."

Something in Dmitry's voice told Marina that she was not at the end of her journey after all.

"I'm going off to fight with Savinkov."

Slowly, she freed herself from his embrace.

"For the Whites?"

"Try to understand. The Bolsheviks want to finish us off; they want to enslave the whole country, and they have the power to do it. I hoped to join Vasily in Samara, but it's too late. Now only the Whites have a chance."

"To do what?"

"Destroy the Bolsheviks."

"And all our hopes."

"You didn't always share those hopes."

"I do now."

"Now that they're doomed? Did you know that they've arrested Spiridonova?"

"Spiridonova must be avenged!" said Marina bitterly.

His eyes became hard. "Yes! Spiridonova must be avenged! And your friends the Sterns and tens of thousands more."

"And how many people will the Whites destroy?"

"Marina, there's no other way. Only they can save Russia."

"Last winter, you believed that only the Bolsheviks could save the country."

"They betrayed us. They betrayed Russia. Everything has changed."

"Something else will change! Spiridonova will loathe you for the rest of your life for what you're doing!" Her heart was breaking. "Dmitry, I love you. Don't do it."

He took her hands. "Marina, I love you too, but I must—"

"Fight for what you believe in," she said bitterly.

"Yes."

"And if the Whites win, if the monarchy is restored, what will you fight for then?"

He was silent a moment; then he said, "If I should live to that day—I'll die fighting to destroy the monarchy!"

"So that one day, after a million deaths, two young people can again stroll by the Neva in springtime and be in love?"

Sergei was at the door.

"Marina," he said, "it's time to go. I have some apples for your journey."

It was nearing midnight when Anna and Marina left Sergei's apartment. Carrying their bags, Sergei led them through the maze of unlit back streets to a side entrance of the station. They passed through an unguarded gate to a platform where a train made up of boxcars stood, its engine under steam. Sergei helped them up into one of the crowded, smoke-filled cars.

"Adieu, ladies," he said. "May we all meet again in happier times." Looking at Marina, he added, "Good-bye Marina, I shall write a poem about you."

With a flourish of his imaginary hat, he walked away, not looking back.

*O*f our journey to Moscow, packed in the freezing boxcar along with some fifty other silent, frightened refugees fleeing the war-torn countryside, I retain one clear memory. I had just fallen asleep when, after creeping along the tracks all night, the train came to an abrupt stop. Passengers rolled open the heavy door. We were in the middle of a snowfield merging with a pale gray sky. People dropped to the ground to stretch their legs. Steam hissed from the engine. Ahead, down the tracks, was an abandoned railway station.

Suddenly, one by one, like bats out of a cave, small figures scurried out of the building. A band of children ran toward the train. The passengers who had gotten down from the boxcar climbed back inside and tried to pull the door closed as small bony fingers clutched at it. For an instant, I saw the children's faces. Their eyes were huge, their cheeks drawn. All had but one face, the face of hunger. They struggled to scramble aboard the train, boosted up by their companions. "Bread! Bread!" they cried. I threw them one of my apples. The train began to move. The cries of the *bezprizorniye*—the abandoned children who roamed in packs over Russia in those years—soon grew faint. The memory of them has haunted me ever since, but in fact it was my mother who was most deeply shaken by what we had witnessed.

Chapter Thirty-two

VASILY HEARD DEEP VOICES SINGING IN THE SWIRLING SNOW.

Behind him, his comrade Volsky yelled out, "We're lost, Vasily."

"We're going south!" Vasily shouted back. The wind rose, and icy snow stung his face. When the wind died, he could no longer hear the singing.

Volsky drew up his horse next to Vasily's. "How do you know it's south?" he asked. Their four companions reined in too. When Vasily looked back through the blizzard, his friends appeared to him as ghosts on ghost horses. Soon, he reflected, they would disappear altogether. They were six. In Omsk, they had been two hundred.

"South is this way," he called out, pointing into the swarm of white ahead of him. Though he had no compass, he was certain of it. He had the map of Russia in his head. Ufa lay ahead of them, the Volga was to the right, the Urals to the left.

Their comrade Sobolev cried out, "It's been three weeks since we left Omsk. Where are we?"

"Ufa is straight ahead," Vasily called back.

The six rode on.

"And the Whites?" asked Ivanov.

"Gone," said Vasily.

"How do you know?" asked Volsky.

Vasily let the rising wind answer for him.

He was thinking of the tidy, stark village of Old Believers where they had spent the previous night. The inhabitants had heard that a Red Army division was moving in from the west and had carted away the village signposts in an attempt to confuse the invaders. Doors had slammed in the travelers' faces, until finally a frightened old woman admitted them into her isba.

"The Bolsheviks will soon be here," she said. "Do you know the prayer against them?"

"What prayer, babushka?"

"The prayer against the Bolsheviks. When one of them comes to your door, you say the prayer, and as hard as he tries, he just wriggles there and can't step over the threshold."

"I don't know that prayer," said Vasily.

"Do you know how to find it?"

"No, I don't. I wish I did."

That night, they had slept on straw piled around the woman's tiled stove. Snow continued to fall. As they were leaving the isba in the morning, they had seen the women of the town, kerchiefed heads bent, filing up to the church halfway up on the hill.

"They're going up there to pray," the old woman said, crossing herself with two fingers in the manner of Old Believers. "Maybe they'll find the prayer in church."

The snow had stopped. It was growing dark. The men rode on, their horses stumbling in the iced ruts. In the distance ahead, they heard shooting. After a while, the sky began to clear, and to their left appeared black hills, rising against a rose sky in which shone a single star. Vasily did not grasp the importance of the star. Volsky, riding next to him, did.

"That's Polaris, my dear Vasily," he said. "We are not going south. We are going north."

At first, Vasily refused to believe that they had been traveling in a circle all day. He had been so sure of his way! Glaring at the star in the wrong heaven, Vasily felt that a malevolent power was sapping his strength. He thought of Anna with tenderness, wondering where she and Marina were, praying that they were safe.

In the twilight ahead, they saw the town with the sullen wooden houses and the church halfway up on the hill that they had left that morning. The church was a mass of fiery rubble.

As they entered the village, Vasily again heard the singing, wavering faintly, receding into the distance. Straining to hear, he could just make out the hymn: "God Save the Tsar."

Without a word, the six went to the house of the woman who had asked Vasily for the prayer against the Bolsheviks. They found her sitting by the window, firelight from the burning church wavering on her stricken face.

"The Bolsheviks locked some of the men of the village inside the church," she said. "You could hear their screams. If only I'd known the prayer."

"They weren't Bolsheviks," Vasily told her gently. "We heard them singing. They had to be Kolchak's men. They were Whites."

She stared at him uncomprehendingly. "Is there a prayer against them too?"

Vasily and his comrades spent a second night in the old woman's isba. When he awoke the next morning, sunlight was streaming through the small isinglass window by the door. The other five men were already awake. From their silence and troubled looks, he realized that they had been talking among themselves. As Vasily sat up, Volsky spoke first.

"Vasily, we hold you in the greatest respect."

"All of us," said Ivanov.

"However, we are all of the opinion that we should not try to go on to Bashkiria. Gavril Zorin is no doubt a formidable fellow, but he's no match for Trotsky and his generals. You have done what you could, far more than most men could accomplish—"

"But you can't harvest straw in a windstorm," put in Sobolev.

"In a word," Volsky went on, "we propose to return to Moscow."

Piqued by the conspiracy in his midst, Vasily said hotly, "And abandon our cause? Never. If need be, I shall continue on to Ufa alone."

"Unwise," said Sobolev. "It's a long way. One can get lost."

"Especially alone," said Ivanov.

"Besides," said Volsky, "you wouldn't be abandoning our cause. Lenin organized in the cities first. Perhaps we should do the same."

They fell silent. Again, in the distance, they heard men singing. As they listened, the voices grew steadily louder. This time, the song was not the Whites' anthem—it was "The Marseillaise."

"Bolsheviks," said Ivanov.

Vasily went to the window and saw peak-helmeted cavalrymen approaching from the north.

"Only a small detachment," he said.

"An advance guard for the main army, no doubt," said Volsky.

As the mounted troops jangled through the slush outside, they now were singing the song of the Revolution:

> Red apple, red apple,
> Where are you going?
> You've rolled to the trenches,
> You've rolled to the forests.
> If you roll to Bashkiria,
> You'll never come back.

The six were silent as the soldiers' voices gradually faded in the distance. Nor did the old woman speak as she served them groats and the venison they had brought with them.

"Zorin will wipe them out," said Vasily at last, but without conviction.

"Zorin may well prevail in Bashkiria," said Volsky, "but you must return to Moscow with us and launch a new campaign against Lenin."

Vasily was silent for a long time.

"Above all," he said at last, "we must remain united."

After that, he and his companions ate heartily. That morning, they set forth on the road west.

Chapter Thirty-three

IT WAS LATE MORNING WHEN MARINA AND ANNA DISEMBARKED AT Kazan Station, cold and hungry, having eaten the last of Sergei's apples. They had no idea where they would spend the night. The city was in the grip of winter. Bundled figures with steaming breath trudged toward them along paths through huge snowbanks. Moscow was silent. There were no horse-drawn cabs, no automobiles, no trams.

"Let's try the Logorovs," said Anna. "They're nearby."

The year before, secret party meetings had been held at the Logorovs' place behind Kazan Station. Now their apartment house looked abandoned. Anna and Marina entered and felt their way up a dark stairway. On the fourth floor, they tried to read the numbers on the doors, but the numerals had been scraped off, as if the occupants had hoped thereby to efface themselves. Anna knocked at one of the doors on the landing at random. A frightened old man opened it a crack.

"The Logorovs, please?" she said.

"Gone," whispered the old man, quickly shutting the door.

Weak from hunger, they groped their way down the stairs.

"We must get something to eat," said Marina.

"We still have the green chiffon dress. We'll sell it at the Sukharevka market, and then something good will happen. You'll see."

·   ·   ·

In those days, north of the Kremlin in the shadow of Sukharev Tower, there was a sprawling bazaar known to Muscovites as Sukharevka. This marketplace, where stolen goods and heirlooms were traded for a few days' supply of food, was neither allowed by the Soviet authorities nor quite forbidden. There, bound together in the community of hunger, worker mingled with aristocrat, Communist with bourgeois, peasant with intellectual.

They reached the bazaar in a state of exhaustion. Marina surveyed the jumble of objects offered for sale—icons, Chinese vases, Bokhara rugs, walking sticks, smoking jackets, court gowns, furs, books. There was food here too, and it made Marina feel faint: bacon, butter, milk, flour, sugar at five hundred rubles a lump, moldy pre-Revolutionary chocolate, tinned fish, biscuits. A well-dressed man was exchanging a gold watch for a sack of flour and a few potatoes. A peasant traded a Sèvres vase for a pair of army boots. Sharp-eyed dealers scanned the crowd. Children in rags gazed wide-eyed at the spoils of the Revolution.

Summoning her courage, Anna went up to a stall where clothes were bought and sold. Opening her suitcase, she offered for sale the green dress with the velvet trim which Marina had worn to the Chaliapin concert. The red-cheeked young woman at the counter made no attempt to hide her appreciation of the gown.

"No wonder you bourgeois looked lovely when you had dresses like this to wear," she said, holding it up for everyone around to see. "Now we'll wear them for a change."

Anna agreed to trade the dress for a tin of biscuits, a slab of bacon, and a small sack of rye flour. The young woman weighed the flour, sliced the bacon, and then, ostentatiously, she threw in an extra slice.

"Here, *ladies*," she said. "Satisfy your hunger for once."

Without losing her composure, Anna thanked her. They were leaving the market when they heard a familiar male voice behind them: "Quel dommage. C'était une bien belle robe!"

Ilya Ehrenburg was thinner than when they had seen him last on the North Sea crossing almost two years before. His hair was cut short, and he was wearing a threadbare overcoat under his plaid shawl. In a low voice, he said, "Come with me," and started to guide them toward the exit. Suddenly, he stopped behind a rack of military uniforms, motioning for them to stay where they were.

"A friend of yours is here," he said. "She mustn't see you."

Tamara Sermus, wearing a full-length sable coat, her red hair now bobbed, was carrying an armful of dresses toward the stall they had just left. With her was a short man with a sleek, bloodless face. He wore an astrakhan hat and an English trench coat. Traders greeted the couple with respectful bows. Tamara threw the dresses onto the counter.

Impulsively, Anna started toward her. Marina tried to stop her, but Tamara had seen them. Her face hardened. Then she turned her back to them.

Ehrenburg hurried them away from the market in the direction of the Kremlin.

"You must be careful, Anna," he said. "Tamara is not your friend. Nor is that nasty fellow with her."

"Peters?" asked Marina.

"Now the Cheka knows you're in Moscow."

"Poor Tamara," said Anna. "She's their prisoner."

"No doubt," said Ehrenburg skeptically. "As for Peters, he is yet another Okhrana graduate. Like Dzerzhinsky himself, some say. And Madam Sermus herself, of course."

"How do you know that?" demanded Anna.

"How does anyone know anything these days? True information is counterproductive to the building of socialism. Facts are counterrevolutionary. Where are you staying?"

"We just got off the train," said Anna. "We haven't found a place yet."

Ehrenburg lit a cigarette, inhaled deeply, and then held it out and studied it reproachfully. "I swapped a warm pair of socks for ten of these damned things"—he gestured to his feet—"when what I really needed is a pair of pants." His ankles were bare. He grinned.

"Socialism won't be built in a day, Lenin tells us. But abundance will follow, including pants. As Korolenko wrote, 'Man is made for happiness as birds are made for flight.' Meanwhile, I think that you should meet a young couple who recently came here from Orel, Fyodor and Nina Ilyanov, both dedicated SRs—not Left SRs but passionate followers of Vasily Nevsky. Fearless. They publish an underground newspaper called *Liberation* and are in touch with what's left here of the SR community. They live nearby. Come with me."

"You see, Marina," said Anna. "I knew something good was going to happen."

Ehrenburg led them into one of the narrow streets of the Arbat, past ancient pink stuccoed houses which had been the residences of Moscow aristocrats and wealthy merchants. The air smelled of charred wood.

They had walked a short distance when, ahead, they heard the sound of steadily repeated blows. Turning a corner, they came upon a grisly spectacle. Five young boys in ragged clothing stood around a dead horse, its legs splayed, while one of them swung an ax, dislodging chunks of half-frozen flesh, which the other four gathered with bloody fingers. Marina noticed that their faces were strangely impassive, like those of the children she had seen at the abandoned train station.

She felt sickened. Anna stared at the scene in silent horror.

Suddenly, from a side street, a man wearing a red armband ran toward the boys, waving a pistol. He fired a shot. The boy with the ax dropped it in the middle of the street, and he and his companions scattered. The man with the armband picked up the ax and hefted it with approval. Ehrenburg hurried Marina and Anna into a side street.

"Don't look back," he warned, as they turned into yet another lane in the maze of the Arbat.

They walked on without speaking, their steps cracking the crisp film of ice.

Anna broke the silence, speaking in a voice Marina had never heard before, rising from a depth of rage she had not known her mother to possess.

"We *must* do something to help these children!"

"Impossible," said Ehrenburg softly. "It's the same all over the country. Millions of them, homeless and hungry, roaming like wolves."

"We saw a band of them north of Saratov," said Anna. "Vasily must know of this. We must organize a worldwide campaign to save the starving children."

Ehrenburg glanced at Marina in bewilderment.

"What a great pity," he said to Anna, "that you, who are the most disposed to help the suffering people of our country, are now the least able to do so."

"But there must be something that can be done," Anna insisted. "What about the Red Cross? What about Peshkova?"

Ehrenburg did not reply. Marina saw that he was vexed by her mother's questions.

"An extremely delicate situation," he said at last. "Peshkova is committed to aiding the political prisoners, and the Bolsheviks tolerate this up to a point. However, in matters concerning the young, they wish to remain in absolute control. They see themselves as the sole educators."

"What about the SRs from Orel? You said that they're admirers of Vasily, and fearless. Perhaps they can be enlisted."

"The Ilyanovs," replied Ehrenburg in a voice that had turned hard, "are indeed fearless. But to tell you the truth, I'm not really sure that I should be taking you there. These brave young people are living on the edge of a crumbling precipice."

The Ilyanovs occupied the former kitchen in the courtyard of what had once been a prince's townhouse. The mansion itself had been destroyed by fire. It was now a skeleton of blackened beams silhouetted against the pale winter sky.

As they came into the cavernous kitchen, Fyodor Ilyanov, an emaciated man of about thirty, with quick, intelligent eyes magnified by thick glasses, was working at an ancient flatbed printing press in the center of the room. Recognizing Ehrenburg, he welcomed his visitors with a wave of his ink-stained hand. Ehrenburg presented them.

Fyodor's wife, Nina, rose from a chair near the huge walk-in fireplace. She was wearing a gray shawl over her thin shoulders, her light brown hair framing a gentle, narrow face that reminded Marina of a Memling Virgin. She came toward them, her arms outstretched in greeting.

"Vasily Nevsky's family! We are honored," she exclaimed.

"For weeks, we've been gathering news of Vasily Nevsky, for a special edition of *Liberation*," said Fyodor. "The reports are sketchy, but an extraordinary saga is emerging."

"We only know that he left Samara for the east," said Anna.

Fyodor pulled up chairs around the fireplace and stirred the embers in the hearth.

"For a while last summer, it seemed that a government of the

Constituent Assembly on the Volga would become a reality. SR forces took town after town, and then drove north and seized Kazan." He hesitated, staring at the embers. "Unfortunately, the Red Army soon recaptured the city."

"Vasily Ivanovich and his comrades then attempted to coordinate peasant uprisings in the vast region between the Volga and the Urals," said Nina. "At first, their efforts met with success, but they failed to gain the support of the strongest partisan group, Antonov's Greens. However, Vasily Ivanovich's perseverance and courage in the face of extreme adversity sustained his SR comrades to continue the struggle beyond the Urals.

"His life was repeatedly threatened, both by Reds and by Whites. In Yekaterinburg, three separate plots to murder him were uncovered. Disillusionment was spreading among the SRs. One by one, Vasily Ivanovich's comrades were going over to the Whites. And then the blow fell: Kolchak assumed power throughout the region, and all the SRs who could not escape were arrested, and many were killed."

Nina took up the story. "This was Vasily Ivanovich's most heroic hour," she said in an emotional voice. "At a hotel in Omsk, in hiding with a handful of SR survivors who had not gone over to the Whites, he laid plans for a war on two fronts. They would organize a new People's Army and depose Kolchak, and then turn around and attack the Bolsheviks. Despite the odds, still convinced that an uprising of the peasants was imminent, he resolved to undertake the struggle, preferring death in a courageous fight to capitulation. However, he found that because the Whites had already recruited most of the region's anti-Bolshevik manpower, there were few volunteers.

"So with a small remnant of loyal SRs, he started south for Ufa, the capital of Bashkiria, hoping to join forces with his friend, the former secretary of the Bashkiria soviet, Gavril Zorin. It appears that from his previous conversations with Zorin, he believed that Bashkiria would resist Reds and Whites alike, becoming an independent state, the Canaan of liberty-loving Russians everywhere. According to the last report we had, he and his comrades had started for Ufa in the teeth of an early blizzard. On the way, they narrowly escaped capture by the Whites. Eventually, with the Red Army closing in from the north, his companions became disheartened.

Vasily Ivanovich was determined to go on alone, but fearing for his safety, his comrades persuaded him to return with them to Moscow to lead the underground struggle for a government of the Constituent Assembly. We heard this from a certain Volsky, one of his comrades."

"Then Vasily must be here in the city," said Anna.

"Very likely," said Fyodor.

"How will we find him?"

"He still has friends here, and so do we. He'll find you."

There was a silence; then Nina said, "I am certain that Vasily Ivanovich will be successful."

No one spoke. At last, Ehrenburg said gently, "I fear that the odds of success now are small even for a man of Vasily's faith and courage."

"We must all have faith and courage," said Nina. "Odds mean nothing. The peasantry is behind us!"

Dear God, thought Marina, the pure SR gospel.

"We would be honored if you were to stay here with us," said Nina, "until Vasily Ivanovich comes for you."

As the cold spring of 1919 approached, Muscovites faced the nightly threat of predawn arrest and summary execution. Lenin had declared that only extraordinary measures could save the Revolution, and the events of the previous year had steeled his resolve: the murder of Uritsky, the attempt against his own life; the seizure of central Russia by the Whites; the Greens' guerrilla tactics; the struggles of my father and other disaffected socialists to establish a rival government to the east; and the opposition of Boris Savinkov's fanatically anti-Bolshevik paramilitary organization, known as the Union in Defense of the Motherland and Liberty.

Lenin continued to deal with these threats by intensifying the Red Terror. In a letter to his wife, Dzerzhinsky wrote of the nightly shootings in Moscow. "Here we are witnessing a dance of life and death, a moment of truly bloody battle."

Yet despite the repression, the Bolsheviks were still far from feeling secure— and now were all the more determined to arrest my father.

Chapter Thirty-four

THE WOBBLY SLED CARVED RUTS IN THE FRESH SNOW. DENSE MIST crept through the streets. Marina stopped, looking up and down the deserted Tverskoy Boulevard. She adjusted the bundle on the sled and towed it across the broad thoroughfare toward the Arbat, in the heart of Moscow.

It was here on Tverskoy the day before, on another errand to the University Printing Office, that she had seen Gorky riding by in a shiny black American automobile, Max at the wheel. For an instant, her godfather had stared straight at her, but her face had been hidden in the cowl of her mother's winter coat and he had not recognized her. As the car sped away, she caught a glimpse of Peshkova in the backseat, conversing with a man with a long lean face and a sharply pointed beard. She was sure, from descriptions she had heard, that he was Dzerzhinsky.

The encounter had shaken her: her godfather and the high-principled Peshkova in the company of the head of the Cheka, the man responsible for the deaths of thousands of innocent people. She too could fall into his hands at any moment, be stopped and taken to the Lubyanka. Then the persistent question of whether she could keep silent under torture would be answered. And all of it to what purpose? Vasily's struggles to form a government beyond the Urals had failed. Any notion that he might have had of establishing an SR base of power in the Ukraine, much less in Moscow, was nothing but a dangerous dream. How could Anna and the Ilyanovs not see this?

Nonetheless, she had volunteered to transport newsprint for the illegal press whenever it was needed.

Now she could make out the burned rafters of the prince's house against the gray sky.

"Marinotchka!"

She stopped, startled.

"Over here, Marinotchka."

It was her father. He was standing in a doorway, dressed as a peasant, his face blackened with soot, a rag wrapped around his neck. She went over to him, and he drew her to him and embraced her. In a low, urgent voice, he said, "How I've missed you, Marina. Is your mother all right?"

"Yes, she's all right. When did you return? How did you find us?"

"Ehrenburg told me. It was foolish of him to bring you here. It's dangerous for all of us. For the Ilyanovs too."

"Where are you staying?"

"In a safe place." He looked up and down the street. "It's better that you don't know the address. What's important is that you and your mother leave the city as soon as possible. You mustn't stay on at the Ilyanovs. Go tomorrow to the home of the Bratsky brothers on the other side of the Arbat. You remember them—we stopped for a night at their apartment when we arrived from Petrograd. They're expecting you. Be sure you're not followed. I'll make the arrangements for your departure from Moscow. Within three days, I'll come to the Bratskys to see you before you leave."

"Where are we to go?"

"I'll tell you then. There's no time now."

"Will you be coming with us?"

"I'll be joining you as soon as I can. I am organizing a secret SR network to resist Bolshevik authority."

Vasily embraced her again. In the fading light, she saw fear in his eyes.

"Tell your mother that I love her," he said. "I love you too, Marina, very much. Only don't try to find me. Above all, tell no one that you're going to the Bratskys. I'll see you there in three days."

Glancing up and down the narrow street, he walked quickly away in the direction of Tverskoy and disappeared around a corner.

Long into the night, by the light of broken-up Louis Quinze chairs blazing in the fireplace to keep them warm, they discussed Marina's encounter with Vasily. Neither her mother nor the Ilyanovs seemed convinced that the meeting she was describing had actually taken place.

"Didn't he say where he's staying?" asked Anna for the third time.

"I told you," said Marina, exasperated. "He said it's better for us not to know. He said that you and I were to go elsewhere at once, that he was making arrangements for us to leave the city."

"Did he say anything about the Ukraine?" asked Nina.

"No."

"Did he say where you were to go?" asked Fyodor.

Marina hesitated, glancing at him and at Nina. "He did," she said—and nothing more.

They fell silent, firelight wavering on their troubled faces.

When they went to bed in the small servant's room off the kitchen, Marina told Anna about her father's request that they wait for him at the Bratskys while he made arrangements for their departure from Moscow—for a destination he had not revealed.

"Won't he be coming with us?"

"He said he would follow us as soon as he could."

"How did he seem?"

"Under some terrible strain. Not himself."

In bed that night under layers of curtains that served as blankets, Marina tried to tell herself that her father's fearful look reflected the sabotage of the Constituent Assembly, the SRs' failure to reestablish it, and the violent deaths of comrades, but she could not shake off the feeling that something else was weighing on him. She drifted to sleep, dreaming of the cemetery on the hilltop in Khvalynsk, of the steppes reaching into endless space, of Kiril Golovin. The knowledge that such a man existed, when everyone else seemed to be failing her—Dmitry going over to the Whites, Gorky and Peshkova associating with Dzerzhinsky, her father behaving so strangely—kept her from despairing.

. . .

Early the next morning, she and Anna bade farewell to Nina and Fyodor. With their suitcases loaded on one of their hosts' small sleds, they walked to the northern edge of the Arbat. There on a narrow lane they found the ramshackle, two-storied building in which Mark and Yevgeny Bratsky occupied a small apartment. The brothers were retired schoolteachers who had been active in the SR party since their early youth, yet by some miracle they had apparently not yet been identified as "insects" to be squashed.

Yevgeny, the younger brother, greeted his visitors warmly. He made them linden tea, explaining that Mark had gone out in search of wood but would be returning soon. Then he added, "Don't be put off by my brother. He's not well. Life has been very hard for us."

When Mark returned, he barely greeted them. In silence, he spent a long time stacking kindling by the stove. Then he sat down at the table.

"You are welcome here," he said at last. "We promised Vasily that we would help you leave the city, and we shall. But the time has come for him to understand that his cause is lost. Vasily is courageous, God knows, but now it's time to admit defeat and prevent others from making useless sacrifices."

For a long time, no one spoke. Then Anna said softly, "I know that you are right, Mark."

Mark smiled and covered her hand with his. "You don't really believe a single word of what I said, do you, Anna? And yet how many of our friends have perished! We can't let this massacre go on. As for us, I hope we can die soon, here and not in the Lubyanka."

On the morning of the third day, moments after both brothers had left the apartment to forage for food, Marina and Anna heard steps on the stairs followed by a knock. The familiar two double raps. Anna ran to the door. Vasily, wearing a sheepskin coat and carrying two parcels, rushed in, shutting the door behind him quickly. He set the parcels on the dining table, and embraced her. Then he took a copy of the Ilyanovs' *Liberation* from his pocket and spread it on the table.

"Wonderful news!" he said.

Marina expected to see the edition devoted to him that Fyodor had been preparing. Instead, she read:

BASHKIRIA INDEPENDENT!
Bolsheviks Yield to People's Demand for
Autonomous Republic

The paper was dated that very day.

Marina said uneasily, "Yesterday, I read *Pravda* on the wall near Pushkin Square. There was nothing about Bashkiria."

Vasily stood his ground. "The Reds don't want it known that they're not gaining control of that part of the country. But they're granting travel permits to SRs willing to settle there. Anna, you and Marina must go there at once. I've made the arrangements through Bolsheviks who secretly favor accommodations with the SRs. A train leaves this evening at six o'clock." He pointed to the smaller package on the table. "Here are your tickets, permits, some rubles, some provisions for your trip. My friend Gavril Zorin will meet you at the station in Ufa." Vasily spoke in an impatient voice. Marina felt a growing sense of alarm.

"Why aren't you coming with us?" asked Anna in a breaking voice.

"I'll come as soon as I can, I promise," he said. "But I have party responsibilities here first. You'll be all right. The Bratskys will help you get to the railway station with your luggage. It's safer for all of us this way."

Marina said, "But we heard time and again at the Ilyanovs that the Red Army was advancing on Ufa."

"That was weeks ago, Marina. You can read about it in the paper. They were driven back."

Anna was trying to remain calm. "But what should we do if something goes wrong? How can we get in touch with you?"

"Nothing will go wrong," Vasily declared with an edge of despair in his voice. "We'll soon be reunited at Zorin's in free Bashkiria."

Anna looked anxiously at the larger package on the table.

"It's a coat for you, Anna," said Vasily. "I'll bring Marina one like it when I come."

He embraced them both and left hurriedly.

Chapter Thirty-five

WHEN HE HAD GONE, MARINA PICKED UP THE NEWSPAPER. THE INK stained her fingers. "How would the Ilyanovs know what's happened in Bashkiria?"

"What does it matter?" said Anna in a devastated voice. "It's wonderful news."

"Aren't you going to look at the coat?"

Fearfully, Anna opened the parcel. In it was a full-length raccoon coat.

"How beautiful," she said, looking stricken.

Where had he gotten it? wondered Marina. She knew that her mother was asking herself the same question.

That afternoon, the Bratskys loaded Anna and Marina's suitcases on their sled and walked them to Kazan Station. Bundled in their shabby winter clothes, they were wearing blankets as shawls over their overcoats. At the station's entrance, they thanked the brothers for their hospitality. Yevgeny warmly bade them farewell, wishing them good luck. Mark said, "I too wish you good luck, but please remember what I said. The times are different now, and Vasily must know that he is putting us all at risk. Do tell him that."

"We may not see my father for a long time," said Marina, before she realized how these words would sound to her mother.

In the station, they had expected to find a crowd of non-

Bolshevik socialists leaving for freedom in the distant republic, but most of the travelers in the waiting room turned out to be Red Army recruits bound for the front to the east. There was no sign indicating a departure for Ufa. At last, they found an elderly, grim-faced railway employee.

"Is there a train for Bashkiria leaving tonight?" asked Marina.

The man looked at them both oddly and pointed to an unmarked gate at the far end of the station.

Beyond the gate was a train made up of three third-class coaches. On each of the cars was a hand-lettered cardboard sign: UFA. There were only a few people on the platform, waiting in silence. Marina saw no SR acquaintances there, no one she recognized. She felt close to panic. However, sensing that her mother too was desperate, she said nothing.

They settled in a barely heated, vacant compartment, spreading Anna's new raccoon coat over their knees. Marina's heart was racing. She wiped the fogged window and looked out. The platform was almost deserted. Suddenly, their compartment door rolled open.

Two frightened-looking women wearing identical white shawls over their threadbare coats stood in the doorway. They were about Anna's age and looked like sisters. With them was a child, a beautiful blue-eyed boy of about ten.

"May we?" said one of the women.

"Please," said Anna with a welcoming smile.

SRs, thought Marina, good people unwilling to believe that there is no place for them in the former empire anymore. With what superhuman ingenuity did they keep their shawls so white?

The women and the boy settled in the seats opposite them. The boy sat there with his fluffy white fur hat balanced on his knees, looking at Marina shyly.

What a charming child, she thought. Everything he feels shows in his face. What a calamity for a Russian today.

"What's your name?" she asked.

The boy flushed. "Sasha," he whispered.

"I'm Marina."

He tried to smile but only shivered and looked away. His hat fell to the floor. Marina tried to pick it up, but the boy snatched it up first. One of the women took the hat from him and put it on the shelf overhead. She rummaged in her bag and took out a children's book with a blue cover and gave it to the boy. He buried himself in it.

Again the compartment door rolled open. A portly conductor with an upswept mustache like the German kaiser's stood in the passageway. Cold air rushed in.

"Departure is delayed," he announced. "Snow on the tracks. It is not permitted to leave the train."

It quickly became very cold in the compartment. The boy began to shiver, warming his hands between his knees. On an impulse, Anna wrapped the raccoon coat around him. The women watched disapprovingly, but the boy smiled and snuggled into the fur.

The woman sitting next to the boy stared at Anna and Marina for a moment. Then she looked at her companion. They nodded to each other, and then turned to Anna. The first said, "Thank you."

"That's very kind," said the other.

"He looked cold," said Anna.

Now the women competed with each other in taking the Nevskys into their confidence. They were twin sisters, Natalia and Vera. Natalia was a librarian; Vera, a teacher. The boy, Sasha, was Vera's son. His father had been killed at the battle of Tannenburg in 1914. They had been SRs since the turn of the century.

"Mother and I are SRs too," said Marina.

"We knew it," said Natalia. "Didn't we, Vera?"

"Oh, yes. But we weren't quite sure. It's impossible to be sure these days."

"How did you learn about Bashkiria?" asked Anna.

"Through *Liberation*," replied Natalia. "Whoever publishes it is a hero of the party."

Vera said, "Without *Liberation*, we'd never have known. So many of our friends have"—she hesitated, glancing at her sister—"gone."

"We were sure we'd be next," said Natalia.

"It has become impossible to trust those who haven't been arrested."

Natalia looked at her sister disapprovingly.

"Vera doesn't mean you," she assured them.

"We understand," said Anna.

Marina glanced out the window. On the platform, the conductor pulled out a large round pocket watch and frowned at it.

Natalia leaned across the aisle. "Where will it end?" she asked in a low voice. "Only a few days ago, a friend of ours, a librarian who wouldn't hurt a fly, was taken to the Lubyanka. They released her, but others haven't come back."

"The Stepanovs," said Vera. "And the Fedotovs."

"And the Ilyanovs. Such courageous young people."

Marina started. "The Ilyanovs?"

"Fyodor and Nina?" said Anna.

"You know them?" asked Natalia.

"When were they arrested?" asked Marina.

"Our friend the librarian saw them in the Lubyanka—the day before yesterday, wasn't it, Vera?"

Marina looked at Anna. "Then the article in *Liberation* about safe haven in Bashkiria must have been planted by the Cheka," she said in a low voice to her mother, who looked stunned.

Now the boy was staring at her in fear. The sisters' eyes hardened. Natalia drew her snow white shawl closer around her. Vera did the same.

"You must get off the train!" Marina whispered. "The story in *Liberation* has to be a fabrication."

The sisters stared at her in silence.

"This trip to Bashkiria must be a Cheka trap. Try to get away!"

The sisters continued to stare at her, too frightened to speak.

Natalia started to pull the coat off the boy's knees to give it back to Anna.

"Keep it, please," said Anna.

She and Marina took their suitcases down from the overhead shelf, hoping that the sisters would follow their example, but they did not. They think we're Chekists, thought Marina.

"Do get off the train," she said one last time. The sisters still only stared at her.

Marina could not look back at the boy as she and Anna left the compartment.

No one stopped them. The conductor was no longer on the platform. They hurried through the station and out into the freezing night. Marina was certain of one thing: they could not go back to the Bratskys. The streets were empty, yet she was sure that they were being followed. It was snowing lightly.

"Where shall we go?" asked Anna in a dull voice, and Marina

realized that for perhaps the first time in her life, her mother was looking to her for guidance.

"The prince's house," she said. "We can't harm the Ilyanovs—they're no longer there."

They started toward the Arbat, dragging their suitcases along frozen drifts. Marina's arms ached. At Tverskoy Boulevard, they stopped and looked back. A man was flogging a horse hitched to a sledge loaded with two coffins. A bent old woman in black limped along behind the sledge. It was now snowing hard.

They went up the lane that led to the ruins of the prince's mansion. Marina looked back. The woman in black was coming toward them through the snow. No longer limping, no longer bent nor old, she was in fact a sturdy, square-shouldered woman of about forty. As she was catching up with them, she raised her right arm. Down the street, headlights came on, and a heavy van roared toward them.

The woman rushed up to Anna and Marina. "Is he there?" she screamed, pointing to the burned-out mansion as the van drew up beside them.

"Who are you talking about?" asked Anna calmly.

"You know damn well who I'm talking about," shouted the woman. She gestured, and two Chekists jumped out of the van and ran toward Marina and Anna, forcing them into the back of the van. Marina and Anna and the woman in black sat down on plank benches, separated from the men in front by a metal screen. The men then ran into the courtyard of the prince's house. Ten minutes later, they returned.

"Well?" said the woman in black.

"Nothing," said the driver. He got in and started the motor.

The woman glared at Anna. "If we don't find your husband soon, Nevskaya," hissed the woman as they drove off, "you'll be praying we do."

Chapter Thirty-six

LUBYANKA SQUARE WAS AN ISLAND OF LIGHT IN THE HEART OF THE darkened city. Blinding electric lights beamed outward from the walls of the former headquarters of the Russia Insurance Company, now the main interrogation prison of the All-Russia Cheka. The lights cast sharp shadows in the freshly fallen snow, rutted with the tracks of vans converging at the prison gates.

They sped into the courtyard, past a sentry box, and stopped abruptly. The woman in black opened the van's rear door and ordered Anna and Marina out. Then she slammed the door, pounding on it twice. The van sped off into the night.

Inside the prison, their escort turned them over to a uniformed guard, a stout woman with a flat round face and a snub nose. She led them down a long corridor, past doors of translucent amber glass with black letters: COMPTROLLER, MARINE RISKS, FIRE AND CASUALTY. At the end of the corridor, they found themselves in a narrow high-ceilinged hall, where prisoners filled out forms at tables set along the walls, before forming a single file in front of a control desk. Posted instructions told the prisoners how to proceed: they were to list their name, date and place of birth, occupation, and social origin. As Anna was filling out her form, Marina leaned toward her to see what she was writing, but the snub-nosed guard stopped her. Marina gave her name as Dubrovin and her occupation as artist-painter, but left the last space blank.

"No social origin?" said the uniformed man at the control desk, thrusting the paper back at her. "Do you come from the moon?"

Marina wrote "Peasant."

The man frowned. "You don't look like a peasant. You'd better not be lying. They'll find you out quick enough."

A few minutes later, the snub-nosed guard brought them to a spiral staircase leading to the floor below. Soon Marina lost her sense of direction. With its mysterious spaces and stairways leading nowhere, the Lubyanka reminded her of prison interiors in the prints of Piranesi, which she had seen in the Louvre as a child.

They reached a heavy metal door marked RECORDS. Their escort took out a ring of heavy iron keys and unlocked it. An enormous room was filled with women of all ages, some weeping, others sitting silently on wooden benches, staring into space. Several rushed up to the guard.

"I'm innocent! It's a mistake; I've done nothing."

"My little boy's home all alone. Please let me go! I promise to come back!"

"They took me for someone else! I've done nothing against the Soviet government!"

"Write a declaration," said the guard, taking a sheaf of paper from her pocket and throwing it at the women. She left, locking the massive door behind her.

For a moment, the noise subsided. The inmates were picking up the scattered sheets of insurance company stationery, and sharing pencils.

Suddenly, the room filled with piercing shrieks. Women at the far end were grappling with a pretty brown-haired young girl. A long green scarf was wrapped around her neck.

"Some flighty actress from the Moscow Arts Theater," said a blond woman with protruding eyes and bleached hair. "Second time today she's tried it."

Marina saw the iron hook over one of the benches.

"I want to die!" cried the young woman. "I want to die now!"

As fellow prisoners tried to calm her, Marina and Anna settled next to a middle-aged woman with flowing black hair and pale blue eyes who was singing softly to herself.

Little red apple,
Where have you gone?
My lover is dead.
When will you come back?

She sang the words over and over.

Marina felt Anna's hand on hers.

Marina hugged her. "Let's decide what we'll say. The interrogators must know who we are."

"We'll give our real names but say nothing that could help them find Vasily. Not a word about *Liberation* or Bashkiria."

The door opened, and a guard called out their names. Slamming the door behind them, the guard led them into the corridor.

"Stupid bitches!" she muttered.

They went up a flight of stairs and down a long carpeted hall. Which of Dzerzhinsky's inquisitors would they face? Marina wondered. Their names were known all over Moscow. Peters? Latsis? Romanovsky? In a case involving Vasily Nevsky, more than one might be assigned.

But the guard did not lead them to the interrogators. Instead, she took them downstairs again, to a row of padlocked doors. Unlocking the farthest one, she pushed them into a cell-like room, filled almost entirely by a plank bed. The room had no windows, only a small iron screen in the door. The guard locked the door and left. A sentry paced the narrow passageway outside.

On the bed sat a tiny old woman with a long, thin face, frizzy gray hair, and piercing, deeply circled eyes. She was smoking a cigarette, her birdlike head cocked to one side.

"No vacation in Bashkiria?" said the woman, frowning in mock commiseration, then laughing raucously until her laughter became a coughing fit.

"You know who we are?" said Anna.

"Oh yes, my sweets." She patted the bed invitingly. "Sit down with me. As you can see, you have no choice."

Anna and Marina sat on the edge of the bed.

"Do you or Marina Vasilyevna smoke?"

"Neither of us does," said Anna.

"I couldn't last a day without cigarettes. My cousin Prince Golitsyn gets them to me. I suppose he bribes the guards. If they were to arrest him, I don't know what I'd do. But forgive me, I am the Baroness Vologdin. As you must already have guessed, Anna Petrovna, I'm expected to obtain information from you about your husband."

"We don't know where he is," said Anna.

"And you wouldn't tell me if you did, that goes without saying. Nasty moment when they called you out from the communal cell, wasn't it? Didn't know where they were taking you, did you, poor lambs?"

"We thought we were being taken for interrogation," said Marina.

The baroness lit a fresh cigarette from the old one.

"That's the nicer possibility. Who is your interrogator?"

"We don't know," said Anna.

"Mine is Yakov Peters. A vile little man, a sadistic child. But what times we do have together, he and I!" She laughed again, choking on smoke. "They all love to play cat and mouse, you know."

"What are you accused of?" asked Marina.

"Of being born. My aristocratic birth is now a capital crime. My husband was shot for that same offense. They keep me alive because I amuse them."

"And because you're useful to them," said Anna.

"That too," admitted the baroness. Lowering her voice, she added, "If only they knew the truth."

She fell silent as the sentry opened the door and set down three bowls on the floor. The meal consisted of gray cabbage soup on which floated a single drop of green oil. Marina and Anna were famished; they ate while the baroness continued in a hoarse whisper.

"Before the Revolution, my husband was a statesman, a liberal member of the Duma. In February, he saw the Bolshevik danger and joined the SR Party—secretly, of course, because of his position. Nevertheless, he was a sincere admirer of Vasily Nevsky—as indeed is our mutual friend, Tamara Sermus."

Marina glanced at her mother. Anna betrayed no sign of surprise. They remained silent.

"You knew, of course, that she used to be Peters's mistress?"

"Isn't she still?" asked Marina.

"Oh no, that's over. Quite recently—and quite dramatically." She looked owlishly from one to the other.

"How did you meet her?" asked Anna.

Again the baroness patted the bed. "Right here, when Peters sent her to pry information from me. Not that my case mattered; I was already in their hands. But the funny thing is that Tamara and I became friends. She said that it was a joy to speak with a person of refinement, who reminded her of her own family in Estonia. German barons, you know. So instead of trying to pry information from me, she regaled me with hilarious stories about Peters and the other high-ranking Chekists. As you know, Tamara has a lovely sense of humor. We laughed together until the sentry thought we'd lost our minds.

"She told me that she wanted desperately to break off with Peters but was afraid. Little by little, only through hints at first, then freely and in such detail that I was sometimes quite embarrassed, she began telling me about her other lover."

"Lianozov?" said Marina.

"Oh no, dear. That was ancient history. This was a man she was seeing secretly these past few months while she was living with Peters."

Anna said, "Wasn't she afraid of confiding in you?"

The baroness looked at Anna as if her favorable first impressions of her had been shaken.

"You don't understand," she said. "We were friends by then. Friends trust one another."

"Who was her other lover?" asked Marina.

The baroness lit another cigarette.

"She knew him as Count Speransky, a former officer in the Imperial Guard. His estate had been confiscated, and he was reduced to selling firewood for a living. Of course, the Count Speransky I knew was married to an American heiress and was an intimate of the Grand Duke Nikolai. *My* Speransky had fled with his family to the West. Tamara said that it could not be the same person, because her Count Speransky was not married and quite obviously had not escaped to the West. But whoever he was, she was madly in love with him. She lost all sense of caution."

The sentry's footsteps outside interrupted the baroness's tale.

"I'll spare you her descriptions of this man and her trysts with him," she said when the soldier had gone away. "According to her, he was a truly prodigious lover. Forgive me, Marina, I have made you blush, though I assure you I am only sharing a soupçon of what Tamara told me.

"As you can well imagine, being so candid with me, she was even more so with her Count Speransky. She openly mocked Peters and the Cheka. She also revealed certain skeletons in her own closet which she would not tell even me. She only learned—"

The baroness broke off, her eyes widening.

"Listen!"

From a distant part of the prison, Marina heard the drone of engines.

"The trucks," said the baroness, crossing herself.

They waited in silence. They had heard that the Lubyanka trucks used to drown out the sound of the nighttime shootings. The baroness's eyes roved wildly, settling on Anna. "It's your fault!" she said in a loud voice. "You SRs opened the door for the Bolsheviks! It's your fault!"

Instantly, she smiled ingratiatingly.

"I didn't mean that." She was shaking. Her trembling cigarette traced curlicues of smoke. "My nerves, you know. What was I saying? Oh yes, Tamara and Count Speransky. Well, yes, it was exactly as you'd expect. He wasn't a count at all. In Cheka circles, he's known as The Seducer. His specialty is female provocation. He can bring women from rapture in bed to death in the cellars in the same night."

Anna turned pale. "Tamara?"

The baroness shook her head. "Her charm saved her. She seduced a guard and managed to escape. In this, I was able to offer her assistance. Knowing the trouble she was in, I gave her the address of a townhouse of mine near the Bolshoi Theater. Most of the rooms had already been occupied by some dreary Soviet agency—residence permits, I believe—but they had graciously allowed my houseman to stay on in the basement apartment—I presume so that he could work for them. I gave Tamara a note to give to the man, directing him to let her occupy one of the extra rooms below stairs. I don't know whether she's there or not, but wherever she is, she won't be able to go about freely in the streets as long as the Bolsheviks are in power. The Cheka is hunting everywhere for her."

"Wasn't Tamara protected by Peters?"

"Latsis set a trap for her. He and Peters are rivals. Latsis was enraged that Peters had told Tamara Cheka secrets." She glanced at the screen in the door and lowered her voice. "Including the Bashkiria scheme." She hesitated, her eyes darting from one to the other. "You knew?"

Anna and Marina looked at each other in silence.

"You're lucky not to be on your way there." A sly smile played across the baroness's face. For a moment, the attractive young woman she had once been came alive.

"By the way, I was Speransky's first victim. I wasn't going to tell you, but now I have."

Anna drew in her breath. "Why didn't you warn Tamara?"

The baroness swayed her head from side to side as if powerful considerations prevented her from answering.

"You spoke of trust and friendship," insisted Anna. "That's not friendship."

The baroness sighed. "I did try to tell her, time and again. I warned her that such a liaison was extremely risky. She wouldn't listen. I would have told her everything I knew, but I feared that then she might have me shot. Tamara Sermus is a lovely person, but when crossed she is capable of the very worst mischief."

Marina cast a cautionary glance at her mother.

"Besides," continued the baroness, "Tamara was radiantly happy. What good would it have done to spoil her last hours with that divine impostor?" She cocked her head and said defiantly, "What would you have done in my place?"

"I would have warned her," said Anna.

The baroness nodded. "I'm sure you would have. She told me all about you. That's just the sort of foolish thing you would have done. But it was not so much about you that Tamara spoke, but of someone else." She smiled suggestively.

"Who?" said Anna.

"Your husband. He must be a remarkable man. Shall we try to sleep?"

Falling silent, the women stretched out on the bed under their coats. Marina and Anna shaded their eyes with their shawls, since by regulation the overhead bulb could not be turned off. Marina dozed, dreaming of her father swimming out to sea. There was a huge fish in the water which he could not see. She dove into the water and began to swim out to him, but someone was speaking to her. She opened her eyes and found the baroness leaning over her, her face inches from hers, staring at her, her breath foul with tobacco and decay.

"Quick! Tell me where your father is!" she whispered. "Peters is releasing me tonight. I can give your father any message you want."

Marina pushed her away. "We told you we don't know where he is. Please let me sleep."

"I can't bear to see you sleeping," persisted the baroness, shaking Marina. "They'll soon be starting the engines again."

"Leave me alone."

"Do you know what the Death Ship is?"

Marina tried to move away, but the baroness was gripping her shoulders.

"It's the cellar on the other side of the courtyard. My first interrogator Romanovsky took me there once. He made me kneel among the bloody corpses. After a very long time, I heard his voice. 'Get up. A strain on the nerves, Baroness? Never mind. Perhaps you'll be a little more tractable from now on.' He had the guard take me back to my cell."

She's working for them, Marina told herself. She's trying to unnerve us. Then she saw that her mother was awake. Anna leaned over and held the baroness by her thin, trembling arms.

"Don't be afraid," Anna said. The baroness fell back on the bed, shielding her eyes with her hand from the pitiless light.

After that, Marina slept. When she awoke, a key was turning in the padlock. Anna was gone. The baroness was sleeping. The snub-nosed guard stood in the doorway. She motioned to Marina to follow her.

Chapter Thirty-seven

MARINA FOUND HERSELF IN A SUMPTUOUSLY FURNISHED ROOM DECO-
rated with crystal chandeliers and huge mirrors mounted on green
damask walls. A heavy-set man with red hair and a neatly trimmed
red beard sat at a desk in the center of the room. Just behind him,
two men sat at smaller desks. In front of the central desk, a stool
had been placed in the converging beams of two powerful photog-
rapher's lights. To one side, a young male stenographer sat at a
typewriter, staring impassively at Marina, flexing his fingers. Behind
the Chekists was a large stained-glass window depicting a green bird
enveloped in orange flame. Over the bird was an inscription in
Gothic letters:

I am Reborn in Fire

"Sit down," ordered the red-bearded interrogator.

The man's eyes were ice blue. He stroked his beard; the nails of
his well-manicured white hand glistened. From the baroness's de-
scription, Marina guessed that he was Martyn Latsis.

"Name?"

The typewriter began to click.

"Marina Vasilyevna Nevsky."

"Not Dubrovin any more?"

One of the men sitting behind Latsis laughed gruffly. Fringes of gray hair framed the sides of his large, bald head. His face was livid. Violet shadows surrounded his small, sunken eyes.

The third interrogator was a young man with dark bristly hair. His narrow face was bathed in orange light.

"Dubrovin is my mother's name."

"We know that," said Latsis. "We know a great deal about you, Marina. Where is your father?"

"I don't know."

"Useless to lie," said Latsis. "Your mother has already told us. When you've confirmed it, you'll both be released immediately."

What a crude lie, thought Marina. Perhaps she had less to fear from these men than she had thought.

"I don't know where my father is, and neither does my mother."

"You're making a very foolish mistake. Vasily Nevsky is no longer our enemy. Our Central Executive Committee has passed a resolution legalizing the Socialist Revolutionary Party."

"Then my father is no longer an enemy of the people?"

"On the contrary, he is the leader of a legal political party which can play an important role in the building of socialism. All we want is to have a talk with him and straighten a few things out."

"Neither my mother nor I knows where he is."

Latsis smiled. On the desk was a heavy crystal inkstand filled with white powder. He dipped the tip of a tiny silver spoon into the powder and raised it to his nose. The diamond glinted.

"So that's the end of it?" he said, sniffing the powder.

"I'm sure it's not the end of it, but it's the truth."

"You must know where he might be hiding. You could find him if you wanted."

"No one knows where he is. That's how he has survived. He tells no one, not even us."

"Why did you get off the train for Bashkiria?"

"Because we came to believe that we would not be well received in Bashkiria."

Again Latsis smiled. "That's odd. You're an SR. You have a great capacity for optimism." Then, in a mild voice, he said, "But tell me, Marina, are you really an SR at heart?"

"Yes!" she said loudly, thinking to herself, Never more than now.

"Because what a tragedy it would be if you were to sacrifice your parents and yourself for a cause you don't believe in."

She said nothing.

Suddenly, Latsis's eyes blazed, and he shouted, "You're not serving your father by your stubbornness! Only after he comes to us voluntarily will he be protected from the people's wrath! You're placing him and yourselves in extreme danger. Do you understand that?"

"I don't know where my father is. I wouldn't begin to know where to look for him. My parents' friends have all left the city."

Latsis nodded to the interrogator with the bristly hair. The man got up and opened a panel at the side of the stained-glass window. From the courtyard, Marina could hear idling engines and smell exhaust fumes.

She was gripped by fear. I must not show that I'm afraid, she told herself, digging her nails into her palm.

"When did you last see Gorky?"

"July 1917, in Petrograd."

"Are you aware that since then he has changed his political views? He now understands that our supposedly brutal acts are performed in defense of the workers and peasants."

"How can he be heard nowadays? You've prevented him from publishing his magazine."

Latsis examined his fingertips.

"We closed *New Life* because your godfather's lackeys permitted it to wallow in counterrevolutionary filth. But Lenin has always known that Gorky would eventually tell our true story to the world."

"Gorky will never serve any party, yours or ours. He believes in—" She hesitated.

"In man?"

"Yes, in man."

"He still believes in man," said Latsis. "In fact, he and Comrade Dzerzhinsky were discussing that very subject only recently. You see, Gorky now recognizes that we are the rightful custodians of Russia's future—*and* of man's."

"You're not rightful custodians of anything; you're murderers!"

Marina felt as if her voice had taken on a life of its own. She was terrified, though her voice was recklessly brave.

Latsis leaned back in his chair. "Yes, it's true: before we build, we must first clean out the rot of the past. This is why Lenin is now in the Kremlin, and your father is crouching somewhere in a cellar."

"Gorky believes in men as individuals, not as slaves," said the brave voice.

"Marina, we aren't carrying out a war against individuals. The first question we ask an accused is—to what class does he belong? what is his upbringing? his background?" In a suddenly threatening voice, he said, "You claim to be a peasant?"

"My great-grandfather was born a serf."

"His son, your grandfather, was a civil servant, a member of the lesser nobility."

"As was Lenin's father."

"Your mother's people were wealthy landowners."

"My mother is a revolutionary," she said. "Our party made your October coup possible!"

Latsis nodded. "An interesting theory." He spoke over his shoulder to the bald interrogator. "No one would deny that the SRs were of some service to us in paving the way for the October victory, would they, Romanovsky?"

"No one," said Romanovsky in a voice so low that it was barely audible. Remembering the baroness's story about the Death Ship, Marina could not look at him.

"In your case," pursued Latsis, "your class origins are mixed. You give your profession as painter. What kind of painter are you? Modernist? Traditional?"

"Traditional."

Marina felt herself falling into a trap. All they want is my father, she told herself.

She remained composed. Latsis asked in an offhanded way, "When did your father last see Boris Savinkov?"

"I don't know."

"When did you last see Baranov?" Latsis waited for her reply, watching her closely now. "Surely you haven't forgotten your learned mentor at the Hermitage. Let me refresh your recollection."

He nodded to the soldier, who opened one of the room's side doors.

Supported by a guard, Andrey Baranov stood there, head bowed, emaciated, his once animated features waxen like those of a corpse.

"Look up, Baranov," said Latsis sharply.

Slowly, the old man raised his head. His eyes found Marina's and brightened for an instant; then his face became expressionless again.

Marina cried out, "You're thugs! An elderly man! How can you treat him this way? He's committed no crime!"

"Untrue. Comrade Baranov is guilty of theft of the People's property. Valuable paintings belonging to the state were found in his apartment. Isn't that so, Baranov?"

Almost imperceptibly, the old man nodded.

Latsis gestured to the guard, who led the prisoner out the side door, closing it behind him. He shuffled through papers, ignoring Marina.

After a moment, he nodded to the young interrogator, who again opened the panel at the side of the window, leaned out, and raised his arm. In the courtyard, the engines of the trucks revved up.

Marina tried to struggle against the stark fear that was overcoming her. The lights blinded her. The engines below were racing at full throttle, filling the room with fumes. The stenographer took out a handkerchief and covered his nose.

"Your father must come in and talk things over with us!" Latsis shouted over the roar.

Marina recoiled, shutting her eyes. The mirrors rattled against the walls. She looked up again, and in the colored halos of light she saw a fifth man in the room.

He stood behind Latsis, his long swarthy hands resting lightly on the interrogator's shoulders. She recognized the sharply pointed beard. Dzerzhinsky!

"So here is the lovely daughter of Vasily Nevsky," said the head of the Cheka. "Russia's great hope."

The three interrogators broke into loud laughter.

Dzerzhinsky did not laugh. He stared at Marina for a long time; then he left through the side door.

The trucks' engines were idling again.

"You are free to leave the Lubyanka, Marina," said Latsis. "The guard will explain the arrangements we are making for you."

Her throat dry, Marina could barely speak.

"I want to stay with my mother."

"Impossible," said Latsis. "You have a task to perform in the service of the people. You will find your father and tell him that there is no reason for him to fear us. Once he comes out of hiding, the three of you will go free."

"But I've told you the truth—I don't know where he is."

"You'll find him. For if you do not, I cannot guarantee your mother's safety. Her fate is now in your hands."

The stenographer ripped the sheet of paper from the typewriter and handed it to Latsis, who pushed the page across his desk, offering Marina a pen.

"Please sign," he said.

Marina tried to read the densely printed words, but they swam before her eyes. She signed her name at the bottom of the page.

"You have until midnight Saturday," said Latsis.

As she got up and started to leave the room, the stenographer was again flexing his fingers, watching her with a cryptic smile.

Chapter Thirty-eight

CARRYING MARINA'S SUITCASE, A CLOSEMOUTHED YOUNG CHEKIST walked her to the nearby National, one of Moscow's most fashionable hotels now requisitioned as a residence for high-ranking Bolsheviks. In Marina's pocket, in place of her passport, was a document known as a "wolf's ticket," which identified her as being under Cheka surveillance. From the curiosity exhibited by the guards at the hotel desk, she sensed that her arrival there was not a routine event.

Her room on the second floor was furnished with a desk and a chair, a loveseat, and a large bed with plump pillows and thick woolen blankets. The radiators were warm. The electric lamp on the desk worked; the electrified chandelier did not. The room smelled of tobacco. She went to the window overlooking Tverskaya Street and tried to open it. It was stuck fast. She could hear in the next room the faint sound of a typewriter being struck one key at a time. She went to the door and tried to lock it, but the bolt was broken. She sat on the bed and inspected her wolf's ticket. It was valid until midnight Saturday. The very hour that her mother was to die if her father had not given himself up. She counted off the days since their arrest. It was Thursday. She had barely three more days.

In the bathroom was a large tub standing on lion's paws. She filled it with hot water and took her first real bath since Khvalynsk.

Perhaps it would clear her head, she thought, but as she was drying herself, she felt a wave of panic. What if she *were* to find her father? Would he give himself up? And even if he did, would her mother be spared? And what would happen to him? She had not for an instant believed Latsis's assurance that the Bolsheviks no longer regarded him as an "enemy of the people."

Where could she turn for help?

She remembered Gorky in her father's study in Alassio: he had foreseen that her parents would need her help one day. Now that that day had come, she felt powerless.

She put on her plaid dress with the narrow waist and small round collar. It was warm and always lifted her spirits.

There was a rap at the door.

"Come in," she said.

Sergei Lomov entered the room. Marina was so utterly worn out that at first she found his presence in her hotel room natural and welcome. Then she thought, Dear God, he is working for them.

"It's not as you think, Marina," said Sergei in a low voice.

"How did you find me?"

"I overheard at the Lubyanka that you were arrested and taken here. I'm a telegrapher there now. So many telegraphers have been shot in Moscow that they transferred me here. It's not an especially secure profession. Our dots and dashes that they can't read make us suspect."

"Why have you come?"

"To bring you this." He held out an apple. "And some bad news about a friend."

She took the apple. "Dmitry?"

He nodded. "Captured near Saratov with a detachment of Savinkov's Whites. They were all shot, every one."

She stared at the shiny red surface of the apple.

"He loved you, Marina."

"I loved him too, very much," she said. Then, remembering Dmitry's words, "You have given me reason to take the highest path," she burst into tears. Sergei came to her and embraced her. After a moment, she drew away from him in alarm. "You must go at once," she said. "You're in danger here."

"First let me ask you something."

Please don't let him ask me where my father is, she prayed.

"How long did Latsis give you?"

She remained silent.

"That's right. Trust no one."

"Midnight Saturday."

"You must go to Gorky."

"Latsis says he's gone over to them."

"It may be true, but no matter what, your godfather will help you. Lenin listens to him. The whole world listens to him. Gorky's is the only independent voice left in Russia."

"Where is he now?"

"Petrograd, but he's expected back here next week for a meeting of his art preservation committee. When he's here, he stays at Peshkova's apartment on Lyalin Lane."

"Does the Cheka follow him?"

"Like his shadow, so you must be extremely careful. Alas, Marina, these are not the happier times I'd hoped for." He took her hands in his. "I'll never forget you." He looked at her for a moment, kissed her on the cheek, and then slipped out the door.

The apple had fallen to the floor. She picked it up and went out into the corridor, but Sergei was gone. The door to the next room was open. An old man with long white hair was sitting at a tall typewriter very much like her father's. He smiled at her. She nodded to him and went back into her room, leaving the door ajar. She put the apple in the drawer of her night table and went to the window. Suddenly, she started sobbing: the realization that Dmitry was dead tore at her heart. To die so young—and for such a cause! For the Whites! For Savinkov! Yet, what did it matter? There were no longer good causes or bad, only early death for no reason. She looked down at the street.

An automobile stood at the curb of Tverskaya Street, vapor curling from its exhaust. She watched Sergei go out and turn right toward Red Square. Suddenly, the car left the curb, made a U-turn, and skidded to a stop next to him. Two men jumped out and forced him into the back. The car lurched forward and sped away toward Lubyanka Square. Marina stood at the window, staring down at the black tracks the automobile had left on the snow-dusted cobblestones.

"May I?"

Marina spun around, startled. A woman in a severe black dress stood in the doorway.

"Excuse me, Marina Vasilyevna," said the woman. "Your door was open. I am Lydia Divilovskaya. My husband is the editor of *Izvestia.*"

Everything about this fleshy, motherly-looking woman with her straight gray hair gathered in a knot at the back of her head put Marina on her guard.

"How do you know who I am?"

"Everyone knows who you are. Everyone's buzzing about Nevsky's daughter being here as a guest of the Excess-ka, as we call the Cheka." She laughed at her witticism. "I thought you might need a friend."

"That's kind of you, but I'm quite all right."

"You must be hungry. Come downstairs and have supper with my daughter and me. We're saving a place for you."

Marina was famished. The smell of food that wafted into the room was tantalizing. She hesitated.

The woman laughed again. "Of course, I understand completely. You feel that you're in a den of wolves. But come along, our teeth aren't as sharp as you've been led to believe."

Marina decided that it was best not to offend this disagreeable woman who was probably dangerous.

"Yes, thank you," she said. "I am very hungry."

As they passed Marina's neighbor's open door, Divilovskaya nodded curtly to the old man at the typewriter. He returned the salutation with exaggerated amiability.

"Ridiculous old fool," Divilovskaya whispered as they started down the stairs. "Don't have anything to do with him."

She led Marina down to a large, low-ceilinged room furnished with heavy wooden tables and chairs, its dark walls lighted by electric sconces. "Before the Revolution, this dining room was for the hotel staff," said Divilovskaya. "Nowadays, it's for us."

A dozen diners looked up at them as Marina followed Divilovskaya to a table occupied by a thin, angular young woman with close-cropped blond hair. She was smoking a cigarette in a long ivory holder.

"My daughter Larissa," said Divilovskaya as they sat down. "The joy and bane of my life."

"Mother!" said the young woman irritably, sliding her chair away from her mother and closer to Marina.

Larissa was about twenty-five, her powdered skin white against her heavily rouged lips and mascaraed eyes. She wore a stylish mauve silk dress, which contrasted with the strict attire favored by her mother and the other women in the room. She smelled of expensive perfume.

Ignoring her daughter, Divilovskaya proceeded to identify everyone in the room.

"Our Commissar of Enlightenment," she said, nodding toward a slender man in his early forties wearing small round glasses, who was conversing with a tall, elegant-looking woman sitting across from him. Anatoly Lunacharsky looked younger than Marina had imagined him, more like an aging student than a Bolshevik commissar. The woman with whom he was talking smiled at Marina, and then glanced with disapproval at Divilovskaya and Larissa.

"And who is the woman?"

"The Red Madonna herself," said Larissa sarcastically. "Alexandra Kollontai, a general's daughter who has insinuated herself into Lenin's good graces. The happy result is that she is now the Commissar of Public Welfare."

Divilovskaya frowned. "The truth is that Madame Kollontai is looking out for the welfare of the people, while Lunacharsky is teaching them to read and write. As I told you, we are not all ogres."

"Some of us are," said her daughter with a wicked laugh.

"Stop this minute!" hissed Divilovskaya, as a waiter in black livery and white gloves served them plates of food. The portions were minute, but to Marina the meal was a feast: potato dumplings with mushroom sauce, cranberry pudding, a slice of white bread.

"Marina," said Larissa, "surely you've noticed the arch-ogre." She nodded toward a far corner of the room. With a start, Marina recognized Felix Dzerzhinsky. He was sitting alone, staring at her steadily as he had done in the interrogation room earlier that day. Feeling dizzy, Marina averted her eyes.

"The head of the Excess-ka," said Larissa in a loud whisper. "Doesn't he remind you of a Spanish inquisitor with his pointy little beard?"

"Any more of this and I'm leaving the table," said Divilovskaya.

Larissa pretended to shudder. "I'm so scared. Aren't you scared, Marina?"

Divilovskaya leaned close to Marina. "It is a tragedy for Russia that your father's valuable contributions to the agrarian question are lost to her people."

"For God's sake, Mother! Don't be ridiculous."

"You would be doing him and our poor country such a great service if—"

"Mother! Marina's not a fool!"

Divilovskaya reddened. "You're the fool!" she said and rose from the table. "Forgive me, Marina, I have some telephone calls to make." She got up and strode out of the room, followed by the stares of the diners.

Larissa smiled coquettishly. "You must forgive me as well, Marina. As you see, my mother and I are not on the best of terms." She leaned closer. The smell of her perfume overwhelmed Marina. "All I want is to leave this ghastly country," she paused. "Is Paris as beautiful as they say?"

"Yes, it is," said Marina, struggling to keep her composure.

"You're very beautiful," said Larissa.

Marina felt herself blushing.

"Perhaps we can help each other. As you may have guessed, my mother works for Latsis. So do most of the Chekists in this hotel. You can't go to your father without being followed. I could. I could warn him of the threat to your mother." Larissa lowered her voice. "Let's go to your room. We can talk there."

"I don't think we have anything to talk about."

"Tamara Sermus, perhaps?"

Marina left the door to her room open. Larissa closed it and went to the window, gazing out toward the Kremlin.

"How I loathe this despicable place," she said. "I would give anything to live in Paris."

"How do you happen to know Tamara Sermus?" asked Marina in a detached voice, sitting down at the desk. Larissa left the window and stretched out on Marina's bed.

"Through my mother's connections. For a while, Tamara was living with Peters."

"Where is she now?"

"In hiding." Then in a casual voice, she asked, "How much do you know about her?"

"Very little. She told us about herself when we first met her, but I didn't know what to believe. Later, I heard that she had been an Okhrana agent."

"It's true. Recruited by Azef himself."

"How do you know that?"

"From dear Mama, who heard it from Peters. Don't be fooled by her boring little Excess-ka jokes. Mama's in the thick of it." She smiled at Marina. "Tamara's very pretty, isn't she?"

Larissa was looking at her intently, her face slack. "And you are very pretty, Marina. Don't blush." She ran her fingers through her blond hair. Then she drew a pillow behind her and sat up. "Come over here."

Marina's heart was pounding. No one had ever repelled her as much as this woman.

"Don't you ever get lonely?" asked Larissa in a soft voice, patting the bed beside her.

At that moment, there was a knock at the door. Marina quickly went to open it. The white-haired man stood in the doorway.

"I'm sorry," he said. "I didn't know you had a visitor, Marina Vasilyevna. I am your neighbor, Kaverin. My wife and I were hoping you might drop in for a visit."

"I'd love to," said Marina.

"Why don't you join us as well, Larissa?" asked Kaverin.

Larissa flounced off the bed. With a toss of her bobbed hair, she stalked out of the room without a word.

The Kaverins' room was filled with books and manuscripts stacked in shelves and on tables. Kaverin's wife, as white-haired as he, had a wrinkled, fine-boned face and a friendly smile. In a flash of recognition, Marina remembered where she had seen Kaverin.

"You used to visit us on the rue Gazan. You were a friend of my father's."

"I was, and I remember you well, dear Marina. You used to sit on your father's lap and look visitors over with a critical eye. You were especially stern with us Marxists."

"For good reason, as it turned out," said his wife.

"As you see," said Kaverin, "Sofia Markovna is even less prudent than I. She is an SR, and I—a Bolshevik."

"Please don't worry, Marina," said Sofia Markovna. "No one here pays the slightest attention to this particular Bolshevik."

Kaverin nodded. "Very true, and let's hope my luck holds. I trust you didn't mind the interruption, Marina."

"I was grateful for it."

"I thought you might be. What do you know about your visitor?"

"Only that she's the daughter of the editor of *Izvestia*."

"Did she mention her fiancé?"

"No."

Kaverin and his wife looked at each other.

"Yakov Peters," Kaverin said in a low voice.

Marina looked at him in astonishment.

"I wish I could help you," he went on. "When I heard that Nevsky's daughter was here, I remembered a night I spent with Vasily Ivanovich in Paris in the summer of 1904. We'd made the rounds of the Left Bank cafés, talking about everything under the sun until the waiters started to pile the chairs on the tables. Toward dawn, strolling across the Pont des Arts, we discovered that we had the same vision of the future Russia. A federation of free communes with no secret police, no death penalty. The fact that we, members of rival parties, should share this simple yet magnificent idea astounded us. We embraced, certain that one day the Revolution would sweep away all barriers between socialists."

"Show Marina what you've been writing," said Sofia Markovna.

Kaverin handed Marina the top page of a thick manuscript lying next to the typewriter.

Against the Death Penalty
by Appolon Kaverin

"My doubts about the notion that the end justifies the means began with that walk," he said. "You must be proud of your father."

"I am," said Marina. "Very proud."

Kaverin sighed. "Unlike him, I first saw the October takeover as a harsh but temporary measure. I closed my eyes to the escalating repressions. The birth of the new society had to be painful, like childbirth, as Lenin never tires of saying."

He took the page from her and put it back on the stack. "Unfortunately, at present a death sentence hangs over every Russian citizen—and over our future."

There was a creaking outside the door. Sofia Markovna got up and opened it and looked up and down the hallway. Closing the door again, she put her finger to her lips. Kaverin went on as if nothing had happened. "Your father's dream of a just society in Russia will be realized, my dear Marina, though probably not in our generation. In yours perhaps, or in that of your children. But one day, it will happen." He took her hand. "When you see your father again, please do tell him that I have not forgotten our night in Paris."

"I'll tell him," she said. "And thank you for rescuing me from a very unpleasant encounter."

She went back into her room and opened the drawer of her night table. Sergei's apple was gone.

For a long time, she could not fall asleep. She remembered Dmitry standing with her on the stone bridge across the Moika Canal, smiling at her in the reflected light from the water. She thought of Baranov in the interrogation chamber, and the racing engines and the shots echoing in the courtyard. Why had Sergei come to see her at the hotel? Could his arrest below her window have been staged?

When she awakened, morning light was creeping around the fringes of the thick damask curtains. She dressed and went out into the hall. From downstairs, she heard a distant clatter of plates. She knocked at the Kaverins' door. There was no answer. She knocked again. She tried the door. It was unlocked.

For a moment, she thought that she was in the wrong room. The Kaverins and all their belongings had disappeared. Everything was gone: the bed had been stripped, and the books and papers and typewriter were gone. Marina went back to her room in a state of shock. Then she remembered Latsis.

"This is Friday," said her brave voice. "I have two more days. I must go to Peshkova's on the chance that Gorky will be there."

Chapter Thirty-nine

Outside the hotel, the glare of damp cobblestones in the sun blinded Marina. Passing the Kremlin on the Savior's Gate side, she came upon a row of frozen corpses laid out against the fortress wall. Emaciated people, their faces wrapped in rags, were silently loading the rigid bodies onto a horse-drawn wagon. Two Red Army men armed with pistols were supervising them. One of them came up to Marina.

"This is your lucky day, comrade," he said. "You have just been appointed a deputy of the Sanitation Committee. Get busy!"

Marina took out her wolf's ticket from the pocket of her coat and handed it to the man.

"I'm under Comrade Latsis's orders," she said.

The soldier gave her back the document as if it had burned his fingers.

"Then carry them out, comrade. Why are you wasting time here?"

On Lyalin Lane, she recognized the building that Anna had pointed out to her on one of their walks the previous winter. It was a contemporary, four-story structure in the art nouveau style. As she started toward it, she heard a shattering roar. She stepped back into a doorway as Max Peshkov, wearing a military tunic and crouched over the handlebars of an enormous motorcycle, sped by. In the sidecar, wearing a cap with a shiny black leather visor, rode Felix Dzerzhinsky.

Max swerved and came to an abrupt stop at the building's entrance, causing the head of the Cheka to lurch forward and brace himself against the cockpit of the sidecar.

"That's enough, Max!" Dzerzhinsky protested, as Max, grinning, shut off the engine. "We're not out for a joyride."

Marina waited until the men had gone inside; then she turned back down Lyalin Lane. She walked briskly toward the center of the city.

A half hour later, she reached the National, passed through the gauntlet of staring guards, went up to her room, and stretched out on the bed, feeling completely helpless. Since childhood, she had thought of her godfather as her protector, but now he was surrounded by enemies—and had perhaps become an enemy himself. She fell into a deep sleep.

A sharp knock at the door awakened her.

Ekaterina Peshkova stood in the doorway.

Marina did not immediately recognize her. She saw a tiny woman with graying hair wearing a maroon overcoat with a worn fur collar and high rubber overshoes. Only her fine gray eyes recalled the beautiful woman Gorky's first wife had once been.

"Get your things, Marina. You're coming home with me."

Marina's thoughts raced. She thought of Dzerzhinsky and Max going into the building on Lyalin Lane. She thought of Latsis warning her not to seek out Gorky. Did Peshkova know of Latsis's ultimatum?

"Thank you, Ekaterina Pavlovna," she said, "but I have to stay here. Comrade Latsis—How did you know I was here?"

"It's all arranged. Come along, child."

In the late afternoon light, the sky turning orange, they set forth for Lyalin Lane, Marina towing her suitcase on the child's wagon which Peshkova had brought for that purpose. The streets were empty.

"My apartment is chilly," said Peshkova, "but there're enough blankets to go around. We manage."

"You and Max?"

"And my mother. Babushka, everyone calls her. She's deaf and

259

cranky, but you mustn't mind her. As for Max, he's never home. He's at the Military Academy all day and out with his wretched theater friends all night, whenever he's not racing around the city on his ridiculous motorcycle. I wish to heaven his father had given him his love of literature instead of that infernal machine."

They walked in silence. Peshkova glanced at Marina with the hint of a smile.

"As a matter of fact, there's someone else at the apartment right now. Someone you know."

"My godfather?"

"Alexey Maximovich has business in Petrograd," said Peshkova coldly.

"When will he be returning to Moscow?"

"Sunday, unless his plans change again."

Marina's heart sank. Even if Gorky were to agree to see Lenin immediately, he would be too late to save her mother.

"However, young Golovin is there, eagerly awaiting your arrival."

"Kiril?" asked Marina, incredulous.

"He told me that you and he became acquainted in Khvalynsk."

"We did," said Marina with a rush of pleasure. "Isn't he still fighting with the Greens?"

"No longer. He came back from the Volga. Soon afterward, his father died suddenly. Kiril has just returned from the funeral in Finland. Now he'll be helping me with Red Cross work."

"Will I be able to see my mother?"

"Tomorrow, we'll go to the Lubyanka. You'll see her then."

"Is she all right?"

"She's a strong woman. Instead of feeling sorry for herself, she comforts others."

Marina glanced questioningly at Peshkova, wondering if she knew of the danger threatening Anna.

"I do know what Latsis told you," said Peshkova.

"Does Mother?"

"I didn't say anything, but she must know. Latsis would make sure of that."

Peshkova was looking at Marina with a mixture of compassion and impatience.

"I want to help you, Marina," she said in a lowered voice. "But for the sake of the political prisoners, hundreds of them, I've had to make certain accommodations which cannot be jeopardized. As for Gorky, don't pin too much hope on him. He has a new friend who is advising him not to pester Lenin for favors."

They dragged Marina's suitcase and the wagon up to an apartment on the third floor. The living room, furnished with a large round table and wicker chairs, was warmed by a fire in the large enamel stove. At one end of the room, there was an alcove with potted palms on either side of an aquarium. In its murky water, a large yellow goldfish with a streaming white tail sculled languidly in place.

In the half darkness, a fierce-looking old woman with a gray shawl drawn tightly around her shoulders was settled in one of the wicker chairs. She stared at Marina, her gnarled fingers slowly winding wool from a pile at her feet onto a ball.

"The electricity's out," she said petulantly.

"It's out every evening, Mother," said Peshkova in a resigned voice. "This is Marina."

"How do you do, Madam," said Marina.

"Speak up, girl. I can't hear you."

Raising her voice, Marina repeated her greeting.

The old woman stared at her. "At least she has manners."

Kiril Golovin walked into the room. Marina caught her breath. Taller, more youthful than she remembered, with waves of dark hair framing a long, handsome face, wearing a dark red blouse with a high collar buttoned at the neck, he reminded Marina of one of Botticelli's thoughtful young men. He came up to her, and they shook hands ceremoniously.

"I'm glad to see you again, Marina Vasilyevna," he said. "I was sorry to have had to leave you so abruptly in Khvalynsk."

"We'd never have reached Saratov without your help. You saved our lives."

Peshkova said, "Come to the table, children. Marina has had nothing to eat all day. Neither have you, Kiril."

"Has Marina her ration coupons?" asked Babushka, taking the chair nearest the stove.

"Mother, please don't fret about such things."

Kiril and Marina sat next to each other in creaky wicker armchairs. From the kitchen, Peshkova brought out a pot of barley gruel and a bottle of sunflower oil.

"Where is the bread, Mother?" she asked wearily.

"Bread? There isn't a crumb in the house."

Peshkova set down the pot and disappeared down the hallway, returning with a half-eaten loaf of black bread.

"Respect," said Babushka, appealing to Marina. "Whatever happened to respect for elders in decent households?"

After the meal, the old woman went down the hallway to her room. Marina and Kiril helped Peshkova carry the dishes to the kitchen; then they sat down in the living room by the warmth of the stove. Peshkova said sternly, "Don't stay up late. Tomorrow, we leave at dawn."

When they were alone, Marina asked Kiril, "Will you be going with us to the Lubyanka?"

"I'll go with you as far as the Red Cross depot on Kuznetsky Most. I'm helping Ekaterina Pavlovna bring food to the prisoners."

She was silent. Kuznetsky Most. The street was familiar to her. It had been there, in the apartment that had been Vasily's sanctuary in 1905, that she had met Boris Pasternak. It now seemed another life.

"I was lucky to see my father before he died," said Kiril. "I'd just left Antonov and come back to Finland to seek his advice. I knew that there must be some better way to help Russia than to fight with the Greens. No one hated Lenin more than my father. Or loved Russia more. He shared your father's political views, and though he was too weak for long conversations, I did have time to tell him about my meeting with you in Khvalynsk. He told me that he remembered Gorky speaking of a goddaughter who wanted to be a Knight of the Round Table."

"I'm pleased that he remembered."

Sorrow crossed Kiril's face. "Gorky and my father had been intimate friends. But even before the Revolution, they parted ways. My father had a clear intuition of Lenin's true nature. Later, he deplored the Bolsheviks' exploitation of Gorky's international reputation to their own advantage."

After a moment, Marina asked, "Will you rejoin the Greens?"

"No, Marina, I can no longer bear the killing. Nor do I believe that there's hope for a democratic government in Russia, not for a long time."

"Kiril—"

He leaned close to her. "Peshkova told me about your mother."

"I don't know what to do," she said. "She said that Gorky won't be here until Sunday. Who is his new friend?"

"A certain Baroness Budberg. Arrested by the Cheka and freed through his direct appeal to Lenin."

"What happened to Andreyeva?"

"They separated. She's become the People's Commissar for Foreign Trade. Among her other duties, she is assigned to sell confiscated artworks abroad for foreign currency."

"And Gorky was so committed to keeping national treasures in Russia!"

Lowering his voice, Kiril said, "He may not know. It's part of the net of lies that are being woven around him."

At that moment, the rumble of Max's motorcycle in the street below filled the room and then died abruptly. Moments later, they heard his heavy steps on the stairs.

"Watch out for Max," said Kiril. "Lenin has enlisted him to bring his father into the Bolshevik fold."

He broke off. A key was turning in the lock.

Max burst into the entrance hall, a military cap cocked over one eye.

"Where is the ravishing Marina d'Alassio?" he asked in a thick voice. "Where is the world's foremost woman painter?" He groped his way into the room, stumbling heavily against the dining table.

"Long live electrification," he muttered. Marina saw that his face was flushed.

"Ah, but who have we here?" he said, drawing back from Kiril in a theatrical gesture. "The Hero of the Steppes. The Avenger of the Rural Downtrodden." He bowed unsteadily to Kiril.

"You're drunk, Max."

"Very true. But at least I'm not an enemy of the people."

Kiril did not reply.

"You make a perfect pair," pursued Max. "Two little finches caught in the whirlwind. Where in the paradise of the proletariat will you make your nest?"

"Go to bed, Max," said Kiril.

"Perchance to dream. That's Shakespeare. William Shakespeare knew all about high and mighty people being destroyed by history."

Marina and Kiril were silent.

"Where's Daddy, Marina? Everyone's dying to know."

"I don't know where my father is."

Max laughed. "Don't you wish you could climb up into your fig tree again and hide from the world? Everything's so tough right now, isn't it? So confusing." He laughed again; then in an ominous tone, he added, "By the way, if you're thinking of involving my father in your schemes, you're in for a disappointment. Gorky has made his peace with the twentieth century."

Crashing against a wall, he left the room. A moment later, he returned, forefinger at his lips.

"Comrades, be vigilant," he said. "Babushka never sleeps."

At last, they heard his bedroom door slam shut.

Kiril drew his chair closer to Marina's. "I want to help you," he said.

"You already have."

"I don't understand."

"You may have told me where my father is. You mentioned Kuznetsky Most. During the events of 1905, an apartment there was his hiding place from the police. I don't know why I didn't think of it earlier."

"And if he is there?"

Marina did not answer.

"Your father will certainly give himself up when he hears of Latsis's ultimatum," said Kiril.

"I must tell him!" she exclaimed. "I won't let my mother die!"

"Gorky will help. There may still be time."

"But he won't be here until Sunday."

"His plans could change. Peshkova says they often do. I'd wait a little."

"Should I? In Saratov, a friend once told me that I had good instincts. Right now, I'm not sure of anything."

Chapter Forty

On Saturday morning, Marina, Peshkova, and Kiril walked to the Red Cross office on Kuznetsky Most. There, after loading two hand-pulled wagons with boxes of food, they separated. Kiril headed in the direction of the Butyrskaya Prison; Marina and Peshkova, toward the Lubyanka. Now Marina could see far up the street the second-floor windows of Number 131 Kuznetsky Most. She was tempted to go there at once, but instead decided to wait for Gorky to return to Moscow before searching for her father, as Kiril had suggested.

When they were entering Lubyanka Square, a military van drew up beside them. A burly Chekist jumped down.

"What's in the wagon, ladies?"

"Red Cross food for the political prisoners," said Peshkova in a clear voice. "Let us pass, please."

"Red Cross," he said derisively. "We'll save you the trouble and deliver the food for you."

"Can you read?" Peshkova asked authoritatively, handing him a sheet of paper.

The Chekist's eyes widened as he read the document.

"What's your name?" demanded Peshkova, snatching it from him.

The man stared at her a moment; then he jumped back into the van and drove off.

"At least they still know they work for Felix Dzerzhinsky," she said.

The guard at the sentry box waved them through. Marina followed Peshkova as she towed the wagon into the wing that housed the women political prisoners.

A female guard stood by the door. She eyed the wagon covetously.

"God bless you, Ekaterina Pavlovna," she said. "I have three starving children at home."

"The food is for the prisoners," said Peshkova firmly. "You filch enough as it is."

The guard glared at her, but unlocked the door.

Marina found herself in a communal cell similar to the one in which she and her mother had been held after their arrest, except that, in this room, the women were completely silent. They were staring toward the far end of the cell.

At the end of the room, Anna was sitting on a wooden bench near a massive steel door. In her arms, she held a young girl with a delicate, almost translucent face. Her long dark hair was undone. She was sobbing. Anna was rocking her gently and stroking her hair.

Peshkova said softly to Marina, "They're taking the girl to the Death Ship."

Marina was horrified. The girl was younger than she, no more than fifteen or sixteen. She thought of André Chénier's "Young Captive," a poem she knew by heart. The French Terror was being repeated in the twentieth century.

Anna looked up and saw Marina. She beckoned to her, and Marina crossed the cell and sat next to her mother.

"Lisa, this is my daughter, Marina," said Anna.

The girl's eyes fluttered and for an instant found Marina's. Then she looked up at Anna.

"Is there a hell, Anna Petrovna?"

"No, Lisa. There is no hell."

Marina heard heavy footsteps beyond the steel door.

The girl seized Anna's wrist. "Then there's no heaven either!" she cried.

"Yes, there is," said Anna soothingly.

"My beloved Paul could not have betrayed me!" the girl cried out as the metal door slowly swung open. A male guard burst in and seized the girl who clung to Anna.

"No, Lisa. Paul loves you. He'd never betray you."

The girl released Anna's wrist, and the guard dragged her through the door and down the stone stairs. The sound of the steel door slamming shut reverberated through the cell.

In the silence that followed, Anna said to Marina, "Her darling Paul was Count Speransky."

The women were beginning to move about and converse in low voices. Some were weeping. Marina put her arms around Anna, whispering, "I think I know where father is."

"Don't look for him!" Anna said sharply.

"At the Kuznetsky Most apartment."

Anna drew in her breath. "Don't go there, Marina!"

Marina searched her mother's face, trying to tell whether she knew about the sentence that hung over her.

Suddenly, Anna embraced Marina, holding her tight.

"I do love you," she whispered. "I know I haven't always shown it, but I love you more than anything in life. No matter what happens, remember that." She looked at Marina as if she were seeing her for the first time.

Peshkova lead Marina out of the cell.

Chapter Forty-one

LATE IN THE MORNING, MARINA AND PESHKOVA RETURNED TO LYALIN Lane. In the apartment, they found Babushka, an unhappy expression on her face, tossing bread crumbs to the goldfish.

"If you feed them too much, they die," she said.

"What happened?" said Peshkova.

"The telephone rang."

"Who was it?"

"Alexey Maximovich."

"Did he say when he was coming?"

"It was impossible to understand him."

In vexation, Babushka threw a whole handful of crumbs into the water. "He mutters. How can anyone hear him?"

"You're sure he wasn't telling you he's coming today?"

"Didn't I just tell you? It was impossible to understand him."

Marina went to the window and looked up and down the empty street. She had no more time. Tonight at midnight, they would come for her mother. She went to the vestibule and put her coat back on.

"My father must know," she said.

"How will you find him?" asked Peshkova.

"I think I know where he is."

"Then you must tell him."

Black clouds raced across the winter sky. It was dark at midday.

Marina ran all the way to Kuznetsky Most, stopping at Number 131. Aware that someone had been walking behind her, she stopped to read the proclamations pasted on the boarded window of the ground-floor shop. A young girl carrying a violin case walked past her, staring straight ahead, looking frightened. When the girl had gone, Marina hurried into the courtyard and up the stairs to the second floor.

She listened at the door. Hearing nothing, she knocked—two quick double raps. Inside, she heard light, rapid steps, then silence. She knocked again.

"Who is it?" asked a woman.

It was Tamara.

"Let me in."

The door opened against a chain.

"Go away. I'm washing my hair."

"You must let me in."

The door closed, and then opened wide. Tamara, wearing a beige silk dressing gown, a towel wrapped around her head, glared witheringly at Marina. Then she shrugged and called over her shoulder, "Vasily, we have company."

Marina went into the room where Boris Pasternak had once bade her farewell by the light of a candle. The kitchen door opened, and Vasily stood in the doorway, looking aghast. Tamara sat down at one of the piano benches, unwrapped the towel, and began combing out her damp hair with an oversized bone comb. Marina was overcome by shame for her father. She could barely look at him.

"You knew that Mother and I were arrested?"

"I only just heard about it. Thank God you've been freed. I'm so glad to see you, Marinotchka. Has Anna been released too?"

"No, and I'm only out on a wolf's ticket."

"To find me?"

"Yes."

"Were you followed?"

"No, Father. I've been well trained. Why did you try to send us to Bashkiria?"

Vasily raised his hands in a gesture of helplessness. "When I read the article in *Liberation*, I thought that you'd be safe there. I'd planned to follow you as soon as I could."

Glancing at Tamara, Marina cried out to Vasily, "You planned no such thing! You did what she told you! She told you to send us to Bashkiria knowing that it was a Bolshevik trap! She wanted us out of her way! She wanted us dead!"

"It's not true, Vasily!" protested Tamara. "I thought the newspaper told the truth, just as you did. Marina will say anything to discredit me!"

"She knew about the Bashkiria scheme from Peters. She had Peters send killers after us while we were at Pavel's—do you know that they've taken him? When they failed to catch us, she had you send us to Bashkiria! Father, how could you have believed her? You too want to be rid of us!"

Stricken, Vasily took a step toward Marina.

"How can you think such a thing?"

Before Marina could reply, Tamara turned to Vasily. "How would I have known about the train? Have you forgotten that I'm high on the Cheka's enemy list, just as you are."

"It's true, Marina. Tamara had nowhere to turn."

"Except to you, her useful connection!" said Marina coldly. "Father, the Bashkiria plot was hatched when she was Peters's lover. For months, she'd been telling him everything she learned from you about your SR friends. Everything! She had them all arrested. Dozens of them!"

Tamara smiled thinly at Marina. "How can you know all this— unless you're working for them yourself?"

Marina suddenly felt herself freed of all restraint.

"You asked about Mother!" she shouted at Vasily. "She is spending her last night in the Lubyanka! Tomorrow, she'll be taken to the cellars and shot!"

In a low voice, Vasily said, "Unless I give myself up."

"Vasily!" cried Tamara. "It's a Cheka trick! They won't dare harm Anna!"

Marina turned to Tamara. "My mother is paying a heavy price for her kindness to you!"

Tamara said icily, "We are all about to pay a heavy price for your stupidity! Vasily, they'd never touch Anna. Never. You're too well known abroad."

"Just as they'd never touch Andrey Baranov?" shouted Marina. "He too is well known abroad! You swore that he would be punished for rejecting you, and you've kept your word. I've seen him with my own eyes. He's being put to death, if he's not dead already. Now you're carrying out your threat against me, and getting rid of my mother at the same time!"

"It's a lie!" cried Tamara. "She'll say anything. Don't listen to her, Vasily!"

"Don't worry, Marina," Vasily said quietly. "I'll not let Mother die."

Marina said nothing. Without looking at Vasily, she walked out of the apartment, slamming the door behind her.

Chapter Forty-two

MARINA WAS STILL SEETHING WITH RAGE WHEN SHE REACHED LYALIN Lane. Three automobiles were parked at the curb in front of the building. One was a large black limousine. Beyond it stood a smaller motorcar with an outsized spare rear wheel. Marina could not see the third automobile clearly. Several Chekists were sharing a cigarette in the building's entrance. When she came closer, one of them started toward her. At that moment, she recognized the third car. Gorky's Ford.

"Papers."

As she was reaching for her pass, the Chekists in the entrance came to attention. Dzerzhinsky, wearing a black leather coat that swept the ground, strode out of the building. One of the men opened the limousine door for him. The car pulled away from the curb and sped down the street.

The Chekist studied Marina's pass for a long time; then he handed it back to her and motioned her inside. She ran up the three floors and let herself into the apartment. A fire was blazing in the stove. Marina took off her coat in the entrance hall and hung it on a rack of pegs against the wall.

On one of the pegs hung Gorky's broad-brimmed black hat.

She stared at the hat, struggling to catch her breath. Kiril rushed out to meet her. "It's what we thought. Babushka misunderstood," he whispered. "He was trying to tell her that he was arriving today."

"Kiril, I've done something terrible."

Peshkova came into the entrance hall and said sternly, "Come in, Marina. We've been waiting for you."

Gorky was seated in a wicker armchair at the table. His head was shaved, the lines of his face deepened. Across from him at the table sat Anatoly Lunacharsky, sipping tea. Behind him, the goldfish was swimming rapidly back and forth.

Gorky rose and embraced Marina in a bear hug. "My favorite god-daughter," he said. "Are you still as unforgiving of us sinners as ever?"

"I'm sorry you remember me that way, godfather," said Marina, kissing him on both cheeks.

"Nonsense," he said. "In the case of Madame Sermus, you were absolutely right. I realized it the moment you were out the door. Anatoly, have you met Marina Nevsky?"

"I've not had the pleasure," said the Commissar of Enlightenment with a formal bow, "though we've seen each other at the National."

Marina nodded politely, wondering whether Lunacharsky knew of Latsis's threat. And whether Gorky knew.

Kiril pulled up a chair for her.

"And where," asked Gorky, "is your dear mother?"

Marina was about to answer when Peshkova shook her head—say nothing, she was signaling.

"My mother cannot be here today."

"A pity," said Gorky, "though I'm delighted to see you. You come at a good moment. We were discussing the future of art in the new society."

"And your place in it, Alexey," said Lunacharsky, "as our fore-most literary artist."

Gorky shrugged. "Anatoly has been saying that in *Mother*, I created the first proletarian hero."

Lunacharsky nodded gravely. "That novel introduced the hero of our time, projecting a realistic vision of the future."

"You see how he flatters me, Marina. What do you suppose he wants of me?"

Your soul, Marina thought to herself. They want you to trade your soul for American automobiles. She glanced at Kiril, who nod-ded as if to say, Yes, this is part of the web.

Dear God, she thought, when would long-winded Lunacharsky leave so that she could speak to her godfather?

"We want only your comradeship in the revolutionary struggle,

Alexey," Lunacharsky continued in an ingratiating tone. "Your hero in *Mother*, the simple worker Vlassov, devoted his life to the Revolution. But now it is no longer enough to sacrifice ourselves: we must require the sacrifice of others as well."

"You were not always so bloodthirsty, Anatoly. Must the revolutionary deny Vlassov his humanity and teach him to kill?"

"Morality and humanity are redefined in this new age. True morality is whatever leads to the triumph of the proletarian struggle."

With a tremor in his voice, Kiril said, "Then Dzerzhinsky is the supreme hero of the Revolution?"

"He is exactly that, young man. He is no less admirable than your early SR martyrs. Can't you still feel his presence in this room?"

Gorky shifted in his chair. "Nonsense," he said sharply, glancing disapprovingly at Peshkova. "Dzerzhinsky has simply gone off to do his nasty work. We don't miss him. Moreover, he *is* still in this room, speaking to us through you, Anatoly."

Peshkova said firmly, "Dzerzhinsky is a caring man driven by his burning faith in the Revolution."

"There is no doubt," said Gorky, "that Lenin showed his genius when he appointed Dzerzhinsky to head the Cheka. Instead of a thug, he chooses a saint with ice in his veins."

"The executioner as savior," said Kiril.

Gorky looked annoyed. "Indeed, Dzerzhinsky is not the noble spirit you and I sought in our revolutionary workshops in Capri, Anatoly. If he is, my Vlassov would be his first victim."

"Not at all, Alexey," said Lunacharsky. "Your hero would grow up with the times."

"As a Chekist?"

"Or as a gifted writer so committed to the Revolution that his pen would ensure its survival."

"Perhaps Vlassov might do that, but I can't. I never engage in politics except as a critic."

Gorky lit a cigarette; then he touched the match to the crumpled package in the ashtray beside him and watched it burn.

"Alexey, you are too modest. Over the years, you have warned our dear Ilyich about the Revolution smoldering in the hearts of a hundred million dispossessed peasants. And Ilyich has listened."

Irritated, Gorky said, "Over the years, I have spoken to Lenin of the need to educate the people through literacy programs."

"Alexey, Ilyich and all of us have been aware of the dangerous backwardness of the peasant masses, but you opened the way for policies in defense of the Revolution, of which the literacy program is but one."

"And a bullet in the back of the head another," said Kiril loudly. "Anatoly Vasilyevich, you would make our godfather bear a responsibility for outrages which he vigorously opposes. This is sophistry."

"You miss my point completely, young man," said Lunacharsky, visibly exasperated. "I commend Alexey. As for terror, it is a necessary step toward the realization of Vlassov's dream."

"Enough politics," said Peshkova impatiently. "Alexey is weary from his journey. It's time for him to retire."

Looking pained, Lunacharsky rose to take his leave. He studied Kiril attentively across the table, evidently making mental notes about this rebellious young man. At that moment, Gorky looked past him at Marina.

"What's the matter, goddaughter? You look upset. Surely it's not our jousting? Deep down, you know, Anatoly is a kindly man. A humanist."

Kiril nodded urgently to Marina. Speak now, he was telling her.

"Godfather," she said in a clear voice, not looking at Peshkova, managing to remain collected, "my mother is in the Inner Prison of the Lubyanka at this moment. I too am a prisoner, released on a temporary pass. I am to help the Cheka arrest my father. Otherwise, my mother is to die tonight."

Gorky stared at her in disbelief. Then he turned to Lunacharsky and struck his fist on the table, causing the tea glasses to clatter and Babushka to peer in from the hallway.

"Is this true?" he demanded.

"I know nothing about it," protested the Commissar of Enlightenment. "Such a thing is impossible without Lenin's direct order. You know this as well as I, dear friend."

"Yet what Marina says *is* true," said Peshkova.

"You knew of it all along?" exclaimed Gorky. "Ekaterina Pavlovna, why didn't you tell me? This is unconscionable!"

He got up, went to the telephone in the alcove, put the receiver to his ear, and shouted into the mouthpiece.

"Gorky here. Connect me with Vladimir Ilyich!"

Chapter Forty-three

"What will you do?" asked Tamara when Marina had gone.

Vasily stared at her in astonishment. In the course of the past fifteen minutes, the quite manageable qualms of guilt he had felt toward Anna on this woman's account had been replaced by an agonizing recognition of his vile behavior toward his wife and daughter. It was clear to him now that, had he chosen to, he could have realized that the Bashkiria opportunity was a ruse. Indeed, it was possible that he had known it in his heart all along. Suddenly, everything about Tamara—the hardness of her voice, her reproachful eyes, the nasty twist of her thin coral lips when she smiled— had become repellent to him.

How very odd, he thought, that the same woman could at one moment be so desirable and, in the next, become a hateful creature whom he would have left long ago, were it not for his imperishable attraction to her incomparable double.

"You can see for yourself, Tamara," he said. "I have no choice."

"Can you possibly believe that they'll release Anna and Marina if you give yourself up?"

"Of course, you know their ways," he said.

"I do," she replied evenly, sitting down on a couch, "and there's only one way you can save them: go abroad. You have influential Socialist friends in the West. Tell them what is happening here. Lenin will listen to them."

"Even if he would, which I doubt, there's no time."

"I tell you, it's a bluff."

"I can't take that chance."

"Then you'll turn yourself in at Lubyanka?"

"I'm going directly to the Kremlin. Lenin must know about the crimes the Cheka is committing in his name."

Tamara laughed. "My poor innocent Vasily, the Cheka is acting on his orders."

"Nevertheless, I shall go to him."

"They'll arrest you at the gates."

"Vladimir Ilyich will not refuse to see his old rival. He will not let such a moment of triumph pass."

Tamara was staring up at him strangely.

"Don't play into their hands, Vasily." Suddenly, she was pleading, drawing him down on the couch next to her. "You and I can go to Paris and work for Anna's release. Marina's too. Then they'll join us there, and we can all be together, just as we were in Alassio."

She was smiling at him seductively, but her smile kept fading. He realized then that she was trying to impersonate the woman with whom he had fallen in love the day he had lifted her out of the sea. He felt sorry for her.

"I'm going to the Kremlin," he said again, touching her face with the palm of his hand.

She sprang away from him and stood up. "You're a pathetic old fool!" she shouted.

Vasily stared at her. He scarcely heard her, scarcely saw her. The burning sense of guilt was overwhelming him. He felt doubly bound, a prisoner of the chaotic times, a captive in the nethermost dungeon of his flesh.

The Kremlin bells tolled seven. Tamara sat down at one of the two pianos, playing with one finger a tune which, whenever she wished to burrow within herself and escape from him, she had played over and over again. It seemed that her picking out the tiresome little melody on the piano now meant that he no longer existed for her. If indeed he ever had, except as a convenience when she needed him for some useful purpose. He went into the bedroom, closing the door behind him.

From a closet shelf, he took down the battered leather suitcase which had served him on his treks since leaving Paris. It was broken at the hinges, cinched by a length of clothesline. He set the suitcase on the bed, undid the knot, and raised the lid, inhaling a musty smell. Inside were a pair of worn-out corduroy trousers, an embroidered peasant blouse, an iron-scorched dress shirt, several discolored collars, mismatched socks, and strewn among the garments, yellowed edicts, ballots, proclamations, and minutes of passionate meetings now long forgotten.

Underneath lay his navy blue suit, not worn since the night of the Constituent Assembly. He took it out and held it up. It was creased in the wrong places but otherwise quite presentable. This suit, which he had intended to wear at the rebirth of the Assembly, he would put on now to wear to the Kremlin.

He pulled on the trousers, recalling the long night of the Assembly. On the podium, he had stood firm against the drunken jeering and the clicking rifles, trying to give Russia a chance to free herself at last from the shackles of her history. He remembered how proud of him Anna and Marina had been. And he remembered Dmitry, warning him not to go to his car.

The suit hung loosely on him, but he hardly noticed. It struck him that in death the goal he had sought for so long would be reached. Gradually, the news would spread throughout Russia, up and down the great rivers, across the steppes and the taiga: the usurpers have murdered Nevsky. They would be unmasked, and democracy in Russia would yet be born, after he was gone. And his own sins would be forgiven. He pulled on his boots.

When he returned to the salon, Tamara was still playing the aggravating little air. He put on his sheepskin coat.

"Good-bye, Tamara."

She went on picking out the notes of the tune.

"Lianozov still has friends in the city who will help you," he said. "You'll be all right. Stay here as long as you want." He searched his pockets and set a thick roll of rubles on the piano.

She kept on playing.

"You still have your ring to sell," he added, noticing how thin her hands had become.

She stopped playing and looked up at him. "You'll never find Ariane," she said.

He stared at her. "What do you know about Ariane?"

"Anna told me about her. You'll never find her, Vasily. She died a long time ago. Go back to Anna."

Chapter Forty-four

"ILYICH WILL SEE ME AT ONCE," GORKY ANNOUNCED, HANGING UP. "The old fox must want something. Call Max."

"Godfather, may I ride with you as far as Lubyanka Square?" asked Marina. It would soon be dark, and she imagined Vasily walking into the floodlit zone at the prison gates. She had to prevent him from giving himself up to the Lubyanka executioners.

Gorky looked puzzled. "You'd better stay here until I've spoken to Lenin."

"Indeed, the streets are dangerous at night," said Peshkova as she went off to get Max.

Kiril turned to Gorky. "I'll go with Marina if you'll take us."

Marina looked imploringly at Gorky.

"Very well," he said, "but we leave now."

Max drove Gorky toward the Kremlin, dropping off Marina and Kiril on Lubyanka Square. They looked around for Vasily, but he was nowhere to be seen. Then they rushed up Kuznetsky Most to Number 131 and ran up the dark staircase to the second floor.

"Why have you come back?" said Tamara at the chained door. "Haven't you done enough?"

"Where is he?"

"Gone to give himself up. Isn't that what you wanted?"

"How long ago did he leave?" demanded Kiril.

"Congratulations, Marina," said Tamara. "You have achieved what the Cheka and the White Guards failed to do; you have entrapped your father. He left for the Kremlin to surrender to Lenin."

"When?" said Marina.

"He should be there by now. Try to undo what you've done, if you can! You despise me, Marina, but I'm glad I won't have to live with your conscience."

The door closed.

It was after midnight. It was now Sunday.

Marina and Kiril raced down the street toward the Kremlin. As they came out into Red Square, they heard a muffled cry. At the far end of the Traders Row arcade, across from the Kremlin wall, in the fading light, several men were wielding sticks over a prostrate form. Marina and Kiril ran toward them, and when the assailants saw them, they fled down a side alley.

Vasily, stripped of his coat and boots, was struggling to his feet. Before Marina and Kiril could reach him, he staggered into the cobbled square and doggedly started toward the floodlit Kremlin wall.

Two uniformed guards rushed out through the arch under the Savior's Tower and ran toward him. Kiril and Marina grabbed him and tried to pull him back toward the shadows of the arcade, but he broke free.

"I must see Lenin!" he shouted, as the guards reached them, pistols drawn.

"Leave immediately!" yelled one. "This is a forbidden zone."

"This man is my father," said Marina. "He's just been robbed and beaten. We're taking him home."

"I am Vasily Nevsky," Vasily announced to the guards. "I must speak to Lenin at once."

The men stared at Vasily a moment, and then grinned at each other.

"The third Vasily Nevsky this week," said one, and to Marina he added, "Take the lunatic away."

"But it's true! I am Vasily Nevsky."

Again the guards looked at each other, uncertain now. They were young Latvians who spoke Russian with a heavy accent.

"We better take him to the captain," said the first.

An automobile sped out from the Savior's Tower into the square, its headlights blinding them.

"Lead me to Lenin," Vasily persisted. Before the Latvians could respond, Gorky's Ford drew up near them. Gorky rolled down the window.

"What's the trouble here?" he asked, pretending not to recognize them.

"My father's been hurt," said Marina. "He doesn't know what he's saying."

"Get him into the car at once," said Gorky. "The man needs medical attention."

"Wait," said the first guard. "We're taking him to the captain."

"You're doing nothing of the sort," said Gorky. "Otherwise, I shall report you to Vladimir Ilyich for making fools of yourselves."

"We're only trying to do our duty, Alexey Maximovich."

"In that case, help get this fellow into the car."

Still protesting, Vasily struggled against the guards who wrestled him into the backseat. Marina and Kiril got in on either side of him. With a squeal of tires, Max pulled away from the bewildered Latvians.

"Where to?" he asked Gorky.

"Lyalin Lane, of course."

"For God's sake," said Vasily, "drive me to the Lubyanka. Anna is to be shot!"

"Calm yourself, my friend," said Gorky. "Lenin telephoned the Lubyanka. Anna is being released. They're bringing her to the apartment."

Vasily sighed with relief. "And Marina?"

"She's also free, on condition that they both leave the country without delay. Dzerzhinsky is arranging the documents for their departure tomorrow morning."

"How were you able to persuade Lenin?" asked Kiril.

"It may well be the last favor he grants me. Ilyich told me in no uncertain terms to concern myself from now on with the millions of ordinary Russians, and to forget about their enemies. However, this time I was able to strike a bargain. He fears that his government may not survive another winter without food shipments from the West."

"And he wants you to issue an appeal," said Kiril.

"That's right. I, who have been vilified by those hypocritical capitalists in the United States for decades, must now approach them with a beggar's cup! It makes me sick."

Babushka stood at the kitchen door as Max and Gorky came into the apartment, followed by Marina and Kiril assisting Vasily. He still appeared dazed.

"So many people," said Babushka. "How will we feed them all?"

"By sharing, Mother," said Peshkova.

Anna rose from her chair by the alcove. In the soft light of the lamps, she looked pale and thin, but radiant. Marina went to her and hugged her; then Vasily enfolded them both in his arms.

"Thank God," he said.

"Thank Marina," said Anna. "And Alexey Maximovich. Peshkova told me what happened. The reprieve reached Latsis just as they were about to take me to the cellars."

"My last miracle," said Gorky sourly, settling into his wicker armchair as Peshkova tucked a robe around his knees. "Dzerzhinsky is sending a car for Anna and Marina. It should be here within the hour. They'll spend the night at the National and in the morning will be driven to the Baltic Station. They'll travel by train to Tallinn, then on to Paris. I have money for them."

"Quick, Babushka," said Peshkova, "help me find that old overcoat of Max's and a pair of felt boots. Hurry! The Chekists mustn't find Vasily here."

"I'll leave at once," said Vasily, and to Gorky he added, "I'm infinitely grateful to you, old friend."

"Never mind about gratitude, my dear Vasily," said Gorky, rising and embracing him. "You're a brave man, but I must tell you that the SR political program hasn't a prayer in Russia and never did."

Vasily shook his head. "The fault is not with the program. The fault is with me."

"I suspect that the real flaw lies in the hearts of our people," said Gorky. "Ivan is far too shrewd to assume responsibility for his own life."

Anna asked softly, "Will you meet us in Paris, Vasily?"

"Yes, Anna. I want nothing more in the world." He turned to Marina, adding, "I have much to reflect upon, much to atone for. Our cause was weakened by having once been stained with blood, and by our own blindness, and Russia is paying the price."

He turned to Gorky.

"Yes, Alexey, we SRs bear our share of guilt, as the first to respond to the tsar's tyranny with violent reprisals, but our victims were individual oppressors, the Bolsheviks victims—our entire people. My friends, from abroad, I shall tell the whole world what is happening in Russia."

There was silence; then Gorky said, "Vasily, your contrition is no doubt admirable, but how the devil will you, of all people, know what is happening in Russia? The moment you set foot abroad, Russia will become a foreign country to you—just as I suspect it has been all along."

Vasily smiled affectionately at Gorky. "You may be right," he said. "The Russia I love, and that you love as well, has never existed. It is an ideal Russia, freed from oppression. It's true that we SRs have lost an important battle, but the seed of freedom is stronger for our having fought that battle. Liberty will one day come to Russia. In the meantime, Alexey, you are still the conscience of the Revolution, the real revolution! You must not surrender your independence to the Bolsheviks."

"And who the devil would you have me surrender it too?" demanded Gorky. "The Whites? The SRs?"

As her godfather and her father jousted, Marina envisioned Vasily going out into the city alone, and she was terrified. Silently, she appealed to Kiril, who sensed her feelings.

"Vasily Ivanovich," he said, "forgive me for interrupting, but you're in great danger here. I know every mile of the Finish border west of Petrograd. There are still people here and in Finland who will do everything in their power to help the SR cause. Let me be your guide."

Marina looked anxiously at her father.

"I accept your offer," he said solemnly to Kiril.

"So, I lose both my assistants," said Peshkova, and to Marina and Anna, she added, "As a matter of fact, I wish I were leaving with you. But what would I do in Paris? Sip wine at cafés and chatter about philosophy and scandals? No, as long as there are political prisoners here, my work is in Moscow."

Quietly, Anna said, "We're forgetting someone, Vasily."

"I don't think so, Anna," he said. "Thanks to Alexey, you and Marina are free, and I have a trustworthy guide. God willing, we'll meet in Paris by springtime."

"But what about Tamara?"

There was a heavy silence in the room. Marina watched her father. He appeared thunderstruck. Then Gorky asked in disbelief, "Madame *Sermus*?"

"We can't leave her behind," said Anna. "They'll find her and execute her. Latsis swore that they would."

"That terrible Estonian woman?" said Peshkova. "You want to take her along with you?"

"What the devil's going on?" demanded Gorky.

Anna said quietly, "In Alassio, I invited Tamara Sermus into our family as a friend. Marina felt that I was making a mistake, and she was right. But now Tamara is under a death sentence—" She hesitated, looking at Vasily.

Gorky scowled. "Then am I to understand—?"

"It's a long story," said Anna. "But we can't leave her to the Cheka."

Peshkova shook her head. "You amaze me, Anna."

"Tamara will be shot if we don't help her."

"This is all very well and good," said Gorky, "but if I'm expected to crawl back to Lenin on behalf of Madame Sermus, it's out of the question. I gave Ilyich my promise not to meddle again. As a matter of fact, he might change his mind about the two of you."

"Lunacharsky has the authority to secure exit papers," said Peshkova. "If you're sure this is really what you want, Anna, I can try to reach him by telephone."

"It is what I want," said Anna firmly, beckoning to Marina. Peshkova went to the alcove and picked up the telephone, while Anna and Marina went into the kitchen.

"Why are you doing this?" asked Marina. "She tried to kill us."

"I know that."

"Then why?"

"I've seen too many women go to the Death Ship. I couldn't live with myself if someone who has once been close to our family were to be taken there without our trying to save her."

"There is something you don't know," said Marina, determined not to let her mother be deceived.

Anna smiled. "Is there?"

"Yes."

"Is it perhaps about the Kuznetsky Most apartment? And your father and Tamara?"

Marina shook her head in amazement.

"How did you know?"

"I was with the Baroness Vologdin shortly before she was taken to the Death Ship. She had learned through her houseman that Tamara had left her apartment and moved to one nearby, on Kuznetsky Most. Then I guessed. By the way, the baroness went to her death bravely. The poor woman had lived through the terror of it so often in her imagination that there was little left for her to fear."

Peshkova came into the kitchen.

"Dzerzhinsky is granting an exit visa to Madame Sermus," she said. "She'll be waiting for you at the Baltic Station. But you'd better hurry; they'll be here for you soon." With a questioning look at Anna, she left, closing the door behind her.

Anna looked pleadingly at Marina. "Try to understand, darling. In that communal cell, I finally made my peace with the fact that Ariane has always been your father's true love."

"Even so long after her death?"

"More than ever, because he believes that he was to blame for it."

"But it wasn't his fault," said Marina. "Your father had him arrested on the day they were to elope. There was nothing he could do."

"But he thought that there was," Anna hesitated, then added, "Don't you see, Marina? I can't leave your father with another martyr to mourn."

Marina sighed and said nothing. How could she ever have imagined that Ariane's spell over their lives would end in the flames at Dubrovka?

·   ·   ·

The two women went off to prepare for their departure. When Marina returned to the living room, Kiril came up to her and held her gently.

"I want to marry you," he said. "As soon as we reach Paris."

He took her in his arms and kissed her. In the hallway, Max was smoking a cigarette, watching them with a sardonic smile.

Now it was time for everyone, including Max and Babushka, to pull up chairs around the table and sit in silence. Marina saw that her father was deeply troubled.

"Anna," he said at last. "Please come into the kitchen. I have something to tell you in private."

"No, Vasily," she said. "We'd only have to sit down again afterward. There'll be time enough to tell secrets."

Gorky rose to his feet.

"It's just as well the Nevskys are leaving," he said gruffly. "Otherwise, they'd be the death of me. The trouble is, Vasily, that when all is said and done, you and your family are the best of Russia, and now you're forced to leave again. It's a damnable tragedy!" He was silent a moment; then he added in a breaking voice, "I hardly know what's happening here any more myself. I may well be joining you in exile." He paused again, and Marina thought that he was going to say something more, but he only smiled sadly at her and winked.

From the front window, she watched her father and Kiril walking down the moonlit street, Vasily hunched forward as if battling a gale, Kiril striding next to him, tall and sure. Long after they had gone, she gazed into the darkness at the end of the street, saying goodbye to Russia.

Early the next morning, a black Cheka automobile stood in front of the apartment building. The young driver was civil, even helping Marina and Anna with their suitcases. Acting on Lenin's orders, Dzerzhinsky had arranged every detail of their departure, including their rendezvous with Tamara at the station.

Leaving Peshkova had been hard. In the apartment, she had embraced them and said good-bye stoically. On the street, just as she and Anna were about to get into the car, Marina heard a sharp rapping on the glass of the third-floor window. Peshkova had drawn the curtains aside and pulled the window open. Max was beside her, and Marina could see then that she was sobbing. Max handed her a handerchief; she quickly dabbed at her eyes and then waved the handkerchief at them wildly, back and forth, as if she would never stop.

$\mathcal{A}$fterword

TO LIVE A LIFE IS NOT TO CROSS A FIELD.
—BORIS PASTERNAK

In early 1920, our family was reunited in Paris. There in 1921, I married Kiril Golovin in the Russian church on rue Daru.

Gorky had been wrong about Vasily Nevsky. Settled with his family in Paris and then in the United States, my father proved to be a far better prophet than Gorky. Sifting through each newspaper article and each new exile's report, he could get his hands on, he proclaimed to a largely unconcerned world that Lenin, and Stalin after him, were using the power generated by the Revolution for the annihilation of millions of Russians.

In Moscow in the summer of 1922, the curtain went up on the tragic last act of his party's story: the trial of the Socialist Revolutionaries. Despite an amnesty granted to the SRs in 1919 in exchange for their desisting from all anti-Soviet activity, some twenty party leaders, including Abram Gotz, were arrested. They were interrogated, tortured, and condemned to death. Then, perhaps because of the protests of prominent foreign socialists, but more likely because of the Bolsheviks' need for hostages to dissuade others from hostile acts, their sentences were commuted to imprisonment. Eventually, they all perished in labor camps and transit prisons. At their trial, Anatoly Lunacharsky served in an honorary capacity meant to lend dignity to the proceedings.

Masterminded by Lenin, the trial of the SRs served as a grim model for

Stalin's show trials of the late 1930s, the spectacular charades that astonished and bewildered the civilized world. All of the elements of those ghoulish proceedings were present in 1922: the breaking down of the defendants' spirits through interrogation and torture, the absurd accusations, the equally absurd confessions, the state-orchestrated campaign to vilify the accused as enemies of the people.

In the ensuing years, hundreds of thousands of SRs were killed or confined in hard-labor camps. Vasily Nevsky's main constituency, the peasant population of Russia, was all but destroyed.

In 1924, Lenin died. Josef Stalin, a secondary figure during the October Revolution, succeeded him, sending his rival Trotsky into exile and to a Soviet-contrived death in Mexico.

When Dzerzhinsky died in the summer of 1926, Gorky sent an open letter of condolence from Capri, where he had settled in 1921. "I am absolutely overwhelmed by the death of Felix Edmundovich," my godfather wrote. "I was rather closely acquainted with him in 1918–1920, and I had occasion to discuss delicate subjects with him. I importuned him about various matters, and because he was gifted with a sensitive heart and a strong sense of justice, we did a great deal of good."

Oddly, Gorky was losing his own sensitive heart and strong sense of justice, traits that had enabled him to save thousands of Russian socialists, artists, and intellectuals during the Revolution. The web that the Bolsheviks were weaving around him was doing its work.

In 1928, he returned home from a seven-year exile, urging Russian intellectuals to become "engineers of human souls" in the service of the Soviet state. Maintained in luxurious isolation, drugged by Cheka operatives, he became a spokesman for Stalin's grandiose, often pointless projects, with their incalculable toll of human lives.

According to one reliable witness of those distant years, in 1934, when Gorky was at last becoming aware of Stalin's genocidal scheming, he was murdered by doctors called to operate on him. His son Max had died shortly before, left to freeze to death in a ditch after a drunken binge in the company of secret police agents. Peshkova alone was allowed to survive.

As for Sergei Lomov, records recently declassified by the KGB reveal that he was shot in the Lubyanka a few weeks after we left Russia.

Boris Savinkov died as he had lived, violently and under circumstances shrouded in mystery. In 1924, the master of intrigue now living in emigration was entrapped by a ruse devised by Dzerzhinsky himself—a bogus organization known as the "Trust," made to appear as a secret alliance of high-level counterrevolutionaries operating within Russia, but in fact an elaborate snare, recalling the Bashkiria deception. Lured from Paris, Savinkov was tried before a Secret Revolutionary Tribunal in Moscow and induced to confess. The following year, he fell—or was thrown—to his death from a window inside the Lubyanka.

Tamara Sermus departed from our lives as abruptly as she had entered them. In March 1920, on our way out of Russia, my mother and I saw her last in the Tallinn railway station, which was still decorated with flags and bunting from the celebration of Estonia's newly won independence. She left us without a word and disappeared into the crowd.